DANGEROUS PASSION

Beneath her soft palms she felt the strength of his arms and the power of his body and the tension that ran like a hot live wire through him. The atmosphere around them was charged with possibility.

"Elizabeth." His tone was unbearably intimate. His rough hands settled on her back and slid up to her shoulders. A wave of sensation the like of which Regina had never before experienced washed over her. Their glances came together.

It was there, the dark hunger she had seen before. Its power and starkness both frightened and compelled her. With a soft whimper she gripped him more tightly, knowing she should not, knowing she was ready to surrender completely.

He knew it as well. She saw it in the blaze of his eyes. Regina clung to him, waiting for him to take her . . .

Other Avon Books by
Brenda Joyce

THE FIRES OF PARADISE
FIRESTORM
SCANDALOUS LOVE
VIOLET FIRE

Coming Soon

PROMISE OF THE ROSE

BRENDA JOYCE

SECRETS

AVON BOOKS ◭ NEW YORK

SECRETS is an original publication of Avon Books. This work has never
before appeared in book form. This work is a novel. Any similarity to
actual persons or events is purely coincidental.

AVON BOOKS
A division of
The Hearst Corporation
1350 Avenue of the Americas
New York, New York 10019

First Avon Books Printing: April 1993

AVON TRADEMARK REG. U.S. PAT. OFF. AND IN OTHER COUNTRIES, MARCA
REGISTRADA, HECHO EN U.S.A.

Printed in the U.S.A.

RA   10 9 8 7 6 5 4 3 2 1

This one's for the men in my life:
for Alvin, Ross, and David.
There is a moral to this story—
love conquers all.

And for Elie and Adam, who don't need any morals yet,
and hopefully never will.

Prologue

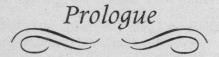

"*A*nd you, my lady? Will you marry a duke as your sister did?"

Regina smiled slightly. "I doubt it, Mrs. Schroener. Marrying a duke was quite a feat for my sister. Generally, one marries precisely among one's peers."

"But your father is an *earl*."

Regina stared out the train's window at the passing scenery, a vista of sunburned saddleback hills thrusting against the sky. "An earl does not rank with a duke." She recalled the last time she had seen her parents, before they had left Texas; she had told them she would not be returning home with them, not just yet. The Earl of Dragmore had not been pleased, but he had allowed her to extend her stay in America with her relatives. Regina's heart twisted. She was not going home with the rest of her family because her former beau Lord Hortense was there, now engaged to someone else after her father had so decisively refused him.

"A beauty like yourself, why, I don't doubt you could have any man you wanted," Mrs. Schroener said enthusiastically, standing with her charge at the window.

"Father will choose someone for me when I return home," Regina said quietly. She and her chaperone were in the club car of the Southern Pacific Railroad's Coast Line amid a dozen other first-class passengers. Most were gentlemen, either engaged in conversation or involved in their dailies. She preferred not being overheard.

Mrs. Schroener's eyes were wide. "He will *what?*"

Regina managed a smile, not wanting the kind old widow to know how much the prospect daunted her. She still loved Randolph Hortense. But it would not be. She could not go against her father's wishes. She was not the renegade her sister Nicole was. And she was no longer eighteen. Had she been going home now, she would be entering her third season. When she did arrive back home, her father would present her with a list of suitable candidates for a husband, and she would have to choose one of them.

"Do you mean to say that in Britain they still arrange marriages? That your father would arrange a marriage for you?"

"It's really the best way," Regina heard herself say.

"But look at your cousin Lucy! No one would have ever arranged her marriage to that Shoz Savage—and look how happy she is! I read all about their wedding just last month. The wedding of the century, they said it was. Now that's true love!"

Regina smiled. "It was quite an event." She and her family had come to Texas to attend the wedding, giving Regina the perfect excuse to escape England—and Lord Hortense and his fiancée.

"Soon you'll have just such a wedding, my dear. Indeed, with your being nobility, I imagine it'll be even bigger and grander!"

Regina murmured, "Undoubtedly," her smile turning wistful. And it wasn't a spectacular wedding celebration she was thinking of, but love. The love she could have had—but her father had denied her. Randolph was not a fortune-hunter, she told herself firmly, not for the first time. Not that it really mattered. He was marrying someone else. Like her, he would do his duty by his parents.

The train seemed to be slowing down.

"We should be in Paso Robles soon," Mrs. Schroener said, peering out of the window. "I think I'll enjoy those famous mud baths myself before I turn around and go back to Texas."

"You certainly should," Regina told her. "The Hotel El Paso de Robles is one of the greatest health resorts on this coast, or so my aunt and uncle have said." She was meeting the D'Archands there. After a long, relaxing weekend, they would head north to San Francisco where they lived. Regina intended to stay with them for the rest of the summer, having had enough of Texas. In September there would be no delaying the inevitable; she would have to go home and face her future.

Regina had opened the heavy gold velvet drapes so she could regard the scenery. They were passing through rolling hills. The summer sun had dried the wild grass to a lemon-yellow, but the gentle hills were spotted with thick, lush green oaks, and the skies were spectacularly blue. From time to time she could glimpse the dry bed of the Salinas River as it snaked alongside them. Regina found the landscape rugged, yet the sheer vastness of it was breathtaking.

"Someone as beautiful and nice as you deserves a prince," Mrs. Schroener declared, unable or unwilling to let go of her romanticism.

Regina smiled faintly. It seemed to her now that the train had definitely decelerated. "Why are we slowing?" She reached into her reticule and removed a well-worn rail schedule. Twenty minutes ago they had stopped at Santa Margarita, and her schedule indicated the train should only be stopping now if flagged. "The next stop is Templeton, but we can't be there yet. And after that we will be at Paso Robles."

"There's probably a farmer flagging us down," Mrs. Schroener said. "Nothing for you to worry about."

Regina could only conclude that her chaperone was

right. Reluctantly, she turned to take a seat. But before she could do so, a gunshot rang out.

Her heart seemed to drop to her feet and the air to rush from her lungs. The sound of the gunshot echoed. It had been fired in one of the other cars, perhaps in the adjacent car, from which could now be heard screams and cries of fright.

Mrs. Schroener gripped her hand. Another shot rang out. The shooting was definitely in the car behind them. Through the chorus of general hysteria, a baby's crying could be heard.

Oh, dear God! Regina thought frantically. *It's a robbery!*

Chaos erupted in the club car. The men were on their feet, milling about, the women pale and shaking with fright and shock. From the other railcar came another gunshot and a woman's long, shrill scream of anguish. Regina had never heard the sound before, but knew it for what it was—terror and grief.

It was at that moment that a man with a mask on his face, holding a huge revolver, burst into the club car from the car behind them, shouting, "No one move! Everyone freeze! Move and you're gonna get yourself killed!"

Regina and Mrs. Schroener were standing at the other end of the car, with all of the passengers between them and the bandit. Regina froze. She could not believe this was happening!

Everyone obeyed the masked gunman, becoming motionless. The women were sobbing, and one of the gentlemen was also in tears. Roughly, the bandit reached out to the person closest to him, a young woman, tearing her ear-bobs from her ears. She screamed, and the man cuffed her. Regina watched her hit the wall and collapse, blood staining her beautiful pink-and-white-striped jacket.

The bandit leaned over her, ripping her necklace from her, too. The woman lay weeping.

"Maybe we'll take you with us," the bandit sneered. When she screamed, he laughed, then rose to his formidable height. He turned to the gentleman closest to him and yanked a wallet out of his pocket, then went for his pocket watch.

Regina was shaking. She was no longer shocked, no longer disbelieving. They were being robbed, and in a violent, terrifying way. The outlaw's threat to the young lady rang in her ears. She could barely think. She was numb, terrified. But she was aware that the door was very close behind her, leading to the platform between this car and the one in front of them. Were there outlaws in that car, too? No sounds had come from it. Yet even if there weren't, the outlaws—and she had not a doubt that there were several—would soon invade it, too. Regina's heart was pounding.

The bandit took a moment to look around the club car. His glance settled on Regina. For an instant their gazes locked. As he turned to rob his third victim, a young man, Regina felt panic overwhelm her. She shook. Sweat almost blinded her as she saw the robber raise his gun and hit the protesting gentleman with it. Her pulse roared in her ears. She swallowed a whimper, watching the bandit pocket a billfold and move to the next passenger. She did not wait to see what would happen next.

She moved. She shoved past Mrs. Schroener, who let out a startled cry. She ran the three steps to the door. She did not have to look backward to know that he had seen her.

"Stop!" he shouted.

Regina ignored him. Terror beat thickly in her heart. She gripped the iron bar and wrenched open the heavy door, stumbling onto the platform. A sob tore from her mouth as she saw how fast the train was still moving. For she would have to jump from the train.

A shot rang out again, this time behind her, close behind her. *He was shooting at her.*

She screamed, catching herself on the opposite rail, for one last second watching the hard ground speeding by so far below her. And then, without another thought, Regina hurled herself from the train.

Part One

Secrets

Chapter 1

"Can you hear me?"

It was hot. The heat was stifling, suffocating. And she was thirsty, her mouth as dry as dust. Her tongue felt swollen and numb. But she heard the words. They sounded far away.

"Are you hurt?"

He was speaking again. His tone was urgent, concerned. Yet she did not want to fight to swim up through the dark depths of sleep, and she wondered if she were dreaming.

"Can you hear me?"

His words were louder, insistent. Interfering. She wanted it to be a dream and she wanted him to go away so she could drift back into the total darkness again.

But it wasn't a dream. The instant he touched her she knew that. He was shaking her gently by the shoulder. She would have cried out in protest, told him to go away, but she could not quite utter the words. And then he touched her head, his fingers sliding over her scalp. Pain burst in Regina's skull. The darkness was sliced abruptly open.

Before she could protest he had swiftly unclasped her jacket and parted it. The cooler air was barely a relief. He was unbuttoning the high-necked collar of her shirtwaist, his blunt-tipped fingers grazing the nape of her neck. And as if he hadn't trespassed far enough, his hands moved over her shoulders and arms searchingly, then grazed her breasts, causing her nipples to tighten instantaneously. He did not appear to notice, intent as he was on probing every single bone of her rib cage.

Regina was frozen, suspended in fear. She was wide awake now, aware of the pounding of her head, the terrible heat, her unyielding thirst, and that she was actually lying upon the ground. And she was acutely aware of him. *Now he was touching her legs.* He was sliding his palms up from her ankles to her thighs, only a thin layer of silk separating his flesh from hers. The fact that the sensation was somehow disturbingly pleasant managed to pierce her fear-benumbed brain.

She lay rigid, not breathing.

"You can quit playing possum. I know you're awake."

Her breath escaped. Very slowly she opened her eyes.

He flipped her skirts down over her legs and rose to stand above her. The sun was behind him and she could barely see him. He was a dark shadow, looming over her. Confusion rose hard. Where was she? A quick glance around showed her that they were alone except for one saddled horse, alone in the middle of a valley surrounded by smooth straw-colored hills and a relentless blue sky. She levered herself up into a sitting position and for one moment, she was dizzy.

Instantly he squatted beside her and put his arm around her, preventing her from falling. His body was hot, hotter than the air. When her head stopped spinning, their glances met and held.

She saw only his eyes, dark and intense, fringed with thick lashes, and so shadowed by his hat that they appeared black. But she was unnerved. She looked away. He pushed a canteen to her mouth and she drank hard and long, careless of the water that spilled down her throat and onto the front of her shirt.

"Slow down," he said. "You'll get sick."

He didn't give her a choice, removing the canteen as abruptly as he'd given it to her. He rose lithely to his full height. The sun had slipped behind a wispy white cloud, and this time Regina could see him. The first thing she noticed were his legs, clad in tight, worn denims, braced apart in a rigid stance, the chiseled muscles of his thighs visible through the thin faded fabric. His fists were clenched on compact hips. He was wearing a gun in a leather holster so well-used it was smooth and shiny except for the rough strap around his thigh. Her stomach clenched up into a knot. Seeing a man with a gun was about as commonplace as waking up to find oneself alone on the range with a stranger.

Her gaze had also discovered the oversized oval silver belt buckle he wore, one that needed a good polishing, and the fact that his white cotton shirt was wet with sweat and nearly open to his navel. His skin was dark, his chest sinewed and sprinkled with coarse black hair, his belly flat. Realizing his state of deshabille and the extent of the inspection she was making, her face flamed. Quickly she lifted her glance to his face, but in the process, she assimilated many more details. His sleeves were rolled up, exposing his muscular forearms. Despite the heat, he wore a heavy leather vest, which was discolored from the sun and wind and rain and also left carelessly open.

She could not help noticing his strong features. His chin was blunt, his jaw hard but not square, his nose perfectly straight. He had a day's growth of beard. His eyes were still shadowed by the dusty gray hat he wore, so she could not determine their color.

Now that her gaze had finally reached his, their eyes met again. His revealed nothing. But she was aware of her accelerated heart rate. This man looked like an outlaw. And she appeared to be alone with him—totally alone. Was he an outlaw? Did he intend to hurt her?

He was astute. "Don't be afraid," he told her. "I'm Slade Delanza."

She felt as if he expected her to know him, but she didn't. "What—what do you want?"

His glance was piercing. "I've been looking for you all afternoon. Everyone's worried. You've got a big bump on your head, and a few abrasions."

Despite the question he seemed to be asking, relief swamped her. She didn't know this man, but she understood that he was here to aid her, not hurt her.

"What happened?"

His question took her by surprise. She blinked.

"I heard you jumped off of the train. Your hands and knees are scun up." His voice had become very tight.

Now she stared.

"Are you hurt?"

Regina couldn't answer. It was becoming hard to breathe. Her mind was not functioning the way it should.

He squatted beside her again. The sun had yet to escape its cloud cover, his face was close to hers, perfect in each and every detail, and she realized he was a very handsome man. That realization could not overly interest her. Not now, not when he was asking these frightening questions, not when the intensity of his gaze was unnerving her.

"Are you hurt?" he demanded again.

She stared at him blankly, tears suddenly forming and misting her vision.

He looked at her oddly.

She managed to tear her gaze away from his. She turned to look at the railroad tracks that stretched out endlessly until the hills swallowed them up. She was trembling.

With effort, he softened his tone. "You need a doctor?"

Another distressing question. He was not just upsetting her, he was backing her into a corner, trapping her, and she didn't like it. She wanted to look anywhere but into his eyes, yet she was helplessly drawn to his gaze. She didn't want to answer his horrid questions. "I don't know." She hesitated. "I don't think so."

He stared at her, then fired the next question with the precision of an army marksman. "What do you mean, you don't think so?"

Regina cried out. "Please! Stop it!"

His hands closed on her shoulders, hard but not hurtful. "This isn't a pretty private school for young ladies! This isn't a London tea party! This is the goddamn real world! That train limped into town, everyone hysterical, a half a dozen people hurt, including a woman, and you weren't on it! A dozen passengers saw you jump off the train and land hard. If you don't want to tell me what happened, you can tell the sheriff or the doctor when we get to Templeton!"

"I don't know what happened!" she shouted back. And then, the moment she said the words, she was horrified, because she realized that they were true.

He stared.

She whimpered as the vast, horrible implications of what she had said sank in.

"What did you say?"

"I don't know," she whispered, closing her eyes and gripping the hard ground. She didn't know. She didn't know anything about a train or about a robbery, she didn't know why her gloves were torn and her hands abraded, and she didn't know why she was stranded alone in the middle of the vast deserted rangeland. She didn't know anything about jumping off a train. She whimpered again.

"You don't remember what happened?"

She still didn't open her eyes. It was worse than that, but she was afraid to acknowledge, even to herself, how much worse it was, so she sat there, trying not to hear him and trying not to think.

"Dammit, Elizabeth," he growled. "You don't remember what happened?"

She was going to cry. She knew he had crouched down beside her again, and she knew he wasn't going to leave her alone, she knew he was going to persist in his questions until she revealed all of the horrible truth. Her eyes flew open. In that moment, she hated him. "No! Go away from me, please go away!"

He rose abruptly, towering over her again. His body cast a long, misshapen shadow as the sun again slid free of the clouds. "Maybe it's for the best. Maybe it's for the best that you don't remember what happened."

"I don't remember anything," she told him desperately.

"*What?*"

"You called me Elizabeth," she cried.

His gaze was black, wide, incredulous.

"Am I Elizabeth?"

He stared, frozen.

"Am I Elizabeth?"

"*You lost your memory?*"

His dark gaze was filled with disbelief. She clasped her face in her hands. The pounding at the back of her skull had increased. And with it, the feeling of confusion, and the feeling of despair. It was overwhelming. The truth was inescapable. Her mind was a blank. She didn't know what had happened; more importantly, she didn't know who she was—she didn't know her own name.

"Dammit," cursed the man called Slade.

She looked up at his dark face. Her tormentor could now become her savior. She desperately needed salvation; in a flash of understanding, she was aware of desperately needing him. "*Please. Am I Elizabeth?*"

He didn't answer.

Torn between hope and fear, she lurched to her knees, clasping her hands tightly to her breasts. She swayed precariously close to his thighs. "*Am I Elizabeth?*"

His gaze slid over her. The vein in his temple throbbed visibly; he had removed his hat. "There was only one woman missing from that train when it arrived in Templeton—Elizabeth Sinclair."

"Elizabeth Sinclair?" She fought for a memory, any memory. She fought to pierce the vast nothingness in her mind. But she failed. Not even a glimmer of recognition came when she rolled the name Elizabeth Sinclair over in her mind. Panic washed over her. "I just can't remember!"

"Can't you remember anything?"

She shook her head wildly.

"What about your companion?"

"No!"

"Don't you even remember being on the train?"

"No!"

He hesitated. "And James? You don't remember him?"

"No!" Her control broke. Her nails dug deeply into the denim on his thigh. She was crying, frightened, clinging.

A heartbeat passed. He lifted her to her feet and awkwardly put his arms around her. Regina pressed against him, choking on her tears and her fear. His chest was slick and hot beneath her cheek. Through the mesmerizing panic, she was aware of behaving in a wildly improper manner.

"Elizabeth." He spoke roughly, but there was strength and reassurance in his tone. "It's all right. We're here to take care of you. And soon you'll remember."

His calm was what she needed. She let him push her away so they were no longer in physical contact with one another. She fought for ladylike control. When she had found a semblance of it, she looked up, slowly and even shyly.

He stared down at her uplifted face. It was an intimate moment after the embrace they had shared. But she did not look away, because he was all she had. "Thank you," she whispered, gratitude swelling her heart. "Thank you."

His cheeks reddened. "Don't thank me. There's no need for that."

She almost smiled, wiping her eyes with the back of her gloved hand. "How wrong you are," she said softly.

He turned away. "We had better get going. Rick should be waiting for us in Templeton. When the train came in without you, Edward rode out to get him."

"Rick? Edward?" Should she know these people? The names were as unfamiliar as all the others.

"My old man," he said tersely. His gaze never left her. "James's father. I'm James's brother, Slade. Edward's another brother."

She shook her head miserably. "Am I supposed to know you? Or know James?"

His face was expressionless. "You don't know me or Edward. But you know Rick. And you know James. You're his fiancée."

His fiancée. She almost succumbed to a fresh bout of weeping. She couldn't even recall her betrothed, the man she loved. Dear God, how could this be happening? Pain filled her skull, almost blinding her. She staggered and Slade caught her. His strength was blatant and comforting.

"You're not okay," Slade said roughly. "I want to get to Templeton. The sooner you see Doc the better."

She was too overwhelmed with her circumstances to respond and only too happy to do as he wanted. In her state, which was compounded by exhaustion, she could not make even the smallest decision or protest. She let him lead her to his horse. She was beginning to feel numb, and because the numbness dimmed her fear and hysteria and encroached upon her despair, it was welcome.

"You're limping a little," Slade said, his hand gripping her one arm. "You hurt your ankle?"

"It's tender," she admitted, unable to stop herself from trying to summon up a recollection of how she had twisted her ankle. It was an exercise in futility. Her dismay must have showed, because for a brief moment she saw compassion flit across Slade's face. He stood inches from her and she realized that his eyes weren't black, or even brown. They were dark-blue, keenly alert, restlessly intent. They were the eyes of a highly intelligent man. An instant later the soft expression was gone, and Regina wondered if she had imagined it.

She looked at the patient buckskin. It had not occurred to her earlier that they would have to share a mount, caught up as she was in her dilemma. Now was not the time to insist upon propriety and she was sensible enough to realize it. He lifted her into the saddle. To her surprise, he did not leap up behind her. Instead, he led the horse forward.

Regina quickly became distressed. She had not thought that he would walk. His narrow-toed boots looked very uncomfortable. And it was unbearably hot. While she did not know the time of day, she guessed it was mid-afternoon and that it would be hours before the sun even began to set. "How far is the town?"

"Ten, twelve miles."

She was aghast.

And he was resolute. He led the horse, his strides long and lithe, the muscles playing in his back, clearly visible beneath his thin, damp shirt, for he had removed his vest.

"Mr. Delanza," she said immediately, unable to call him by his first name. He turned slightly to look at her without stopping. "Please. I can't let you walk. It's much too far."

He squinted at her. "You—a fine lady—are inviting me to share that saddle with you?"

"You have saved my life."

"You're exaggerating a bit, don't you think?"

"No." She shook her head vehemently. "I am grateful. I can't ride if you're walking. Not such a distance. Please." Her color had deepened but she did not care. She meant every word she had said. He had rescued her; undoubtedly he had saved her life. She could not repay him with callous insensitivity. He was all she had and she was acutely aware of it. A feeling of dependency was blossoming and becoming urgent. And she was even more grateful now for his interest in her sensibilities. He did not appear to be the kind of man who would be sensitive to a lady's distress, yet he obviously was.

He studied her with his too-sharp gaze before making a decision and jumping into the saddle behind her.

Regina's instant pleasure vanished at the feel of him behind her. She had not really considered the intimacy of such a position, and briefly, she was stunned by it. Abruptly she told herself that she did not care and that under these circumstances, rules were made to be broken. Yet she could feel the tension in his body, a tension as great as hers. Because he was a gentleman regardless of his appearance, he would ignore it—as she would. And she did not regret offering to share his mount with him. It seemed the least she could do after all that he had done.

They rode in silence. Regina was consumed with thoughts of her dilemma and peripherally aware that he was involved in his own brooding. The seed of panic in her breast, which had abated slightly, took its hint from the silence and rose up quickly to fill the void. It soon verged on fresh hysteria. No matter how often she told herself that she was Elizabeth Sinclair and that all would soon be well, the vacuum of ignorance she existed in unraveled the web of optimism she tried to spin. She had to regain her memory—she *had* to. How could she continue like this? She knew nothing about herself or her family, nothing about the train robbery which had brought her to these dire straits.

"Try and relax," he said gruffly. "Let it go for now."

She gripped the pommel, wondering at his sensitivity, his words a welcome distraction. She must remain calm and sensible whenever these bouts of hysteria threatened. Abruptly she shifted in the saddle so she could peer up at his face. "Please tell me what happened. Tell me about the train robbery. And tell me about James."

He was silent for a long moment, and Regina thought he wasn't going to speak. When he did, his tone was matter-of-fact. "You were on your way to Miramar, to your wedding. My brother Edward and I were sent by Rick to meet you at Templeton. The train arrived late—without you on it. We learned from the other passengers that you jumped off of the train during the robbery. My brother rode back to Miramar to tell Rick what happened. I set out to find you. It wasn't hard to do. I just followed the railroad tracks."

She stared at him, wide-eyed. For a moment she thought she had remembered, for a moment she thought the images were there and she could almost see them: frightened people, a gun, running, falling. But the moment was gone before she could grasp it and make sense of the jumbled, formless shapes and ideas. She didn't remember, but the mere notion of being involved in a train robbery was shattering. A shudder swept through her.

He had been riding with his free hand on his thigh, now he touched her arm briefly. "Don't dwell on it," he told her. "It's not going to help to get yourself more frightened."

"I *am* frightened," she said. She twisted to look into his eyes. Their gazes collided. Neither one looked away.

"There's no reason to be frightened. You'll rest at Miramar until you remember."

She did not relax. "What if I never remember?"

For a moment he did not answer. "You *will* remember. It just may take some time."

"And what about those thieves? What happened to them?" she cried.

"They escaped."

Regina moaned.

"They'll be caught," Slade said firmly. "Don't even worry about them. They're the least of your concerns. Elizabeth, we protect our own. We always have. We always will. Trust me."

She strained to look into his eyes again. There was nothing enigmatic about his regard. It was hard with determination, with promise. Regina believed him. And with the belief came absolute trust. He was James's brother and he was her rescuer, and now, now he was offering to protect her. She would eagerly accept his offer. "Thank you."

He gave her a smile. It was tentative, a small form of encouragement. Very slightly, and just as tentatively, Regina smiled back. His arm slipped around her waist.

She stared at it. The masculinity of it—of him—struck her at once, as did the protectiveness of his gesture.

Then she wondered what would happen when she saw James, which would undoubtedly be in the very near future. He must be waiting for her in Templeton, distraught.

Panic swept through her again. She tried to summon up a recollection of her fiancé. To her dismay, to her horror, Slade's image was implanted irrevocably in her mind now, especially the image of his hard bare arm wrapped around her waist; James was nothing more than a vague, faceless shadow. She didn't even know what she herself looked like, she realized in shock.

"What is it?" Slade asked quickly.

His astuteness was unnerving. "I can't remember James no matter how hard I try. It doesn't seem right."

Slade said nothing, but because they were in such an intimate position, she felt the tension overcome his body again. Abruptly his arm fell away from her.

"I don't even know what I look like," she added.

A long pause followed her words. "Blonde," Slade said roughly. "Your hair is long and blonde. Not pale or silver, but gold, with red in it."

She twisted to look at him, surprised that he would volunteer such a detailed description of her hair. But he would not look at her again.

"Tell me about Miramar. Tell me about James," she said into the awkward silence. She was aware of being pleased that he liked her hair. "Tell me everything I should know."

"Miramar?" His voice softened. "You'll fall in love with it the moment you see it. There's no place on earth like Miramar. Our land lies between the Santa Rosa Creek in the north and the Villa Creek in the south. It butts right up to the Pacific Ocean. Once we had over fifty thousand acres; once our borders reached the land that's now the town of Templeton. We've only got a third of the original grant left, but what we do have is the heart of God's country."

Regina was motionless. This man was in love, she realized, stunned, in love with this place called Miramar. It was almost as if he were talking about a woman.

"The rancho is mostly hills and small hidden valleys, but it's good grazing land. We mostly run beef," Slade said in the same soft voice. "But we've put a few acres to oranges and lemons and we even have an almond orchard." He smiled. "Best almonds around. We've also got a winery and damn if we don't make the best wine in the entire state. By the coast the hills are covered with pine and crawling with wildlife. We hunt venison and elk in the winter and catch freshwater trout in the summer. Not for sport, but to eat. From time to time you can see more than a few gold eagles, and even the occasional baldy. There's damn good fishing in the ocean, too, and all year long you can watch the sea lions there, except for May and June, when they're breeding. The coast at Miramar is probably the most beautiful you'll ever see. Up north it's wild and rough, hemmed in by cliffs, but on the cove where we swim the beaches are flat and smooth, the color of those pearl ear-bobs you're wearing. Even so, the ocean can be dangerous—people have drowned there. You don't swim unless you're strong and fit. We've been swimming there since we were boys."

"We?"

"My brothers and me. Edward . . . and James."

Regina was silent. She was completely caught up in his glowing description of his home. She had never seen a sea lion, and wondered what it was exactly. Miramar sounded too beautiful, too wonderful to be true. And she could imagine three young boys playing there, while the mythical sea lions watched.

"Tell me about him," Regina urged suddenly, aware of the small piercing of guilt. James was her fiancé and she not only couldn't remember anything about him, she didn't even have the slightest feelings for him. She was determined to know all about him before she was reunited with him. She realized that Slade was silent and that he had tensed behind her. "James," she repeated. "Tell me about him."

"Jesus. I don't even know where to start." His voice was rough.

"What does he look like?"

"Big. Bigger than me. Lots bigger. And handsome. Real handsome. Women . . ." He stopped.

Regina could guess what he had been about to say, and she shifted to look up at him again. She was shocked to see his mouth drawn in a grim line, his eyes bleak. When he caught her regarding him he quickly looked away.

"He could always have any woman he wanted. Not just because of his looks. But because he was kind. James was a kind man. There's no one kinder. He was always helping others, even louses—even those he shouldn't have bothered with."

"Then I'm very lucky," Regina said softly, but she still felt nothing at all except an extreme interest in how much Slade loved his brother. He didn't seem to hear her.

"No one's smarter than James," Slade said. "With numbers and with words. Can he write! No one can write a prettier letter, I know that firsthand. And no one is a harder worker. And loyal. James was loyal, he'd never let you or anyone else down. When he made a promise, when he made a commitment, he kept it. No matter what."

"He sounds like a paragon," Regina said wistfully.

For a moment Slade was silent. "There was no one like James. No one. He was a paragon."

It suddenly struck Regina that Slade was referring to her fiancé in the past tense. "Why do you keep saying he *was* this and he *was* that?" she asked.

Slade tensed. For a long time he could not speak, and Regina knew. "Because he *was* strong and he *was* smart," he finally said. "But not anymore. James is dead."

Chapter 2

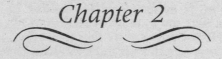

*T*here was only one hotel in Templeton, right on Main Street, although the town's single saloon advertised that it also had rooms for rent. The hotel, a false-fronted, brand-new brick building, was adjacent to the saloon. Neither establishment had a name. The sign HOTEL and the sign SALOON were sufficient, apparently, for both the proprietors and the patrons of these establishments.

An occasional oak tree provided some shade at the southern end of town. There was a boardwalk instead of a paved sidewalk but no streetlights. Main Street was a wide dirt thoroughfare. The railroad ran parallel to it, one block over, on this side of the dry Salinas River.

On the other side of the hotel was a small bakery and cafe. There was also a general store, a meat market, an office of the West Coast Land Company, a barber shop, a blacksmith's, and several other retail establishments in the "business district," which encompassed several blocks. Most of the buildings were wooden and very new; there were many plots of vacant land interspersed between them. The entire town probably had two dozen dwellings.

Slade told her that there had been a fire two years ago which had wiped out most of the town's center.

But by then Templeton had already seen its very brief heyday. It had been a railroad boomtown for just a few short years, founded in anticipation of the railroad's advent by shrewd speculators who had bought out and carved up the original Mexican ranchos. After the fire, many of these proprietors had gone elsewhere instead of rebuilding, leaving Templeton to doze quietly in the California sun, more ghostly than before.

Templeton's saving grace was its setting. It was surrounded by an endless line of sunburned hills and brilliant blue skies; occasionally a translucent silver-lined cloud puffed past them. No matter where one looked, there was beauty, majesty, and eternity in the California landscape.

Now Regina stood alone in the middle of the hotel room, unmoving. Slade had left her there just a moment ago, intent on finding the town's doctor.

Regina did not want to be alone. She trembled. Being alone was frightening. There had been so much comfort in Slade's presence; now there was a void. And anxiety was rushing in to fill the void created by her solitude. There was gaping loneliness in being alone in the hotel room, a stranger to herself.

How she yearned for Slade's presence, as if they were old and dear friends, not actual strangers. But they were really only that. In the hour or so that it had taken them to reach town, they had not furthered their acquaintance. After he had told her that James was dead, they had ridden in complete silence. She had been able to feel his grief. She would not intrude upon it, not knowingly. Her own heart had ached for him.

Suddenly Regina slid the dead bolt on the door. Her nerves, she realized, were shattered, but locking the door did little to soothe them. She turned, facing the room. There were five trunks stacked neatly in one corner. The top one was open. Had she had a maid, she would assume that someone had unpacked some of her things. But she did not have a maid, and she could only think the worst—that someone had been going through her belongings.

She trembled again. Why would someone invade her privacy like that? Those trunks belonged to her. Slade had said so. Even though she had not the faintest idea of what the trunks contained, she had a sense of being violated. But more importantly, would she recognize her things? Would her memory be jarred, and would she finally remember who she was?

Alone, she was desperate to know herself. But she was afraid, afraid that she would look in the trunks and be faced with another blank wall. She did not move.

Instead, her glance jerked over the room. It was small and shabby. The walls were papered in a pretty rosebud pattern, but they were stained and could use a good cleaning. There was a scarred bureau, a rickety armoire, and two upholstered chairs, but they did not match each other or the room. The bed was nothing more than a cot with a thin comforter and there was a hand-loomed rug underfoot which had seen too many trespassers. Regina reflected upon her setting. Although she didn't have her memory, she knew that this hotel room was not up to standard. Or—it was not up to *her* standard. So Elizabeth Sinclair was no stranger to travel, but she was used to somewhat better accommodations.

And then she saw the mirror.

For one second she stared. Then she rushed to it. Pain darted through her sore ankle but she ignored it. She came to a halt in front of the mirror and she blinked, staring at herself. Her hopes crashed. For she was looking not at a dear and familiar face, but at a pale and frightened stranger.

She choked on a sob, clutching the edge of the bureau to hold herself upright. Disappointment immobilized her. Shock made her dizzy. She had to fight to calm herself, taking deep, steadying breaths, until the floor ceased its eddying.

Finally the sensation of being on a moving ship passed. The dizziness disappeared. Still gripping the bureau tightly, she inspected herself as one woman might inspect another who was both a newcomer and a rival. There was a fine coating of dust on her face and dirt stains on her bodice, but Regina barely saw them. Her hair was piled haphazardly on her head, and as Slade had said, it was a rich blonde tinged with red lights, a mass of shimmering honeys and golds. It was a very unusual color. She could understand how Slade would admire it, but the pleasure she had felt before over his apparent interest was gone.

She studied her face intensely. It was oval, high-cheekboned, delicate. Her mouth was full and rosy-red, her complexion pale but touched with gold beneath the dust. Her eyes were light-brown, amber. Her lashes were long and dark, as were her brows. It gave her a dramatic appearance.

Staring at the stranger in the mirror, she could only hope that she was dreaming. She touched her cheek to make sure that she was indeed staring at herself, to make sure that this awful and bizarre episode was real, and not a nightmare. It was real. Her fingertips were smooth on her skin, the floor beneath her feet was hard and solid, the room around three-dimensional, not one.

A rude, unwelcome thought intruded. *She had jumped off the train.* Regina's pulse accelerated. She still could not remember, and trying only caused an instant headache. Looking at herself now, she could understand why she had leaped off a speeding train. She was very beautiful, the kind of woman who could have been singled out by outlaws for more than robbery.

What had happened? A terrible pain pierced the back of her head and a gunshot sounded. She clapped her hands over her ears. For a moment she stood frozen, frightened. Abruptly she turned and ran to the window, looking down at Main Street. It was deserted except for one overburdened dray pulled by two dusty mules. She lifted the window, which opened reluctantly. A warm breeze touched her damp face. She listened intently for another gunshot as a small boy slowly bicycled into view, a balloon tied to the back of his seat, but only heard a dog yapping, wind chimes, and some male laughter from the saloon below.

She knew that she hadn't heard a gunshot. It had been in her mind. Yet it had been so real. Had it been a memory?

Numb, Regina sank into the blue-and-white chair. For many minutes she did not think and she did not move. She did not dare. And when she did think, she found herself yearning for Slade.

Against her will, her gaze settled on the trunks. She made no move to go over to them. Yet she knew she must. She had just had a memory, she was certain of it. Had it been caused by the sight of her own reflection? If so, would her own possessions trigger an even greater recollection? Fear was almost immobilizing her. Sweat trickled down her cheekbones.

Like a somnambulist, Regina stood and moved slowly across the room. She leaned over the open trunk. Someone had indeed been there before her, rummaging among her clothes. They were rumpled, not folded neatly. She lifted out a day dress. The fabric was of the finest linen, and the garment was custom-made. She lifted out another dress. It was an expensive silk. She did not recognize either dress, and by the time she had reached the bottom of the trunk, she was breathing hard, as if she had run a great endurance race. She had been told that these were her possessions, but she had never seen them before. They had not revitalized her memory. And she was not hearing any more frightening gunshots in her mind, gunshots that sounded incredibly real.

She had only gone through one trunk, but she was exhausted. She did not have the strength to move it in order to open the one below, and she sank into a chair. She was perspiring. It was very hot out, but that wasn't why her shirtwaist was clinging to her skin.

Her memory was still blank, but she realized the effort hadn't been entirely in vain. She had just learned an important fact about herself. All of the clothes in that trunk belonged to a wealthy young woman. A very wealthy young woman. Slade hadn't told her that Elizabeth Sinclair was rich. It seemed like a glaring omission.

Dozens of questions were suddenly bubbling up in her, questions that she had to have answered. Was she rich? Who was her family and where was she from? And what about James? Had she been grieving before the train robbery? When she regained her memory, would she be devastated by his death? If only she could, at least, recall him!

Guilt pricked her and she covered her face with her hands. She was aware of waiting for Slade to return, of being eager for his return. Yet his brother, her fiancé, was dead. Even though she could not summon up the slightest feeling for him, she should be dwelling upon that, not upon the brother who had rescued her. She told herself that in the state she was in, it was only natural to need the one and only person she knew, to be looking to Slade for the comfort and strength he so readily offered her.

She bit her lip. She could not deny herself in these circumstances. Slade was the only person that tempered her fears. If she did not have him to rely on she would be so alone. No, she could not deny herself.

He did not look like a hero. She smiled slightly, her first smile in many hours. Heroes wore tweed hacking coats and doeskin breeches and rode gleaming black stallions. Heroes wore jet-black tailcoats and brilliant white shirts and gold signet rings with family crests and precious stones. Heroes did not wear denim pants so worn they were close to ripping, with sweaty cotton work shirts and dirty, oversized belt buckles. He was just a flesh-and-blood man, albeit an attractive one, and apparently one who might be a bit down on his luck, too. But he had rescued her. Gratitude swelled her heart once again, as it had done many times before in the past few hours.

Her warm thoughts were interrupted by a knock upon her door. For an instant Regina thought it was Slade. She eagerly rushed to the door, unbolted it, and swung it open. But Slade wasn't on the other side. And the moment Regina saw the other man she knew who he was. He was bigger and fairer than Slade, and his face was rougher and not as handsome, but their eyes were exactly the same. Burning midnight eyes. Intense, passionate eyes. Relentlessly alert, intelligent eyes. This man was Slade's father, Rick Delanza.

His eyes lit up at the sight of her. He held out his arms. He said, "Elizabeth! Thank God you're all right!"

Slade leaned back in the hardwood chair, his head against the rough wall. He had a cigar in one hand, the tip lit and glowing, and a glass of whiskey in the other. Yet there was nothing relaxed or indulgent about his posture. His legs were bent at the knee and his feet braced hard against the broken tiles of the floor. He looked as if he might erupt from the small chair at any moment.

An open bottle sat on the small, rickety table in front of him. Slade was facing the door. Despite the heavy smoke which hung in the air, he saw his brother Edward the moment he paused in the doorless entrance of the shabby cantina which was in an alley well off of Templeton's main thoroughfare.

Edward strode forward. He was slightly taller than Slade, an inch or so over six feet, yet much bigger in build. Slade was whipcord-lean, Edward was abundantly muscular. Like Slade, he had midnight-black hair that framed a face that could only be described as handsome. But that was where all resemblance between the brothers ended. Edward was much fairer than Slade and his eyes were light-blue. His jaw was broader, his nose larger and slightly hooked. He was well-dressed in a dark suit and a white shirt, a silver waistcoat and a silk tie. Unlike most big men, he wore his clothes well and gracefully. Of course, they had been custom-made for him. His black boots were polished to a high sheen and he wore a dark Stetson, which he tossed onto the table beside his brother. "Goddammit, Slade. Couldn't you find a worse place?"

"Hello, brother."

Edward pulled up a chair and grimaced as he looked at it before sitting down. "You actually like this kind of hellhole? Two blocks over Renee's got the best whiskey in town, and the softest girls."

"I feel at home here," Slade said mockingly.

Edward stared at him. "Bull. In Frisco you wouldn't be caught dead in a rat hole like this."

Slade said nothing. He turned and signaled a fat saloon girl for another glass for his brother.

"You gonna drink that whole bottle?" Edward asked.

"Maybe."

Edward sighed. He took Slade's glass and drank half of it, then pushed it back at him. "I miss him, too."

"Don't start."

"Why not?" Edward's face tightened, and his beautiful blue eyes glazed. "I'm not going to ever get over it, not ever. There was no one like James. But I'm not drinking myself to death."

"You're only screwing yourself to death," Slade said calmly. "If you don't watch out you'll catch something you'll regret."

Edward was angry. "You should talk! You're no damn choirboy! I've met Xandria."

"There's nothing between us and there never was," Slade said flatly.

"Then you're a fool," Edward said just as flatly.

A moment passed. Slade smiled. It was a sad smile, but a smile nonetheless. Edward smiled, too, his expression almost identical except that his was dimpled. The waitress came with a glass. Slade was about to pour his brother a drink, but Edward stopped him. He took a handkerchief from his breast pocket and cleaned the glass, holding the cloth up afterward to show Slade that the linen was now gray. Slade shrugged, refilling both of their drinks. "A little dust never hurt anybody."

Edward sighed and drank. "So what happened? The whole town's buzzing. You found her."

"I found her." Slade's mouth tightened. "She doesn't remember who she is. She doesn't remember anything." An image of her looking at him with near-worshipful eyes assailed him. Angrily he shrugged it off. But it was an image that had been haunting him ever since he had left her at the hotel.

Edward blinked. Then he said, "Well, maybe that's for the best."

Slade looked at him, understanding him. "Did she love James?" If so, it was better that she didn't remember, that she was spared, at least temporarily, some of the grief.

"How in hell would I know? You're the one he wrote those letters to. I got sick of hearing how goddamn beautiful and perfect she was and told him to shut up years ago." He winced, then eyed his brother. "Is she God's gift to man?"

"Yeah."

"I don't recall you and James having the same taste in women."

"She's beautiful," Slade said brusquely. He didn't bother telling his brother that she was more than beautiful. She was sexy. Very sexy. It wasn't even that knock-out body of hers, which he had inspected too closely and too carefully. It was her face. There was something about that face that would make a man crazy and make him think of sex. He shut off his thoughts with a vengeance. She was obviously a lady, but his body didn't seem capable of respecting that.

"So maybe it's not such a bad idea after all. Maybe you and Rick can work things out and . . ."

"No!" Slade slammed his fist down hard and the glasses jumped and fell to the floor, breaking. Edward caught the bottle before it tipped over. Slade couldn't believe himself. Lusting after Elizabeth, his brother's fiancée.

"That sure was smart," Edward said.

"This town hasn't changed," Slade said. "Nothing changes around here, does it? She needs to be examined and I found Doc upstairs with a two-bit whore, passed out cold."

"You see Rick? We got to town hours ago. Rick's been going crazy waiting for you to get back. He'll really bust loose when he hears she lost her mind. That sure puts a kink or two in his plans."

"She lost her memory," Slade corrected. "And I saw him just after I brought her to the hotel. I told him she didn't know who she was. He was very surprised. Last I know, he was going over there."

Edward looked at him. "Something's bothering you. What?"

Slade shifted. "Nothing." He wasn't a liar and he never had been. "It's been a bitch of a day."

But Edward was a clever man. He couldn't possibly be so in tune with Slade's thoughts, but when he spoke, it was as if he was reading his brother's mind. "You know, you've never met Elizabeth. Neither have I, for that matter. Rick's the only one who has, and I guess he's with her now. What if the lady is someone else?"

"Elizabeth was scheduled to arrive on that train," Slade pointed out. "She was on her way to Miramar to marry James. The wedding was supposed to be in two weeks. These plans were made a long time ago. If for some reason she didn't board, if there had been an emergency, she would have wired us. Only one passenger—one woman—was missing." Slade shrugged indifferently. "Besides, she looks exactly the way James described her." Small and stunning, he added silently. And yes, perfect.

Yet his indifference was all show and he knew it. No matter how hard he tried to tell himself that he didn't care, he did. He was a traitor to himself and to his brother and the fact shocked him. Because he was hoping that she wasn't James's fiancée. It was ridiculous, it defied logic, and, more importantly, he had no right to hope like that at all.

Even if she didn't belong to James—and those odds were a million to one—she was obviously a lady, and ladies did not look twice at a man like him. He would rein in his traitorous mind if it killed him.

"What is it?" Edward asked again.

"Nothing," Slade ground out. He might be able to turn off his thoughts whenever they dared to intrude, but it was much harder not to be angry. The anger coiled thick and hot inside him. Rick had better not say one damn word about his latest scheme. Slade would erupt if he did.

"Maybe we should go over to the hotel and find Rick."

Slade didn't move. Sweat beaded his brow. "No." He knew she was Elizabeth. Which was why he did not move. Right now, Rick was undoubtedly there, with her. Removing the last doubt would be crushing when he was far too cynical and wise to be crushed.

"I see," Edward said. He folded his arms and watched Slade drain the glass. "You've made up your mind, haven't you? You're not going to stay. You're Rick's heir now, but you're not going to stay. You're going to go back up north."

"That's right."

Edward was mad. He lunged to his feet and placed his palms down hard on the table, causing the bottle to roll off and spill all over the floor. Neither brother noticed. "Why the hell don't you stay?" Edward demanded. "You're going back there to work like a frigging majordomo for Charles Mann, when you should be here!"

Slade kicked back his chair. For a moment he was an inch from taking his fist and blacking out one of his brother's eyes. But he controlled himself. "Because I like working for Charles," he said. "Because I don't like working for Rick. And because I don't like being blackmailed."

"You're a goddamn fool!" Edward shouted. "Be honest. You're doing this to get back at him, right? You think you're getting back at Rick. You know what? You're doing this for all the years he loved James more than you!"

Slade was white. "Wrong," he said. "*Wrong.* I'm doing what I want to do for me!"

"You're choosing *them* over *us!*" Edward shouted. "They're not your family—we are!"

"That has nothing to do with it!"

"You belong here! Now more than ever. James is dead. Rick needs you! We need you!"

"No." Slade shook his head, enraged. His face was flushed with fury. "Rick needs an heiress, not me. And I am not going to marry her in order to inherit Miramar. I am not going to marry the woman James loved—not for you, not for Rick, not even for Miramar."

Chapter 3

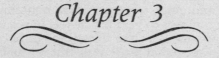

Edward left abruptly after their shouting match. Slade made no move to follow. He drank the awful gut-wrenching whiskey, trying not to think about what Edward had said and trying not to think about the woman he'd left at the hotel. He watched as shadows finally appeared on the hard-packed dirt outside, watched as they gradually lengthened. Dusk settled over Templeton with finality.

It wasn't true. It was ridiculous. He wasn't trying to get back at Rick for favoring James. He had loved James, too. Everyone who had known James had loved him; James had possessed a rare kind of magic, the magic of charisma and kindness, a magic very few men had. Edward had some of that magic, too. He, Slade, was the only brother who had not been touched by that special magic wand.

James had been Slade's hero even though he was only a year older. They had both grown up with the house-keeper and cook, Josephine, acting as their mother, even after Rick had married Victoria; *her* only interest was her own son, Edward. James's mother Catherine had died in childbirth, and Slade's mother had run away when he was only a few months old and too young to know what had happened. He had thought the Negress

Josephine his real mother until James had explained to him the facts of life when he was three years old.

James and Slade had been as inseparable as twins, with Edward, three years younger, tagging along behind them. The brothers were perceived as being as different from each other as night and day, James always sunny-tempered and quick to laugh, Slade hot-tempered and grim. Yet contrary to popular belief, James had had a mischievous streak in him too, although he wasn't the determined rebel that Slade was. But it was James who had the common sense to deter Slade from some of his wilder ideas, just as it was James who was always standing up for Slade when he was caught for a misdeed, hoping to distract the adults or take the blame himself. No one ever believed James, because everyone knew Slade too well.

But Slade could accept that now. It had been harder when he was a boy. As a boy he had thought it grossly unfair to be the one instantly blamed for every misdeed, even if he *had* been the one responsible for most of the pranks, some kind, some mean, that he and his brothers pulled. Unquestionably he had been the leader of the hell-raising pair, which had become a trio once Edward was a bit older.

Today, as an adult, he could look back at that boy and smile sadly, for it was so obvious why he had been an unrepentant mischief-maker. He had desperately wanted attention. The only way he had known how to get it was to cause trouble. And trouble begat trouble. He had been punished countless times, but confinement or an occasional slap were not enough to redeem him.

Yet he hadn't been the one to get fifteen-year-old Janey Doyle pregnant. That still rankled. It still hurt. Even when Edward had come forward to claim responsibility for the deed, no one had believed him, because Edward was only twelve. Of course, no one had thought James would ever ravish their innocent neighbor, but everyone had believed he, Slade, who had in fact still been a virgin, to be the culprit.

There had been no minor slap for that incident. Slade had ceased protesting his innocence way before the punishment began. Edward would not stop proclaiming his guilt and had finally been locked in his room. Rick had whipped Slade. But Slade had refused to cry. Rick had been so angry Slade had truly been afraid, too afraid then to understand what his father had been saying. Rick had been berating him for being exactly like his mother. In retrospect it was ironic, because he was actually as different from his mother as a son could be.

Now he was wise enough and detached enough to know that the whipping had been the trigger for his running away, not the cause. The issue of Janey Doyle's pregnancy had merely been the last and final straw in a never-ending and bitter battle he'd waged for his father's attention. The whipping had been a crushing defeat, not of his body, but of his soul. Rick had not tried to stop him from leaving. Rick had let him go.

James had tried to prevent him from leaving, though. Slade could still hear James's urgent voice and Edward's soft sobbing.

"You can't go. He didn't mean it."

"He meant it. I've got six marks on my back. He meant it." Slade's voice choked.

"Let me get Jojo," James said worriedly. Jojo was their pet name for the woman who had mothered them both. "She's in the kitchen, crying a flood over you."

Slade thought he might cry soon, too. At least she cared—she'd always cared. But tonight that just wasn't enough. He scowled at Edward, standing behind James, now hiccuping. The stable was dark and he was a small noisy shadow. "Tell him to quit it."

"Stop it," James commanded, but his voice wasn't harsh and his hand clasped Edward's shoulder. "It's not your fault. You told the truth."

"Slade's leaving because of me," Edward cried. "I should have been whipped, not him!"

"That's right," James said. "Just forget it. Slade, don't go. I'll be right back with Jojo. She can put salve on your back." His tone was desperate.

"No. She'll only cry harder." He turned, moving stiff-ly, his back hurting. He led the small roan out of the stable. Rick would probably be mad at him for taking the cow pony.

James grabbed him, whirling him around. "You can't go! You can't do this! You can't!"

"Yes, I can," Slade managed, trying to ignore Edward, who was crying again.

"I'm going to get Dad," James shouted.

"Don't you dare!" Slade retorted. Yet half of him wanted James to do just that.

From the shadows, Rick spoke, stunning them all. "He's like his mother. She wanted to leave and nothing could stop her. If he wants to go so badly, let him go."

Those words were all he needed. Slade jumped on the roan. James tried to grab his foot but Slade kicked him, hard, when it was his father he would have liked to hit. And it was Edward who begged, "Please don't go. I'm sorry. Please don't go." Those were the words he wanted to hear from the man who had sired him, not from his brother.

He had ignored his brothers' pleas. And later that night, alone by a small campfire not far from San Francisco, with only the wind and the fog for company, he had cried like a baby. It was the last time he had cried, too, until the day of his brother's funeral.

It was a little more than a month since he had been alerted by Edward—not Rick—and had come home. He had made the short train journey in shock. To this day he could barely remember boarding in San Francisco or the journey south. Charles had been there, he thought, trying to comfort him. But he wasn't sure. His mind had been consumed with denial. James could not be dead, drowned, for God's sake, in a flash flood. Other men might die, but not James, never James.

Miramar was in mourning when Slade returned after Edward's summons. Rick had been closeted in the soli-tude of his study for days; it was weeks before he functioned, and then with an ashen pallor and the automatic movements and speech of a sleepwalker. He barely acknowledged Slade's return, and Slade hadn't been home in two years. Yet Slade could not feel bitter toward Rick. He even imagined comforting him. But Rick held everyone at arm's length, unable to share his grief, and later, he came up with his damned idea to see Slade and Elizabeth wed. Slade instantly realized that he had been a fool to feel any compassion at all for his father.

Edward managed to hide his grief with great self-discipline. Still, his smiles and witticisms were gone. Slade knew that beneath his smooth surface he was as anguished as anyone; there were no secrets between the brothers. Even Victoria, Edward's mother, was somber. Slade was certain it was an act. And when she saw Slade she forgot her grief—if she really was grieving—and her eyes blazed with fury. She wasn't happy that he had come home. Then again, Slade hadn't expected her to be.

The funeral had finally been held four weeks ago, shortly after Slade's return. Until the funeral, the shock had been numbing. Until the funeral, James's death didn't seem real. Didn't seem possible. The eulogy was Slade's undoing; unlike most eulogies, which were bull-shit, this one was not. Father Joseph was not exaggerating when he praised James for his extraordinary kindness and endless generosity, for his compassion and his morality. It was also true that James had been selflessly devoted to his family, to his father and brothers, to his stepmother, to Josephine, to Miramar. Such sincerity, devotion, and commitment were astounding in one so young. All life was God-given, but a young man like James was a very special and holy gift.

Father Joseph ran the mission at San Miguel and he had known James since he was born. He delivered the eulogy with teary eyes and a choked-up voice. He was only halfway through it when Slade lost all control. He wept. Restraint was impossible. Edward proved to be stronger and more disciplined, or perhaps he had already shed his tears, for he put his arm around Slade, offering him what support and sympathy he could.

Slade could not stop crying until the funeral was over and everyone had gone, the coffin buried deeply in Miramar's rich red earth.

The whiskey wasn't doing its job. Tonight the grief was as painful and raw as it had been that day at the funeral. Father Joseph had said it would lessen in time. Common sense said the priest was right, but at the moment common sense was no consolation. He had never missed James more. It was even more heart-rending to face the fact that he was never going to see his brother again—to finally comprehend the utter finality of death.

Eventually the big bubble in his chest began to deflate. He had weathered this latest crisis. He looked around at the dark cantina with its less-than-respectable patrons, so caught up in his grief and memories that he was briefly surprised to find himself there. Edward was right in more ways than one. In San Francisco he wouldn't be caught dead in such a place, but when he came home he didn't think twice about joining this kind of crowd. Even at the age of twenty-five, he still came home determined to rebel. The thought, laced with whiskey, made him slightly uneasy.

He wondered what had happened over at the hotel. Did he really have a doubt? It was obvious that she was Elizabeth Sinclair, not some other woman. When her memory came back, would she grieve, too? Had she loved James? The marriage had been arranged and they had only met a few times because she'd been away at school in London, until last summer. Her father had died and she had come home for the funeral, staying the summer. James had courted her. He had gone to San Luis Obispo as often as possible to see her. Slade knew; James had written all about her. James had sure as hell loved her. Slade's gut grew tight when he imagined their courtship, which had ended in the fall when Elizabeth had returned to London for her last year of school.

He thought about what Rick expected of him and it was almost funny. He was the oldest now. Rick wanted

him to inherit Miramar. Rick expected him to inherit
Miramar. It was tradition, real old-fashioned Californio
tradition. But there was a catch. He had to marry the
heiress, Elizabeth Sinclair, to do so. Because Miramar
was cash-poor, real cash-poor, as it had always been,
and she was bringing all the cash they'd ever need to
the union.

He did not like recalling her wide, trusting, grateful
eyes. Especially not now. He didn't want her looking
at him like that, not ever. He wasn't going to marry her. Slade would never agree. He wasn't staying,
he wasn't inheriting Miramar, and he wasn't marrying
Elizabeth Sinclair. Rick, who had never asked him to
stay the few times he'd come home to visit, would
have to do a lot more than ask him to stay now. He'd
have to beg. As if he would. And as if it would matter.

It wasn't that he didn't love Miramar. He did.
He always had. He always would. But Miramar had
belonged to James, just as Elizabeth Sinclair had belonged to James. And he loved James, his death didn't
change that. He wasn't going to betray James, not even
in death.

Tomorrow he would return to San Francisco, where
he had worked for Charles Mann for almost ten years.
San Francisco was his home now. Rick might not have
James, but he had Miramar, and Edward could take
over when Rick got too feeble—which wouldn't be for
another twenty years, Slade imagined.

But the irony was that Slade knew he could turn
Miramar around and pull it out of the hole it was in.
They'd been cash-poor since he'd been born, because
times were changing. Slade was no longer a green
boy. He'd traveled enough, worked enough, and seen
enough to know that it was time to get rid of the
old in favor of the new. He saw it up north. The
old ranchos were not making ends meet. Modern
industry, technology, and agriculture had come to
California with a vengeance. The great self-sufficient
ranchos like Miramar were obsolete, empires which

belonged to the past, dinosaurs which could not survive in the future. They were no longer viable. The future belonged to other enterprises such as mining, lumber, farming. Already there were vast agricultural enterprises in California that were making big profits in oranges and lemons, wheat and barley. Miramar had an abundance of land, and plenty of it was fertile. The few orchards they had yielded the sweetest fruit in the county, the best wine. They had forests aplenty, too, and with careful management Slade knew that a portion of them could be harvested, cultivated, and regrown, not raped and destroyed. It was time to make changes, to take Miramar into the twentieth century, and it was the ultimate irony because Slade knew he could do it, but he wasn't going to.

Instead of turning Miramar around, tomorrow he was going to ride out of town right back to the big city where he now belonged.

When Slade returned to the hotel it was after dark. He was sober. He'd gone to the cafe, which had been closing up. Mrs. Burke had seen who it was at her door and had immediately invited him in and fixed him up. She had served him a thick rare steak, which he'd washed down with lots of strong coffee. He'd even managed to eat half of a piece of her apple pie. She seemed to take pleasure in hovering over him, although he couldn't understand why, because as a boy he'd pulled a few good pranks on her, too. She was his own age. He finally decided she was so friendly because she felt sorry for his loss.

"Come back now, Slade," she whispered at the door when he left.

He nodded, thanking her, feeling her staring after him. He finally understood her invitation, but not why it had been issued. She was pretty enough, but he could not imagine ever taking her up on it.

He took his key from the hotel clerk and went slowly up the stairs. He grew intensely aware of the fact that Elizabeth's room was at the top of the stairs. The exhaustion which had settled over him quickly lifted. He was more resolved than ever to leave the county tomorrow.

But he paused in the corridor and glanced at her door. His body tightened. He was instantly assailed by an image of her heart-stopping face, her wide golden eyes. The question he had avoided all evening rushed in upon him. His traitorous mind dared to wonder if she were someone other than Elizabeth Sinclair.

He didn't want to think the thought. Not now, not again. He was too tired to hope, but deep in his heart, there *was* hope. How foolish could he be? He made a fist, the key digging into his hand. Tomorrow he was going back north. She would solve her own problems. He tried not to remember her weeping in his arms, clinging to him, regarding him hopefully as if he were a hero. He was the farthest thing possible from a hero.

A door further down the hallway opened. Rick stepped into the hall, a tall, powerful figure clad in thin red wool pajamas. "Thought you were out here." He eyed his son.

Slowly Slade looked at his father. "I'm going to bed." But he waited, waited for Rick to reveal what he knew about her identity.

"You been over at Dom's?"

Slade nodded.

"Take a bath. You smell of smoke and liquor and cheap perfume."

Rick was imagining things, because he certainly did not smell of a whore's perfume, but Slade did not refute him. If he wanted to think the worst, he would. "So what?"

"I don't want Elizabeth seeing you like this."

"At this hour she's sleeping." *So she was Elizabeth. So she was James's fiancée.*

"I want to talk to you."

"I don't want to talk. I want to go to bed."

"Looks like you've already been to bed."

"What the hell do you care?" Slade bristled. Rick *always* thought the worst of him. "What I do is my business, not yours."

"Wrong. You have the morals of an alley cat and you always have. I don't want Elizabeth finding out."

Slade stiffened. Sometimes he felt like telling his father the truth. But Rick wouldn't believe him. It would be pointless. "It doesn't matter if she finds out," he gritted. "Because I'm not marrying her."

"Then you're not getting Miramar!" Rick roared.

"I don't want Miramar!"

"You liar. You want it. You always have. And now's your chance to have Miramar." Abruptly Rick grabbed Slade's arm and pulled him into his room. Slade shook him off as Rick shut the door.

"You miserable old bastard," Slade hissed. "Now is my chance! Is Miramar all you can think of? Your son is dead. James is dead. Miramar belonged to him. You think I can step into his shoes so easily?"

"I think you have no respect," Rick raged. "No respect for me, for your grandfather, for Miramar, for tradition. *You have no choice.* You're the oldest now. The oldest inherits. It's always been that way in our family. Always. My father was the second son, but he made something of himself! He fought in the war for Mexico's independence, and later was rewarded—with Miramar. He worked hard from the day he gained title until the day he died, but not for himself. He worked to leave a legacy for me—for you. You are my heir now, and one day your son will be your heir! That is tradition, and tradition doesn't change!"

"You're living in an age that doesn't exist! Give up! Move on! Forget the past! For God's sake, in a few months we're going to be in the twentieth century!"

"Then do it for James," Rick shot back. "He knew how much you loved Miramar. We'd discussed it. He would want you to take over now. He would—"

"Don't you speak about him as if he were still alive!" Slade was enraged. James had always been Rick's favorite, always, but then he had been the heir. In that instant it occurred to Slade that Rick really loved Miramar best—better than his own son.

Rick gripped Slade's arms. "If you don't marry her, we're losing Miramar."

Slade went still. "What kind of bullshit is this?"

"The rancho has been mortgaged. I had no choice. Times have been bad and getting worse. The depression of '93 really hurt us. But I never thought it would come to this."

Slade stared.

"I haven't been able to make a mortgage payment in over two years. But that was fine—until six months ago when some fancy banker from New York took over the Bank of San Francisco. They've threatened to call in their loan. They only changed their tune because of James's impending marriage—and the dowry Elizabeth is bringing to us. They don't know James is dead. When they find out, all hell will break loose. They'll foreclose in a flash. They won't try to operate the rancho. They'll break it up, sell it, all of it, in tiny little pieces. You've got to marry Elizabeth, and soon. If you don't, they're going to take Miramar away from us."

Slade was shocked speechless.

"It's the truth," Rick said, releasing him. He paced away. He turned to look at his son. "We're not just broke. We're bankrupt."

Slade stared in disbelief.

"If you don't marry her, then Edward will. We need her money and we need it now."

Slade heard himself say, "Edward doesn't care about Miramar. He never has."

"You're right. The only thing he cares about is women and an occasional game of cards. But he's young. And he's smart. And he'll do what he has to do." Rick left the rest unspoken: *not like you.*

"Wouldn't Victoria be happy," Slade said sarcastically. That woman would do anything for her son, even if it meant forcing him into a loveless marriage with his dead brother's fiancée so he could inherit the rancho. Of course, contrary to what Rick thought, Edward would not agree. Or would he? Edward was loyal, too; it was a Delanza trait.

"Well?"

Slade felt trapped, backed into a corner. He didn't want to stay. He didn't want Miramar. Miramar belonged to James, who wasn't yet cold in his grave. But . . . the very idea of losing Miramar was abhorrent, sickening, frightening. And he didn't like the idea of Edward marrying Elizabeth any better.

"What in hell is so hard about marrying a pretty little lady like that in order to get what you've always wanted anyway?" Rick asked.

"That's not true," Slade said tersely. But if he dared be honest, he would admit that it was true. Deep inside, he had always wanted what he could not have. Now, an impossible dream was within reach. But only because his brother was dead.

He turned on his booted heel. At the door he paused, his expression hard. "I'll think about it. Give me some time."

Rick was equally grim. "We don't have time."

Chapter 4

The doctor was a thin, wiry man of indeterminate age. Regina sat obediently in a chair while he probed and prodded her head. She did not have much confidence in him and she worried her hands in her lap. His eyes were bleary and bloodshot, and she smelled a strong mouthwash on his breath, as well as the whiskey which he couldn't disguise. Regina kept her expression impassive, but her heart was fluttering anxiously. Even though this man seemed thoroughly disreputable, he was a doctor. Rick Delanza, who was waiting outside her door, had brought him to her. And she was afraid of his diagnosis. For although it was a new day, although she had gone through all of her trunks, her memory was as blank as it had been yesterday when Slade had found her. In fact, she hadn't experienced another moment of recollection as she had with the gunshot.

"Got a nice-sized bump on the back of your head." The doctor smiled at her. He had a kind smile. "It hurt you any?"

"I've had a headache since yesterday afternoon."

"You got a knock on the noggin for sure, but you don't seem to have a concussion. Still, you should take it easy until your memory comes back."

"So it will come back?" She could not imagine living in such a mental abyss for very much longer.

"Probably." He saw her dismay and patted her back. "There, there, don't fret. That won't help. Truth is, I've never had a case of amnesia before. It's pretty rare. Still, most folks recover, given time."

Most folks recover, given time. Not for the first time since she had regained consciousness yesterday and realized that she had lost her memory, Regina faced the possibility that she might never regain her faculties, that she might never know herself. The notion was shattering.

Rick knocked upon the door impatiently. "You through, Doc?"

"C'mon in, Rick." The doctor began packing up his black bag slowly, in no hurry at all.

Rick walked in, radiating the kind of energy she had witnessed in Slade, but with a difference. In Slade, it was almost explosive, in the father it was merely vital. Again she wondered where Slade was. She had not seen him since he had left her at her hotel room yesterday afternoon. She had thought about him too often. She was disappointed he was not with his father.

Rick smiled at her but focused on the doctor. "Well?"

Regina did not listen as the doctor told Rick what he had already told her. She got up and walked over to the mirror, staring at the stranger she saw there, the stranger who was herself.

Regina had bathed using a pitcher of water on the bureau and the washbasin beneath. She had dressed in one of her suits, a smart navy jacket and skirt with a cream-colored blouse and a string of pearls which had been among her things. This morning she thought that she looked more than wealthy and attractive, she looked regal and elegant. It was an observation, devoid of any vanity or conceit. It was still disturbing to look at herself. Whenever she did so, the lack of familiarity caused a lump to lodge in her chest.

There was another knock on the door; Regina's first thought was that it was Slade and she smiled, her first genuine smile that day. She stole another quick glance at herself in the mirror, but every hair was in place. She reached the door before Rick and opened it. A hotel valet stood there holding a breakfast tray. Disappointed, she watched him deposit it on the small table between the two upholstered chairs.

"I know you didn't eat last night so I ordered you breakfast," Rick said. "You look like a new person today. How do you feel, Elizabeth?"

"Better." Her reply was automatic. She could smell freshly scrambled eggs and warm buns, making her realize that she was ravenous. But she made no move to sit down. "Where is Slade?"

Rick scowled. "Still in bed. That boy has a tendency to laziness."

Regina glanced at Rick in surprise. She did not know Slade well, but she was positive that he didn't have a lazy bone in his entire body. Quite the opposite, in fact. She didn't think she had ever met a more restless man.

"Go ahead, Elizabeth. Eat. We're not much on manners here."

Regina was about to sit down when, from the open doorway, Slade said, "You wouldn't know good manners if a book of them were shoved right in your face."

Regina and Rick turned. Slade's face was red and angry; he'd obviously heard his father's derogatory remark.

"And the apple don't fall far from the tree," Rick said. "It's ten o'clock. She's got every right to sleep all day. You don't."

Slade stalked in, using the toe of his worn boot to slide the door closed. "You my boss? You feed me, pay me my wages? I don't recall getting a paycheck from you."

"Charlie Mann let you sleep till ten in the morning?"

"When I'm in Frisco, I'm working," Slade said.

Rick hooted. "Like hell! Maybe if you got to bed at a decent hour you could get up in the morning."

"Maybe what I do—at night or any time—is none of your damn business."

The two men glared at each other. Regina was gripping the back of one chair, her eyes wide and riveted upon father and son. She was witnessing what she had no right to witness and she was appalled by the relationship she saw between them. Why had Rick attacked Slade? How could a father do such a thing—and in front of other people? And why had Slade risen so eagerly to do battle? Into the ensuing silence, she said, her smile overly bright, "You're just in time for breakfast! Come, sit down. We'll send for more plates."

Slade and Rick both turned their attention to her, which had been her intention. "I already ate and there's plenty of coffee," Rick said. He pulled up a chair. "Sit down, Elizabeth."

Regina didn't move, regarding Slade, who hadn't responded to her offer. Now that he was no longer focused on his father, his glance had settled upon her. His gaze was sharp, as she had come to expect, meeting hers. The question was there in his eyes. "Anything?"

Regina understood what he was asking. She shook her head, unable to look away—and not wanting to. Disappointment showed plainly on his face when he realized that she had not recovered from the amnesia.

Regina could not help stealing a more thorough glance at him as she sat down. He looked good, and the realization was jarring. His dark thick hair was damp and slicked straight back. He was clean-shaven, and it showed off his perfect features. She really hadn't realized just how extraordinarily handsome he was until that moment. His cotton shirt was snowy-white and freshly laundered, his denims dark-blue and spanking new. He was not wearing his gun. His boots had been wiped clean of dirt, mud, and dust. And Regina thought she detected a whiff of a pleasant, woodsy cologne.

He caught her staring. Regina smiled in response, because she was glad to see him and because she hadn't forgotten for a moment that he had rescued her and that he had also offered to be her protector. He did not smile in return. His gaze was enigmatic. His thoughts, whatever they might be, were well-hidden. The intensity and fire he had evinced yesterday were securely guarded and thoroughly banked.

"Well, now that the patient has been examined, I'm going," Doc said cheerfully from the position he'd maintained near the bed.

Regina started. She had forgotten the doctor was present. And he did not seem at all astonished at the exchange he had also witnessed, or in the least bit discomfitted. Rick walked him to the door, thanking him.

Slade's gaze slid over her, making her skin tingle. Softly, he asked, "What did Doc say?"

"That I'll probably recover—in time."

Slade said nothing and Rick returned to them. Regina was intensely aware of Slade and had lost much of her appetite. She poured both men coffee, asking them how they liked it and fixing it for them. She pretended to eat. Both men sipped their coffee in silence, waiting for her to finish, Rick sitting in the one chair at the table with her, Slade lounging against the bureau behind her. In the dead quiet of the small hotel room, she was powerfully aware of Slade. His presence was strong, definite. She could feel him watching her. She was reminded of a tiger she had once seen in a zoo, dangerous if released, unfathomable caged, and predatory if stimulated.

"Elizabeth," Rick said when she was done, "we didn't get a chance to really talk last night. But we have to talk now, because I have to go back to Miramar today."

Regina started. His words made her realize that her situation was fragile and uncertain. Rick was going to return to Miramar. She could only assume that Slade would, too. And where did that leave her?

She clutched her napkin. Had James been alive, she would be going with them, to her wedding. But James was dead. Where would she go, what would she do? Last night Rick had answered all the questions that she had had about her home. She had been raised in San Luis Obispo although she had been attending a very exclusive school for young ladies in London since she was thirteen years old. Her father had died last year, and her stepmother had already remarried. Regina wondered if her stepmother would welcome her into her household. "I suppose I will be going home," she said uncertainly, and she found herself turning so she could look at Slade. Her gaze locked with his, questioning.

But he said nothing. His expression was grim.

"That's what I want to discuss with you," Rick said. "I don't think it's a good idea for you to be traveling now, when you don't have your memory. Especially not alone."

She agreed with him wholeheartedly. The thought of traveling alone was unappealing when she was in such a vulnerable condition, even for such a short trip, but the truth of the matter went beyond that. She was already establishing a niche here, while home was nothing but a concept, one that should have been inviting, but that, under the circumstances, offered her very little comfort. "I suppose," she said slowly, wanting to look at Slade who was still behind her, "that when my companion recovers we can travel together."

Rick hesitated. "Mrs. Schroener died yesterday, after the train came in—before you and Slade even arrived."

Regina was shocked.

"I could always send you home with one of my boys," Rick said, "but even with an escort, I'm not sure you should travel right now. Doc has advised against it."

Not being able to remember her chaperone helped Regina recover her wits quickly. "I must send word to her relatives, if we can find them."

"Don't you worry about that. I've taken care of everything, but if you want to send a note, I'll pass it on for you."

Regina nodded. "Would my stepmother welcome me if I returned?"

Rick frowned. "Susan remarried six months after George died. Since you returned from London last month you were her guest, and I doubt she was very happy about it. She's not so much older than you and you're too damn attractive. I don't think she'd be very happy to have you move in with her now."

Regina said nothing. She wasn't surprised. It only made sense that a newly married woman would want privacy with her husband, and the fact that Susan wasn't much older than she herself made her even more unwelcome. She had a headache now. Her glance finally did turn to Slade. Now he was sitting on the bureau and he was studying the contents of her breakfast tray as if he found them fascinating. She wanted to catch his eye, but he seemed determined to avoid her. If she did not return home to San Luis Obispo, where would she go?

"You can stay here for a while. With my family. At Miramar," Rick said.

"That's very kind of you! Too kind!" She thought she heard Slade snort, but wasn't sure. "Why would you take me in?" Regina asked. "Why would you do something like this? It might be a long time before I regain my memory." *Or never*, she thought with a touch of panic.

"Because I believe in family," Rick said. "James loved you. He was my son. As far as I'm concerned, you are family. Your place is with us, at Miramar. We'll take care of you there until you get well."

Regina gripped her hands hard. He was offering her a sanctuary in her time of need. She was grateful. And Slade was there. She couldn't help thinking of that, too. "Thank you," she whispered. She dared to glance at Slade.

"You have every choice." He spoke stiffly. "You want to go to San Luis Obispo to your stepmother, I'll take you. You want to go to London, I'll find you a chaperone. You're an heiress, Elizabeth, so you're not without means."

She gasped. "You don't want me to stay?"

"I didn't say that," he said. "I'm only pointing out to you that you are a woman of substance."

He didn't want her to stay. The fact practically blinded her. It nearly swept her from her chair. Not only didn't he want her to stay, Slade was offering to help her leave. She felt betrayed. But most importantly, she was anguished, because she trusted him, needed him.

"Can't you be nice to your brother's fiancée?" Rick shouted. "Can't you see how upset you've made her?"

Slade was rhythmically tapping one booted heel against the bureau now, an outlet for the hot flow of lava-like energy in his veins. There was something ominous about the steady thump-thump-thump. "Just how *nice* do you want me to be?" he said softly.

Regina looked from one man to the other. Again she was witnessing an intimate and powerful conflict, one she had no right to even be aware of. "Stop it," she said.

They both looked at her in surprise.

She gripped the edge of the table, not looking at Slade now, even though she knew he was staring at her. She refused to look at him after he had made himself so clear. "Let me at least learn all of the facts. Am I close to my stepmother? Or was I, before her remarriage, I mean?"

"No," Rick said bluntly. "Susan was furious with the terms of the will. George knew you were going to marry James, and he'd left most of his fortune to you."

"Why?"

"George and I grew up together. George was an orphan. He was raised at the mission at San Miguel. As kids we ran wild together and became friends. But let's face it. George was always aware of the differences between us, that I was the heir to Miramar while he was an orphan working in our winery. Back in those days, my father was like the old Spanish dons of centuries ago. He was the king of this entire county and everyone knew it. The law answered to him. Whole towns answered to him. You couldn't breathe without his okaying it. See what I mean?"

Regina nodded, fascinated.

"But George was smart, I gotta hand it to him. He took off at sixteen and soon opened a store in San Luis Obispo. He made himself a fortune, not as a merchant but by speculating in real estate way before everyone else jumped on the bandwagon. He saw the railroad coming in the early '80s. We stayed in touch. An' one day we agreed on an alliance between our two families. George was getting for his grandson—your son—what he'd always wanted for himself: to be boss of Miramar. To be the king."

Regina understood it all then. She could sympathize with the man who had grown up as an orphan and consequently was determined to secure for his family the land and position, the power and the roots, that Miramar would bring. And to secure that, he would do it through her, his daughter. Of course, she was only an acceptable bride to someone like James because she was a wealthy heiress. She didn't have to ask to know that had George remained penniless, friend or not, Rick would not have affianced his son to her. But Regina accepted that as the way of the world. And in accepting it, she realized that she was a somewhat worldly young woman, another clue to her character. And she was sorry for the father she couldn't remember, because his dreams had died with James.

"George and I were like brothers," Rick said. "He's dead and James is dead, but you can count on me, Elizabeth. You can count on me to be a father to you."

Regina was moved. How could she not be? She was no longer marrying his son, no longer marrying into the family, and Rick did not have to extend himself the way that he was doing. "Thank you."

Slade had stopped back-kicking the bureau, but now he thumped it once, hard, reminding everyone that he was there. "My father, Mr. Kindness himself."

Rick lunged to his feet. "You got something you want to say?"

Slade slid abruptly to his feet. "No. But don't you? Don't you have something to add?"

Regina regarded the two men in shock and fright, wondering if they might actually come to blows. Both of them were suffused with anger, while she didn't understand the hidden meaning in Slade's question.

"You leave her alone," Rick said.

"Oh, so now you want me to leave her alone!"

Rick controlled himself. When he turned to Regina, he managed to smile. "Your daddy would turn over in his grave if I didn't take care of you."

Regina looked at Rick, who was now smiling warmly at her, and she looked at Slade, who wasn't smiling at all. What on earth was going on? And did she have any choice?

"Thank you," she said, making the only decision possible. "I'll take you up on your offer of hospitality, for a while anyway." She could not speak calmly. She was shaking inside and afraid to look at Slade and witness his reaction to her decision. It had somehow become important to her that he approve, not just of her decision, but of her.

And she didn't think that he did. His next words confirmed her fears.

"I guess that settles it," Slade said darkly. "Let me guess. You're gonna head out now, right, Dad? And you want me to escort our guest to Miramar once she's ready."

Rick scowled. "Do you think you might extend yourself to do that?"

Slade didn't answer. Without even looking at Regina, he strode from the room, but not before Regina saw how angry he was.

Rick and Regina were left alone. Regina was stunned. And she was dismayed. Why was Slade so angry? Why would her visiting his home upset him so? She had thought him to be her friend. She looked up at his father. "What have I done?"

Rick came around the table and patted her shoulder. "It's not you. Trust me on that. You're pretty and sweet and a man'd have to be blind not to see that. It's me. We don't get along. We never have. When I want something, he's got to fight me. He's always been that way. He's always been a hardheaded rebel. Just like his mother."

Regina stared up at the older man. She heard the regret in his tone. And she heard more. She heard the love—the love he'd hidden so well in front of his son.

Chapter 5

*T*hey left Templeton behind. A few miles from the small town was a dirt crossroads where they turned west, passing a crude white sign which read MIRAMAR in hand-painted black lettering. The three other signs directed traffic north to Paso Robles 5 miles, east to Fresno 112 miles, or south back to Templeton 2 miles. Once they turned, the railroad tracks, which ran north and south, soon disappeared from view. An endless sea of golden hills surrounded them. Dark pine-clad mountains hovered behind them. Hawks took wing above them, gliding high into the vividly blue sky. Regina would have been awed with the scenery had she not been stricken with tension.

For Slade sat beside her on the front seat of an old-fashioned buggy pulled by two spirited bay mares. Her half a dozen trunks were piled in the backseat behind them. He had not said one word to her since he had arrived at her hotel room to load her luggage. Nor had he given her more than a cursory glance or two. He could not have made his displeasure with her more obvious.

The sign directing them toward Miramar had not indicated how far away it was. Yet even if it were only minutes from them, she could not endure this kind of silence. "Your father is too generous," she said softly in an attempt to make conversation.

Slade said nothing.

"I am very grateful to him." She could not believe he would refuse to talk with her at all.

"I'm sure you are."

His tone was civil, if unenthusiastic, and she breathed with relief. "He didn't have to offer me his hospitality," she offered.

"That's right. Rick doesn't do anything he doesn't want to do." This time he looked at her hard.

"You almost sound as if you're warning me."

"Maybe I am."

"He's your father."

"Don't I know it."

Regina opened her mouth to tell him that Rick loved him, then she shut it. She would be trespassing. That was a subject that was much too personal for her to broach.

"I know you're angry," she said very softly. "I'm sorry."

He looked at her again. There *was* anger in his eyes, but not the uncontrolled blaze she'd seen in the hotel room that morning just before he'd strode out.

"I'm sorry," she repeated, dismayed. "Angering you is the last thing I would want to do, not after the way you saved me."

His grip tightened on the reins. "Stop talking like that. I didn't *save* you. I found you and brought you to town, that's all. If I hadn't found you, someone else would have."

"Would they? Or would I have woken up, wandered until I dropped, maybe even died?"

His glance skewered her. "I'm not asking for your gratitude."

"But you already have it."

Slade stared straight ahead, out over the horses' heads at the faded blue horizon. "Damn it," he said very softly.

Dismayed, Regina said impulsively, "Turn around. Take me back to Templeton. It's all right. I'll stay at the hotel until I feel better and then I'll go to San Luis Obispo. I'm sure Susan would not turn me away in my condition. I will not impose on you any further."

He grimaced, swiveling to look at her. "Do I seem like such a heel?"

"No! Not at all! I just don't understand why you're so angry with me."

He swallowed. His gaze slipped to her mouth before moving back to her eyes. "This isn't your fault. I'm not angry with you."

"You're not?"

"No."

Regina was relieved, more than relieved; she was terribly glad. But his dark, brooding expression instantly chased away her smile. "If you're not angry with me, then it must be your father you're so angry with."

"That's right." From his tone, she knew she was crossing into territory where he had put up inviolate boundaries. Yet she could not stop. For she kept remembering the last time she had seen Rick, she kept hearing the regret in his voice, and the love, and something else she hadn't identified at the time but which she could label now in hindsight—the resignation.

Regina could not restrain herself. "Because of what he said?"

Slade looked at her.

"Because he insulted you?"

"It would take a lot more than a lousy insult from Rick to get my goat," he said sharply. "Stop pushing."

"Then it *is* me. You're mad at him, but it's because of me!"

"I was angry with Rick long before I ever met you, and I'll be angry with him long after you're gone."

His words dumbfounded her. Her heart wept over his relationship with his father, a relationship she wanted to heal, one she wanted to interfere in—which she absolutely must not do. And the assumption that she would be gone, while the conflict remained, dismayed her.

She didn't dare question herself too closely and ask herself why.

And of course, she knew that she was somehow involved in his roiling emotions even if he hadn't said so. She sensed it; she felt it.

She had been staring at him and he was finally compelled to turn his head toward her again. Their gazes leaped together, held, then darted apart. His profile was hard and handsome, almost too perfect, but he was clenching his jaw. He said through gritted teeth, "What in hell do you want from me?"

Regina did not hesitate. "Friendship."

He jerked toward her, his expression amazed. She was motionless, unable to believe that she had been so direct. The incredulity on his face told her that he was disbelieving, too. Her palms began to perspire. She did not need her memory to know that ladies did not offer friendship to strange men, unless it was a certain kind of friendship, an illicit one, and that had not been her meaning at all.

"Friendship isn't possible between us."

Regina looked carefully at her gloved hands, folded in her lap, just as he carefully stared out over the horses' heads. She should let this entire topic drop and they would both pretend it had never even been raised. Instead, she heard herself say, "Why not?"

Abruptly he halted the mares, this time pulling down the brake and winding the reins around it. He sat very still, but Regina felt the incredible wave of energy rushing through him, coiling up in him. She mistook it for anger, and she regretted her brashness completely.

He looked at her. Whatever secrets he had were no longer hidden in dark shadows—if she could only decipher them. His eyes were bright and intense. His needs were raw and powerful, they were needs she did not understand, and she was both attracted to and frightened by him in that single moment.

"Unless you mean a certain kind of friendship—and even that would be impossible."

Regina could not speak. His regard was mesmerizing. His words might have shocked her had she not been consumed by the heat of his gaze. She was a woman and he was a very handsome man, and the attraction she barely understood was growing stronger with every heartbeat. She found it increasingly difficult to breathe and she was wondering, just wondering, what would happen if she dared to lean slightly forward.

"Don't." He said the one word, but it held a volume of meanings, all warnings.

Warnings she chose to ignore. Unable to tear her gaze from him, she swayed forward. It was not even an inch. But it was enough.

"*Elizabeth.*"

She waited. Time was suspended. She knew he was going to kiss her. The desire was there in his eyes. She yearned uncontrollably for the touch of his lips. He dipped his head. She didn't move, and finally, finally, it came—the merest brushing of his mouth upon hers. Almost immediately he jerked away from her.

Her heart thundered in her ears. She gazed at him, wide-eyed. He was staring at her too, his expression aghast. Abruptly he unwound the reins, lifted the brake, and urged the mares on, all in one smooth, well-practiced movement. The team leaped forward instantly.

Unsettled was too gentle a word to describe how Regina felt. She could still feel his lips on hers; her entire body was clamoring for more, for so much more. She could not take her eyes off him. Dear Lord, he was so handsome—more than handsome. She clenched her hands in her lap.

"That was a mistake," he said harshly without looking at her.

"What?"

He refused to look at her. "One damn big mistake."

She straightened her spine. A wash of hot color crept up her cheeks as she realized that he was regretting the kiss, while she was cherishing it. Her pink flush deepened when she was struck with how brazen she had been in enticing him. "Oh, dear," she whispered.

"It's too late for 'oh, dear.' "

"Oh, dear," she said again, trying to imagine what he must think of her.

"But of course, it's just what Rick wants."

She looked at him.

"Don't look at me with those big brown eyes!"

"You mean my coming here to Miramar, don't you?" Or did he mean the intimacy they had just shared?

"I mean everything. I'm no damn saint. And I never wished I was—until now."

"You are a good person," she said fervently. "A very good person."

He whipped around, staring at her. When he recovered, his voice was hoarse. "Lady, you have one hell of an imagination—either that, or you're too good to be true. Don't make me out to be something I'm not."

"I'm not."

"I won't sit here and argue about my character with you."

"All right," Regina agreed, shaken now to the core of her being. She had made him very angry. It was the kiss, or her prying, perhaps even both. But she pondered his dark and complicated nature, unable to help herself, and she found herself berating the man who had raised him. And the memory of his kiss still lingered.

The road they traveled on wound steadily west and steadily upward, surrounded by the summer-burned hills. The hills seemed to become bigger and bigger, the swatches of bent oaks sparser. Cattle flecked the countryside. Rounding the corner of one slope, they emerged suddenly onto a bare ridge.

Slade had not spoken to her since the kiss, but he urged the team to the cliff's edge and halted them at the overlook. Regina gasped. Although she was very much struck by the view he had offered her, she was also well aware that he was watching her closely.

The edge of the ridge, where the buggy stood, dropped precipitously to a valley below. Across that valley, a sea of bronze saddleback mountains rose up to face them, huge and bare and stark. Cattle grazed the lower elevations. Etched against their rippling rim was the steel-blue Pacific.

Regina looked at Slade. "Miramar?"

He nodded, unable to contain the flash of pride in his eyes.

Regina had never been faced with such raw majesty. The land was forbidding in its immensity and starkness, yet it was spectacular, too.

Slade pointed north, in the opposite direction, across the other side of the narrow ridge. "The big valley's there. Where we have our groves and the vineyard. On the hill above is the house. You can't see it from here."

The mountains were tamer on that side, resembling the hills he had described to her earlier. Oaks and pine softened the landscape. The ocean stretched out against that horizon, too, dusky-blue boldly juxtaposed against summer gold.

Regina breathed deeply. The air had a cleaner, sweeter smell, and it was distinctly cooler than it had been in Templeton. Slade lifted the reins. The road wound gently down through the hills now. Not many minutes passed before they entered the valley. And just before they actually arrived at the hacienda, Regina knew they were approaching the sea. She could taste the salty tang on the slight breeze that lifted the tendrils of hair on the back of her neck.

The ranch house was at the end of the valley where the ground slowly rose to meet the sky. Numerous barns, paddocks, and wood-sided buildings, all weathered gray, gave the rancho the appearance of a small, secluded village. Privately, Regina could imagine just how wonderful Miramar would look freshly whitewashed, but she would never say so.

They passed acres of orange groves. Slade had not been very communicative since they had kissed, but now he could not refrain from telling her about his home.

"My grandfather, Alejandro Delanza, chose to build his home here rather than at the other end of the valley."

"I don't blame him," Regina murmured. The Spanish-style hacienda was silhouetted boldly against the pastel-blue sky, framed on one side by pine-clad hills, and gave the distinct appearance of reigning above all the land, people, and other living creatures below it.

Slade gave her a long look. "There were no towns down-valley back then, just the mission at San Miguel."

"Even so, your grandfather had an eye for grandeur."

The road wound toward the house, which was where it ended. As they approached the outlying barns, passing blooded colts frollicking in one pasture, Slade said, "Once we had a hundred men in our employ, and Miramar supported not just them but their wives and children, too. In those days we were a traditional hacienda, meaning that we were self-sufficient. Everything we needed was raised, grown, or made right here."

"That's very romantic."

Slade gave her another thoughtful look. "But not productive, and by the time California reached statehood, not competitive. Now we have a dozen vaqueros in our employ, one tanner, one butcher, and Cookie. Not including some help up at the house," he added.

It was a far cry from the old days, Regina thought. It was somehow sad. Slade might have guessed her thoughts. "I wouldn't turn back the clock even if I could," he said.

He drove past the outbuildings and barns, taking them directly to the house. A man who bore no real resemblance to Slade, but who somehow reminded her of him, came through the courtyard toward them.

"Welcome to Miramar," the smiling young man said. "I'm Edward."

Regina smiled back at him. His open, direct friendliness was very welcome after the complicated, tangled state of her relationship with Slade. He helped her down from the carriage. "Now I know why James was in love with you," he said.

Regina was aware that his flattery was rather smooth, but he was such a handsome man, his charm innate, that she did not mind. Here, surely, was the classic ladies' man. His flirtatiousness did not unnerve her, not at all, and she had the feeling that she was well-versed in this kind of exchange. "That is too kind of you," she said.

"I guess you must hear flattery all the time. Does it ever get boring being told how beautiful you are?"

From behind them, Slade began heaving her trunks on the ground.

She was not embarrassed and she laughed. "You, I think, are a rogue."

"A rogue?" His grin was devilish and handsome. "I've never been called a rogue before. I like it."

Regina laughed again. She had most definitely played this flirtation game many times before; not only was she well-schooled in it, she was comfortable in such an exchange. But then she wondered how it was possible if she had spent the past few years cloistered in a private school for young ladies. In such a setting she would not have had the opportunity to flirt with handsome young men; briefly, she was perplexed.

"Well, you'll certainly hear it from now on," Edward said, grinning, "until you do get bored."

Regina flashed another smile, but it was only a facade. "I don't think a young lady ever tires of flattery," she said automatically. She was uneasy with her last thought. She did not have time to brood upon the contradiction, however, for Slade made a contemptuous noise, gaining both their attention.

"You think women really fall for that?" he said.

Regina regarded Slade in surprise, wondering why he was angry when his brother's words were merely a game.

Edward smiled at her again. "He's jealous. He's jealous because he wouldn't know how to sweet-talk a woman if his life depended on it."

Slade looked at Regina before answering his brother. "I have no use for 'sweet-talking.' But you seem more than adept at it."

"I'm wounded," Edward said jokingly, but he seemed puzzled by Slade's response.

Slade threw another accusing glance at Regina. "You *both* seem more than adept at it."

Regina could not believe that he would attack her so. Beside her, Edward looked equally surprised. "Slade," he protested.

Slade ignored them both. He heaved the last of her trunks on the ground and disappeared into the house.

Regina's feelings were wounded but she was very careful to hide them. She turned toward the house so that Edward would not see her flushed face. "You have a beautiful home," she said unevenly.

"The house was first built in '38," Edward said quickly. Then he touched her arm. "He didn't mean it."

"Yes, he did. And I seem to be very accomplished in the art of flirtation."

"Sometimes even I can't understand my brother," Edward said grimly. "Most of the ladies I know flirt."

His words did not soothe her. In the past few hours she had pushed Slade away, when that had not been her intention at all. She owed him her life, she was sure of it, but all she had done was to anger him.

"Come on, let's go in, it's much cooler inside," Edward said, taking her arm.

He was hoping to distract her, and Regina wanted to be distracted. She looked at the house and realized that it was indeed beautiful. Huge oleanders, red and pink and white, surged up against the sides of the sprawling, U-shaped adobe house. Through the arched entryway she could see that the house was built around a vast courtyard with apricot-hued stone floors, a limestone fountain, and a profusion of exotic blooming plants. There was an opening at the back of the courtyard, and it looked as if another courtyard was behind the first.

"Of course, it's been added onto quite a bit since '38," Edward said. "What you see now is actually only a part of the original structure. We are a real Californio family, one of the last ones. Most have sold out."

"I see," Regina said, thankful that he was succeeding in his attempt to bring a degree of normalcy back into the moment.

"You'll probably hear this over and over again, but the Mexican governor, Juan Bautista Alvarado, awarded this land to us in '37. All of the Mexican ranchos were originally Spanish missions; when Mexico gained her independence from Spain in '22, she claimed California. Mexican soldiers and settlers, even some foreigners, petitioned and received large grants of land. Our grant was one of the first. My grandfather was a soldier. Of course, when California became a state, we lost most of our land. But we fared better than the rest of the Californios, most of whom lost everything. And those that didn't lose their land soon divided it up. Rick would never do that."

Despite herself, Regina finally let her thoughts slip free of Slade, and she turned to face Edward. "Why did you lose your land?"

"The Americans wanted it. The Californio claims were old, the original grants often lost or unreadable, boundaries often—and usually—marked by nature: a pair of boulders, for example, or the turnoff of a creek, or a tree that was struck by lightning. As you can imagine, in a half a century creeks change course or dry up completely, boulders are removed, trees are chopped down or uprooted by storms." Edward shrugged. "Most of the Californio grants were overturned, the land given to the newcomers by the newcomers' courts. We spent a dozen years defending our claim, at a great expense, and fortunately we retained a third of our holdings." He smiled. "Truth is, the original grant was so large it was not just unmanageable, it was obscene."

A woman entered the courtyard from the far side of the house and began walking toward them.

Regina watched her, saying, "But that seems so unfair."

"Is life fair?"

She looked at Slade's brother, who was no longer smiling, who was suddenly serious and intent. She did not have to know him well to know that he possessed a sunny and pleasing character. Yet in that instant, she saw the shadow in his eyes. A shiver touched her. For he was right. Life was most definitely not fair. She had only to recall the tragedy of James Delanza's death or her own plight in order to agree with his assessment.

"Edward," the woman called.

Regina turned to her curiously. She was a slender woman with gleaming auburn hair that was pulled back into a fashionable and classic chignon. She moved forward with resolute strides. As she came closer Regina saw that she was an older woman, perhaps forty, but a beautiful one. Regina also noticed that her pastel-green dress had once been designed to accommodate a bustle. It had been altered, but there was no mistaking its original intent. It was more than a few years old and hopelessly out of fashion.

"This is my mother, Victoria," Edward said.

"And you must be Elizabeth." The woman smiled, extending her hand. "How very nice to finally meet you after all these years."

Regina shook her hand. Although the woman's words were warm, they rang false. Her smile seemed as brittle as glass. When Regina looked into her eyes, she saw that they glittered. A chill crept up the back of her neck.

"I hope you are not too upset over the trauma you have suffered," Victoria said.

"I feel much better today," Regina said. "Thank you."

"Come with me. Slade will bring your luggage in. I'm giving you a guest room which also faces the ocean. It's the coolest room in the house. There's almost always a breeze."

Regina hadn't realized that they were that close to the Pacific Ocean. She was hurried along, leaving Edward leaning against the thick wall in front of the house with a cigarette in one hand, rummaging intently in his pockets with the other, apparently no longer even aware of her.

Regina followed Victoria into the house, and it was like entering another world in another time and place.

The furniture was dark, heavy, and old. The Oriental rugs were exquisite but very faded and so worn that she actually discerned several tears. A Spanish chest in the central salon caught her eye because of its immense proportions—it was at least chest-high—and the chunky engraving upon its sides. As they passed the dining room she glimpsed a large old trestle table and a dozen heavy chairs, upholstered in studded, worn tan leather, with a massive tapestry on one wall, much of it faded and cracked and in great need of repair. Unquestionably, everything was Sephardic and, Regina suspected, dated back to the era of the original land grant or even earlier.

"Did the first Delanzas bring the furnishings with them?" she asked curiously. "It's all so unusual, but so handsome." She realized she was used to marble floors and gilded moldings, to wrought-iron and stained glass, to electricity and telephones, not stone tiles, whitewashed stucco, gas lighting, and old, dark wood.

"Of course." Victoria's reply was cool and almost disdainful. They had left the house and entered the interior courtyard, this one smaller than the one in front of the house. Another fountain sprayed cool, inviting water in its center. It, too, was graced with many shade trees and an abundance of blooming shrubbery and flowers. They crossed the courtyard quickly, passing the fountain. The air around it was cool and moist with tiny droplets of water.

"Here we are," Victoria said, entering a room directly off the courtyard. She swiftly moved across it to open the doors on the opposite wall. Regina was greeted with a breathtaking glimpse of a summer-yellow hill sliding away abruptly to the shimmering gray ocean.

"What a wonderful view!"

Victoria turned, smiling. The smile was cold.

Regina's own smile died. She began removing her gloves, her heart lurching uneasily. She carefully took off her hat. When she looked at the other woman, she saw her staring at her pearls.

"How beautiful," Victoria said, with no warmth whatsoever.

"Thank you."

"I will have Lucinda bring you lemonade. This is the guest wing, and as you are the only guest, you have it to yourself." Somehow, her words were not kind or hospitable, but quite the opposite.

"You will want to freshen up before dinner," Victoria continued. "I'll have Lucinda run you a bath. We dine at seven."

"One of the few breaks with tradition Rick has allowed," Slade said from the doorway, holding two of her bags.

Regina was terribly glad to see him. Edward's mother was not just unpleasant, but disturbing. She was certain the woman despised her. Yet she could not even begin to fathom why.

Slade entered, dumping her bags on the floor. "Rick is up and out at the crack of dawn, so traditional dining at ten or eleven in the evening is out of the question."

"I see," Regina said.

Without another word Slade turned and left. Regina gazed after him, wishing he had stayed. She did not relish the idea of being alone with Victoria any more than was necessary.

At that precise moment, Victoria moved quickly across the room, closing the doors that opened onto the courtyard and closeting the two of them together. Regina stared at her.

"So tell me," Victoria said unpleasantly, "is this a ruse?"

"What?"

"Is this a ruse? A charade? This loss of memory of yours?"

"No! Of course not! How I wish I could remember!"

"I see." Victoria moved slowly to the bed, fingering the brightly colored cotton coverlet. "Then why did you come here—Elizabeth?"

"I . . . Rick invited me. He said I was welcome, as if I were actual family."

Victoria laughed mirthlessly.

Regina realized that she was standing with her back against the hard wooden door. "What is it?"

"Don't you know what he intends for you? Don't you realize why he's invited you here? Can't you figure it out?"

"No." Regina was dismayed by the woman's innuendos, dismayed to realize that there might be some kind of motivation other than what Rick had professed.

"Hasn't Slade told you? Or hinted?" Victoria asked.

"Hinted at what? Told me what?"

"Rick intends for you to marry Slade."

"What!" Regina was shocked. "But—I was supposed to marry James!"

"And James is dead. Now Rick plans to see you married to Slade. Come hell or high water."

"I don't understand. Why?"

"Why?" Victoria laughed. And she looked pointedly at Regina's perfect pearls. "For your money, of course."

Chapter 6

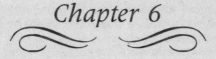

*R*egina was incredulous.

Victoria had left in triumph. Regina paced the room, wringing her hands, too shocked to think clearly. Rick had seemed so sincere. But he hadn't been sincere, not at all.

The double doors of her room which opened on the courtyard banged open. Regina halted. Slade stood there with one of her larger, heavier trunks. "Where do you want this?" he asked.

Anger overwhelmed her. She moved toward him before she knew what she was even going to do. He was as much an accomplice to this deception as his father was. For he had known. And she had trusted him. He had said he would protect her. Oh, how she had trusted him! But he wasn't trustworthy at all. *He had lied to her. He hoped to use her.* The betrayal was devastating.

She raised her hand. He immediately understood what she intended and dropped the trunk in order to catch her wrist and restrain her.

"Blast you!" Regina cried furiously. His grip hurt her and brought her to her senses. Ladies, even ones with no money, did not strike gentlemen, no matter what the provocation. But it was too late. For he had caught her other wrist, hustling her up against the wall.

Instantly he pressed his steel-hard body on hers in order to immobilize her. He was successful. She was unable to move her hands or her body and her back seemed to sink into the rough stone wall.

"What is it?" he demanded.

She slumped beneath him, physically drained from their brief yet strenuous tussle. But she had the strength to look into his eyes, and hers were tearful and accusing. "I trusted you!"

"A mistake," he said grimly. "Are you calm? I didn't realize a lady like you could have such sharp claws, and I don't relish wearing your mark."

She realized that she couldn't speak further. Her anger and hurt had not dimmed, but awareness of another sort was rapidly dawning on her. She thought that she could feel every interesting male inch of his body. They were closely pressed against each other. Somehow, his knee had slipped between hers, and his thigh had aggressively inserted itself against her loins. It was shocking. Her body's response was even more shocking.

Regina realized that he was staring at her, but not with any interest in what she might have to say. He was studying her mouth, and the line of her neck, then the full curve of the top of her bosom, crushed beneath his chest. His intent perusal quickened her already keen senses. Restraining the anticipation flooding her body was impossible.

Regina found herself looking at him with equal intensity. It had never occurred to her before that the thick fringe of a man's eyelashes could be erotic, or that the slim line of his nose could summon up an urge to feel his face nuzzling hers. His lips were parted. His face was very close to hers. Close enough that she could see how smooth and unblemished his dark skin was, except for the tiny crow's-feet around his eyes that testified to his many years of squinting into the sun. For they most certainly were not laugh lines.

His gaze slowly lifted. His body pulsed against hers. Regina stared.

"Maybe you should stay mad," he said in a low, rough voice.

He was right. She *was* angry, just as she was hurt, and while his betrayal could be ignored for a moment, it could not be forgotten. "Please remove your person from mine," she said, trembling.

A smile, ice-cold, mocking the heat of his body, curved his mouth. It was thoroughly unlikable. "Have I finally been demoted?" He stepped away from her with apparent indifference.

She had no idea what he was referring to. "I think you should get out of my room."

"I thought I was your hero." He didn't move.

"Heroes don't lie."

"So I *have* been demoted. What did I lie about?" His voice was flat, as if devoid of even the tiniest spark of interest. "Is that why you're crying?"

"I'm not crying. My eyes are—wet."

"An allergy."

"Yes."

He lifted a brow. "What has brought on this . . . allergic reaction?"

"Don't you dare mock me." Her anger blossomed again.

"I wasn't aware that I was mocking you. Maybe you're mocking me." His glance slid over her, not quite indifferently.

Her eyes widened when she guessed his meaning. "I assure you, I am not leading you on!"

"No? You led Edward on. Maybe you led James on. Did you?"

She stiffened, incredulous. "I was not leading your brother on!"

"You were grinning at him like an idiot. Is that kind of talk what a woman really wants to hear?" He strolled around the periphery of her room, not looking at her.

"It was a game. A game of words. That's all."

He leaned his back against the opposite wall, his arms crossed. "But you seem to like to play it. Edward definitely likes to play it."

"It's not a matter of liking it or not." Somehow, he had maneuvered her into a very defensive position, and her back was against the wall in more ways than one.

"No?"

"No! It's a matter of being polite. Of being a lady. Edward was just being a gentleman."

"And if I tell you how pretty you are, does that make me a gentleman, too?"

She went still. Her heart was pounding erratically for an unfathomable reason. His gaze held hers. She sensed the serious nature of his question. "No. No, it does not."

"I didn't think so."

How could he deflate her anger so easily, and turn the topic onto another course? "You try very hard not to be a gentleman, don't you?"

He grinned, but it was forced. "Do I?"

"I can see through you, Slade."

His grin died. He pushed himself off the wall. "I don't really care what you think you see. And if you want to flirt with Edward and call it polite, go right ahead, I sure as hell won't stop you. But maybe I should warn you. Edward may be a gentleman in your book, but he's also a man."

"What does that mean?"

"It means he wouldn't mind stealing a kiss or two. In fact, if you encourage him, I'm sure he will."

Regina drew herself up. "I am not encouraging him." But her face grew red when she recalled, very clearly, how she had encouraged Slade.

Slade looked at her. "Do what you want."

She trembled. He thought the worst of her. He thought her immoral. But she was, wasn't she? Not with Edward, who, as handsome as he was, did not elicit the slightest interest from her. But with Slade. She had asked for his kiss in the buggy, and just a moment ago she had wanted another.

They stared at each other. The silence was thick with tension. Regina was quite certain that he knew exactly what she was thinking. "I think I had better return to town," she said unevenly.

He regarded her before walking past her to the balcony. Heavy clouds had suddenly appeared to cast long, almost purple shadows on the ocean. The breeze was becoming more noticeable, too.

"No," he said, his back to her. "With your pretty smiles and pretty speech, *as polite as you are*, you'd be prey for every man drifting by. Rick is right. You had better stay here until you regain your memory."

She was unsure. She had come to Miramar because she had no place to go, and because she had trusted Slade to protect her in these bizarre circumstances. But she no longer trusted him. He had lied to her. Yet she still wanted to trust him, as incredible as that might be. She wanted that very much. But how could she? She could not trust a man who hoped to use her. And it hurt to be Slade's hapless victim.

And now there was the undeniable fact of her interest in him as a man. She did not want to remember the feel of his kiss or his body. She did not want to be aware of how handsome he was, how male and virile he was. She did not want to be interested in him.

In that moment Regina was afraid. Not of her circumstances, of her loss of memory, of the truth of her identity and what had happened, but afraid of the enigmatic man standing on the other side of the room with his back to her. And maybe, just maybe, she was afraid of herself. "Why didn't you tell me?"

He didn't move, watching the clouds sailing toward them. "Tell you what?"

"That Rick intends for us to marry."

He turned. "Victoria been flapping her gums a bit?"

Regina waited, well aware that her eyes were bright again with unshed tears that signaled a fresh wave of hurt. "Why did you tell me?"

"I can see you're not too happy about the prospect."

"I trusted you."

"I didn't tell you because I haven't made up my mind yet," Slade said brusquely. "Truth is, I haven't agreed to marry you."

"What?"

"I told Rick I'd think about it."

"You told Rick you would think about it."

"That's right."

She could barely believe her ears. She had assumed that Slade was planning to marry her for her money. But he wasn't. He was considering it. That he hadn't agreed and forced her to make a choice should relieve her, but it did not. The situation was no less conspiratorial just because he had yet to put his final stamp of approval upon it. "I trusted you."

"That's the second time you've said that."

She closed her eyes, resolved not to cry, at least not until he had left her room. She inhaled and it gave her strength. "You realize that it would be absurd?"

"How absurd?"

"Completely absurd."

"How come I get the feeling that your objection has everything to do with me—but not one damn thing to do with James?"

She stepped back reflexively, shocked at his rage. In truth, she had forgotten all about her dead fiancé, and that Slade was his brother.

"I thought so."

"I can't even remember James," she protested.

"But I can," he said.

His pain was as primitive and dark as his other emotions had been earlier in the buggy. She knew she should not be witnessing it, just as she should not have glimpsed even briefly so deeply into his soul. "It's not my fault. James's death is not my fault. That I can't remember him is not my fault. Believe me, I wish I could remember him—and I wish he were not dead."

He glared at her, inexplicably furious. "You know what, Elizabeth? Damn you." He wheeled past her and slammed out of the room.

Regina cried out. His curse immobilized her, then she ran to the double doors and caught them before they banged again. She did not pull them shut. She stared after Slade, tears finally slipping free to stain her cheeks, tears very similar to the ones she was sure

she had just glimpsed in his eyes. But they were crying
for very different reasons—or were they?

Regina had no intention of remaining at Miramar
another moment. Coming here had been a mistake.
For Miramar was no longer an inviting sanctuary. She
could not get past the fact that Slade had betrayed her
trust. The wound was unbearable. It shouldn't matter
as much as it did; in reality he was only a stranger, but
logic did not rule her heart. He most certainly was no
longer her savior. And that brought forth a new urge to
weep.

*She needed him. Didn't he realize that? How could he do
this to her when she needed him so!*

Yet even as she prepared to leave, she could not
shake him from her mind, she could not stop thinking
about him. She remembered everything she shouldn't
remember, from his concern when he had rescued her,
to his conflict with his father, to his kiss. And she found
herself thinking "if only." If only she did not have amnesia, if only she were not James's fiancée. But the reality
could not be changed by wishful thinking.

She would leave all of her things. Because it had been
so blazingly hot and sunny down-valley she exchanged
her perky little hat for a wide-brimmed straw bonnet,
even though the sky had become overcast. She also
donned low-heeled walking shoes. They looked brand-
new, but she was afraid to tarry and search for another,
broken-in pair. Because she was in a rush, there was no
time to plan. She decided that in Templeton she would
wire her stepmother for assistance. Within minutes she
was ready to leave. Her instincts urged her to flee before
she might change her mind. She knew better than to ask
Slade or any member of the household to take her to
town. They would refuse, or attempt to talk her out
of leaving. Because they wanted her to marry Slade;
because they wanted her money.

The house was built on a hill. She went to the terrace
overlooking the sloping grounds outside, and beyond
that, the frothing ocean. For one second she wondered

if rain was on its way—the sky was becoming positively dreary; and the ocean had become quite rough. She shrugged off the moment of hesitation. She had to protect herself and her own interests, for there was no one else to do it for her. Not anymore.

Regina walked out onto the terrace and debated climbing over the railing and dropping the ten or twenty feet to the ground. As she stood there in indecision, a shadowy image formed in her mind, and, just for an instant, Regina thought she could see someone she knew, someone dear to her, laughing and telling her that she could do it. For one split second it was so real that she could see the person, and then the instant was gone.

Regina froze, gripping the railing. The memory was gone—and it *had* been a memory. She had remembered somebody, someone important to her. She was certain of it. But now, that person was shrouded in the darkness of her amnesia.

Who was it that she knew who could leap off terraces so bravely? She yearned for the answer, and she was terribly disappointed that the identity of the person eluded her when she had grasped it seconds ago. Frustration brought stinging tears to her eyes.

Nevertheless, Regina turned to the task at hand. She did not have to have her memory in order to know that she was not the type to leap off terraces, and she moved away from the railing. Not stopping to think, because it would only make her hesitate, she slipped out into the courtyard. She ran across it and then through the adjacent front courtyard as well. When she reached the front gate she paused against the wall beneath two lemon trees, panting and trying to catch her breath. The wind was picking up. It lifted her skirts and whipped them against her legs. She strained to hear, waiting for shouts of discovery, but there were none.

Her heart beat wildly now. Running away made her feel like she was committing a criminal act. She peered through the iron gates. Perhaps because of the weather, or perhaps because of the time of day—it was mid-afternoon, siesta time—there was no one about. When they had arrived at the house several hours ago there had been a great deal of activity around the stables and corrals. The timing could not have been better. Regina darted out of the courtyard.

She hadn't planned on taking a horse, but now she knew she would have to do so if she wanted to reach Templeton by nightfall. Traveling on foot was out of the question. There had been no traffic on the road when she had traveled it with Slade, but even if there had been, she would not even consider trying to get a ride to town with a stranger. The very idea was unacceptable.

She wasn't thrilled with the idea of taking a horse out by herself, either. That afternoon she had learned that she was a poor horsewoman. But she would manage; she had no choice.

She saw no one as she crossed the grounds and approached the stables. Amazingly, a glance into the barn showed Regina that not even a groom was within. It could not be any better. She ran inside. It was dark within but she didn't dare turn any lights on. She found the tack room and dragged a saddle and bridle from it. She was quite certain that she had never saddled a mount before.

Regina chose the most placid-looking animal in the stable. Although the horse seemed oblivious of her, it took Regina a very long time to manage to lift the saddle and secure it into place, and even longer to bridle him. By now the bay gelding was looking at her, although he stood motionless. Regina praised him in high, nervous tones. Moments later she led the docile animal from the stall.

The worst was over. Relief filled her. She dragged open the barn door and assured herself that no one was about. On the slope slightly above her, the sprawling adobe house appeared deserted and lifeless.

Trying to remain calm, Regina led her mount to a bale of hay, stepped up on it by sweeping her skirts up and out of the way, and, ignoring the awkwardness and utter lack of decorum of riding astride, she slid onto the saddle. She grabbed the pommel as the bay jiggled.

Ordering herself not to lose her head, she found the reins, shortening them to an appropriate length. Even though she was no expert horsewoman, it was obvious that she had received some training.

They walked out of the barn. The wind blasted them. The horse leaped abruptly, almost throwing her. Regina clung to the reins and his neck at the same time. The horse danced a little. "Not now, please, boy," she cried, glancing around desperately. No one was in sight. She nudged the bay with her heels, determined to get down the road and away from the house as quickly as possible.

The bay responded instantly, breaking into a bone-jarring trot. Regina hung on for her life, her body bouncing uncontrollably.

The wind wrenched her straw bonnet from her head. Regina, gripping the pommel and the reins, looked up, watching it fly away. Her skirts flew up about her thighs. Just her luck. A storm was coming.

It occurred to her to turn back.

She saw Slade's dark face again. His intense midnight-blue eyes. Her resolve faltered. And then she did not have to worry about changing her mind. Her skirts frothed up again even more wildly than before. Her mount snorted and, as a gust of wind lifted his tail, he broke into a canter.

Regina's scream died in her throat. All she could concentrate upon was not falling off. The bay was galloping now, the bit between his teeth. She felt herself beginning to slide off the saddle. He ran faster. She tried to hang on, but it was hopeless. The scream she had wanted to emit burst forth as she lost her grip and tumbled to the dirt.

She landed on her shoulder and her back with a force that left her breathless. When she could breathe, she took great reassuring gulps of air. She was regarding the low, oppressive sky. Very cautiously, she sat up, expecting her body not to work. But it did, albeit with some amount of internal protestation. She sighed in relief.

The horse was gone.

She glanced around, but there was no sight of him—
or of the house. She wasn't sure whether to be relieved
or dismayed. Trembling, she got to her feet. She looked
at the sky. In the distance, over what must be the ocean,
it was black. But she did not turn back. She had come
this far; she would continue on. As she half-ran and
half-walked, the wind worked with her now, pushing
her from behind. She cast many glances over her shoulder, but there was no one in pursuit. Slade was not in
pursuit.

Regina felt as if she had been walking forever. Her feet
hurt so badly that she limped, and she was exhausted.
The wind had changed direction with a vengeance and
now it blasted her in the face, making her fight for every
step she took away from Miramar. Even the tall, solid
pine trees shuddered under the wind's violent assault.
The pines were becoming scarcer, giving way to more
and more oak, but their very existence told her that
she had not traveled more than a few miles from the
house.

The sky was darkening quickly. She had run away in
the late afternoon, but soon it would be early evening.
Soon the Delanzas would be sitting down for supper—
soon her disappearance would be noticed.

She choked on a long-repressed sob.

She was not going to make it. She had come a few
miles, but she guessed it had taken her two hours to
travel that small distance. If she remembered at all
correctly, the crossroads, which were so close to town,
were a good dozen miles from where she was. Was she
going to have to spend the night alone in the middle
of the mountains? The prospect was frightening. Slade
had talked about the wildlife so abundant at Miramar
when he had brought her there earlier. She could only
imagine that there were many hungry wolves roaming
about looking for deer. She shuddered at the thought
of being discovered by a wolf pack. And then, to make
matters worse, the first few drops of rain began to fall.

She stopped in her tracks, looking up at the threatening sky. "Oh, no," she moaned. As if on cue, the heavens opened and released a deluge.

In an instant Regina was drenched. She had been cold before; now she was freezing. The wind roared. The rain pelted her face and body fiercely. She could not continue to stand in the open; she ran beneath a thick, stooped oak tree.

She collapsed at the bottom of the tree, regretting what she had done. The leafy canopy above her filtered some of the falling rain, but she was already soaked to the bone. Even had she wanted to turn around and go back, she did not have the strength, and the rain was an added deterrent.

She was exhausted and frozen, regretting her foolish, childish escapade. But crying would resolve nothing. She swallowed her tears. If she were very lucky, her disappearance had been noticed and she would be rescued. Again.

And then she heard her name.

She tensed. Surely she had been imagining it. She listened acutely, but heard only the howling wind— or was it a wolf? The rain beat the ground loudly, adding to the din. She strained to look back up the road, but already it was too dark to see. She hugged herself, shivering.

"Elizabeth!"

Someone was calling her, and if her ears had heard correctly, it was Slade. She wanted to run. Not away from him, but into his arms.

She was such a fool.

"Elizabeth!"

His voice was growing stronger. She crouched, remembering his betrayal. It did not seem to matter. "Slade! Slade, I'm here!"

A light flared, wobbling toward her. She heard his horse snorting.

She stood. "Slade!"

He emerged from the dark like a phantom emerging from the mist. His shadowy outline grew stronger and briefly he appeared to be one with his horse, like a mythical centaur. Then he leaped to the ground, striding forward, leaving the horse behind. His poncho swirled about him. The lantern he held up shone in her eyes, momentarily blinding her. When he saw her, he broke into a run.

Regina didn't move. She sagged against the tree, sobbing in relief, waiting for him to rescue her.

Chapter 7

Slade grabbed her. It was not an embrace. He was angry. Regina brushed away the hot tears that were suddenly spilling forth. Once again, he was rescuing her, and once again, she was utterly relieved.

He gripped her. "You know there are wolves and mountain lions in these parts?"

"Wolves and lions?"

"Yes!" He shook her once for emphasis. Regina bobbed in his hands like a cork on water. "Jesus! You're soaking wet!"

Regina hugged herself as a few drops of rain found their way through the foliage overhead and continued to sprinkle down on her. He backed away from her, staring. "I don't want to hear a word of protest out of you," he said grimly.

No longer thinking of flight, Regina could freely succumb to exhaustion, and to his will. She was so tired that she wanted him to take charge of her. "All right." She began to shiver uncontrollably. The cold was creeping across every inch of her flesh.

Abruptly, he removed his poncho, his thick leather vest, and his soft cotton shirt. Regina started, forgetting all about being cold. His upper body was beautiful. He was beautiful. He was not really a big man, but every inch of him was sculpted muscle, every inch of him was exquisitely defined. He was the essence of power and masculinity.

He stared back at her gravely, swiftly slipping his vest back on over his bare torso. "Take off your clothes."

She could not have heard correctly. "What?"

"Take off your clothes before you catch your death and put on my shirt."

She was incredulous, disbelieving. It was a moment before she could speak. "You are joking."

"No, I'm not." He reached for the shiny brass closures of her jacket. Before she could react, he undid them with swift fingers and pulled the jacket off.

"What are you doing?" she cried, trying to push his hands away as they performed the exact same procedure on her ruffled blouse.

"You're getting into dry clothes," he said, yanking off her shirt. "And we're not going to waste time arguing about it."

"Your intentions may be legitimate, but this is unacceptable!" she cried, shielding her chest with her arms, and backing away until her head hit a low branch of the tree.

He reached for her corset.

She gripped his wrist with surprising strength. "Don't you dare." She meant it. She was shivering, but was oblivious to her discomfort in the face of what he was intending. It didn't matter that he obviously feared for her health; his intentions were beyond the pale. If he tried to remove her chemise and corset she would scratch his eyes out.

A long moment passed. "You are not the first woman I've seen naked," he finally said.

She blanched. That was not reassuring, nor was it comforting. To the contrary. She bristled, even more resolved to remain fully clothed.

He did not attempt to persuade her again. He whirled her around before she could even comprehend what he was doing. As he yanked on the ties she shouted at him. He was just as adept at removing a lady's corset as he was at removing her jacket and blouse, and Regina found this revelation as unpleasant as the first. Upset with his proficiency as well as his actions, she squirmed like an eel, forcing him again and again to cease his efforts to divest her of her corset and jerk her back to him. By the time he triumphed, they were both panting and flushed with exertion.

"Stop!" Regina cried. She was acutely aware of wearing nothing on her breasts but a sheer silk chemise, and she was equally aware of his gaze, which slid to inspect its contents. "Enough! I am not disrobing! Give me back my clothing!" As an afterthought, she added, "Please."

"You're getting out of your clothes before you catch pneumonia. I won't look."

She was furious. "Why should you? When you've already had your fill?"

"If you think I've had my fill, you are sorely mistaken."

Regina hugged herself harder, as if that might erase the glimpses of her person that he'd had; her flush deepened. She dared not analyze his statement. "I am not disrobing," she repeated firmly. "May I please have my clothing back?"

He shoved his balled-up shirt at her. "Take off your clothes and put this on."

Regina eyed him defiantly, refusing to take it. It was out of the realm of possibility. She was not going to give another inch. Distress made it difficult to breathe normally. "No."

"I don't want to do this any more than you want me to do this," he muttered.

Regina was relieved. Her relief lasted all of two seconds.

Determined, Slade gripped the chemise. Regina protested immediately, incoherently, trying to pull the fabric out of his hand. The thin delicate material ripped completely in two.

For one instant she was the object of his undivided attention. She quickly covered herself with her hands.

She was aghast, too shocked for words. She could not believe what he had done.

He had the grace to redden as well. "I didn't mean to tear the damn thing off of you. If I was trying to tear your clothes off, you'd sure as hell know it."

She was motionless, clutching her arms to her bare bosom, shielding herself. His words drummed up an image she shouldn't entertain, one of him ripping her clothing from her in a hasty prelude to his lovemaking. She shook. She was shocked that she would think such a thing. How could she think such a thing?

"Elizabeth, I just want—"

"No!" she cried, hysteria pitching her voice upward. "I don't care what you think you were trying to do! Look at what you've done! How could you? How could you treat me this way?"

His color deepened to a shade of beet-red.

Their gazes connected sharply, then they bounced off of one another. "I'm sorry. You're right." He shoved the shirt at her; she took it without removing her arms from her chest. "Put my damn shirt on. I'm going to get my bedroll."

Regina was still shaking, but not entirely from the cold. She was terribly aware of being half-naked. She was terribly aware of him. She was aware that he had seen her breasts. Thank God he stepped out of the glow of the lantern's light, disappearing into the darkness.

She blinked at the shirt, *his* shirt. Her color heightened again. How could she put on his shirt? The shirt was snowy-white and cotton. It was soft from too many washes and too many wearings. It was warm from his body. She swallowed. How could she put it on when it had covered his body a moment ago? How could she put it over her own naked breasts? If she put it on, it would be the most intimate act she had ever shared with a man, she was quite certain of that. Yet the idea, *the very idea*, made her light-headed and breathless.

How could she not? Slade would return at any moment.

"You are not a real gentleman," she whispered to the night. "If you were a real gentleman, you would not force me to do this."

"I am not a gentleman, and more importantly, I never said I was," Slade said tightly, stepping back into the circle of light beneath the oak tree.

He was carrying a blanket. His eyes automatically went to the shirt she clutched to her bosom. Regina did not have to be a wizard to know that he was thinking along the same lines as she—or worse. She surrendered. "Turn around," she whispered.

Slade's gaze met hers. The moment seemed agonizingly intimate. He turned his back to her.

Quickly she slipped his shirt on, fumbling with the buttons. As the soft cotton teased her bare breasts, she felt dizzy and dazed. Her skin tingled with illicit pleasure and hungry expectation.

He turned, but his glance slid past her, as if he were determined not to look at her. "Just get rid of those soaking skirts and forget the rest."

Her skirts *were* soaked, heavy and impossible to move in, but she had gone far enough. She would not strip down to her petticoat and drawers. When she did not answer and she did not move, he looked at her grimly. She choked when she realized that he was implacable.

Regina's fingers dug into her palms. The shocking fantasy she'd entertained so briefly in response to his words, of him ripping off her clothes and embracing her, swelled in her mind. She could not look away from him. And she knew, she absolutely knew, that in not moving and not turning away, she was issuing another invitation, one that was infinitely dangerous.

Slade moved. Lithe and graceful, he came toward her. His hands reached for her. Her body shook in response, her heart missed a beat. Anticipation almost wrung a cry from her mouth. For one second she was frozen, gripping his bare arms, her breasts straining against his shirt. In that second he froze too. Beneath her soft palms she felt the strength of his arms and the power of his body and the tension that ran like a hot live wire through him. The atmosphere around them was charged with possibility. If he had dared to strike a match, Regina thought that most likely the air itself would have blazed into a fire.

"Elizabeth." His tone was unbearably intimate. His rough hands settled on her back and slid up to her shoulders. A wave of sensation, the likes of which Regina had never before experienced, washed over her. Their glances came together.

It was there, the dark hunger she had seen before. Its power and starkness both frightened and compelled her. With a soft moan she gripped him more tightly, knowing she should not, but ready to surrender completely and knowing that too.

And he knew it as well; she saw that in the blaze of his eyes. Regina clung, waiting for him to take her. Instead, he reached under her shirt, and a moment later her heavy skirts fell down around her ankles. Instantly he released her, moving away from her. She buried her face in her hands with a small sob. His scent, male and sexy, filled her nostrils, wafting from his shirt, the final crushing blow.

He tossed his poncho and bedroll at her. She caught them reflexively. He would not look at her. His expression was strained. "Let's get out of here before you do get pneumonia."

Regina did not have the strength or the will to argue. Trembling, she wrapped the blanket around her and awkwardly slipped on his poncho. The slicker was lined and toasty-warm. It smelled strongly of him. She hugged it and the blanket to her body.

When Regina stepped forward, her knees gave way and she fell against Slade with a whimper. Her feet were raw from the endless walking she had endured. Instantly Slade was kneeling before her and yanking off her shoes. Regina cried out.

"Jesus," he said tightly. "You must hate me a hell of a lot to keep on going with blisters like these."

"No," she whispered, very close to tears. She spoke to the top of his head. "I don't hate you."

If he heard her he gave no sign. He hoisted her into his arms and strode into the night. The rain whipped them fiercely, the wind howled, and the trees danced in a helpless frenzy around them. Slade deposited her on his mount and jumped up into the saddle behind her.

Abruptly he lifted her crossways onto his lap and pushed her face into his shoulder. "Hold on," he said, shouting to make himself heard over the wind, one arm firmly around her waist.

He didn't have to repeat himself. She buried her cheek against his bare chest, wrapping her arms around him, wondering if the night would ever end. She tried not to think about what had happened—and what had not happened. She tried not to be aware of the warm, strong man gripping her as tightly as she gripped him. It was impossible. He spurred his horse into a canter and then they galloped into the storm, back to Miramar.

Slade carried Regina through the courtyard in the pouring rain. She was protected by his slicker, he was not. Now he was drenched, his hair sticking to his head, water running in rivulets down his arms and chest, his vest heavy and sodden, his pants plastered to his legs.

Rick appeared at the door that led from the dining room. "You found her!" he cried in relief.

Slade didn't stop. "I found her," he said. He moved with aggressive strides toward her room, mindless of the rain, which was coming down now harder than before.

Victoria came to stand by her husband. "Is she all right?"

"Soaked. Have Lucinda draw a bath and bring her some hot food."

"Slade!" Victoria called. "You can't go into her room with her!"

Slade didn't acknowledge her comment. He disappeared into Regina's bedroom carrying her in his arms.

Victoria started to go after them.

"Don't you dare," Rick said, gripping her arm.

"Ow! You're hurting me!"

Rick did not release her. "Why did you do it? Why did you interfere?"

Her eyes widened innocently. "Do what?"

"Cut it out!" He shook her. "Slade told me it was you. You told Elizabeth of my plans."

"You're hurting me," Victoria said calmly.

"Let her go, Father," Edward said. He moved out of the shadows of the hallway.

Rick released his wife. "Your mother's meddling in my affairs again."

"So I gather," Edward said, unsmiling. His glance was on Victoria. "Why, Mother? Why are you trying to obstruct Father?"

"I'm not trying to sabotage your father!" Victoria cried. "I'm only trying to look out for all of our best interests!"

Rick laughed.

Edward grimaced. "Mother, I know you are doing what you think is best, but it's time we spoke freely. *I am not going to take Miramar away from Slade. I don't even want it.* Slade is now Father's heir. Slade is going to marry Elizabeth and inherit the rancho. Not me."

"Why not?" Victoria cried furiously. "Why the hell not? You're here. You've been here your entire life, working alongside Rick and James. Why should Slade be the chosen one! Why him? He left his home ten years ago, turned his back on all of us. He hasn't even bothered to come home more than three or four times in all those years. Do you know it's been two years since he was last home? And if James hadn't died, God knows, maybe he would have never come home again!"

"He would have come home," Edward said.

"What's the point of all this speculation?" Rick asked. "He's home now, ain't he? He's the oldest. He's the oldest like I was the oldest. It's our way, Victoria, and you knew it when you married me."

"He doesn't want to marry her," Victoria gritted. "He only wants to get into her drawers—and that's certainly continuing one family tradition!"

Edward smiled slightly. "Who the hell wants to get married anyway? You can't blame Slade for that. You can't blame him, but maybe if you gave him some time he'd come around. I think he would."

"We don't *have* time," Rick growled.

"Even if he never marries her, he's still the oldest," Edward pointed out. "Miramar would still rightfully be his. My vote is in, Mother." With that, he turned and walked away.

Victoria was speechless.

"Edward's right, at least on the last point. I don't want you butting in," Rick said coldly.

"Do you really think I should just stand by and watch while you give that ingrate everything you've worked so hard for? When you have another son, a worthy one, one who didn't run away and turn his back on all of us? On you?"

"If I find out you've interfered again, I'm going to toss you out on your ass, Victoria."

She looked at him for a long moment, assessing his intentions, then she smiled. "You won't."

"Oh, no? You think your acrobatics in bed are going to stop me?"

For a moment Victoria appeared uncertain. Then she said, smiling, "You won't throw me out, Rick. You may despise me, but you need me. Nobody understands you the way that I do, and certainly not another woman. And I am not referring to our sex life."

"Maybe that's the problem," Rick said, his smile threatening. "Maybe that's the real crux of it, Victoria."

She stared.

Rick grinned, enjoying his power.

But Victoria recovered quickly. "Edward is also your son. Edward did not turn his back on you. Edward, if you asked him, would do everything you want. Slade will never, ever do anything if you want him to, as you damn well know."

Rick looked at her. "For the last time, you stay out of this. Slade is going to marry Elizabeth, and he is going to inherit Miramar. Slade will bend. This time, he is going to do what I want, you wait and see."

Chapter 8

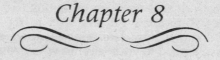

*S*lade deposited Regina abruptly on the bed.

She bounced once on the soft mattress and settled into its thickness and warmth. She lay unmoving, staring up at him.

His expression was blank. She sat up, then remembered her state of undress, and she quickly pulled the coverlet over her. The cold, wet, wild ride had chased away the insanity which had possessed her. She was still too aware of him, and she could not forget what had almost happened, but she was in control of her faculties once more. "I don't think you should be in here."

"You're right. This is the last place I should be." He did not move.

She looked at the water running down his face, his vest, his naked chest and perfectly flat stomach. His dark skin had a sheen to it. She lifted her gaze. She was in control of herself, but his presence was too potent and too unnerving. Especially here in her bedroom. "Now *you'll* catch pneumonia." She laughed uneasily.

"I'm tough. I've survived a hell of a lot worse." Abruptly he flicked the ends of the coverlet off her feet. "That wasn't smart," he said tightly. "You've got a dozen blisters all broken and bleeding. Don't you have any common sense? After your bath take some gauze and antiseptic and wrap your feet up. Stay off of them."

"All right." She looked at the door, which was closed. "I think you should leave, before I'm compromised."

His glance was hard. "I'm not going to compromise you, Elizabeth. If that were my intention, we'd still be down-valley. Tomorrow I'll take you to the Southern Pacific. If I'd known how determined you were to leave, I would have agreed to your leaving when you spoke of it earlier."

His last words made her feel guilty, nonsensically so. He was interpreting her attempt to run away as a personal indictment of him. But wasn't he right? Hadn't it been a very personal indictment? And why should she be upset that his feelings might be hurt? He did not act hurt. In fact, he acted as if nothing untoward had happened between them. "Tomorrow you'll take me to town?" she asked uncertainly.

"Unless you'd rather someone else take you. Like Edward—my gentlemanly brother."

She blushed. Slade hadn't been a gentleman half an hour ago, but he had rescued her—again. And she seemed to have a weak spot for him, regardless of what he said and did. She also did not like it when he mocked himself. "I understand what you were trying to do," she said softly. "I was just . . . shocked . . . at the time."

"Why are you trying to spare me? You were right. Don't mince words now. I'm no gentleman and I never will be. I don't even aspire to being one. And you are obviously a lady. To tell you the truth, I don't have the foggiest notion of how to act around you." He flushed.

"No."

"You're not a lady?" His mouth curved slightly.

It was the very first sign of a sense of humor that she had witnessed in him and she smiled. "Of course I'm a lady." Her smile faded. "Slade, I'm sorry I said that. It's not true. You have a rough appearance, but you are very much a gentleman, and there is nothing wrong with your behavior around me."

His mouth tightened. He was no longer amused. "I can swear on the Bible that I didn't have a single gentlemanly thought in my head a few minutes ago, and my behavior was just about borderline."

She opened her mouth to reply, and shut it. What could she say? Her thoughts hadn't been exactly ladylike, either. In fact, they were becoming less ladylike by the second. Had his behavior been borderline? Hers had certainly been worse. Finally she whispered, "We can't always stop our thoughts, but we can control our actions. That is what's important."

He gave her a dark look. It was challenging and skeptical.

Regina regarded her hands nervously. He had every right to doubt her. Still, she owed him an apology. "I'm sorry for running away. It was foolish. I was frightened, confused."

"No one would ever force you to marry me," he said roughly.

"I . . . I didn't even think that way."

"You were upset enough to take off on horseback when you're a poor rider. You were upset enough to walk until you bloodied your feet. I'd say you weren't just upset. I'd say you were damn determined."

She could not respond. She *had* been very determined. She could no longer fathom why.

"Having a change of heart?"

"I don't know," she whispered.

Their glances held. His grew dark. "The southbound train goes through Templeton twice a day. You won't be able to make the morning stop, but you can catch her tomorrow evening. Rick has a schedule, I'll check it now."

She had the feeling that he was very intent on taking her to that train. "M-maybe I should rest tomorrow and leave the following day."

"I'll take you tomorrow," he said flatly. "Before things really get out of control."

She understood. She understood everything too well. He knew as well as she that desire had bloomed between them, dangerous desire, and it was not going to go away just because they both wished it would. They certainly could not reside together under the same roof without tempting fate. He was determined that she leave his home as quickly as possible. Obviously he had decided he didn't want to marry her after all.

She lowered her eyes so he wouldn't see that she was actually hurt. There was no reason to be hurt, because marriage was out of the question. Wasn't it? She did not look up as he crossed the room, until he had shut the door firmly behind him.

Regina fell back against the pillows. She was distraught. Yet she should be relieved that he was taking charge and compelling her to leave. But she wasn't relieved. She was torn, confused, dismayed. What if she did stay? What if they did marry? Dear God, what was she thinking?

She had no time to reflect upon this ghastly turn, for suddenly there was a knock on her door. At Regina's request, a woman entered. She was fair-skinned and dark-haired and just a few years older than Regina. Her simple skirt, shirtwaist, and apron told Regina that she was a servant. The maid set a tray down on the small wooden table by the terrace doors, then turned slightly, regarding Regina.

Regina sat up. "You must be Lucinda. Thank you. The food smells delicious."

Lucinda murmured a response. Regina had the distinct impression that the maid was studying her, but that made no sense at all.

"Do you need anything else?" Lucinda asked. "I'll draw your bath now."

Regina shook her head. The maid left quickly. Regina slid from the bed. Her feet throbbed painfully now and walking was very difficult. She hobbled across the room and sat down at the table, but food was the farthest thing from her mind. Broodingly she wondered what she should do—and what she wanted to do.

* * *

Slade awoke her the next day. He walked into her room, throwing the doors to the balcony open so that the brilliant sunlight suddenly poured inside. She stirred. She was exhausted, she did not want to move, yet she knew there was a reason—an important reason—for her to get up and face the day.

"Elizabeth." Slade's voice penetrated the thick mist of her fatigue. "Wake up."

It took a great effort to force her way up through the heavy cloak of sleep. As she did, she became aware of Slade's voice, urging her again to awaken. When she opened her eyes, it only took a moment for her sleepy senses to distinguish Slade standing over her, regarding her.

Regina became fully awake. She gripped the covers which were down by her waist and pulled them up to her chin. "What are you doing in here?"

His gaze lifted to her face reluctantly. "It's almost noon."

She sat up, making sure not an inch of her person was revealed to his wandering eyes. "Why didn't you knock?"

"I did knock. I've been pounding on that door. You sleep like a dead person, Elizabeth." His gaze finally met hers. His emotions, whatever they might be, were very carefully shadowed. "The train comes through around six tonight. It will take us three hours to get back to town. I don't know much about women, but I do know they need a lot of time to dress and such. You had better get a move on."

It was on the tip of her tongue to tell him that she was too tired and too sore to leave today, which was the truth. Yet there was more to the truth than her physical condition. Last night she had spent many hours considering her dilemma, unable to convince herself with all of her heart that Slade was right and she must leave. She was still not welcome at her stepmother's; it would be a last resort. The idea of lingering alone at any hotel was equally unpleasant. Solitude was not what she craved, not in her state. Now that she knew what the Delanzas really wanted from her, might she not be able to deal with it forthrightly? She might even be persuaded to consider marrying Slade. After all, last night had proved that there was potential for their relationship. But of course, she would need time, and if she did decide to marry him, it would have to be when she was in full possession of her memory.

But how could she possibly explain all of that to him now, when it was so painfully apparent that he was determined that she leave Miramar? When it was clear he had decided not to marry her? Her pride rose quickly to the occasion. "I can be ready in an hour."

His gaze suddenly settled on her mouth, disconcerting her. He nodded, turned abruptly, and left.

Regina leaned back against the pillows. There was no doubt about it. She was hurt again, hurt that he could so easily dismiss her, not just from Miramar, but from his life.

Despite her best intentions, she soon saw that it would take more than an hour for her to pack her belongings, much of which had been unpacked for her by an unknown maid, perhaps Lucinda, and for her to dress. She did not like the thought of Lucinda going through her things. She was also reminded of the fact that someone had gone through her luggage once before—but not to unpack it—at the hotel in Templeton.

Her physical condition slowed her down. Because of the many blisters on her feet, she now limped. And all of her muscles were stiff and sore; apparently she was unused to the amount of exertion she had endured the day before. Very honestly, if she had a choice, she would sink back into bed and not get out all day.

At one-thirty she decided she did have a choice. She did not like being rushed. She was fatigued, physically and mentally. She needed another day of rest, at least. Dear Lord, it seemed like ages ago, but it had only been the day before yesterday that she had lost her memory. She did not look forward to confronting Slade, but the sooner she told him she would not leave today, the sooner she could relax. Moving somewhat awkwardly, she crossed the courtyard, apprehensive about his reaction, guessing it would be too eloquent. He was not the kind of man to mince words when he was angry.

Her steps soon slowed. She could hear Rick's voice raised in anger. Although she knew she should go back, she continued to approach, more cautiously. As she came closer her suspicion was confirmed; Slade was the other participant in the argument being waged. It was impossible not to hear what they were fighting about now, and she became as still as stone.

"You go out of your way, don't you, just to get my dander up!" Rick roared.

"I haven't gone out of my way for you in years," Slade responded flatly.

"But you had to volunteer to take her back now!"

"Looks like I'm the only sane one around here."

"Like hell. You don't care if she goes or stays. You just want to piss me off."

"You flatter yourself if you think I do anything because of you."

They were in the dining room. Regina could see the two of them standing on opposite sides of the trestle table, squared off the one against the other. She decided in that moment to turn around and flee.

But Slade said, "She wants to leave. She wants to leave so bad she ran away, got thrown from a horse, and walked her feet raw. But you know what? At least she's smart. At least she's got you figured out."

"Maybe she's got *you* figured out!" Rick shot back.

"Maybe," Slade agreed calmly.

Regina was nearly disbelieving. She was stunned to see a son slur his father so, and a father attack his son even more strongly. How could they throw such painful stones at each other? And she was angry. She was angry at Rick, recalling how, at the hotel in Templeton, he had accused Slade of laziness; then, when Slade was gone, he'd dropped his armor and revealed the love he kept so carefully hidden.

Both men had seen her. Regina's anger turned to embarrassment and she wished she were anywhere but there. Now they were silent, watching her.

"You ready?" Slade said brusquely.

She had no choice but to enter the dining room. Once inside she could see them clearly. Rick had relaxed and was regarding her in a friendly manner—as if he had not just been engaged in a violent verbal battle with his son. But Slade wasn't relaxed. He sat on one of the studded leather dining chairs, but he looked as if he might explode from it like a cannonball at the slightest provocation. His dark gaze made her unaccountably nervous.

"Mornin'," Rick greeted her.

"Good morning," Regina said politely to both men. But she felt like giving Rick a good tongue-lashing, which he could use. It was up to parents to set a good example for their children, and the example he was setting did not fall anywhere near that category.

"You ready?" Slade asked again. "We have just enough time for you to eat something if you're hungry."

Her anger boiled over at Slade now. She faced him, her eyes flashing. "No, I am not ready. Not only am I not ready, my feet are so raw I can barely walk. I have come to tell you that I am not leaving this afternoon. This afternoon I am going to rest."

Rick flung a look of triumph at Slade and moved toward her. "Come on, Elizabeth, sit down, have some breakfast. You don't have to leave at all. And we had better have the doc out to tend to your feet."

Regina recovered her senses, remembering that this man had lied to her; still very aware of how he had been fighting with Slade, she whirled. "That's quite all right. I have tended to myself; thank you for your concern." Her words were very clipped and precise because of her anger, but she did not raise her voice even a decibel.

Rick's expression was hangdog. "You're mad."

She lifted a brow.

"Look, I don't blame you, but it's not fair for you to be mad at me without even hearing my side of things."

"I *would* like an explanation. I do not believe I am used to being deceived."

Slade stood, almost knocking over his chair. "You're making a big mistake," he told her.

She looked at him. He stood before her, a relentless and volatile force, tension seething about him so hotly it was almost visible. "I'm only going to talk with your father. He owes me some honesty."

Slade was angry. He looked at Rick. "Just how honest are you going to be with her? Don't you think you can give her a break? She doesn't even know who she is, for Christ's sake. *Leave her alone.*"

Regina was stunned—Slade was trying to protect her from Rick.

"You stay out of this, boy," Rick said tightly. "This is between me and her. An' don't think I've forgotten for a second that she's got that amnesia."

"Slade," Regina said, touching his arm. She gave him a warm aching smile. "I'll be fine."

"Like hell."

"Give me a chance," Rick cajoled her.

Regina turned toward him. "All right."

Rick took her arm. He glanced darkly at Slade. "You're not invited. We all know where you stand."

"No," Slade said. "No one knows where I stand!" He strode from the room.

Regina didn't have a chance to watch him go or to call after him. Rick was guiding her into the corridor. "Let's go to my study where we can have some privacy," he said.

He was smiling and friendly. He seemed so genuine that Regina had to remind herself that this man was not as he appeared. She had to remind herself that he had lied to her, that he had attempted to use her.

His study was cool and dark. Rick closed the heavy redwood door behind them and led her to a leather easy chair. He sat opposite her behind his desk. "I wish you'd come to me first, before trying to leave like you did, in the middle of a storm," he said.

"I was angry."

Rick shook his head ruefully. "I guess I don't blame you."

"You lied to me," Regina said coolly.

"I didn't lie to you. I just didn't tell you everything," Rick said.

"I fail to see the difference."

"There *is* a difference, a big difference. Your father and I did grow up together, and you can ask anyone around here if you must. We arranged the marriage between you and James because we both wanted it. George wanted you to be mistress of Miramar, and he wanted your son to be the boss."

"And you wanted my money."

"I won't lie. I didn't lie. We need your money, Elizabeth. We're cash-poor. Most big spreads like this are cash-poor. It's not unusual and it's no secret. Just like it's nothing to be ashamed about. *But we're land-rich.* And we're rich in cattle, horses, and heritage." Rick's eyes snapped with excitement. "Money can buy land like this, but not the tradition, the heritage, the past that goes with it. But it sure as hell can buy the future. Yes, we need some cash. But look at what you're getting!"

Regina followed Rick's bright gaze, thinking that father and son had so much in common in the love they shared for Miramar. She looked out the open doors of the terrace to the south, at the jagged line of starkly gold, treeless, imposing mountains where they painted a sharp line against the vivid blue sky. Directly ahead of her, the hillside sloped down, disappearing when it collided abruptly with the Pacific. And to her right, pines pointed at the sky. The view was breathtaking. She couldn't help but agree with Rick. He was right. Money could buy a lot of things but it couldn't buy a home like this. Regina doubted there were two such places in existence in all of God's creation.

"Honey," Rick said, smiling, "I may want cash, but that doesn't mean you're not family to me. George was like my brother—like the brother I never had. You're his daughter. And James loved you. He was my son, my first child. Your welfare is important to me. How could it not be?"

Regina tore her gaze from the splendor that was Miramar and looked at him, filled with conflicting needs. She didn't really want to leave. And there was no question that she found Miramar very appealing. Right now she was a woman without a home or a past, and the idea of finding that here was very seductive. Yet the instinctive need to protect herself balanced the scales. But why should she think he was lying? Caring about her and needing money were not mutually exclusive propositions. Not necessarily. Not when one considered the entire set of circumstances, not when one considered the history between Rick Delanza and George Sinclair.

Rick smiled. "Is it so wrong to hope you and Slade might like each other and want to marry? Is it so wrong for me to want to bring you into the family as George and I intended? Slade is now my heir. He's fighting that, because he plumb likes to fight me, but he'll do his duty, you wait and see."

"Meaning he'll marry me?" Her tone was calm, but inwardly her heart had skittered.

"I didn't exactly mean that," Rick said, leaning back comfortably in his chair. "I meant he'll inherit Miramar. Like he should. Of course, I hope he'll come around and want to marry you. But I can't force him to it, just like I can't force you."

Regina tried very hard to be calm. She tried very hard not to let his words sway her. She tried very hard not to think about the possibility that she and Slade might eventually "like each other and want to marry."

"I still want you to stay here, Elizabeth, until you recover, anyway, and maybe by then you'll decide you want to stay—maybe you'll decide my son isn't so bad. God knows, there's lots of women who would give their right arms just for the chance to marry Slade."

Regina's hands were trembling, and she clasped them firmly so Rick wouldn't see. She could well imagine that most women would take one look at Slade and do just about anything he asked.

Slade was filling her thoughts. But suddenly she sensed the presence of another man, someone who seemed intent on struggling up through the depths of her mind. She tensed. For an instant his image was there, but it was dark and shadowy and unformed. Then it disappeared, and she wondered if her mind was playing tricks upon her, if she had been about to remember someone at all. Yet if she had, had it been James?

"What is it?" Rick asked sharply, peering at her.

She touched her throbbing temple. "I think I was about to remember something, someone, but then it disappeared. Yesterday the same thing happened."

"Well, that's just great!"

Regina barely heard him. Yesterday, she was almost positive, she had been about to remember someone else. Was her memory trying to return? She could not contain the hope swelling in her breast. And then it occurred to her that if she had loved James, when her memory returned so would that love. She grew very still.

"As soon as you remember something, you tell me," Rick was saying. "The sheriff wants to speak with you when you do remember, even if it's still hazy."

Regina was motionless. The excitement was not only gone, now there was fear in her heart instead. Some things were definitely better left unrecalled.

Her fear must have shown, because Rick leaned across the desk and patted her hand. "Don't you worry none about the sheriff. It's just routine."

It wasn't the sheriff she was worrying about. She was worrying about how she would feel about James when she recovered from this mental lapse. And when she did recover, what would happen to her relationship with Slade?

"So?" Rick smiled. "You gonna accept some old-fashioned hospitality?"

Regina looked at him. She fought for a smile. Suddenly there was comfort in the fact that her memory had yet to return, forestalling what might be a horrible dilemma. "Yes, I will stay."

Rick beamed. His smile was so hearty that Regina had to smile back.

Chapter 9

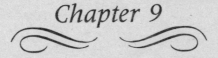

Rick closed the door to his study, thinking about the girl. He had concluded his interview with Regina Shelton a few moments ago, convincing her to stay.

He heaved a sigh of relief. It had been a close call. Close, but not fatal. Slowly he smiled, hands clasped behind his back, staring out the wide-open windows and across the sloping hillside. The sweep of saddleback mountains in the south and the expanse of steel-gray ocean in the west never failed to thrill him. Pride swelled his chest as he regarded the land that was Miramar, that was his, and that would one day be Slade's.

Thinking of Slade made him grim, and in the next heartbeat, he thought of James. Pain crashed over him. It would never go away, he knew that. It was worse than anything he'd ever experienced, and he'd been through a hell of a lot. His first wife had died in childbirth, and although that had been an arranged marriage, he'd been fond of her, and no woman deserved such an untimely death. Catherine had been the only gentlewoman in his life; neither Pauline, Slade's mother, nor Victoria, deserved such an appellation.

It occurred to Rick that Regina Shelton was also a gentlewoman, and that she reminded him of Catherine.

Catherine's death had only been the beginning of the series of personal tragedies besetting him in his lifetime. He and his father had been running the rancho together until a heart attack had struck his father, leaving him alive but paralyzed and incapable of speech. Rick had loved his father, but that day his father had seemed to die, leaving only a shell of a man in his place. He had watched him physically waste away over the course of two long, agonizing years until death mercifully claimed his body as well as his heart and soul.

Pauline had left him by then. She had been the only woman he'd ever loved, and she'd been nothing more than a whore in disguise. To this day he couldn't be sure if it was him or their impoverished circumstances which triggered her desertion. He suspected that she had never really loved him, and had only been seeking to marry a fortune, something the Delanzas had never had. Their marriage had been brief, little more than a year. He had almost gone after her, almost begged her to stay. But he had some pride, because she was leaving him to go to another man. Letting her go had been impossibly hard and impossibly painful.

And like his mother, Slade ran away also, fifteen years later. *Just like his mother*. It was a second betrayal that he had barely been able to survive, and it hurt so much more than the first. Of course, from the time Slade had been toddling Rick had seen the nearly unbearable resemblance between mother and son. Slade's astounding looks, which were almost too pretty when he was a young boy, had come from his mother. So too had his defiance. Rick had spent fifteen years trying to tame that wild streak, without success.

And now, finally, it had come to this, the death of his first son, James, who was as different from Slade as white was from black. James hadn't had a defiant bone in his body. They had rarely argued. No son could have been more dutiful and more loyal. No man could have been more honest or more sincere.

He couldn't bear thinking about James, not even now, so he forced his thoughts back to the girl.

He had known her real identity before Slade had found her by the train tracks and brought her to Templeton. Rick had sent Slade and Edward to town to meet the train, expecting Elizabeth. Rick had not informed her of James's death yet. He was not intending to do so until she was at Miramar, because he wanted to convince her quickly to marry Slade, and he was certain he could do it in person. The week before she was due to arrive— two weeks before she and James would have been married—he had wired her at her home in San Luis Obispo. The telegram had been a simple welcome. He hadn't expected a reply, and he hadn't gotten one, but he most certainly had expected her to be on the train at the prearranged date.

Yet the train had limped into Templeton after the holdup, without Elizabeth. It was detained by the sheriff as he attempted to interview the overwrought passengers. A dozen gentlemen were quick to point out that a very beautiful, elegant young lady had fled the club car during the holdup. Hot on her heels had been one of the thieves. So Slade and Edward had split up. Slade had ridden out to find her while Edward had galloped back to Miramar to inform Rick of the disastrous events.

Rick hadn't hesitated. He and Edward had returned to Templeton immediately. The normally sleepy town had been in an uncharacteristic frenzy and the train had not yet been allowed to leave. One of the passengers who had been seriously wounded was the chaperone of the young lady who had fled the train. From eyewitnesses it had been learned that she had attempted to block the thief chasing her charge and he had shot her, perhaps purposefully, perhaps accidentally. It had been hard to tell. The chaperone had been unconscious since the train had arrived in Templeton, so no one had spoken with her.

Rick was the first and only person to speak with her when she regained her senses. Slade had yet to return with the woman everyone assumed to be Elizabeth. Rick was afraid that Elizabeth had been hurt.

The chaperone was dying. Rick was sorry for that, but there was nothing they could do to stop her from meeting her maker. Doc Brown had left the room to see if Father Joseph had arrived, having done all that he could for her. Rick knelt beside her, taking her hand.

"What can I do for you, ma'am? What can I get you?" Rick said kindly. Death was final, and Rick had seen it too often to be callous about it. He was no fool, he knew there was no glory waiting for anyone, no ever-after, just nothingness, dirt, and dust.

The woman shook her head, unable to speak at first. She was weak from having lost so much blood. "Harold," she said.

"Harold?"

"I'm finally going to be with Harold again." She smiled faintly. Her voice was reed-thin. "My husband."

If she believed in an ever-after, it was better for her. He patted her hand. "Can you tell me about Elizabeth? Is she all right?"

The woman didn't seem to hear him. "R-Re-Regina?"

Rick leaned closer. "Is Elizabeth all right?"

Tears filled the woman's eyes. "R-Regina? W-where . . . is she?"

"Who is Regina?"

It took all of her strength, but five minutes later, she had explained quite a bit. Mrs. Schroener was not the chaperone of Elizabeth Sinclair. Her charge was Regina Shelton, the daughter of a British nobleman. She had been hired by the girl's grandfather in Texas, and he was none other than the very rich, all-powerful Derek Bragg. In fact, her charge was a very great heiress, and the woman was distraught at having failed in her duty to see her safely to her destination.

Rick was nearly in shock. But he recovered. Apparently Elizabeth was not on the train—he could only assume that she would arrive on a later one. At least he could rest assured that she was all right, although he wanted to know why in hell she wasn't on the Southern Pacific when she was supposed to be on it.

The woman slipped back into unconsciousness, but fortunately Father Joseph arrived then, while she was still breathing. Ten minutes later she died.

And then Slade arrived in town and told Rick that Elizabeth had lost her memory.

Rick could not help seeing the opportunity that some awfully mighty God was hand-delivering to him. In fact, it seemed like a miracle. And if he hadn't quite believed in God before, he did now.

Regina Shelton was a much greater heiress than Elizabeth Sinclair. What if he could arrange a marriage between her and Slade as he'd intended to do between Elizabeth and Slade?

It seemed that was what fate had intended. Her amnesia gave him the perfect opportunity to foster just such an alliance. She was alone and vulnerable, and while he didn't like preying on her condition, she couldn't be left to go her own way. Obviously he would bring her to Miramar, so she could rest and recover while being cared for. In that interim, she would be convinced to marry Slade, whether her memory returned or not.

Unfortunately Rick could still not reveal to her her real identity, not yet, because she would be whisked away by her relatives, and this golden God-given opportunity would be destroyed. So what if he just happened to mistake her for Elizabeth? He had only met Elizabeth twice—five years ago when she was thirteen, and then last summer at her daddy's funeral—but then she had been swathed in a dark veil. No one would ever know that the mistake was calculated. If everyone believed her to be Elizabeth, she would continue on her way to Miramar, as planned, despite her condition.

Although everything was going to work out perfectly—and Rick was certain of it, despite his hardheaded son's determination to oppose him—he did not have time on his side. Right now he knew there were Braggs looking for Regina, worried about her. He was no fool, and he'd figured out right away that she would be missed when she did not show up at whatever destination she had been traveling to. As soon as he had learned from Slade that she had amnesia, and as soon as he had briefly spoken with her, he had wired the Pinkerton agency to send one of their men. He wanted to know who was looking for her, where she had been going, and more about her background.

It had been a very close call. Just yesterday her uncle, Brett D'Archand, a San Francisco millionaire, had been in Templeton, searching for her. He had interviewed Sheriff Willow, who, fortunately, was not the smartest of men. Sheriff Willow hadn't been able to tell him anything about Regina Shelton, for the sheriff didn't know anything about her. Everyone in Templeton assumed that Regina was Elizabeth. D'Archand had been very worried, and he had left for Lompoc, determined to find out if his niece had been on the stage, apparently uncertain whether she had been on the train or not because of her failure to arrive in Paso Robles as scheduled. Rick knew all of this because the Pinkerton agent had sent a rider with his first report last night. It answered most of Rick's questions, and he was impressed with the agent's efficiency.

Rick shuddered to think what would have happened if Regina had made it to Templeton yesterday. D'Archand had just missed crossing paths with his niece by a hair.

Rick had also asked the agent to find out what the hell was going on with the real Elizabeth Sinclair. The last thing he needed now was for her to show up at Miramar.

Rick didn't really feel guilty. Back in Templeton three days ago, when the chaperone had died and he had made the decision to "mistake" Regina for Elizabeth, there had been guilt, but desperation had been driving him. He just could not lose Miramar. Then he had told himself that even if she were promised to someone else, she would become the mistress of Miramar. There was nothing terrible about that. And she would be marrying his son Slade. Although Slade was a callous womanizer, Rick knew that all women mooned over him madly. In this instance he was hoping it would be the same.

And it was. That was why he no longer felt guilty. It had taken him about two seconds after seeing them together to learn that Regina Shelton was falling hard for his son, and fast, too. She could barely take her eyes off of Slade and the invitation she was issuing was obvious. He didn't think he'd had to really persuade her to stay a few minutes ago. In fact, he'd bet a substantial amount that she'd wanted to stay, and that she was relieved he'd supposedly had to talk her into it.

As for Slade, he belonged at Miramar. He always had, and he always would—even if James were still alive. Despite his rebel ways. The boy loved the land, with passion, and in that one way he was like Rick. And he was twenty-five, old enough to settle down. A lady like Regina Shelton was just what he needed. She would set him the kind of example he, Rick, had never been able to. In the end, she might even have him falling in love with her. Rick had seen the way Slade looked at her, too. And every man needed a good woman. His son was no exception.

It was ironic, but he was actually playing matchmaker. He looked forward to having an obviously well-bred, classy lady like Regina as his daughter-in-law. Because he was a good judge of character, from the moment he'd laid eyes on her, he'd known she was more than a blue-blooded aristocrat. She was honest and genuine and soft. She was as different from Elizabeth Sinclair as was possible, except for the fact that they were both stunningly attractive.

Even five years ago Rick had seen right away that Elizabeth was a very spoiled coquette. She was selfish and manipulative. Rick knew the type too well, because Pauline had been that way, and Victoria had it in her too, when she chose to play the game. James, of course, hadn't seen that; he'd been mesmerized by Elizabeth's blinding blonde beauty and he'd fallen for her limpid gaze and quick, pretty smiles instantly. The one thing that had been bothering Rick when he'd realized that Slade would now have to wed Elizabeth was that he knew Slade would despise Elizabeth Sinclair on sight.

Fortunately, he no longer had to worry about that.

James had been honest, kind, and good, too. Maybe it would always be an attraction of opposites in this world. God knew, with James gone, his family needed someone like Regina Shelton in their midst—and Slade needed her most of all.

No, he really didn't feel guilty, not at all.

Trapped. It was a very definite, distinct feeling, and it had been growing ever since he'd found Elizabeth Sinclair not far from the railroad tracks a dozen miles from Templeton. Last night Slade had begun to feel as if his collar were too tight—or as if there were a noose around his neck.

She could not stay. The attraction that had been there between them from the first was rapidly growing to uncontrollable proportions. Last night had proved that. Last night had been dangerous. She was James's fiancée, but Slade had forgotten that and just about everything else. He had been oblivious of their circumstances, who she was, and her state of amnesia. She was obviously a well-bred lady and a virgin if he had ever seen one. Yet he had forgotten that too. He could no longer trust himself around her. Last night he had been consumed with desire. To this moment, he did not know how he had been able to control himself and take her home without seducing her.

He supposed that the real irony of it was that she was everything James had described. Not just blindingly beautiful, but a real lady, a lady from the top of her head to the tip of her toes, a lady from the elegant clothing she wore right down to the too-generous and forgiving tendencies of her heart. She was gracious and kind and good. He was not very familiar with those traits, but he could recognize them in her easily enough. Last night when he had confessed that he had been so near to acting out his fantasies, she had said it was actions that counted, not thoughts. He almost smiled, but couldn't. She was such a damn lady she had been trying to make him feel better, she had been trying to relieve his guilt, when she was the one exhausted and suffering from amnesia, when she was the one who had been frightened enough to run away from him.

God, she would have been perfect for James. How they had suited each other. But she didn't suit him, Slade, not at all, and she never would.

He wasn't noble like James, and, as she had pointed out, he wasn't a gentleman. Even though he knew it, her subtle slander had hurt. He was so ungentlemanly he had nearly taken advantage of her last night, and the more they crossed paths, the harder it was going to be to resist her—to resist himself. He wanted to condemn her for her responsiveness to him, but he could not. It was the only earthy quality she had. Somehow, on her, it made her even more of a lady, perhaps because it was in such contrast to her obvious propriety. He could only regret it profusely, but for every sigh of regret, there was a competing and secret breath of elation.

He had been trying to push her away, hoping to push her away. If he was himself, he was sure she would be repulsed. But she refused to see him as a bastard, no matter what he did; she saw only her rescuer, and maybe even her hero. How could he fight her gratitude, coupled as it was with her incredible face and too-generous heart? How? He was trying so damn hard. But every time she looked at him with those big brown eyes it was all he could do not to haul her into his embrace.

Maybe the real problem was that the need to push her away was not as strong as the urge to protect her. She was an innocent young woman. It was so very obvious that she had led a proper, genteel, sheltered life, an easy life. Now her innocence and naiveté were compounded by her loss of memory. How could he not respond, how could he not feel compelled to look out for her? God knew, a woman like that had not the faintest idea how to look after herself outside of a gilded salon.

The noose was there around his neck. He was damned if she left and damned if she stayed even if for a while. He couldn't forget Miramar. Rick had said that if he didn't marry the little heiress soon, Miramar was going to be taken from them. It was possible that Rick was exaggerating. The old man had been known to do that from time to time, especially when the stakes demanded it. In another minute he was going to go over the books himself.

And if she did stay, he was going to have to fight himself very hard in order not to betray James. And it wasn't just his fantasies or his damn body that he was thinking about. For he suspected there was a small part of him that refused to bend to his iron-clad will, that refused to accept the *fact* that she was off-limits, that might even *consider* the notion of marriage to her.

Slade was determined to do battle with himself until the end of time, if need be, but he was not touching her and he wasn't marrying her, and somehow, he would sort things out and save Miramar—if Rick were telling the truth.

He no longer considered leaving Miramar and returning to Charles Mann in San Francisco, where he was a crucial man in Charles's far-flung empire. He couldn't leave now, not when his home was in such financial jeopardy. Charles had told him to take as much time as he needed in order to be with his family, but Slade would have to send him some word soon about his plans. Of course, he was not staying forever and he was not taking James's place. He was not. But he could not abandon Miramar now. He would not leave until some kind of arrangement had been made with the bank, until Miramar was on less shaky footing. And, being home for this long, he couldn't escape the truth. Elizabeth aside, he was glad to be staying a little longer. Miramar was in his blood and always would be. It occurred to him suddenly that if James hadn't died, maybe he wouldn't leave Miramar at all.

Slade pushed such morose considerations aside. He strode toward Rick's office. He was aware that whatever Rick and Elizabeth had been discussing, the interview had ended some time ago. He hoped grimly that Rick hadn't convinced her to marry him. He had little doubt that they had discussed that issue. Of course, it was crazy for her to agree to such an alliance, but then, it was crazy for her to look at him the way that she did, too. There was going to be one hell of a battle around here if Rick had managed to persuade her. And Slade was used to winning his wars.

But then, so was Rick.

His stomach clenched at the thought.

Rick's door was open. He saw Slade and smiled. Apparently he was in a fine mood. "C'mon in, boy. You ready to do some work?"

Slade ignored what he perceived to be a slight slur and entered his father's office, a place he hadn't entered in years. Memories swarmed over him. Memories of being outside this door, while James and Rick were on the inside. "You strike up a deal with her?"

Rick closed the door. "Not the kind of deal you're thinking of."

"How in hell would you know what I'm thinking?" Slade asked.

"She's gonna stay a while," Rick said, ignoring the bait. "And I'd appreciate it if you didn't run her off first chance you get."

"I meant it when I said I'm not going to marry her." If Rick even guessed he waged a private battle with himself over the woman, he would attack with every weapon he possessed. Slade knew it, so he spoke with nothing but conviction.

"You'll change your mind when you go over the books. When you see that we really are bankrupt. Then you'll agree to marry her and you'll agree to do it fast."

Slade looked at his father. Rick believed what he said. And if Miramar were really bankrupt . . . He could almost feel the damn noose tightening. And he had started to sweat.

"Let me see the books," he said abruptly. In that moment, he hated Rick, really hated him.

Rick smiled. "Better sit down. It'll take some time."

Slade's jaw was tight. He walked over to the desk and sat down in Rick's oversized chair. He looked up. Rick slapped three big thick ledger books in front of him. "You look like you belong there," Rick said pointedly.

Slade ignored the remark. "How far back do these go?"

"Nine years. They go back to the last year we made a profit."

"Tell Lucinda to bring me coffee and sandwiches," Slade said, snapping on the desk lamp. "I can see I'm gonna be in here all afternoon."

It was black outside. The sun had long since set, and Slade had been closeted in Rick's office since the early afternoon. He had just closed the last of the ledgers and he was in shock. Not only were they in debt, but they had been operating at a loss these past two years. *At a loss.* Even if they could make up the back payments on the mortgage, how in hell could they make future payments and operate the rancho? It was practically impossible.

Unless, of course, he married an heiress.

But she would have to be a mighty big heiress.

The noose was tight now. He could feel it. And he didn't think there was going to be a way out of this particular hanging.

He lunged abruptly to his feet and paced to the open doors of the balcony. The night was black but starry and bright. To his left the mountains were a darker, jagged shadow against the night sky. Ahead, if he looked hard enough, he could see the ocean glinting silver against the night. And if he strained hard enough he could hear the waves beating upon the shore with drumlike insistence. Usually he could be lulled into a momentary peace by the rhythmic throbbing of the surf against the sand, but not tonight.

He would have to make a choice.

He could continue in his refusal to marry Elizabeth Sinclair, which would be tantamount to turning his back on Miramar. And it would change everything. Because if he did so, Miramar would be taken away from Rick, from his family, from himself. The banks would take it away, divide it up, sell it off in pieces and parcels. Miramar would go the way of almost all the other great ranchos in the area. It was unthinkable.

He knew that if he should choose to stay and take up his birthright, that alone would not be enough. Had Miramar not been in such a deep hole, it would be enough. But it was too late for that. If he stayed, if he took over Miramar, he needed money and he needed it soon. From the correspondence he had perused, he had learned that the bank had made it clear that they had ninety days to make up the back payments or Miramar would be foreclosed. The ninety-day notice had been given when the bank had been taken over by a New Yorker—two months ago exactly. Time was most definitely running out. Slade had thirty days to get his hands on the sum needed just to prevent foreclosure.

It occurred to him that he could borrow the thirteen thousand dollars they needed now from Charles Mann. Charles would gladly lend him the money, although Slade had never asked him for anything, and he dreaded the prospect. Yet that sum would not get them very far. It would not make next month's payment, or October's, or November's or December's. It would not give them the capital they needed to make the changes necessary to take Miramar into the future as a profitable enterprise. Slade had always been very good with numbers. In his head he could calculate the kind of cash and the kind of time necessary to turn the rancho around and have it operating in the black. Five years would be a realistic assessment of time, but the monetary figure was astronomical. Never could he ask his friend for such a sum.

And Rick, who despised Charles, would never bring him in as a partner. And Slade would never bring a third party who wasn't family in as a partner. The kind of money the partner would bring would mean he would have control—assuming such an investor could be found, which was probably unlikely. The options available were decreasing with every passing second. Especially as he dismissed the very notion of Edward marrying Elizabeth. He would not even entertain the possibility.

Yet Rick was right. Miramar needed an heiress—now.

To even consider staying at Miramar—with Elizabeth—made him pause. Feelings long denied tumbled forth. He loved Miramar. He *loved* Miramar. This was his chance, his excuse, to stay. Even James would understand the necessity of his remaining. But marry her?

This was the excuse he needed to marry her. The perfect excuse. But would James understand that? Would James, if there were a heaven, look down on him and approve of him taking his woman as his wife?

"I don't want this," Slade said desperately to the night. Or maybe he spoke to his brother's ghost. At that very moment, he could actually feel a presence, as if James were there with him in the night-darkened room. "I don't want to marry her. I don't."

James was dead, but dead or alive, he would never share what was his. Not ever. Slade knew his brother well enough to know that.

He touched his neck, as if to loosen an actual hangman's knot. But his fingers merely brushed the sensitive skin of his throat. The noose, which seemed so real, was only a figment of his imagination.

Desperation washed over Slade. He didn't have a choice. He turned from the balcony, his eyes piercing the gloom. "I don't have a goddamn choice," he gritted. He almost expected his brother to materialize out of the night, his finger pointed, accusatory.

His brother, he knew, would never forgive him his lewd fantasies—fantasies he'd had nonstop since he'd first met Elizabeth, fantasies that were thoroughly carnal—much less the fulfillment of those fantasies. Could dead men read live men's minds? Slade fervently hoped not. Some secrets were meant to be kept forever.

But James did not materialize. If he had been present—and Slade was torn between hope and dismay—he wasn't any longer. There was no one in the ink-black office except for Slade himself.

The solution washed over Slade with stunning swiftness. It was so obvious—and so impossible—that he laughed with absolutely no mirth whatsoever. He could marry her and get her money, save Miramar. But it would be a marriage in name only. And everybody who counted would be satisfied: the bank, Rick, James. Even Elizabeth would be satisfied, being the lady that she was. Everybody would be satisfied—everybody except himself.

He knew he was a bastard. He had been told he was a bastard by his father more than a few times, and the few women who had slipped through his life had also been quick to malign him. Even his own mother had found him somehow lacking and had abandoned him as an infant. His revulsion with the solution to this dilemma proved they were all right. But for once he would be honorable. For once he would be selfless. He would marry her, providing her with his home and his name and the protection she so obviously needed. It would be a marriage in name only. To the union she would bring her inheritance, and Miramar would be saved.

A marriage in name only.

He wondered if he could really do it.

Chapter 10

Slade left the office. He didn't bother to turn on the lights in the hallway for he could make his way through the entire house blindfolded. In the den he poured himself a hefty glass of tequila and sipped it, all the while staring sightlessly at the wall. In his mind he kept seeing Elizabeth, and because the solution was a marriage in name only, it was in a way he didn't want to see her, in a way he had no right to see her—in a way he would never actually see her.

The light snapped on.

Slade scowled. "Thanks."

"Knew it was you," Rick said. "We celebratin'?"

"Celebrating?" Slade smiled coldly. "*You're* celebrating, old man. I'm just drinking."

"You're gonna do it."

"Did you have any doubt?"

"Not really."

Slade tossed off the last of his drink and poured himself another one.

Rick came to stand beside him. "Pour me one, too."

Slade obeyed.

"Don't look so happy," Rick said. "Jesus! I see the way you look at her, like a goddamn tom that's been locked in an attic for a month! What in hell is so god-awful about marrying that pretty little gal?"

"Nothing," Slade said tightly. Rick was right on the mark. He felt exactly like the tomcat his father had described, although it had been at least three months since he'd had a woman, not one. "Nothing at all."

"You just hate doing anything that might make me happy. That's it, isn't it?"

"Believe it or not," Slade said slowly, "you really have nothing to do with my decision. I'm doing this for Miramar."

Rick winced. "You have a way with words, don't you? As long as you're being honest with me, why don't you try out some of that honesty on yourself?"

"What does that mean?"

"It means we both know you love Miramar and we both know that being my heir is no hardship. We both know you're being a stubborn fool just to fight me."

"You really flatter yourself, Pop. The problem here has nothing to do with you, except that it's your damn idea for me to marry Elizabeth. Has it ever occurred to you that I might not like the idea of marrying James's woman?"

Rick looked at him, frowning slightly. "James is dead."

Slade was furious. "Damn right. And that makes me the oldest," he said very tightly. "And after the wedding, we do things my way or not at all."

Rick had always known when to back off, and he backed off now. "Well, that's good enough for me," he said. "Look, don't go getting riled. We both know you were loyal to James when he was alive."

"And we both know if he was still alive this conversation wouldn't be taking place." Slade stared at his father. "None of this would be taking place."

"But he's not alive," Rick said abruptly. He turned his back on his son, refilling his own glass. When he faced him again, he was smiling. "Of course, now you got your work cut out for you."

Slade regarded his father over the rim of his glass.

"How come I get the feeling I'm not going to like this very much?"

Rick grinned. "You probably won't. Edward would see it as a challenge, but not you."

"Edward would see what as a challenge?"

"Courting."

"Forget it." He slammed his glass down on the sideboard.

Rick leaned close, dropping his voice to a whisper. "We need cash and we need it fast. We don't have time for a prolonged engagement. I think you had better set a date for next week. And in order to do that, you got to get the little girl to agree."

"Next week?" Slade was shocked. But at the same time, he knew Rick was right. The sooner the better. *But next week?*

"Put on your courtin' clothes," Rick said, trying not to laugh. "And maybe a courtin' face, too."

Slade stared.

Rick said encouragingly, "I know you can turn her head if you try."

Slade said nothing. It was then and there that he realized that his agreeing to marry Elizabeth Sinclair solved nothing. Somehow, he was going to have to propose to her. Vaguely the fairy-tale image of a knight in shining armor, down on one knee, before a woman clad in what might be medieval dress, came to mind. The woman looked suspiciously like Elizabeth, the knight resembled James. He grew even grimmer. He shoved such ludicrous thoughts from his mind. He had not the faintest idea how he should propose—or even approach her. And Rick was right. What if she rejected him?

A feeling very much like dread swamped him. Of course she would reject him. Every woman he had ever spent a few nights with had rejected him. His mother had rejected him. And not one of those women had been ladies by any stretch of the imagination—and that included his mother, who had run off to live with a man other than Rick. But Elizabeth was a lady. She was not going to accept his proposal unless that knock on the head had made her insane. Regardless of the attraction between them.

"You're thinking, what if she says no, right?" Rick was asking. "You can't just go up to her and ask her. She's not stupid. You better put on some courtin' manners, boy."

Slade barely heard. Now that the decision was made, he felt a touch of panic. He gripped his glass tightly. He did not think he would be able to take rejection from Elizabeth Sinclair lightly.

"You can't take no for an answer," Rick continued. "You seduce her if you have to."

"I am having difficulty even believing this conversation," Slade said, setting his glass down very carefully. "I am not seducing her. Keep your advice to yourself. You're the last person I'd listen to anyway when it comes to the subject of courtship and marriage." Slade pushed past his father, heading for the courtyard.

"Then maybe you'd better get some advice from Edward. God knows you need it from somebody!"

Slade wasn't listening. Outside, the air was cool and sweet with the scent of the orange roses that budded against the thick adobe courtyard walls. In the center, the fountain had been turned off, but the water bubbled up against the sides of the pool. His gaze drifted past, and settled abruptly on the doors of her room. They were closed.

Seduction was out of the question. Rick didn't know that it would be a marriage in name only. Slade wasn't about to tell him. It wasn't his business, and he knew his father's response would be ridicule. Rick was too much like him. He wasn't noble, either.

He stared again at her doors. Closed against the night, or against somebody like him. Anger suddenly washed over him. If she hadn't been engaged to James, he wouldn't be going through this. He wouldn't be staring at her room and, despite his best intentions, he wouldn't be beginning to tremble. The solitude and the silence of the night were his undoing, allowing him to become aware of his body and his most basic, primal urges. Need he hadn't felt since his brother's death had hit him hard the moment he'd seen her, and it had been growing uncontrollably ever since. If she weren't James's woman, maybe he'd have seduced her long before now, even though unmarried ladies were outside of the boundaries he'd set for himself. If she weren't James's woman, he could walk into her room and take her, right now, instead of staring at her doors and feeling as if he might explode right out of his own skin.

If she weren't James's woman, it wouldn't have to be a marriage in name only. He was aghast when he realized how enticing the idea of a real marriage could be. But she was James's woman, and if he could get her to accept him, it would never be such a union. Which brought him back to the starting gate. How in hell could he persuade her to agree to a marriage? Because he could not take no for an answer.

Clearly, this time Rick was right. He would have to forget his pride and do the unthinkable, he would have to court her. But the problem was, he didn't have the slightest idea how a man went courting. While she, undoubtedly, had been courted very thoroughly by his brother just last summer.

Regina found that walking was much easier the next morning. A full day of bed rest had done wonders for her entire body, for that matter. And she had purposefully spent the day in her room, not wanting to confront any of the family, not wanting to confront Slade, in order to attain the rest and serenity she so badly needed.

Her mind felt much clearer today, too. The cobwebs of confusion and indecision were gone. She had made the decision to stay at Miramar, come what may. And she had done so with Rick's encouragement and blessing. Now that her departure from Miramar did not loom anywhere on the horizon, she was actually cheerful. She told herself it was because she had nowhere else to go, and would not analyze her emotions any further.

Her current state of amnesia no longer dismayed her. In fact, remembering might bring more problems into her life than it would solve. She certainly did not want to regain her memory to find that she had loved James madly, not when she could not keep her mind from wandering to Slade. Nor did she want to remember the trauma of the train robbery. She felt strong enough now to accept her amnesia for as long as necessary—forever, if need be.

And she blithely refused to think of where she might be heading—of the destiny that awaited her if she did not leave Miramar.

At mid-morning she entered the dining room and though it was empty, one place was set there, undoubtedly for her. Regina moved to take her seat. She had just sunk down into it and was about to ring the small silver bell to alert the servants to her presence when a rustling movement caught her attention. She had thought she was alone, but Slade stood in the shadows at the far side of the room, which, being windowless, was cloaked in darkness. He was watching her. At the sight of him she became still and strangely expectant.

He came forward, leaving the gloom behind. She wondered if he had been waiting for her. She regarded him intently, searching anxiously for a clue to his disposition. Yesterday he had wanted her to leave and he had not been happy that she had stayed. Today his face was impassive.

"Good morning," he said. He wasn't smiling. His tone was as guardedly neutral as his expression. He slipped into the chair opposite hers.

"Good morning." She noticed that his hair appeared to be finger-combed. And he had left the first three buttons of his faded red shirt open, exposing a swath of swarthy skin on his chest. The skin there was moist—it was already a warm day. Then she realized that he was inspecting her precisely the same way that she was inspecting him. She lifted her glance quickly, as quickly as her heart now beat.

He shifted. "Feeling better today?"

"Yes, thank you."

"You look . . ." he hesitated. "You look better."

"I beg your pardon?"

"You look better," he repeated. "A good night's rest . . ." His words trailed off. He flushed.

Regina straightened and very cautiously said, "I did have a good night's rest. Thank you." What was going on? Clearly he had been waiting for her. But why was he attempting to make polite conversation with her? She expected an attack for staying, if anything. This sort of interaction was out of character; if she didn't know better, she would think that he was trying to flatter her.

A dull-red color was definitely creeping up his cheekbones. "You look good today, Elizabeth."

She could not have heard his low, muttered words correctly. "Excuse me?"

His eyes finally found hers. They were bright. "You look good today. You look . . . very pretty." His tone had become intense, intimate.

Regina had picked up her napkin and now it fell from her numb fingers and fluttered to the floor. Slade looked away. He was a brilliant shade of red. She realized he had just given her a compliment. A very sincere compliment. Pleasure flooded her. Her own cheeks flushed brightly pink.

At that moment a plate of food was plunked down on the table in front of Regina. She started. Her glance quickly met Lucinda's. The maid's eyes were dark. Comprehension rose quickly. The poor girl had some kind of *tendre* for Slade. Regina felt sorry for her, because no matter how casual the situation might appear at Miramar, Slade was the son and heir, and men of his station did not condescend to notice serving girls.

"Please bring me some coffee," Slade said to her.

"Maybe you should get it yourself," Lucinda retorted.

All the sympathy that Regina had felt for her fled abruptly. She was shocked.

Slade looked up at Lucinda sharply.

Lucinda turned on her heel and left the room. Regina stared after her.

Slade was grim. "She was born in Paso Robles and has worked here her entire life, like her parents before her. In a way she's a part of this family—but that doesn't give her special rights."

"No, it certainly does not," Regina agreed. "I think— I think she's taken with you."

"Yeah, well, she's no more taken with me than she is with any other young, strong male around here." Slade looked her directly in the eye. "Eat your pancakes before they get cold," he instructed.

Their gazes met again and held. Regina did not pick up her fork. She no longer thought about the maid. Slade's glance was so intense it was practically unnerving. He wanted something from her, desperately, but she did not know what.

"Eat," he said again. Then he smiled slightly. "Jojo makes the best flapjacks between here and the Big Sur. Believe me, I know." His tone was affectionate.

She heard the fondness in his voice and wondered at it. She had met the warm, friendly housekeeper yesterday. But how could she eat now? Slade had purposefully joined her at the table, he had sought her out. And he had not attacked her for staying, nor was he being cool, indifferent, or mocking. To the contrary, he was being pleasant, and, as unpracticed at it as he was, he had complimented her. She was certain his compliments to ladies were rare, making his even more precious. "You call Josephine 'Jojo'?"

His lips curved slightly. "A hangover from childhood."

She instantly imagined Slade as a child. He would have been beautiful as a boy, almost pretty. She imagined he would have been the kind of boy to always be in trouble. "She's been here since you were a child?"

"Since I was born." He hesitated, the smile gone. "She raised me. Me and James."

Regina hesitated, too. She could only assume that the boys' mother had died. "I'm sorry."

He regarded her. "For what?"

"That you did not have your mother to raise you."

"Don't be." He waved indifferently. "She was a tramp."

Regina gasped. "Slade!"

His expression was set in stone. "She didn't die, which is what I can see you're thinking. She ran off, abandoning me, leaving Rick. She was a selfish, dishonorable woman."

Regina was so shocked she could not speak for a moment, although she certainly agreed with his assessment of his mother. And her heart broke for him. How could a mother abandon her own child? "How . . . how old were you?"

"Three months."

She almost cried. "And James?"

"You don't understand. James and I are—were—half-brothers. His mother died birthing him. But that put us both in the same boat, with Jojo. She was plenty of mother to us both." Then he smiled unexpectedly. "She's still not afraid to box my ears."

Regina smiled, too, but tears still lurked close to the surface. She had the urge to take Slade in her arms as if he were still a child, to comfort him in a motherly way. Yet he was no small boy to be mothered by her, and she folded her hands in her lap.

"You're not eating," he remarked.

"I'm not very hungry."

He hesitated. "You want to take a drive? Maybe down to the bathhouse in Paso Robles?"

She was still. If she did not know better, she would think that this man was courting her. Of course, that was impossible. She had been engaged to his brother. Not only had she been engaged to James, yesterday Slade had wanted her to leave his home, and he had been adamant about it. "That might be nice," she said slowly. Then: "You aren't angry with me?"

"Why would I be angry with you?" he asked. His attempted smile fell strangely flat. There was a vast difference between his expression now and the genuine smile he had shown her earlier. Slade had no facades.

"Because I didn't leave yesterday." Regina trembled. "Yesterday you wanted me to leave."

"Yesterday's not today." He hesitated. "Yesterday what had happened between us was too fresh." His eyes swerved to hers, collided with hers.

She was remembering exactly what he was obviously remembering, being half-naked, clad in his shirt, and in his arms. Too clearly, she could feel the thick web of desire that had ensnared them that night, as if it were ensnaring them again. And in fact, it was. Her own body told her that, as did the look in his eyes.

She swallowed hard. Her smile was too brilliant, her tone overly light. "You are forever my rescuer. Do you make a habit of rescuing damsels in distress?" She wanted to change the dangerous direction that both of their thoughts had too quickly veered in. She was almost certain that his reference was deliberate, that he wanted her to remember every detail of that night.

"You know I don't." He would not buy into her casual flirtation. "Only you. It's only you I seem to be rescuing." His eyes darkened.

Regina managed to swallow the lump that had risen in her throat. "You *are* angry," she said, her voice surprisingly steady. "You would prefer that I leave."

He denied it with a shake of his head, but he refused to meet her glance. "I didn't like the idea of you traveling alone, or being alone at the hotel, from the start. I still don't like it."

Regina picked up her fork. She kept her expression carefully blank to hide her uncertainty. Her heart wanted to leap and embrace his words, but she did not quite believe him. "I am going to stay for a while," she said, spearing a piece of bacon, also avoiding his gaze. "I need to rest after the train robbery and my foolish attempt to walk to town."

"Good." Again he hesitated. His gaze slid to the table, over it, and up one wall. Anywhere but at her. His jaw was tight. "I want you to stay."

Regina froze.

Cautiously he looked at her.

His words were too good to be true. And he failed to look her in the eye. In the precise instant that she realized he was manipulating her, for whatever reason, her pleasure crashed. It crashed hard at her feet, the way a pine tree might when felled with a logger's lethal axe. It crashed so hard it left her robbed of her breath.

He had been about to touch her hand. Seeing her expression, he withdrew it.

"What are you doing? Why are you saying something you don't mean?"

He gripped the table hard. He didn't raise his head. "I do mean it, dammit."

The hurt that stabbed her was intense. She should have known that he was being less than honest. It was certainly obvious now that he was not being honest. He could not even look at her. She sprang to her feet.

"Elizabeth . . ."

She cut off his protest. "You must think me a fool!"

"I don't think you're a fool." He was standing, too.

"You are a very poor liar."

His face was a mask, except for his intense eyes. "I do want you to stay," he managed.

"For a moment I believed you," Regina quavered. "For a moment I thought you didn't mind my staying, that you had a change of heart. That since the other night you . . . liked me."

"I do have a change of heart," he said grimly. "I do . . . like you."

"Somehow I don't think so!" Regina cried. Her anger rose hotly, saving her. "Was this some kind of a game? An amusement, perhaps? To toy with me and my feelings? Or do you want my inheritance now, too? Is that what this is all about? Are you going to offer me marriage now?"

"Dammit," Slade said angrily. "Dammit!"

Furious, Regina whirled. But Slade was very fast. He caught her by the shoulder before she had left the room, spinning her around to face him. He appeared desperate. "This isn't a game. You're mistaken. Look,

Elizabeth, we can be friends. We *are* friends. That's all.
I thought about it and realized that—"

"We are not friends! You wouldn't know the meaning
of the word *friendship* if a dictionary were open and
staring you in the face!" Regina cried. "Friends don't
deceive one another! Friends don't lie to one another!
You're lying to my face and doing a blasted poor job
of it!"

"Elizabeth . . ."

"No!" she cried furiously. "Don't say another bloody
word!" She turned, realizing she was crying, and rushed
into the courtyard.

What a fool she was for staying after all. She was much
too vulnerable as far as Slade was concerned, and she
was frightened to realize it. She was halfway across the
courtyard when she realized he was following her. Frantically she broke into a run. So did he. Regina wrenched
open the doors to her room and turned to slam them
shut. Slade barged through them. Accidentally Regina
was flung backward and onto the floor.

The floor was oak, but the homespun rug there broke
her fall, preventing it from being worse. She landed on
her backside and, after the fall from the horse, it hurt.
For a moment she lay still on her back, nearly stunned.
Then she became aware of him kneeling beside her on
one knee, the other almost level with her eyes. There
was a rent in the denim fabric there.

His hands closed on her shoulders. "Jesus! Are you
all right?"

"Don't touch me," she whispered. His thighs filled
the legs of his pants completely. He wasn't an overly
large man, but he was all muscle and so much bigger
than she herself. Using her hands, she skidded back
a few inches on her fanny, putting a safer distance
between them.

He didn't move. When she lifted her gaze he was
regarding her with blazing eyes. "I'm sorry," he said.
"I apologize. I'm sorry."

He meant it. She saw it, heard it. "What are you sorry
for, Slade?"

"For barging in, for knocking you down like I did. *For everything.* I don't want to hurt you, Elizabeth."

She didn't move. His regard held hers. His palms still gripped her shoulders. She tried to fathom if his last words meant what she thought they did—what she hoped they did—that he had not meant to hurt her feelings the way that he had.

He looked her grimly in the eye. "The one thing I'm not is a damn liar." He winced. "Sorry. I haven't known too many ladies. Ladies like you, anyway."

The time his compliment was inadvertent but so genuine she was moved to tears. "That's all right," she said softly. "I don't understand."

"I should have never listened to Rick. I've never courted a woman before, it just isn't in me."

"Courted a woman?"

"I was trying to court you." He looked at the floor. "It was a stupid idea."

The thought of him courting her might have been thrilling, given different circumstances; it could not be pleasing now. Her tears welled uncontrollably. For she knew that his courtship had nothing to do with love. She covered her face with her hands.

"Don't cry," he whispered, agonized. "I'm sorry. I am."

She shook her head. "I'm not really crying." But all she could think of was that his courtship had everything to do with her inheritance and nothing to do with his feelings for her. His flattery must have been a lie, too. She was crushed.

He lifted her to her feet as she wiped her eyes. His hands were warm and strong, inexplicably offering comfort. She pushed them away. "Let's talk," he said, watching her.

"About why you were courting me?"

"Yeah."

Regina stared at his somber expression, her vision still misty. "I already know. It has to do with the marriage Rick wants, doesn't it? You've agreed. Somehow he talked you into it."

Slade's posture became defiant. "He didn't talk me into anything," he said shortly. "I'm used to Rick. He might be able to sweet-talk you, but not me."

Regina did not bother to dispute him. "Why would you court me if not with marriage in mind?"

"I didn't say that," he said grimly. "Marriage is on my mind. Do you . . . would you . . . want to get married?"

She stared. Never had she seen such determination in a man's eyes before—yet desperation lurked right beneath the surface. She supposed that she had just received a marriage proposal, as offhand and awkward as it was, from the most handsome, virile man she had surely ever met. But it was not made out of love, or out of any honorable intention whatsoever. Tears crept back into her eyes. Her emotions were dangerously overwrought. Before this moment, she might have said yes. No more. "No."

He was very still. There was no expression on his face. A long silence ensued. Regina wished he would leave—so she could cry—and pack.

"I figured you'd say that," he finally said. "Even Miramar can't entice you into saying yes."

It was a flat statement. Her fists clenched. She wanted to shout at him that Miramar was not on her mind, and that he could induce her easily enough if he wanted to, if he would only try, if he would only care, just a little, but she did not. She was not going to be a fool, she was not. This man offered her nothing but pain. She wanted love.

"I want you to listen to me." He paced toward her.

Regina shook her head. "No. Don't bother. There's nothing you can say to change my mind."

Yet she did not move, and he did not cease coming. Her heart hammered impossibly hard. He wasn't through and she knew it. A part of her had to hear him out. That foolish, hopeless part of her. He didn't stop until he stood directly in front of her, so close that she could easily touch his cheek if she dared. His warm, strong hands closed on her tense shoulders. "You would be mistress of all of this," he said, his voice uneven.

She wished desperately that he would move away. This close, his magnetism was just too dangerous. "And you would have my money." Her voice was even less steady than his.

"Not me. Not me personally. I need your inheritance to save Miramar. We're bankrupt, Elizabeth, and if we don't make our back payments soon, the bank is going to take Miramar away from us."

Regina gasped. "Is that the truth?" But even as she asked, she saw the fierce determination in his eyes, the desperation, and she knew that it was. And maybe it was then that she knew, too, that her fate was sealed.

"It's the truth," he said harshly. But his eyes glowed. "But have you ever seen a place like this, ever?" He shook her once for emphasis. "Have you ever seen mountains so breathtaking? Where else can you go and look one way, out across the infinite ocean, and the other way, down into a sweet-smelling valley? Have you ever seen skies like this—skies that are so blue they're almost the purple of irises? Have you gone down to the beach yet? I'll take you," he said, not waiting for her to answer. "There were whales playing out at the point this morning. Have you ever seen a mama whale playing with her one-ton pup?"

Tears were slowly falling from Regina's eyes. Slade wasn't hard. He wasn't hard at all. He was a romantic. He was in love with Miramar, and maybe, just maybe, she was in love with him. "N-never."

"I can't let all of this go," he said, gripping her hands. His eyes were bright and midnight-blue. "I can't, I won't. Can you understand that? Dammit, Elizabeth, I'm sorry I didn't just come right out and be honest with you from the first. I wanted to. I really did. Rick pushed me into the god-awful idea of courting you." He winced, closing his eyes briefly. "I knew I couldn't do it."

Tears slipped down Regina's cheeks. Whisper-soft, she said, "You could do it, Slade. You *are* doing it."

He didn't hear her. "But would it be so bad? You'd be the mistress of all of this. You'd be the mistress of one of God's most spectacular creations. You were going to be the mistress of all of this anyway. You'll be the mistress of Miramar." His gaze was scorching. "The mistress of Miramar."

He still held her hands, tightly, but she knew he wasn't aware of it. He was consumed with Miramar, not her. "But I can't remember," she whispered, her last protest. "I have no memory." And she left it to him to see how illogical and unthinkable such a proposition was.

"And maybe you never will get your memory back," Slade said bluntly. "But you'll always have this. You'll always have your place here, you'll always belong here. Miramar is forever. Don't you see?"

She saw; she saw everything, she saw too much. She tried to pull her hands free, and he suddenly realized what he'd been doing, because he let her. She wiped the tears from her cheeks.

"It wouldn't be so bad," Slade said intensely. "How could you say no to all of this?"

Regina wet her lips. How could she say no to this man?

Suddenly he cupped her chin in one large palm. Their gazes locked. In that fleeting second, Regina thought she knew all the secrets of his soul, thought she knew all of the raw desperate need filling his heart.

"You're our only hope," Slade said. "You're my only hope."

It had been an illusion, of course, and the feeling of knowing him more intimately than she knew herself passed. Regina pulled her face free of his palms, then regretted the loss. "You're not being fair," she whispered.

But she already knew her answer. And she knew she was more than stupid, more than a fool. She didn't know who she was, couldn't remember her past, or her fiancé, but she was going to marry Slade. And she wasn't doing it for Miramar, she was doing it for him. And maybe—probably—she was doing it for herself.

Chapter 11

*T*hey walked past the house toward the beach. The hillside sloped gently down to the ocean where the waves beat the sandy shore. When they reached its edge, they were standing on top of an immaculately clean, cream-colored dune. A path wound on down to the beach where a small inlet faced them. On both sides of the cove the dunes gave way to tawny-hued rock and finally to soaring, pine-ridden cliffs.

They paused, staring out at the vista. The sun dappled the ocean, gulls glided above them, cawing, and the surf was snowy-white against the pearl-hued sand. They were the only people in sight; it felt as if they were the only ones in existence. Regina felt her breath catch at the majesty of it all.

Slade said nothing. He had not said a word since she had agreed to marry him. The impending marriage should have created a degree of intimacy between them, but instead it seemed to have created awkwardness and tension. Regina wondered at his thoughts, but did not dare ask him what they might be. In truth, she was afraid to know. She hoped he was not regretting their decision. It seemed, still, monumentally foolish. Yet she was not regretting accepting him. How could she? He had rescued her, offered to protect her, and now, his passionate proposal haunted her.

She sought to break the silence and the tension. "Is this where you swim?"

"Yes, but it's not as calm as it appears. It's rough. Don't you try to swim here."

She stole a glance at him. She hoped he was concerned about her welfare. And if he wasn't quite concerned about her yet, she was determined that one day he would be. He was staring out at the sea, unwilling or unable to look at her; maybe he was staring out at China. His profile was hard and perfect and too handsome for words.

"And the whales?" she asked, not seeing any sign of the big mammals.

He pointed toward the northern point of the cove. "They're gone," he said, and he could not quite keep the disappointment from his tone. "But they were out there earlier."

"Oh," Regina said, disappointed as well.

Slade still didn't look at her. "But they'll be back. They always come back. They can't stay away from here."

"Like you?" Regina whispered.

He finally turned to her. "Yeah," he said roughly. "Like me. Let's go. There's no point in staying now. They won't be back today or even tomorrow. They won't be back again until next year."

Regina reached out and restrained him. "And if you were leaving, you wouldn't be back for another year either, would you? Or even two?"

"You seem to have learned a hell of a lot about me in the few days you've been here."

"How could I not hear some of the things Victoria has said?"

"Victoria is one person not worth listening to."

"Why, Slade? Why did you leave home to begin with?"

He stiffened.

Regina realized the extent of her audacity. "You are going to be my husband," she whispered.

In answer, he began walking down the path, and Regina hurried to follow. The sand was deep and soft, making it difficult for her to keep up with him. Finally he spoke, not looking at her. "Rick. I got tired of being told how rotten I was."

Regina's heart twisted. "I don't believe that. A father couldn't possibly tell his son that he is rotten."

"Not in so many words," Slade admitted. "But he was always on my back. It was clear he thought me a loser, while James was perfect."

"Rick loves you." The words popped out before she could stop them.

He whirled. He was livid. "What the hell do *you* know?"

She trembled but stood her ground. "I know what I see and hear."

He cursed. "You've been here, what? Three, four days? You don't know anything!"

"I'm sorry," she said quickly. She had known from the first that Slade would not be receptive to her opinion of his relationship with his father, and now she knew when to retreat.

He began walking again, faster now, as the path spilled onto the beach. Regina hesitated. He was working off his anger, she saw it in his long hard strides. She was afraid that he was not just angry with Rick, but with her. She kept her distance, staying behind him, letting him walk off the tension. She was certain that angering him at this new and fragile stage of their relationship was not a good idea.

She breathed deeply, sucking in the fresh salty air, trying to soothe her taut nerves, letting him outdistance her. She would be more careful in the future. Alienating him had not been her intention. They had their whole lives to learn about each other, to share deep—and painful—secrets. Then she realized that unless she regained her memory, he would be doing all the sharing, and she would be doing the listening. She tensed a little at the thought. Yet regaining her memory now would definitely cause more problems than it solved.

Forcing her mind elsewhere, she gazed around her. The slate-blue ocean appeared to be endless, seamlessly blending into the faded-blue horizon. Above the cliffs on her right, two hawks were gliding, etching circles into the sky around one another. It was an effortless and spectacular ballet. On both sides of her, the beach rolled away, glinting almost white with the iridescence of pearls. She inhaled deeply again, a feeling of contentment suddenly washing over her. She would never grow tired of this beach, of Miramar. Her heart told her that.

Slade had paused near the point where the whales had played that morning. Wistful, she wished she had seen them. She watched him turn, gazing toward her, a dark silhouette against the soft pale sand. Slowly he began to make his way back to her. She smiled. There was no anger in his leisurely strides. Still smiling, she walked down to the water's edge, making sure to stay just out of reach of the breaking waves. It was a fine moment to share with a man like Slade, with the man who would one day be her husband.

Careless of her pretty shoes, she dipped her toes in the rivulets of water. He was a complicated man. But she did not mind. She found him fascinating and now, engaged, she could freely admit it. Perhaps he was a dark man, but she did not really think so. She had seen his soft, sunny side once too often. She thought that she could be a good helpmate to him. She intended to be. She would make sure there was more sunshine in his life than shadows. She greeted him with a smile. "It's lovely here! The tide doesn't appear rough now, the breakers are so far from shore. What about wading?"

His glance was not quite closed. "Wading's okay."

Regina wondered if she dared. Then she grinned, sat down in the sand, and pulled off her shoes and stockings.

He glanced at her bare feet and ankles. Regina knew she was behaving shamelessly, but they were engaged, and his interested regard thrilled her. She smiled up at him.

His mouth almost quirked. "Is this what they teach ladies about deportment in fancy private schools?"

She laughed, the sound as clear as a bell. "You do have a sense of humor! Unfortunately, sir, I do not remember, but I do not think so!"

The corners of his mouth finally lifted. "Proper deportment is boring, anyway."

Regina was about to get up when he held out his hand. Her heart careened. She took it, allowing him to lift her to her feet. The warmth and strength of his hand did funny things to her pulse. Recovering, she gave him a look, then skipped past him to the surf. "How would you know?" she teased.

He grinned. "You're right. How in hell would I know?"

Regina paused, her skirts clenched in her fists, her feet buried in soft, wet sand, water trickling over her toes. Slade's smile was devastating. "You are very handsome when you smile, sir," she said. It was an understatement. She tried to keep her tone light and flirtatious, and she thought she succeeded. But she was reeling, not just from the impact of his good looks, but with the powerful desire to shower him with sunshine so he could smile freely and more often.

Slade's smile died swiftly. He stared at her.

Regina felt heat suffusing her face and she quickly stepped into the bubbling foam of a small, retreating wave. She felt Slade's eyes boring holes in her back. She had meant what she said, but she had never intended for him to take her flirtation so seriously. She wondered if he would wade with her.

Lifting her skirts, she ventured out further, the water lapping her calves, but not far enough to come close to the breakers. She dared to glance back over her shoulder. Slade had been watching her; he quickly eyed the sand at his feet.

Slade was obviously not going to play in the water with her. Instantly, a very calculating notion came to her mind. She tried to dismiss it. But it just refused to go away. Could she really be so deviously feminine?

"You're going out too far," Slade called.

Regina turned with a smile and a wave. The water was knee-high now, and the hem of her skirts, even though she lifted them, was soaked. "It's not deep," she responded, flashing him a smile. And then she gasped, eyes widening, and plunked into the water with a splash. "Oh!"

Even as she floundered, beating the water with her arms, she heard Slade thrashing through it at a run. A bare instant passed. His strong hands gripped her beneath her arms and lifted her to her feet. She clung to him, soaked from head to toe.

"Are you all right?"

She coughed, exchanging folds of his shirt for a death-grip around his neck. "S-something bit me!" she gasped. Her little lie was already worth its weight in gold.

"Probably a crab," he said, his hands splaying out on her hips.

Regina was not listening. How could she? She could barely think. She was in Slade's embrace, clinging shamelessly to him, and she could feel every thrilling inch of him. "Slade," she murmured, raising her face to his.

She watched his gaze darkening, felt his hands tightening on her body. Triumph claimed her. This man was going to be her husband, this man was her fiancé, and she was thrilled. Passion, sweet and heavy, flowed through her body.

"Damn," Slade said very softly. He started to push her away from him.

Regina reacted immediately. She shrieked, falling down again. Slade was taken by surprise and he went tumbling down with her—helped by the fact that she did not relinquish her grip on his neck for a single second.

For an instant the water claimed them, washing over them both. When Regina's head broke the surface she was in Slade's arms and between his legs, bobbing in the shallow water. She still had her hands looped about his neck, and their faces were very close.

His hands slid down to her bottom, pulling her even

closer. As another breaking wave raced toward them, petering out, his hands tightened. The waved eddied around them. "Are you all right?" Slade asked hoarsely.

"Yes," Regina whispered.

He didn't speak again. His eyes moved to her mouth, settling there enviously. Regina was not adverse to being brazen. She twisted until she was practically lying on top of him, the water supporting them both. If he'd needed a hint, he got it now—either that, or he'd lost the last of his willpower. His lips covered hers. Regina was both surprised and pleased to find that his mouth was open, wet, and warm, salty from the sea, and demanding. Never had she dreamed a kiss could be so intimate, so powerful. His tongue stroked hers. Their mouths fused. Her breasts strained against his chest, while he kept her pressed firmly against his loins. The feel of him there was hot, hard, and electric.

A renegade wave, bigger and bolder than the rest, broke close to them and swept over them in a froth of whitecaps. Slade lunged to his feet, taking her with him, breaking the kiss. Regina could not stand. Her pounding heart was thundering in her ears. Slade lifted her effortlessly into his arms, plowing through the surf and to the shore.

Regina stole glances at him, breathless and dazed. Reality crashed hard over her when he finally slipped her to her feet in the warm sand. She staggered against him and he steadied her, but with one hand, careful to keep her at a distance. She gazed at him hopefully but his face was inscrutable. There was no sign of the passion they had just shared.

"Slade?"

His jaw flexed. His eyes sped from her anxious expression down her wet, clinging clothes to her naked toes. "We'd better go back and change."

"Of course." She plucked at his sleeve. "I don't mind," she said, very bravely, "I don't mind that you kissed me."

He gave her a long grim look. His obvious displeasure stunned her. Abruptly he took her hand, but there was nothing personal about the gesture. It was exceedingly difficult to walk in her wet, heavy skirts and he was only supporting her. He led her up the beach toward the path, not speaking again. Regina was dismayed, unable to think of anything other than the wonderful intimacy they had shared, which had somehow escaped them as swiftly as it had embraced them.

Just before supper Slade came to her doors. They were closed for privacy, although she would have preferred leaving them ajar in order to enjoy the evening's sea breeze. She had been reading and now she set the magazine aside, her palms growing damp at the sound of his voice. Quickly she patted her hair into place, smoothing down her skirts, going to the door.

"We're sitting down to eat," he said. "I thought I'd come and get you."

For a moment she didn't move. His presence emitted a restless, forceful energy that filled up the space around her, that she could actually feel. She wondered if he had been half as preoccupied that afternoon with thoughts of her as she had been with him. She doubted it. The screen doors, closed between them, obscured his expression from her view, but even if they hadn't, she was sure that she wouldn't see what she wanted to see in his gaze.

He moved impatiently. Regina slipped outside. She could see Slade clearly now and his expression was guarded. What she wouldn't give for another earnest smile! She guessed that it was an old habit for him to hide his thoughts and emotions from everyone; she also thought that he tried even harder to disguise them from her. But the day would come, she hoped, when Slade would eagerly share his feelings with her. She felt determined to make that day happen.

Regina had entertained a few logical doubts about their marriage that afternoon. It had occurred to her that it would not be easy marrying a man like Slade under the best of circumstances, much less the worst. Yet logic could not convince her to change her mind. She had cast her lot in with his, for better or for worse. She wanted to see Slade's soft side again for her own reassurance, but her anxious smile did not change his set expression. She was stricken with the horrific thought that he had been having logical doubts that afternoon as well.

They moved across the courtyard. Outside of the dining room, he paused, touching her lightly. "I haven't said anything yet. No one knows. I'll tell them now."

Her stomach had been knotted; now it relaxed. He wasn't going to change his mind. So, if logic were to rule the day, she would have to be the one to naysay him. She hesitated, then knew she would not. Unreasonably, she could not.

Her brief moment of doubt must have showed, for he suddenly straightened. Very coolly, he said, "Gonna back out?"

"No," she whispered. "I gave you my word and I intend to keep it."

"A lady with honor," he said flatly. The tension slowly drained from his shoulders. "Let's go in."

Everyone was waiting for them in the den. Victoria had dressed for supper, as had Regina. Edward's mother was slim and beautiful, and elegant despite the fact that her red gown was more than a few years outdated. A strand of rubies was looped around her throat. Regina could see at a glance that they were glass and paste; of course, she was clued in to the dire straits at Miramar and rubies were outrageously expensive.

Edward slouched against one wall, sipping a glass of red wine, the perfect picture of a splendid male in a moment of indolence. Dressed in a dark suit and tie, he was the epitome of refinement, and terribly handsome, more so when he flashed her his fabulous smile. Rick had been pacing the living area, still in his work shirt, the sleeves rolled up to his elbows. He had not bothered to dress for dinner, but then, neither had Slade.

Slade wore a worn white shirt and blue jeans that were so faded they were dappled gray. Until that instant Regina had not looked closely at him, but now she was shocked. The shirt he was wearing was the one she had worn the night of the storm. Her breath caught in her chest and then her blood began to race.

Hot color flooded her face. No one else could possibly know that they had shared that shirt, but she knew. For an unguarded instant she stared at him, remembering how the shirt had felt on her naked breasts, how it had smelled, remembering the intimacy the dark stormy night had created, remembering the urgency that had throbbed to life between them.

"There you are!" Rick exclaimed. "I'm so hungry I could eat a bear!" Then he grinned. "You two look cozy."

Slade's hand found the middle of Regina's back. She tensed, surprised at the intimate gesture, but that was nothing compared to the surprise his next words generated. He said, very quietly, "Elizabeth has agreed to become my wife."

His choice of words rooted her to the spot. He could have chosen a dozen other ways to declare their intentions; he could have merely said that they were getting married. Their marriage was ultimately a sham, yet he had made the statement very possessive and very personal. Regina did not know what to think.

Victoria stared. Edward was still. Rick was the only one who didn't seem surprised and he shouted with glee. "This calls for a celebration! We'll open a bottle of that fancy French champagne that James brought home when . . ." He stopped abruptly. A vast silence filled the room and Josephine could be heard singing in the kitchen several doors away.

"That James brought home the last time he went to London to visit Elizabeth two years ago," Victoria finished.

"Aw, hell." Rick shoved his hands in the pockets of his corduroy pants. "Me and my big mouth."

"Don't bother apologizing," Slade said tightly. He had removed his hand from Regina's back.

"It was an innocent slip," Rick said. "There's no cause to get all fired up."

"Drop it," Slade warned.

Edward came to life. He moved quickly forward and smacked Slade on the back. "All I can say is that I'm glad you've come to your senses." He grinned. Then he turned to Regina. "You, my dear, are the perfect bride—every man's dream, in fact." He looped his arm around her shoulders. "Welcome to the family."

She swallowed nervously. Slade looked like he wanted to kill his father. Or maybe it was Edward he was less than thrilled with now. "Thank you."

"I want you to know that I've had my fingers crossed regarding this particular event," Edward said, winking. "I cannot think of a man and a woman better suited to one another. Trust me on that, Elizabeth."

Slade lanced them both with a dark look. "Don't trust him too much."

Edward looked back at him very thoughtfully and then removed his arm from Regina's shoulder. He turned to Victoria. "Aren't you going to say something, Mother? Other than what you've already said?"

Victoria smiled a bit stiffly. "Congratulations."

Regina managed a thank-you.

"You two set a date yet?" Rick asked.

"Sunday," Slade said.

Regina started. Quickly she turned to Slade, who still stood beside her, and she touched his wrist. Instantly she had his complete attention. "Don't you think," she began, her voice low, "that maybe we should wait just—"

He cut her off. "No. Sunday. This Sunday."

Her heart was pounding harder than it should now. When she had agreed to marry him she had not thought that it would be in a few days! She had assumed it would be in a few months or even longer. Ripples of shock much like the waves she had watched that day washed over her.

"Well, Sunday is just fine!" Rick cried, coming over to them and hugging Regina. "Don't fret so. It's usual for gals to get all nervous and fluttery before a wedding. That right, Victoria?"

Everyone turned to look at Victoria, who had walked over to the sideboard and was pouring herself a glass of white wine. "I wasn't nervous before my wedding," she said. "But then again, I wasn't engaged to your brother before I married you, now was I, Rick?"

"That's enough," Rick said angrily.

Regina had the childish urge to run from the room. Why hadn't Slade told her that they would rush this wedding through? Did he doubt her word? Did he think she would change her mind? She wasn't, even though it was insane to marry a virtual stranger. Yet it was becoming more and more apparent that marrying into this family would be no easy task. There were too many hidden currents eddying around her, too many strong personalities and too much conflict. Everyone, it seemed, was a player in this little drama that should have belonged exclusively to her and Slade. She wanted their marriage to belong exclusively to her and Slade! And there most definitely was a plot, one which hinged around her. Regina did not like remembering that she was an heiress and that Miramar was bankrupt.

"Damn right it's enough," Slade said furiously. "Let's put all the cards out on the table, why don't we, Victoria? We all know you can't stand me and the truth is, I only stand you because you're the mother of my brother. And we all know why you're so damn unhappy right now. Well, it's too bad. I—not Edward—am marrying Elizabeth, and I am inheriting Miramar—not Edward. And if you really cared about your son, you'd be happy, because he doesn't want to be tied down to any woman just like he doesn't want to be tied down to Miramar."

Silence greeted Slade's harsh words. Regina was shocked. Victoria wanted her to marry Edward? Was this some kind of backup plan? If Slade had refused to marry her, would Edward now be courting her? She was appalled; she felt sick.

"Bravo," Edward said finally, clapping. "I couldn't have been more succinct myself, Slade. Mother, could you possibly apologize to the lucky groom and his bride?"

Victoria's breasts were heaving. "No," she said. "I won't apologize. I won't apologize for wanting for my son what this hoodlum is getting." She strode from the room.

Rick sighed. "That woman is impossible. And I'm getting tired of it." He looked at Edward. "If it weren't for you, I'd toss her out on her ear."

Edward shrugged. "Then it's a good thing that I'm here, isn't it?" He turned to Regina with a friendly smile and held out his hand. "Let's go in and sit down. Don't worry, Mother will grow accustomed to the idea of your marrying Slade, eventually."

Regina accepted his hand, but she could not smile. She could not even reply.

Victoria was so angry that she was shaking. Damn Slade! If only he hadn't come back! If only he would go back to Charles Mann and his life up north! He didn't deserve this—not Miramar, not the heiress, not any of it. Edward deserved it all.

She paced her room, the bedroom that she shared with Rick. It was an oversized chamber, the ceilings high, the floors warm pine that were covered with colorful throw rugs. A massive brass bed sat in the center, one big enough to accommodate her and Rick when they weren't speaking to one another and chose to lie back-to-back; it also accommodated them quite nicely when they were engaged in their enterprising sexual activities.

She paced the room relentlessly, all the while thinking. How could she break up Slade and Elizabeth? How could she manipulate Slade into returning to San Francisco?

She knew, just as the entire family knew, that Slade loved Miramar. She wished that Edward possessed just a drop of his brother's passion for their home, but he didn't. She also knew that Slade was hot for Elizabeth; his lust was obvious to anyone who cared to notice. Yet Slade had had to consider the prospect of marrying her; for a while Victoria had thought he would refuse to do as Rick wanted, and that he was intending to leave Miramar as he always did. But she had been surprised.

They had all been surprised. He had suddenly had a change of heart.

Perhaps, with a little prodding, he would suddenly have another change of heart.

There was another angle, an easier one, because Slade, when he set his mind to something, was one of the most stubborn men she knew. That was a Delanza trait. The other angle was Elizabeth. She did not seem to be exactly thrilled with the idea of the marriage. She did not seem thrilled with Slade. She was anxious. A few minutes ago she had seemed actually horrified. Perhaps she needed a little prodding, too.

And why should she be thrilled with Slade? He was a bastard and a boor. Edward was handsome and virile, and he was a gentleman. It shouldn't be too hard to get Elizabeth to run away from Slade—and into Edward's arms.

That would solve one half of the problem.

Abruptly Victoria left the bedroom. She crossed the courtyard quickly, staying close to its walls and the shadows they cast. The doors to the dining room were open, the conversation of the family clear enough for her to understand most of what they were saying. It was mostly a dialogue between Edward and Rick. Slade, as usual, was his boorish, taciturn self, and Elizabeth was being meek and saying nothing at all.

Victoria slipped inside Elizabeth's room. It was dark within and for a moment she stood motionless, listening to the night outside, to the murmur of the diners across the way, to the faint sound of the waves breaking down at the beach; her eyes slowly adjusted to the dark.

Then she moved. She shut the bedroom doors and snapped on a light. Her glance swiftly took in the entire room, the made-up but rumpled bed, the chair and table, the open magazine. She swiftly crossed to the armoire and opened it. A row of ironed, hanging dresses greeted her. She rifled through them, not yet knowing what she was looking for, but aware that she was looking for something, a key that would unlock the door to the not quite tangible puzzle she sensed Elizabeth presented, a key that would solve all of Victoria's problems.

The gowns were all beautiful, all custom-made, all very expensive. She slapped shut the armoire's door and strode to the pile of trunks and lifted the lid of the one on top. Carelessly she pushed through the garments there. More clothes, suits, and underwear, nothing of interest. At the bottom of the chest was an assortment of beautiful shoes. At another time Victoria might have paused to admire them and covet them and even try them on, but not now.

In one of the smaller compartments she found jewelry. Regina never seemed to take off the stunning pearl necklace she wore, but Victoria didn't blame her, for it was so valuable only a fool would leave it around to be stolen. Still, the items she had left in the trunk were not fakes. There were several beautiful filigreed gold bracelets and a dramatic topaz necklace. For a moment Victoria weighed the necklace in her hand. One day she would have jewels like these, one day she would have better: she would have rubies and sapphires galore.

She tossed the topaz necklace back down, irritated. If she knew what she were looking for it would be so much easier. She didn't have that much time, it wouldn't do to get caught. It would be very hard to talk her way out of such a situation. She didn't care what Rick thought, or Slade or Elizabeth, but Edward's opinion of her mattered very much. It was everything.

Then her glance fell upon a small, insignificant-seeming locket. She scowled, for it was the kind of locket a child would wear, not a grown woman. She didn't have to inspect it to know that it was not valuable. Then it occurred to her that if Elizabeth had bothered to bring it with her to her wedding, it must be very significant. She picked it up.

There was a small daguerreotype inside of a young girl that resembled Elizabeth but was obviously not her. Victoria guessed that it was her mother as a young woman, Dorothy Sinclair, whom she had never met, for she had died way before Victoria had married Rick. Victoria sighed, annoyed and impatient. She turned over the locket carelessly and scowled at the boldly scripted *S* engraved there. Then she froze, staring.

At a glance, the initials on the back of the locket might appear to be *ES*. But they were most definitely not *ES*. Nor were they *DS*.

They were *RS*.

RS.

Those were not Elizabeth's initials. They were not her mother's initials. *Who was RS?*

Why were the initials RS engraved upon this little locket?

There was no reason for Victoria to be suspicious of Elizabeth except for the fact that Victoria had been scheming to gain her own ends since she was a homeless child. In those long-ago but never-forgotten days, she had connived in order to survive. She had more than attained her ends when she had married Rick Delanza twenty-three years ago—until Miramar had fallen upon bad times.

Now she spent her days scheming to gain for her son everything that he should have, which would concurrently solidify her own position as mistress of Miramar. So Victoria instantly wondered if Elizabeth's amnesia was false and if Elizabeth was someone other than who she claimed to be. Her very first thought was that if she were a nobody and a young woman, she would gladly pretend to be Elizabeth Sinclair in order to marry into the Delanza family and gain the power and prestige that came hand-in-glove with being Miramar's first lady.

But if that were the case, wouldn't Rick have known? Maybe, Victoria mused, flushed with excitement, but maybe not. After all, Rick had not seen Elizabeth in five years, except that once at George Sinclair's funeral, and then she had been so heavily veiled that no one could see her features.

Victoria leaped to her feet, trying to tell herself to be calm. There were many reasons why Elizabeth might carry a locket with intials other than her own upon it. The locket might have been given to her by the woman whose initials were RS. It was that simple.

But perhaps Elizabeth was not who she said she was—
perhaps she was an imposter, a fortune-hunting imposter who was very cleverly pretending to have amnesia
and manipulating them all. For if she did not know
very much about the real Elizabeth Sinclair or James
or Miramar, what better way to pull off her charade?

Victoria ran from the room. Tomorrow she would go
to San Luis Obispo herself to visit Elizabeth's family to
ascertain if the woman calling herself Elizabeth Sinclair
was really Elizabeth Sinclair after all.

And somehow, Victoria knew that she was not.

Chapter 12

*A*fter supper Slade escorted Regina across the court-yard and back to her room. Supper had not been the most pleasant of affairs. Victoria's absence was glaring. Edward was charming, but he was clearly trying too hard to make up for his mother's hostility. Rick's joviality was genuine, but overwhelming. His obvious pleasure at their impending marriage reminded Regina that he was looking forward to her inheritance as much as— or more than—her advent into the family. Enough to have considered her marrying Edward instead of Slade. She could not eat, she could barely hide her distress. Nothing could have made her feel more like a sack of goods, to be handed over to whichever brother proved more convenient.

Slade had not spoken during the entire meal, either. But he had been seated next to her, and she had felt his glance on her more often than not. Outside her doors, they paused. It was dusky out, but a multitude of stars were beginning to cast their lights, glittering faintly above their heads. All around them the heady scents of roses and hibiscus wafted, thick and sweet. The faint sound of the surf rushing at the shore was a lulling melody, a serenade, and the night air was so soft and pleasant it felt like a velvet caress upon Regina's cheek.

It was a night ideally suited to romance. Such a night dismayed Regina even more. Romance could have been so easily on her mind. Instead, she was considering how she might broach the subject of their marriage, if she dared broach it in regard to Edward. She could not let this topic alone. She had given him her word in accepting his proposal, but she was ready to go back on it.

There was no delicate way to bring it up, either. "I cannot believe what you said in there."

Slade leaned against the rough stone of the house. "I thought that was coming."

She stared up at him. "Is that the way it was going to be? If I wouldn't marry you, they'd bring forth Edward?" Tears laced her voice.

He hesitated.

Regina closed her eyes in misery. No answer was answer enough.

"It wouldn't have come to that," he said forcefully. He gripped her wrist, causing her to look at him. "I know it sounds bad. I—"

"It's horrible!"

"Elizabeth," he said, very firmly, "you were engaged to James, or have you forgotten? And that was arranged, just like our marriage is."

Her head began pounding. "I can't remember James. That's why it doesn't feel wrong to marry you." There was more than that, so much more, in her heart, but she would never tell him so.

Slade hesitated again. "James is dead. Dead, and in the past." For a scant instant, he turned his face away from her. "Rick was using the threat of Edward to break me, that's all."

She moaned. "He had to force you into the idea of marrying me?"

Slade uttered an incoherent curse under his breath. "Rick can't force me to do anything. He just likes trying, that's all. Forget about Edward. You're not marrying him. It was never a possibility, except maybe for Victoria, who would do anything if she thought it would benefit Edward. Sometimes I think she'd commit murder if it would help him."

She regarded him in dismay. How she needed some small sign from him that he cared, even a little, about her!

He shifted. "We're really not so bad. It just may seem that way right now. The Delanza men may not be gentle poets, and we sure as hell aren't very subtle, but we're strong and we take care of our own. Once you're married into the family, you can count on Rick and Edward as if they were your own father and brother, for anything. I want you to know that. Once you marry into the family, you won't be alone, not ever again. Delanzas are notorious for their loyalty. In fact, with the amnesia, you need us."

He had paused. She was hugging herself, expecting him to say, "And you need me." But he didn't. He shifted again. "You're not making a mistake, Elizabeth."

She wanted more than words from him—unless they were the right words. "And you?" Her heart was thundering. "Are you notoriously loyal, too?"

"And me," he said somberly. "I'm a Delanza, too."

Her heart beat harder, faster. Was he making her a promise? The idea of having his loyalty was overwhelming. It was a powerful lure. Yet she could not quite get over the fact that Edward might have been foisted on her had Slade not agreed to marry her, regardless of what Slade had said.

"I don't know," she whispered.

"You were engaged to James, you knew that, but you agreed to marry me. What would have been the difference if you agreed to marry Edward?"

She looked at Slade, trembling. Did she dare respond truthfully? He was marrying her for her money. How could she tell him that she was marrying him for the promise of the future? His eyes seemed black in the shadows of dusk. Black, but so intense. "I wouldn't have agreed to marry Edward."

He didn't move. "Why not?"

It was a painful admission. "He's not you," she managed softly.

Slade didn't even blink. It was his cue, but he did not take it. He turned his head away, staring God knew where. He did not offer her hope.

Regina almost moaned, perilously distraught. "Lord, I f-feel like a b-bag of oats." Her head swam. There was so much desire, and so much pain. She had to think, sort out this mess, before it was too late, but she couldn't think clearly now. She turned, anxious to leave him.

He caught her, taking her loosely in his arms, causing the hopefulness and the wishing to spin dizzily out of control. "Lady, you are the farthest thing from a bag of oats I have ever seen."

Their gazes locked. Very naturally, Regina's hands settled on his shirt, pressing against the rock-hard muscle of his chest. She did not mean to touch him and she did not mean to cling, but she was doing both.

Her senses were only peripherally aware of the stars and the song of the sea and the scent of the summer blooms. She was in Slade's arms. She could not look away from him. Finally he was offering her something of himself. Greedily, she would take whatever he gave her. "B-but that's h-how I feel. Like goods. I-it's awful."

"I'm sorry," he said roughly. He leaned toward her. Regina froze, eyes wide, thinking he was going to kiss her. Despite her second thoughts, her body reacted with enthusiasm. But kisses were not his intention. Low and intense, he spoke. "I'll be a good husband. At least, I'll try to be. I won't . . . I won't make you unhappy. Not on purpose, anyway."

She was stunned. Instinct told her that she was getting a promise from this man that he had never given before—and that he would never give again. Any battle she had been waging with herself was lost. She gripped his shirt. "And—I will be a good wife to you."

His face was close enough to hers that despite the darkness—and night was settling over them rapidly now—she could see the blaze leap in his eyes. His powerful palms almost crushed the delicate bones of her shoulders. Exhilaration swept through her. They had just made a pact, and although it was incomplete, it was a promise for the future, for their future, a future she knew would be glorious. She strained toward him on tiptoe. She wanted his kiss. She wanted another kiss like the one he had given her on the beach that day, a kiss both powerful and intimate, a kiss both agonizing and electrifying. She craved him, not just with her body, but with her heart and soul.

He stared down at her, tension straining his features. His eyes were even brighter than they had been the instant before. Beneath her fingertips, she felt his heart pounding in a mad gallop. Regina trembled, knowing that before she took another breath his mouth would be on hers.

"Dammit, Elizabeth." He dropped his hands abruptly, and just as abruptly, he moved away from her.

Regina could not understand why he had not kissed her. She was unable to move, filled with shock and disappointment.

"You're playing with fire, lady," he said, stalking away from her. He circled the fountain, not once but twice.

She watched him. Again he reminded her of the caged tiger she had seen in the zoo. His rigid strides hinted at a hot energy, at an imminent explosion. "What does that mean?"

He paused, legs braced, hands clenched into fists. He had put the fountain between them. "Better you don't know."

Regina had not ceased shaking. Her next words came unbidden, surprising not just him, but herself. "Don't you want to kiss me again?"

"No." He was suddenly, inexplicably, furious. She watched him whirl across the courtyard and slam into the house, into his bedroom, as forceful as a hurricane. The heavy oak doors thundered behind him.

She nearly collapsed against the rough stone wall. She stared after him, shaking harder than before. Now what had she done? What could she have possibly done to bring on such anger? He could not be angry because she had wanted a kiss. He had wanted one too, she was almost certain of it. Was it possible that he was trying to be a gentleman, trying to be honorable, trying to avoid touching her until their wedding night?

There was no other explanation. Regina should have laughed, she should have been happy with such consideration, but instead, she choked on a lump in her throat. Moments ago she had been so certain that their future would be glorious. Now, she wasn't quite so sure. Slade was not going to be an easy man to get to know, not on any level.

But she knew her duty. And regardless of how difficult it might be, she would be patient, endlessly patient, if that was what it took. And it dawned on her that she could cultivate the softness and sensitivity he had dared to reveal more than once, cultivate it gently and carefully, the way one would tend the most precious and fragile of exotic blooms. She would encourage him to leave his hard edges and anger behind.

The notion was heartening. Finally calming, she opened her doors and stepped swiftly inside her bedroom, where it was dark and still warm from earlier in the day. She took another deep breath. Feeling much less shaken, she snapped on the lights—and gasped.

The lid of one of her trunks was open, and even from a distance she could see that someone had been rummaging through her things. She ran to the chest, kneeling beside it. All of her neatly folded clothes were rumpled and mussed. Just as they had been that day in the hotel in Templeton.

Regina froze, frightened.

She had not dwelled upon that first incident, feeling safe here at Miramar. Yet someone had trespassed again. Someone had invaded her bedroom and gone through her private possessions. But why? And, just as importantly, who?

She had to wonder if the culprit had thievery on his mind. She did not think so, because if that were the case, the thief would have taken all that he wanted back at the hotel and would not have needed to return a second time. Unless he had been interrupted the first time.

She shuddered. At least now she knew what she possessed and she could determine if anything was missing. She hurriedly turned to the trunks. A lightning-fast search through the compartment which contained her jewelry, all that she had of value, revealed that nothing was missing except for a small, worthless locket. The locket had contained an old and faded photograph of a young woman, but Regina had not recognized her. It had been engraved with the initials *RS*, causing Regina to assume that some family member had given it to her.

She was angry as well as frightened. Although she did not know anything about the locket, it had been the most personal of all of her possessions, and she felt a distinct sense of loss. Obviously the locket had been of value to her or it wouldn't have been among her things. Slowly Regina stood up and went to a chair, where she sank abruptly down.

Why had someone been searching through her things if not to steal? And why had they taken the locket instead of the bracelets or the necklace? It did not make sense. And who was the culprit?

Victoria had not been at dinner, but Regina could not believe that she would bother to snoop and steal. Lucinda disliked her, but wouldn't a maid take something of value? Perhaps the thief had been someone she did not know, but someone who knew her.

She shivered. Someone had been here in her room, violating her privacy and rifling through her possessions. Someone had stolen the locket; she sensed that the thief was interested in her, not her belongings. She could not be more powerfully reminded of her vulnerability, trapped as she was in the mental darkness of amnesia, and she was afraid.

Regina realized that she had left her doors open, and that with the bedroom lights on, anyone might be watching her from the dark night outside. Quickly she crossed the room and closed them, her heart beating rapidly. She tried telling herself that she was being a silly fool, that no one was watching her, that her imagination was running wild because of the small theft. But the jittery feeling in her breast did not ease.

Her instinct was to run to Slade. He had said he would protect her and he had meant it. She was certain he would be angry that someone in his home had dared to steal from her. He had strength, strength that she would heartily welcome right now. But she knew better than to seek him out in his bedroom. Not after he had just left her in anger. She reminded herself that whoever had been snooping had apparently not meant to harm her, but she was not relieved. Tomorrow, first thing, she would tell Slade all that had happened.

Slade could not stand it. He jerked himself from the bed, standing very still, his head cocked toward the courtyard. He had his doors open but the screens were in place, a matter of habit. Inside the room he had one small lamp on which emitted a very dim light, and the night outside was terrifically black.

He was hot. Sweating hot. And it had nothing to do with the weather. A midnight fog had started to roll in, and this close to the ocean, there was nothing unusual about that. The night was cool, misty, and sweet. He wore nothing but a pair of short cotton drawers. Sweat left a sheen on his bare chest. Three months without a woman was more self-denial than he could handle. Especially now.

He closed his eyes. Every time he managed to shove her out of his thoughts, she invaded his mind again. This time he wasn't remembering her eyes or her hair, her gratitude or her graciousness. This time he was recalling how she had been clinging to him, her hands locked around his neck, kissing him back, openmouthed and eager, uninstructed and passionate. And after such a long period of celibacy, it only took an instant for him to become aroused. He could not stand it. He could not stand this.

There was a soft rapping on his door. Slade froze. He knew who it was. It was Elizabeth.

He wished she would go away. He wished she would stay. He did not move. He did not dare. When the knocking came again, more insistent, he turned slowly to face the screens. His eyes widened when he saw Lucinda standing there instead of Elizabeth.

Lucinda had the screen doors ajar. "Slade." She smiled, but it was questioning. "Can I come in?"

He should have guessed. This was not the first time she had come to his room. He was immensely relieved . . . he was vastly disappointed.

"Slade. Can I come in?"

His jaw flexed. She had been after him for years. He was the only brother who had not taken her. She did not interest him. She had slept with everything male that was human and capable of fornicating on this side of the county line. She'd slept with both of his brothers, although not recently. James had ceased dallying with her many years ago, way before his engagement, and Edward had found greener pastures before he'd reached fourteen. Still, boys talked the same as men did. He knew she was a good lay, an insatiable lay. Tonight he needed a woman, badly. Then he looked past Lucinda's blurred features, toward Elizabeth's room. The dark woman standing at his door could not possibly substitute for his bride.

"No," was all he said, turning away. But even as he gave her his back, his body hurt, and his mind thought about the fact that he would never have Elizabeth, because he was not going to betray James. Not ever.

Yet he was human—a man. He was not foolish enough to think that he would become totally celibate after his marriage. He wished he could, but it was not in his nature; he wished he would not have the aching hunger inside him, now focused only on her. Elizabeth was a lady, and although he was not too familiar with ladies, he was a fast learner, and in this case he promised himself he would be even faster. He would treat her as she deserved to be treated to the best of his ability. When his body reached the breaking point and he had to seek comfort outside of their marriage, he would be discreet. He intended that she never know.

"Slade," Lucinda whispered, behind him.

Slade wheeled, furious. He had not heard her enter. "Get out."

Her eyes had a wild light. "You need me." She smiled, her hand cupping his stiff sex.

He knocked it away. Never, ever would he take a woman just days before his wedding to Elizabeth, even if that marriage would never be consummated, and certainly not under the same roof as his bride. "When I say no I mean no." He dragged her to the doors. He pushed her outside, into the cool, misty darkness. "Don't you dare come in here again."

Lucinda stared at him. "What's wrong with you?" she whispered. "I know it could be good, I know it! Why are you this way? Why do you have to make everything so serious? Why do you have to take everything so seriously?"

Slade had known her his entire life. Honest, he grimaced. "Damned if I know, Lucinda. Damned if I know."

She looked at him, somber and regretful, then turned and faded into the night. Slade stared after her, almost calling her back.

He had not chosen to live in a mostly celibate manner out of preference. But as a bachelor his choices were few. The gentlewomen who were available to him—the married ladies who took lovers behind their husbands' backs—disgusted him. He had never accepted an invitation from that kind of woman and he never would. Unmarried ladies were looking for marriage, and as they obviously would not be interested in him, they were out of bounds. For a bachelor, that left two alternatives, a mistress or a whore.

Slade had never kept a mistress. These women seemed no different to him than prostitutes or the married women masquerading as proper ladies. They were bought and paid for like the former, and as immoral as the latter. He did not want a woman in his bed who preferred the material favors he would give her over him. Not on a steady basis. That left prostitutes as a last and rarely pleasant resort.

He was a sexual man and he knew it. He'd known it since puberty. He did his best to ignore it. When the hunger got too great, he frequented the cleanest establishment he knew of. By then the need was out of control, but the resulting night of endless fornication was never satisfying. No matter how many times he found physical release, being with a prostitute was about as much fun as masturbating. Sometimes even less so.

Before he'd come home, he'd been about due for one of those long feverish nights. But James's death had effectively killed the lust in his body. Until the moment he'd laid eyes on Elizabeth Sinclair.

Unfortunately, that was all it had taken, one moment, and he'd felt the hot hard hunger begin to uncoil deep and low inside him. It had a different feel to it this time, enough so to frighten him and make him avoid thinking too hard about why it was different. Tonight he had reached the breaking point. Tonight he had almost thrown all his resolution to the wind, all his vows, all of his promises to James. And she would have been willing. Very, very willing.

He had come close to taking her. One kiss would have led to the final act. His hunger was that raw, that explosive. How he had wanted to kiss her! Even now, he could feel her lips soft and open and hungry but innocent beneath his. Slade cursed.

He paced away from the bed, his body lean and sinewed, his phallus hard and erect. He moved to the big oak bureau and poured himself a glass of brandy from the decanter there. He sipped it. It did not numb his aching body. He needed release and he needed it badly, he needed it soon. There was more frustration—and more need—than he'd ever experienced before.

God, how was he going to survive his marriage?

Again Slade looked toward the courtyard. She wouldn't leave him alone. Damn her! Or was it that *he* couldn't leave *her* alone? He could just barely distinguish the shadowy outline of the house on the opposite side of the courtyard. Soon the fog would be so thick he wouldn't be able to see even the fountain. But he didn't have to see clearly; just knowing she was so close—and so far— was enough.

He stalked toward the screen doors.

He paused in front of them. He stared hard through the tendrils of mist at her closed doors, as if staring hard enough and long enough might enable him to penetrate the thick wood with his vision and see within. She would be sleeping in that high-necked nightgown she wore, her hair loose and flowing, her mouth softly parted.

His sex reared up fully again, a partner to his imagination. For he had quickly stripped her naked in his mind, had quickly pushed her beneath his hungry body. Slade gripped the doorknob, for an instant about to wrench the door open and go to her. *God, he needed her!* But James was between them. He would always be between them. She was his bride, but it was a sham. She would always belong to James, even though he was dead. His hand tightened on the brass knob, and he pressed his tortured body into the screen mesh. His breathing came faster.

It was too damn easy to imagine Elizabeth in his bed, and it was hell. He saw her sprawled and restless and waiting for him, but it wasn't her beautiful body he concentrated on, it was her face. He'd be merciless. He wouldn't stop. He wouldn't be able to stop. He would make love to her until they both dropped from exhaustion.

He would make love to her . . . His breath caught. He was afraid. He had guessed the reason why the lust was so different this time. He had never in his life made love to a woman before, but that's what he wanted to do to her. Badly. Very, very badly.

Slade closed his eyes, leaning hard against the screen. He couldn't stand being in his own body another moment, was ready to jump out of his own skin. Forget surviving his marriage—he wasn't sure he could make it through these next few days.

Chapter 13

*U*nable to sleep, Regina got out of bed just after sunrise.

She had watched it. It had been glorious. In the east the sky had begun to turn gray. Then abruptly it had glowed pink and a burning orange ball had emerged from behind the rim of wheat-hued mountains. For many minutes the canvas-colored sky had been splashed with rainbow colors of pink and green and apricot, as if assaulted by the mad hand of an abandoned modern artist, so vivid they had taken Regina's breath away. And the morning had become alive with birdsong.

Regina had spent most of the night tossing and turning. Her wedding was just three days away. And while she had gone to bed worrying about the intruder and wondering what his invasion signified, she soon forgot the theft of her locket, recalling Slade's promise, his declaration of loyalty. Her mind swam with his image, playing with the possibilities the future might bring. They were all glorious. Slade would gaze deeply into her eyes as they exchanged vows, and afterward he would take her in his arms, kissing her with the kind of passion she had only read about. And later, later when they were alone, before he would ravish her, he would tell her he loved her, and that he had loved her since they had first met.

Regina chastised herself for being as foolish as a dreamy young girl, but in her heart she was yearning so hard for the realization of her dreams that she just knew they would come true.

She had heard that brides often grew so nervous before their weddings that they were afflicted with second thoughts. She was marrying a stranger, she had amnesia, and his family sometimes frightened her, but she was not hesitating at all. She could not wait for Sunday, the day they were to be wed.

The idea left her breathless. Slade beckoned her like a beacon light beckons a lost, wind-tossed ship in a dark and stormy sea.

Naturally she imagined walking down the aisle of a church, where Slade would await her at its end, magnificent in a black tailcoat. Her dress was every bride's dream, custom-tailored by Worth or Paquin, the bodice the most delicate lace, beaded with pearls, the abundant skirts frothing tulle and glinting with diamants.

Regina paused, frowning. Where *was* her wedding dress?

She grew very still. Her wedding was this Sunday, in three days. She had gone through all of her trunks. There was no wedding gown among her things. She knew that for a fact.

Regina sat down hard on a chair, stunned. She was getting married on Sunday, today was Thursday, and she did not have a wedding gown.

It must have been sent separately, she thought instantly. But that was so risky that it was utterly foolish. For if the trunk got lost, as it apparently had, she was up a creek without a paddle. But there might not have been a choice if the gown wasn't quite ready when she had left London. Or perhaps there were other trunks of hers that had been missed in the confusion that had ensued when her train had arrived in Templeton without her on it.

She realized that she was also missing her trousseau.

Regina did not even breathe. Did that mean that two trunks were missing? For a bride's dress would be packed so carefully that it would take up an entire trunk by itself. But there was no reason for a trousseau to have been shipped separately. Her trousseau would have been prepared well in advance of her departure date.

But didn't the very same logic apply to her wedding gown? Her heart began to thud heavily. She had been engaged for five years. She had known the date of her wedding for five years. One did not wait until the last minute to have a wedding gown made when one had such a long engagement. Of course the gown would have been ready. There would have been absolutely no reason to ship it separately.

Then why was it not among her things?

Because, she told herself with flaring panic, it was still at the train station in Templeton. Regina covered her face with her hands, trembling. She did not want to listen to the ghostly voice inside her head that was insisting upon another possibility, one she did not want to entertain.

What if she were not Elizabeth?

She jumped to her feet and began pacing wildly. Of course she was Elizabeth! What a foolish idea! Rick had met her once five years ago, and again at her father's funeral. He knew her! But . . . people change in five years. And at her father's funeral she would have been veiled. If she bore a superficial resemblance to Elizabeth Sinclair, then he might have mistaken who she was.

She gripped the bureau and stared at her shocked expression in the mirror. If she were not Elizabeth Sinclair it would explain why she had no trousseau and no wedding gown among her possessions. It would explain the locket with the initials *RS* upon it. It wasn't possible, was it? Could such a mistake have been made these past few days?

"No!" She shook her head in denial. "I *am* Elizabeth— I have to be! Slade and I are getting married in three days!"

But the thought had been planted in her mind. It frightened her. For if she weren't Elizabeth Sinclair, then who was she?

Very cautiously Regina approached Edward. She was certain that he would help her. There was no one else she would even think of turning to, not even Slade— especially not Slade. She had waited until all of the family had left the house. Victoria was gone for the day. And Slade and Rick had ridden out before breakfast; Regina had not even glimpsed them. She was relieved for that. Slade would take one look at her and know that she was distraught. He was too sensitive, despite his wanting the world to think otherwise. Until Regina solved the riddle of her wedding dress herself, she did not want to see him. Even more important than the issue of her missing gown was her own doubts, her very secret—but foolish, she told herself—anxiety that she might not be Elizabeth Sinclair. She did not want Slade to even guess that she had such thoughts. And it was no longer important for her to tell him about the theft of her locket the night before.

Today Edward was not impeccably dressed. He wore denim pants and a faded pale-blue flannel work shirt. Even in a working cowboy's attire, though, he was striking. Regina saw him leaving the house. She ran after him, calling out his name.

He turned with that devastating smile of his, one she was sure had caused many hearts to flutter and break, even though, she had learned, he was only twenty-two years old.

"Good morning," he said, his glance sliding over her appreciatively. "You know what? I think I could become jealous of my brother."

Regina did not blush, yet she sensed that he was being sincere. "You are very flattering, Edward."

He smiled. "There are few women who could deserve flattery more, Elizabeth. I hope Slade appreciates his good fortune."

Regina hoped so, too. Very much.

"Is something on your mind?"

"Yes, there is." She smiled back. "Edward, I need your help. I have a problem. But—" She touched his arm. "I really don't want to worry Slade."

He smiled again, but it did not reach his eyes this time. He was gallant, but Regina almost felt as if he understood they were forming a secret pact. "I would never worry my brother needlessly, especially now, a few days before his wedding. How can I help you?"

She took a breath. "I've gone through all my things and my wedding gown is missing."

He raised a brow. His glance was unreadable. "Ah. A definite problem."

She opened her mouth to tell him that not only didn't she have a dress, she didn't have a trousseau, either. Instinct stopped her. She did not want Edward, or anyone, to know of those unsettling circumstances. She was afraid that if *she* had become suspicious of those facts, if *she* had become suspicious of her own identity, so would everyone else. Indeed, Edward's smile and unfathomable expression were almost worrisome. He did not appear ruffled by her revelation. "The dress must have been shipped separately, of course," she said instead, "and obviously it has been lost."

"Yes, that would seem to be the case." Edward took out a cigarette and lit it slowly.

"Or could I have more trunks in Templeton?" Regina asked casually. "Perhaps a bag has been overlooked."

Edward lazily blew out a stream of smoke. "You don't have any luggage in town. There was a lot of confusion, but after all the passengers had reboarded and claimed their bags, yours and your chaperone's were all that were left."

"Oh, dear." Regina was pale. She had been praying that one of her trunks was missing—and that it would be found in Templeton. "Edward?" She forced a smile. "Did my luggage have name tags?"

"No, it didn't." His glance was keen as it met hers. "But that's not so odd, you know."

Regina froze. Edward guessed. She was certain of it.

But how could he be suspicious of who she was? And if he was, then why hadn't he said something, not to her, but to Rick, or Slade? She stared at him, but he wasn't looking at her now; he was blowing a series of playful smoke rings into the air and watching them drift apart.

Regina tried telling herself that she was wrong, that she was overwrought, and that Edward did not even fathom the possibility that she might not be Elizabeth Sinclair. She had a pounding headache now. She tried to think through the stabbing pain about the lack of name tags on her bags. It could mean something, or it could not. Many people traveled with tagged baggage, many did not. *I am Elizabeth*, she told herself fiercely. *I'm getting myself upset for no reason! Obviously the gown was sent ahead, ahead, and it got lost!*

"Are you all right, Elizabeth?"

She jumped, praying her eyes were not as wild as her nerves. "What am I going to do?"

"Relax," Edward said, regarding her. "What do you want to do?"

She wondered if there was a double meaning to his question. It was impossible to guess at Edward's thoughts, hidden as they were behind his handsome face and easy smile. "I need a dress."

His smile broadened. "Don't fret. I was supposed to put in my time and mend fences with Rick and Slade today, but I think we'll make a trip into Paso Robles instead."

"And?"

"We're going hunting," he told her evenly. "Hunting for a wedding gown."

"But I'm getting married this Sunday!"

"I'm sure we can find something new and white and pretty. And by offering a slight bit of encouragement—in dollars, of course—we can have that dress altered and ready by noon on Sunday."

"I hope you're right," Regina breathed. And she firmly shoved all her doubts from her mind—until Edward's next words.

He said, looking at her, "And we don't have to tell anybody."

"Where the hell *is* everybody?" Rick demanded.

Slade shrugged. The two men were alone in the den as the supper hour approached. Rick was pouring them both drinks. After being out on the range all day, both men had bathed and put on clean, comfortable clothes. Slade's hair was still wet. He wanted to know where everyone was too; he particularly wanted to know where Elizabeth was. It hadn't escaped his attention that Edward was also missing.

Lucinda appeared, carrying a plate of cut-up melons, all homegrown, which Slade had requested. She set it down on a big engraved chest which served as a coffee table, gave him a smile, and walked out. Slade was reminded of last night. He sank onto the couch and began eating, ignoring the drink Rick offered.

"You better stop fooling with her," Rick warned. "Your little bride won't be too happy if she gets wind of it."

Slade didn't look up, licking the juice from his hands. It wasn't easy to remain calm. Anger boiled up in him. He wasn't sleeping with Lucinda and he never had. Last night had been sheer hell. Last night he could have found a cold kind of comfort in her arms, and he hadn't. He was not in the mood to take this kind of criticism from Rick, not today, not when he was waging a constant battle with himself, and coming so close to losing. "Drop it," he warned.

But Rick wouldn't. "Elizabeth's a real lady, and real ladies are sensitive. She's not going to put up with philandering. For once, be smart. You don't know how lucky you are."

Slade kicked his feet up on the chest and put his hands behind his head. Lucky? That was a laugh. He was the unluckiest man alive, to be marrying a woman like Elizabeth Sinclair, a woman who belonged to his brother, a woman he could never have. But if he could have a real marriage with her, then he would be very lucky, and he was well aware of it.

"You want her to find out and run, right?" Rick said.

Slade scowled. "You know, you've been judging me guilty ever since I can remember. And I'm getting sick and tired of it."

"What am I supposed to do when I see you doing damn fool things? Like foolin' with Lucinda? Leave the damn maid alone. Elizabeth is the best thing that's ever happened to you, boy, I'm telling you that now."

Abruptly Slade's boots hit the floor and he sat up. "You know what? You're the goddamn fool."

"Like hell I am."

He gritted his teeth. "You won't believe this, but I have never touched Lucinda, and I doubt I ever will."

Rick snorted, incredulous.

Slade flushed, both angry and embarrassed. Why in hell had he bothered explaining anything? Rick wanted to believe the worst, he always had, and Slade had stopped defending himself ten years ago—the night he had run away. "I want to talk."

Rick settled back comfortably. "What's on your mind?"

Slade got to his feet. "After Sunday, I'm calling the shots around here."

Rick blinked, and then he hooted. "Over my dead body!"

"Oh, no," Slade said very softly. He stalked around the big Spanish chest and confronted Rick. "I'm marrying Elizabeth. I'm going to control her money. I'm holding the purse strings around here after Sunday, and we're gonna do things my way."

Rick's face was red. "Like hell!" he shouted. "You're my heir—but I ain't dead yet and I'm a long way from it!"

"Then you don't get a frigging penny!" Slade shouted, the artery in his neck bulging.

"You miserable son of a bitch!"

"It takes one to know one."

"What the hell kind of game is this?"

"It's no game," Slade said firmly. "You shouldn't have shown me those books, old man. They're the proof that I need to take over the reins from you. You've made a mess of things. We can run this place together—but we do it my way."

"And what's your way?" Rick raved, his face darkening dangerously. "What's your way that's so much better than my way? You think you're so smart—huh, boy? Well, let me tell you something! You don't know shit about what it takes to run Miramar! You left here when you were fifteen, so don't you go telling me that you can do a better job than I can!"

"But I can, and I will," Slade said. "First thing we're gonna do is sell off two-thirds of our herds."

Rick froze. His eyes bulged.

"We're overstocked. The next thing we're gonna do is clear five hundred acres. We've got three fertile valleys perfect for growing wheat and oats. By next spring, we're going to be planting every single available acre."

Rick was now purple. "Sell off our herds? Turn five hundred acres into farmland? *You want us to be farmers?*"

"In five years, barring a drought, Miramar is going to be in the black."

"*Farmers?*"

"My way," Slade said softly. "Or no *dinero.*"

"Farmers!" Rick shouted. "Goddamn farmers! You've lost your mind!"

"Are we interrupting?" Edward asked calmly from the doorway. Regina stood beside him, her eyes huge, her face white.

Slade's gaze passed right over his brother and slammed to a halt on her. She met his gaze briefly before glancing away.

"To the contrary," Slade said, never taking his gaze off her, his mouth curling very slightly upward. "Your timing has never been better."

Rick paced his bedroom, enraged. When the door opened he whirled to see his wife standing there in her dusty traveling suit. "Where the hell have you been all day?"

Victoria smiled and closed the door behind her. "Shopping. Why are you shouting?"

Rick didn't hear. "Do you know what that bastard intends? Have you any idea what he intends?"

Victoria took off her hat and gloves and turned to face her agitated husband. "You must be referring to Slade."

"Who the hell else has the power to upset me like this? Not even you can upset me like this!"

Victoria went to him, her hands going to his shoulders, kneading them. "You had better calm down, Rick," she said, meaning it. "I haven't seen you this mad since he ran away at fifteen. You'll have a heart attack."

"You're right!" Rick shrugged free of her. "He'll be the cause of my death and he'll dance on my grave. I won't give him the satisfaction."

"What has he done?"

"It's not what he's done, it's what he intends to do. Dammit, Victoria, he's gonna try and take Miramar from me, try and run it himself—and turn it into a farm!"

Victoria's eyes went wide. "He told you that?"

"He said he's gonna control Elizabeth's money and run this place and the first thing he's doing is selling off our herds and turning five hundred acres into farmland. *Farmland!* He wants us to be farmers!"

Victoria's eyes narrowed. "Kick him out. Now. Right now. And don't ever let him come back."

Rick stared at her, thinking about it.

Victoria gripped his wrists. "Edward would never take over from you. Not ever. We both know that. Let him marry Elizabeth. He'll be more than happy to let you control her inheritance and run things here, as long as he has enough to live on. You know it. We both know it."

Rick walked away from her. "Slade's the oldest. He's my heir."

"Slade's trouble! He's been trouble from the day he was born!"

Rick turned and regarded her.

"If Slade says he's going to do something, only a freight train can stop him," Victoria warned.

"And maybe I'm that freight train," Rick said.

"And maybe you're too old to stop him! Kick him out! Disinherit him!"

"I can't break tradition. Miramar *is* tradition. The oldest has always inherited, always. It's our way, and you knew it when you married me, knew I already had two sons."

"And we've always been rancheros!" Victoria cried passionately. "Always! But if Slade inherits, he's going to break with tradition and become a farmer. Isn't it better that you break tradition to preserve it—rather than he break it to destroy it?"

"Damn him!" Rick cried.

"Send him away!" Victoria cried.

"Enough!" Rick strode past her. "He's my heir, he's the oldest. That's not changing. But if it's a fight he wants—well, then that's what he's gonna get. Because we're not turning the rancho into a farm—at least, not until I'm dead!"

Victoria watched him. "Where are you going?"

"I need another drink." He left.

When he was gone, her expression changed. She laughed, exultant. Her day was getting better and better!

Slade had stupidly told his father his intentions, and now there was a new wedge between them, one that would be fatal for their relationship and fatal for Slade's future at Miramar. Victoria would see to it. He had given her an opportunity and she would utilize it the best way that she could.

And once Slade was gone, Edward would be the only one left, Edward would inherit everything.

And it didn't matter, either, that Slade was marrying the girl on Sunday. Victoria laughed again.

Because the girl wasn't Elizabeth Sinclair. Elizabeth Sinclair was in San Luis Obispo. Not only was she in her hometown, last fall she had never left it to go back to her school in London. She had been in San Luis Obispo this entire year. Victoria knew, because she had visited her and they had had a long chat.

Elizabeth had never intended to come to Miramar to marry James. She had received a telegram from Rick, but hadn't bothered to answer it. Victoria, having met her, understood it all so clearly now. Elizabeth was living in the fancy house she had bought herself, with a bevy of servants, indulging herself left and right as if she were a queen. She had been wearing diamond ear-bobs, a diamond necklace, and a diamond ring in the middle of the morning while still clad in her dressing gown—and the diamonds were real. She had told Victoria that she had no intention of leaving the city. She was not about to marry a rancher, live on an isolated ranch, and give up all of her money.

Victoria did a little jig around the room, triumphant.

The girl, whoever she was, was nothing more than a fortune-hunting imposter. And Victoria knew now why she never took off the pearls she wore, not out of fear that they would be stolen, but because they were fakes and she didn't want anyone to take too close a look at them. Victoria had looked closely at the jewelry in her trunk and had thought that they were real, but now she knew that everything had to be fakes. Good fakes, but fakes, just like the girl herself.

The bottom line was that the girl was a fraud and a liar, an imposter, and nothing more. Slade wasn't marrying an heiress, so he wouldn't have an inheritance and he couldn't save Miramar. He wasn't going to control any purse strings at all.

And Rick was going to be furious when he found out how he'd been deceived and that there wasn't any inheritance. Slade would be useless to him without the money they needed to save Miramar.

Soon Slade would be out on his ass, penniless and powerless, forever fallen from Rick's grace. Soon Edward would take his place as Rick's heir. Victoria was going to find him an heiress *toute de suite*, and it would be Edward who would be Miramar's savior. Not Slade.

Chapter 14

Slade had been watching her throughout the meal. Regina was uneasy. She had been uneasy all day, although Edward had done his best to distract her and keep her smiling. They had found a dress and paid the seamstress well, and it would be ready the night before her wedding. Not once had they again spoken of the fact that they were keeping their day's errand a secret from Slade and everyone else; they had not discussed how odd it was that she did not have a wedding gown; they had not even alluded to what this circumstance could signify. Edward was so witty and charming that she could only pray that she had been wrong earlier to think that he was a partner to her suspicions about her identity.

Something was on Slade's mind. It was obvious. His glances were long and enigmatic. Regina grew more distraught as the meal progressed. She worried that he had somehow begun to have doubts of his own about her. She was afraid that he was going to seek her out after the meal and confront her. She would avoid being alone with him tonight—and tomorrow, and until the wedding—at all costs.

She excused herself from the table immediately after dessert, which she refused. To her dismay, Slade leaped up and fell into step beside her.

"What's the hurry?" he asked as they strolled into the courtyard. The night air was cool, the breeze whisper-soft. The first fingers of fog were reaching out to them.

"I'm—I'm very tired. It's been a long day."

"I guess so. Where were you?"

She froze up inside. She was afraid to tell him that they had gone to Paso Robles. She did not want to answer any questions about how she had spent her day. She did not want to lie, but she was not going to tell him the truth. For if Slade hadn't begun to have doubts, he surely would if he knew about her missing wedding gown. She managed a false smile, pausing outside her door. "I needed a few things, toilet items."

He crossed his arms, leaning one shoulder against the adobe wall. His posture was too negligent; it belied the gleam in his eyes. "You and Edward have a nice day?"

"Well—" She smiled too brightly. "—it was hot and dusty in town. But we had a very nice lunch at the hotel."

Slade's jaw tightened. "I see. He take you to the bathhouse, too?"

Regina hesitated. She did not want to lie. "No."

"You sure had to think about it, didn't you?"

She blinked at him, dread kicking up in her heart.

"What was so important that you had to go all the way to town today?"

"Just a few things. You know. Soap—for my hair. Some powder. Those kind of things."

"Those kind of things could have waited."

Regina was unnerved. He knew she was lying. She could not respond.

"Couldn't they?" he demanded.

"I'm very tired," she cried.

"You and Edward must have had quite an outing if you're that tired."

"*What?*"

He was grim. "He wine you and dine you in that fancy restaurant over at the hotel? He flash his pretty smile at you? Did you smile back at him? The two of you spend the day flirting? Did he sweet-talk you? Kiss you?"

Regina was speechless.

"Well?" He was no longer braced against the wall. "He change your mind?"

"What?"

"Have you decided you'd rather marry him now? Are you suddenly hankering after my brother, Elizabeth?"

"No!"

He stared coldly, his eyes glittering.

"Are you jealous?" Regina was shocked. She had thought he was after the truth, that he had somehow guessed what she was up to, but he was jealous of Edward!

He did not answer.

Her heart began to speed. He was jealous that she had spent the day with his brother! She was thrilled. No matter what Slade said, no matter how he acted, he cared about her or he would not be jealous. But she did not want him to be jealous. She did not want to see dark hurt in his eyes. "I needed a few things. That's all. Really, Slade." She touched his bare forearm. It was tense with coiled muscle, so tense she wondered if the tendons there would snap. "Edward was only helping me out."

"I'll bet." His glance dropped to her hand, pale and white against his darkly tanned skin, small and fragile next to the sinewed strength of him.

He looked up. Their glances held. "You're lying to me," he said very softly. "I don't like it. I don't like this."

"No! I'm not!"

"Tell me the truth." Before she could react, he slipped his hands around her waist, manacling her. "Did he kiss you? Because if he did, I might kill him. Either that or be real noble, and let the two of you have each other."

She reeled under the impact of his gaze. "Slade, we're engaged." Her tone grew intense, desperate, matching his. "I do not take that circumstance lightly. I do not take my vows lightly. I would not kiss another man. Never. I would never betray you."

He stared at her. "But do you want to?"

She had to press her lips together so that the words which were on the very tip of her tongue would not slip out. She wanted to tell him the truth, all of it. She wanted to tell him that she was afraid, terribly afraid, that she was not who she was supposed to be, and that she did not have a wedding gown, and that she had gone to town to buy one for their wedding. And she wanted to tell him more, so much more. She wanted to tell him that she was in love with him, not Edward.

"No, Slade," she said, very softly. She was acutely aware of his large hands spanning her waist, of his strength and power. Very bravely, she lifted her palms and cupped his face. "I don't want Edward, I never have. I only want you."

A silence descended. His cheeks were warm beneath her hands. His eyes were wide. She could hear her own heart beating, she thought she could hear his. Neither one of them was relaxed. If ever he would kiss her, it would be now. She could barely stand the suspense. And then he released her, expelling a shaky, drawn-out breath, flinching away from her. "I'm a bastard. I'm sorry. I *was* jealous."

Relief flooded her. But so did disappointment. Her face heated. She had thrown herself at him, but he had not responded. "Slade?"

"I'm sorry." He was grim. "I already have your loyalty, don't I?"

"Yes!" she cried. "Yes!"

Something flickered in his expression. "I can't figure out how in hell I earned it." He shoved his hands in the pockets of his pants as if not trusting them. "I can't figure you out."

How she wanted to share her feelings with him! Her pride prevented her from doing so, as did her fear. She would settle for revealing that part of the truth which was innately safe to reveal. "You have my loyalty, Slade, now and forever."

He stepped away from her. "But will I still have it when your memory comes back?"

She cried out. James loomed between them, a shadowy ghost. For an instant she could almost see him, but it was her imagination playing with the incoming mist.

He smiled bitterly. His glance skimmed her features, one by one. "I guess we both know the answer to that."

"Maybe I won't remember," she whispered, too late. He had already walked away, into the shadows of dusk.

Edward was spying.

He stood in the unlit interior of the den, by the open windows, watching them and listening. He grimaced when the discussion involved him.

He would be careful not to flirt with her again. It was harmless, he didn't mean anything by it, and Slade should have known that. Edward had no idea that Slade was so far gone on the girl that he would be pea-green with jealousy over his spending time with her and taking her into town. Yet even if he had known, he would have still come to her rescue.

He watched Slade leave her and shook his head. He'd heard every word. What was wrong with his brother? She stood sadly in the evening's lengthening shadows, staring after Slade. Slade should have kissed her, made love to her. She had been waiting for him to do so. She was in love with him; it was obvious. Edward wondered if he dared interfere, then decided to let nature take its course.

She turned and slipped inside her own room. Edward took a packet of papers from his breast pocket, tearing one off. Adding tobacco, he deftly rolled a smoke, licking both ends of the cigarette to glue them together. A moment later he had lit it and was inhaling deeply, still staring out at the courtyard, which was becoming dense with patches of fog.

It would have helped if she had told him the truth. But she hadn't. She hadn't told Slade why they had gone to town. Not for the first time, Edward wondered if she knew all of the truth, if she really had amnesia. Up until today, he had been convinced that she was suffering from the loss of her memory. Now he was no longer sure; in fact, it looked to be just the opposite case. But it did not matter. Edward's mind was made up.

He was certain he was doing the right thing in keeping his silence. He was not going to reveal the fact that she was not Elizabeth Sinclair.

He'd had his doubts from the beginning. James and Slade had never had the same taste in women. Yet he'd shrugged it off. And he'd watched with great interest the fireworks that Slade and the girl set off. The instant, spiraling attraction heightened his doubts.

It was coincidence that Edward had been in Templeton two days after the train robbery, at the same time as Brett D'Archand. Templeton was a small town, so the very wealthy stranger who had closeted himself with the sheriff was an instant object of speculation. Edward barely paid attention to what the very pretty Hetta Lou was telling him; he was much more interested in maneuvering her to bed. It was only when she told him, greatly excited, that D'Archand was looking for his missing niece and offering a thousand-dollar reward for information that he jerked to attention.

D'Archand's niece, Regina Bragg Shelton, was twenty, British, small, blonde, and very beautiful. That description fit Elizabeth Sinclair exactly, right down to the accent, which she'd been forced to acquire at the private school in London.

It made sense. It made more sense that the girl was Regina Shelton than that she was Elizabeth Sinclair, whom James had loved. It made enough sense for Edward to disappear one day. San Luis Obispo was an hour away by train. He was not surprised to find Elizabeth Sinclair there, although he was surprised to find her in the circumstances he did, and he was greatly saddened. For the first time in his life he hated. He hated Elizabeth, and was glad James did not know the truth, would never know the truth.

His trip south had been days ago. He wondered about his father's role in this masquerade. Rick had obviously stumbled upon the truth as well. He was too shrewd to mistake a stranger for Elizabeth Sinclair, whom he had met twice. Obviously an alliance with the powerful, very wealthy Bragg family was his motivation.

Edward would not say anything. This girl who was posing as Elizabeth was the best thing that could happen to his brother. His brother had been shafted his entire life. And his brother was the finest man he knew. Slade and James had been so alike. As always when it came to his brothers, Edward felt left out. James and Slade had both been noble and selfless. He knew he was selfish, not selfless, and that basically he was a hedonist. He only worked hard when he had to, while James and Slade both thrived on hard work. Edward tried not to dwell upon it. He enjoyed life's pleasures too much to want to give them up.

To Edward's way of thinking, Slade did not deserve misery, he deserved happiness. But Slade was not a happy or contented man. To this day, Edward felt guilt. To this day, Edward remembered the night Slade had run away. To this day, he could see the welts on Slade's back from the whipping Rick had given him for getting that girl pregnant. Slade hadn't even cried. *He* had cried. He still wanted to cry when he remembered. Of course, it was all his fault. He had been banging her, not Slade, he had gotten her pregnant. No one had believed him. It was his fault that Slade had been whipped, and, more importantly, it was his fault that Slade had run away. Slade had left Miramar and his family, turning his back on both, because of him. A day didn't pass that Edward did not remember it.

Shakily, Edward inhaled hard on the cigarette. It wasn't very manly of him, but even at the age of twenty-two, thinking so hard about what he had done to his brother brought him to the verge of tears. But now he was going to make it up to him. Edward had not one doubt that his brother was in love now. And Slade was not like him. Slade was loyal. Like James, he would love one woman forever. Finally, after all these years, Slade was going to take his place at Miramar with the woman he loved, regardless of who she was. Finally, after all these years, Edward was going to atone for his sins. Which was why he wasn't saying a goddamn word about Elizabeth really being Regina Shelton.

She managed to sleep a few hours, but only because she was exhausted. And when she slept, she had a strange dream.

There was a train. She was on it as it sped through the darkness. She was afraid. And then the darkness became light, bright vivid sunlight, but the train was going even faster and she was even more frightened. There were people. Shadowy, faceless people, frightened people.

She woke with a start.

She was covered with sweat and shaking. She snapped on the lamp by her bed, panting. It was only a dream, she told herself. But the fear did not ease. Her head ached. And then she thought about how real it was, how it felt like it had actually happened. And she gasped, wondering if it had been a dream or a memory.

She covered her face with her hands, shaking. The feeling of being on a train filled with frightened people haunted her. She could still feel her terror. And it was so real. *As if it had happened.* She suspected that it *had* happened.

What if her memory was returning?

God, she didn't want to know!

She was getting married in two days. Married to Slade. She didn't care about what had happened during the train robbery, and, more importantly, she did not want to remember James or her feelings for him. And most important of all, she didn't want to know who she was—just in case she wasn't Elizabeth Sinclair.

Regina got up to change her soaking-wet night-clothes. Her body still trembled. She could not stop the encroaching feeling of dread. She had to face it. She was almost certain that she had been remembering the train during the robbery, not just dreaming. "I don't want to remember!" she cried frantically. "I *am* Elizabeth!"

She yanked open the drawer to her bureau, trying not to succumb to hysteria. Blindly, she pulled out another nightgown. When she did, something which had been tucked in its folds fell to the floor.

Regina stared at her locket.

She cried out, going down to her knees. It was the same locket which had been stolen from her trunk yesterday. She clasped it to her breast. She was wildly glad to have it back, as if it was terribly meaningful to her, yet she was shocked that it should appear among her things after being stolen. Her gaze flew to the doors of her room, the set which was barred to the corridor, and the set which was barred to the courtyard.

Whoever had stolen it had decided to return it. Whoever had stolen it had been here, in her room, again. Whoever had taken it in the first place had decided that he or she no longer needed it. But why? What could this locket have told someone?

Regina whimpered, opening it. The pretty girl who looked up at her from the daguerreotype was unfamiliar, but her heart leaped at the sight, as if in welcome. She turned the locket over, staring at the initials *RS*. Suddenly a pain lanced through her skull so severely she reeled and was dizzy.

If she closed her eyes and thought, she knew she would know the identity of the young lady in the locket.

Regina jumped to her feet, pacing the room in a frenzy, the locket on the floor. Did the thief know her identity? Was that why the locket had been returned?

The young lady's image returned with a vengeance to her mind. "I am Elizabeth!" she cried again, clapping her hands over her ears and screwing her eyes shut.

She could see a locomotive chugging into a station, the words *Southern Pacific Coast Line* painted boldly in gold on its sides. She began to pant. Surely she had seen a hundred trains like this pulling into a hundred depots like this. Surely this was not memory, merely imagination!

But a perfectly clear recollection came to her. She was dressed in her beautiful ivory-and-white ensemble, the same suit that she had worn the day she had arrived in Templeton—the day of the robbery. It was not dirty, stained, or wrinkled, but crisply pressed and spanking-clean. She was about to board the train. The depot was crowded and busy. But she was not alone. For a small, older woman stood beside her dressed in navy-blue and white. Mrs. Caroline Schroener.

Regina sobbed.

And another image formed swiftly upon the heels of that one. A splendid stone mansion set in the midst of wet, rolling green lawns with vibrant red roses creeping up its walls. Dragmore, her home.

As clear as day, her parents' faces loomed before her, the Earl and Countess of Dragmore. The countess—the young girl in the locket.

She was not Elizabeth Sinclair. She was Regina Shelton.

She dropped her hands and opened her eyes and listened to the wild beating of her heart. She should be ecstatic. Her memory had returned as suddenly as it had gone. But she sat frozen, shocked. She was not Elizabeth Sinclair after all. Her suspicions had been correct. Dear Lord.

It took a moment to adjust. She began to breathe more normally. She was Regina Shelton. She was no longer mentally crippled. Relief started to flood her. She was Regina Bragg Shelton. Her world was no longer a vacuum of nothingness, a long dark tunnel that she, a blind person, attempted to traverse. She was Regina Shelton. She was not alone in the world. She had parents she loved, parents she trusted, parents whom she could count on. She had two fine brothers and a wonderful sister, the Duchess of Clayborough. And she had many relatives here in America.

Then she recalled how it had all begun, with the train robbery, and she froze. She sat absolutely motionless, remembering how the outlaw had viciously robbed the woman in the pink-and-white dress, tearing her earbobs from her ears, ripping her necklace from her throat. She cringed, recalling too vividly how he had struck the young gentleman with his gun. Oh, God.

Just remembering made her head hurt. Remembering made her heart pound with the same wrenching fear. No wonder she had been afraid to remember. No wonder she had bolted and leaped from a speeding train. She did not dare try to imagine what might have happened to her had she not jumped to safety. And that was the last thing she remembered, hurling through the air, time suspended, the ground reaching up for her. She remembered thinking, terrified, that she was going to break her neck. And that was the very last instant she recalled, the split second before impact.

She didn't know whether to laugh or cry. She did both. She sobbed and choked on laughter for a long time. She hadn't broken her neck, she had escaped the vicious outlaw, and she was alive. She had been daringly brave, acting in a manner more suited to her sister, a hoyden, than to herself, the so very proper Regina Shelton. She laughed again, exultant. She was Regina Bragg Shelton—she was not alone in the world anymore.

Suddenly Regina straightened. Dear Lord! How everyone must be worried about her. She had been on her way to the hotel in Paso Robles to visit with her Uncle Brett and Aunt Storm, to enjoy the baths, before going on to San Francisco with them. But she had never arrived. Not only had she never arrived, she had just disappeared.

Oh, God! And Mrs. Schroener was dead! *She* was alive, but that sweet old woman was dead! Regina's heart broke. She remembered being told that Mrs. Schroener had tried to interfere with the bandit chasing her. Fresh tears spilled. Mrs. Schroener had died because she had tried to protect her.

When Regina had calmed somewhat over the kind chaperone's death, she began to worry about her family. By now her parents would have arrived back in England, only to receive word of their daughter's disappearance. Her grandparents would also have been informed. They must all be hysterical, and as had happened when Lucy had been abducted in '87, a massive search for her had undoubtedly begun. She would have to inform her grandparents and aunt and uncle of her whereabouts immediately. She was certain her parents had boarded the first steamer bound for America, and even now were on their way back across the Atlantic. She thought of how frightened they must be. As soon as her parents stepped upon American shores, they would be informed as well, but until then they would be suffering over her disappearance needlessly.

She swallowed. She would have to inform Slade and his family that she was not Elizabeth Sinclair, too.

Regina became still. The ramifications of the truth hit her. Trembling, she covered her face with her hands, all the jubilation gone. She was not Elizabeth Sinclair, she was not George Sinclair's daughter, she was not the girl Rick loved as if she were his own daughter. He was going to be very surprised when he realized that he had mistaken her for Elizabeth after not seeing her for five years. But Regina did not care about Rick. James no longer stood between her and Slade, but she could not be glad. The truth stood between her and Slade now.

It hit her hard. She was not going to marry Slade. The wedding would be called off. For undoubtedly the real Elizabeth Sinclair would be found. Perhaps she was already on her way to Miramar. And Elizabeth would be persuaded to marry Slade once she had been informed of James's death. No woman could be indifferent to Slade, and she was expecting to marry into the Delanza family, had been expecting that for five long years.

Her stomach lurched. She felt cold and clammy. She would tell everyone that she was Regina Shelton and she would go on her way. She would in fact be handing Slade over to the real Elizabeth Sinclair.

She clenched her fists. She did not want Slade to marry the real Elizabeth Sinclair. She did not want him to marry another woman. She could not bear the thought. She wanted to be his wife.

For a moment she tried to think calmly about what would happen if she told the Delanzas that she was Regina Shelton. She was also an heiress. Could she persuade them to allow her to marry Slade instead of Elizabeth?

She didn't know. Rick had been so adamant about how he felt about George and Elizabeth. She was afraid. If she took the chance and failed, she would lose Slade to the other woman. And what if her father demanded she wait until he could approve of Slade himself? What if he disapproved of Slade?

The risks were too great. She could not give Slade up to another woman. She could not.

Hot color flooded her cheeks. What she was thinking of doing was wrong, terribly wrong. Did she dare? Did she dare to not tell everyone the truth? Did she dare to continue this deception? Did she dare to pretend to be Elizabeth Sinclair? And marry Slade on Sunday as planned?

Regina covered her mouth with her hands, aghast. Oh, God! She wanted to marry Slade! She loved him! She could not give him up to another woman, she could not! She had no other choice!

She would have to keep her identity a secret. She would have to lie. Knowing herself now, again, she knew she was not a liar. She had never been a liar. She had always been docile and obedient, even when she had mistakenly thought herself to be in love with Lord Hortense. Of course, now she knew she had never been in love before. How glad she was that her father had rejected Hortense! She had respected his decision. She had always been the ideal of a proper lady. Since she had come to Miramar, there had been little that was proper or ideal about her thoughts. And now she was about to do the unthinkable, something no proper young lady would ever do. She was about to violate the code of conduct every gentlewoman lived by.

She got to her feet. She had a monumental decision to make. To tell the truth and go on her way, or to continue this charade and marry Slade Delanza.

Chapter 15

"Do you, Elizabeth Sinclair, take this man, Slade Delanza, to love and to honor until death do you part?"

The judge had repeated the question.

Regina stood beside Slade in the den. Behind them stood the family; in front of them was Judge Ben Steiner. There were no guests, no organ, no minister, and there were only two small floral arrangements in the room. She was being married on a simple ranch in California, not in a soaring cathedral in London. Her parents weren't there, her brothers weren't there, her sister and her husband weren't there. None of her family was there.

She wore a simple white dress with a high lace-edged collar and leg-o'-mutton sleeves. It was pretty enough. But it wasn't the fantastic creation she had always envisioned. She carried a bouquet of orange roses picked from the bushes in the courtyard outside, but she had no veil. Nothing was the way she had always dreamed her wedding would be.

And now was not the time to notice the difference, or to regret it, or to worry about what she was doing.

Slade hadn't looked at her since she had first entered the room. He stood stiffly by her side, like a soldier at attention. But when she had first appeared on Rick's arm, he had done more than look. He had stared, his eyes visibly brightening. Regina had been overwrought with nerves, and his open appreciation of the pretty picture she made had soothed her instantly. But only temporarily. When Judge Steiner started the ceremony, nervousness beset her, along with guilt.

Slade finally turned his head. His eyes were wide, incredulous. Regina met his gaze and knew that if she didn't get the words out, if she humiliated him now, he would never forgive her.

Could she really do it? Could she really continue this deception? What she was doing was wrong, so terribly wrong.

Judge Steiner looked at her. From behind them, Rick coughed. Victoria's pink dress rustled. Josephine sniffed. She had been crying all day. A floorboard creaked as Edward shifted his weight. And beside her, Slade had turned to stare straight ahead, rigid and stolid, like a martyr accepting his fate.

"I do," she whispered.

The judge sighed with relief.

Regina regarded Slade. Tears blurred her vision. She had done it, she had done the unthinkable, she had deceived the man she loved. He refused to meet her gaze, staring at the wall behind the judge.

"Then I pronounce you man and wife," Judge Steiner said. He smiled at Slade. "You can kiss the bride."

Slade didn't move. A muscle in his jaw flexed. Regina was perspiring profusely, more now than before. Dear God, she had done it! But her hesitation had upset her husband immensely. How could she explain her behavior to him? Worse, how would she explain her deception to him later?

Abruptly Slade shifted and leaned forward and touched his mouth to hers. It was the barest brushing of their lips and it was over before it had begun. For an instant he looked at her. Regina managed a fragile smile in return, a tear slipping down her cheek. His expression tensed. Their gazes remained locked for another heartbeat. And then, to her utter surprise, he wiped the tear away with the blunt tip of his forefinger.

He turned from her just as they were swamped by the family.

Judge Steiner sighed again.

Regina swallowed hard. She quickly found her handkerchief and dabbed at her eyes. Any regret or worry she might have had was gone. She was now Slade's wife. At least, she thought that she was. She fervently hoped that she was. She had married him under an alias, but it had been she, Regina, standing beside him making her vows, it had been she, Regina, not Elizabeth Sinclair, who had received his ring, which she now wore. She was the one who had pledged to love and honor him for the rest of their lifetimes, until death separated them. She trembled, and watched Edward congratulating Slade. Edward was smiling, but Slade was not.

Over Edward's shoulder their glances met again, for a longer moment. Regina's breath caught. She could not decipher his expression, just as she had not been able to comprehend what his tender gesture had meant an instant ago. She prayed he was coming to care for her. Why else would he wipe away her tear?

Regardless of what his well-hidden feelings might be, there was no escaping the fact that she was married to him now, that she was his wife. He was the most complicated, and the most sensitive, man that she knew. He was an enigma, but she loved him. She gazed openly at him, studying his extraordinary profile, relishing the sight he made. She was certain he would always take her breath away. Her heart twisted. Anticipation and excitement fluttered wildly to life inside her.

If she had to do it all over again, she would.

Rick had come forward. He hugged her with real enthusiasm, almost crushing her in his embrace. "Welcome to the family."

"Thank you," Regina managed.

But Rick had already turned and was pumping the judge's hand. Out of the corner of her eye, as Victoria approached, she watched Josephine embrace Slade. He favored her with a rueful smile. Regina strained her ears. Slade said, "Bet you thought you'd never see the day."

"I been prayin' fo' yeahs to see this heah day," Josephine returned. "You gonna be fine now, sweetie, trust ol' Jojo."

Regina wished she could hear Slade's rejoinder, but she had no choice and she turned her attention to Victoria. To her surprise, Edward's mother was smiling. "Congratulations, dear," Victoria said, kissing Regina's cheek. "Welcome to the family, *Elizabeth*."

Regina could not move. Victoria's eyes glittered with mirth and utter comprehension. There was no mistaking the tone she had used when speaking the name which Regina was using. She knew that Regina was an imposter.

"Elizabeth?" she asked. "Is something wrong? Are you feeling ill? Can I get you something, Elizabeth?"

Regina regarded her wide-eyed. Edward's mother knew about her charade. *She knew*. And Victoria disliked her, she had from the start. Victoria did not want her in the family. Regina would not put it past the other woman to do something awful, such as expose her now, in front of the judge, moments after being wed. She shuddered. She could not imagine what Slade's reaction would be if he were told in such a way instead of being told by Regina herself.

Victoria laughed. "Don't worry, dear, you can count on me." With that enigmatic threat—and it was a threat—she swept away.

Regina closed her eyes for an instant. She was sweating again. Dear Lord, what had she done? She should have anticipated someone finding out about her deception and been prepared to handle it. But she hadn't. What was Victoria going to do? Regina was afraid; she expected the worst.

She would have to tell Slade soon. Very soon.

But the truth was that she was afraid to tell him. She had yet to think of a good way to do so. She wanted time, time to have him fall in love with her, so that he would be forgiving when he did learn the truth. More importantly, once he loved her, she would be able to tell him all of the truth—that it was her love for him which had propelled her into keeping such a secret in the first place.

Edward paused by her, smiling broadly. Regina had a moment of severe doubt. She liked Edward very much, but she was still unsure whether he knew the truth about her. In the past few days, since he had helped her find the dress, she had begun to think her suspicions were rooted in her own anxiety and guilt and were therefore baseless. Now she could not help regarding him distrustfully. It would be very easy to conclude that he had known about her and had shared his knowledge with his mother. She stared at him. There was nothing but cheer in his sparkling gaze. Any other thoughts he might be having were obscured by his obvious pleasure in today's event.

"How's the beautiful bride?" he asked, grinning.

Regina wet her lips. "Fine." She did not want to think that Edward had, in a way, betrayed her. She liked him. She did not know what to think.

"What's wrong?"

She bit her lip, her glance darting past him, looking for Slade. He stood on the other side of the room, with his father and Judge Steiner, watching them like a hawk. She managed to smile at Edward, wishing Slade would come to her. He did not. "I'm just a little faint."

Edward took her arm. "No wonder. I would be more than a little faint if it were me who just said those vows. Are you having second thoughts, Elizabeth?"

She regarded him carefully. "Not as far as Slade is concerned."

He studied her. When his smile came, it was as dashing and disarming as before. But she saw a shadow in his eyes. He had understood her innuendo. Gentleman that he was, he chose to ignore it. "Good. The two of you are perfect together." Then his smile disappeared and he was uncharacteristically serious. "Trust me."

Regina smothered a gasp. He had not ignored her double meaning after all; he was sending her one of his own. She could not respond.

He bent and brushed his warm mouth on her cheek. "There is no one I care for more than my brother," he told her, the smile back, graced with dimples. "And now you are his wife."

Regina watched him walk away. So Edward also knew. She was certain he had just implied that, regardless of her real identity, as Slade's wife he would be loyal to her. Dear Lord, was there anyone other than Slade who was not a partner to her masquerade? Unwillingly, her gaze slipped to her father-in-law. Rick had been watching her, as was Slade, who was still beside his father, his face inscrutable. Beaming, Rick raised a fluted glass. "To the bride," he cried. Then he cast a warm glance at his son. "And the groom. To the newlyweds. To the future."

He didn't come. He wasn't going to come. Regina knew that now.

It was almost midnight. Regina had been waiting for him since supper had ended three hours ago. She wore the thin ivory silk nightgown that he had been so fascinated with the one time he had seen her in it, when he had entered her room to wake her up. High-necked and long-sleeved, the fabric was nevertheless so fine that it skimmed every curve of her body. It was scandalous, but she wore nothing beneath it at all. The silk was unbearably exquisite upon her body.

She had bathed, perfumed herself, and spent an inordinate amount of time on her long, honey-blonde hair. She had carefully arranged herself in the bed, the sheets around her waist, her position enticing, alluring. But he hadn't come and by now she knew that he wasn't coming at all.

She was upset.

He had married her for her money and he had been open about it. Yet Regina had expected him to be a husband to her in every sense of the word. Had she been a fool? She could not help thinking that he hadn't wanted a wife, he had only wanted an heiress. It was she, Regina, who had wanted a husband—who had wanted Slade as her husband.

Regina slid her bare feet to the floor, tears of hurt and
anger filling her eyes. Tonight she had left one of her
bedroom doors invitingly open and she looked outside.
There was no fog. The sky was ink-blue, lit brilliantly
by an incandescent full moon. Her gaze lowered. In his
room across the courtyard the lights were on.

He was also awake.

In an instant she made a decision, one she dared not
dwell on. She hurled herself from the room. A quick
glance around showed her that the rest of the house
was cloaked in darkness. As she passed the fountain,
her steps slowed.

He had both doors fully open, the screens closed.
Regina's heart began to pound too fast and too hard.
Her chest felt heavy. The night was cool, but she was
too warm, even in her thin nightgown. What she was
doing was unbelievably daring, unbelievably aggressive. Most ladies would be thankful to be spared their
husbands' attentions. Regina almost paused. She had
never acted so impulsively before, or so decisively. Yet
she could not stop, not even to wonder at herself. Regina
moved into the full glow of the room's lights. She gazed
through the screen doors.

About to knock, her hand froze. Her heart slammed.
Slade was sitting up in his bed wearing only a pair of
short summer drawers. There was a glass of brandy
on the table by his bedside, the same table that held
the small lamp he had left on. He wasn't reading or
smoking or doing anything that she could discern. He
was just sitting there, awake and alone.

She trembled. As far as she was concerned, he was
naked. She should not look, but she could no more
look away than will her heart to cease beating so madly. His skin glistened with a sheen of sweat, despite
the cool sea breeze. Although relaxed, he was so sinewed that the muscles in his arms rippled with his
slightest movement, as did the tendons in his abdomen. His chest was washboard-hard. His legs were long
and hard and sculpted of sinew and muscle and flesh
and bone.

A salty breeze teased the hem of her thin nightgown. It caressed her bare legs, her buttocks, her breasts. Her nipples were hard, aching. She folded her arms tightly beneath her bosom. She was not going to go back to her room, where she too would sit in bed, awake and alone.

She swallowed. Despite her determination, she was beset with cowardice. She raised her hand to rap upon the door.

He said clearly, "How long are you gonna stand out there?"

Regina jumped. She had not realized that he had seen her. All of her color drained from her face. She felt like a truant caught in a criminal act.

He stood up and stared at her. His stance was rigid and his eyes blazed. He appeared angry, prepared to do battle.

Regina almost felt like fleeing. Almost. "S-Slade."

"What are you doing?"

"I . . ." She was at a loss. "I c-can't s-sleep."

He took one step toward her and halted. He stood in the middle of the room now, bathed in warm light, while she stood on the other side of the screens. His gaze swept her from head to toe. His expression hardened. "You're not going to fall asleep standing there."

She could not believe she had come this far and he would not invite her in. In a flash she recalled their wedding supper. He had sat beside her but he had said very little. He had not been rude, but he had been tense and withdrawn. He had not touched the champagne or wine, which was not usual for him. Regina had been too overwhelmed herself to even attempt to understand him then. She dared not understand him now.

"Just what the hell are you doing outside of my door?"

"I . . ." She could not think of any reason that might seem plausible. Her cheeks flamed again. He regarded her steadily, careful now to look only at her face. He was grim.

Trying to speak was nearly hopeless. Her gaze kept slipping down his bare, damp torso and past his flat, hard abdomen. She had never seen a man in his underwear before. But this was not just any man, it was her husband, the man she loved. His shorts drew her eyes like a magnet draws metal. The linen fabric was opaque.

"Go back to your room," Slade ordered.

"T-tonight is our wedding night."

Slade's face was darkening with anger. "You think I don't know it?"

Dread filled her. "You're not going to invite me in?"

His gaze slid over her. "No. Go away. I'll see you at breakfast in the morning."

She was shocked.

Despite his words, Slade did not turn his back on her. In fact, he did not move. His thighs were still braced hard apart. His diaphragm indicated that he was breathing somewhat unevenly and too quickly. His summer drawers seemed fuller, the linen billowing.

"I'm warning you," he said.

Regina swallowed hard. Wives were obedient. She had just sworn to obey him. But if she was obedient now, she would be crushed. She could not understand why he was sending her away, but every womanly instinct she had told her that his words belied his feelings. Gripping the door, she swung it open and stepped inside.

His eyes were wide. "What the hell are you doing?" And he looked at her as if he could see right through her nightgown.

She was reminded that she wore nothing beneath it. Her body flamed. A strange wet heat gathered near her thighs, where she seemed to hurt. She hugged herself. "Tonight is our wedding night."

"Oh, no," he said. "Get the hell out. Now."

She could not believe what he had said. "W-what?"

"You heard me," he said stiffly. His face was strained, flushed more deeply than hers. The sheen on his dark skin was brighter, too. "Out. Now."

Regina did not think. If ever there was a time for action, that time was now, and she acted. Swiftly she moved to him, laying her palms on his damp, hard chest.

He tensed. He was incredulous.

She could barely get the words out. "W-we should b-be together tonight."

He recovered, gripping her wrists hard enough to hurt her. "No."

She did not feel the pain in her wrists. Her thighs brushed his. The blood inside her was churning wildly. Her body throbbed. She shook her head, unable to speak, and she leaned against him.

He shuddered when their loins met, heat against heat. Regina gasped, shocked.

His jaw clenched. "Don't do this." He did not push her away.

"Do what?" she asked. Her eyes were fluttering closed. Her hips had a will of their own, undulating against his male hardness. Her breasts swelled against his chest. Her nightgown clung to her, wet with his sweat and transparent.

He still didn't move, except for where his shaft pulsed against her. He was sweating more heavily now, and his breathing had become harsh. His grip tightened on her wrists and Regina whimpered, but not in pain. He rocked her body back an inch. "I don't believe this," he said thickly. "I'm playing the saint and you're playing the fool."

She opened her eyes. She had not expected to see such carnality in his gaze. Her heart seemed to stop; she had not expected to see such wicked promise. Then it beat even harder. She felt faint, weak-kneed. His gaze slid down her body, inspecting her raised nipples, the joining of her thighs. She was well aware that he could see through her nightclothes. She heard herself moan, a sound she could not restrain. Their bodies no longer touched, and she could not stand it. She strained against the grip he had imprisoned her with, strained for him.

"I give up," he said, his eyes blazing, his tone dangerous. "I give up."

His words, his tone, his expression, made her cry out.

Slade moved. He took her face in his hands. He began kissing her the way a man might kiss a woman if he loved her very much and hadn't seen her in a very long time.

With a sob, Regina threw her arms around him while he kissed her endlessly. It was nothing like the kiss they had shared in the buggy. It was not gentle, soft, or teasing. It was not even like the kiss they had shared at the beach. This kiss had no limits. It was bruising and terrifying; it was exhilarating. It was deep, openmouthed, and intimate. He tasted all of her that he could, plumbing her mouth, and she let him. He didn't touch her body, only her face. His hands never left her face. Regina had never been kissed like this in her entire life, and she was certain that she would never be kissed like this again. She lost all sense of time and place. She lost all sense of everything other than Slade. And when he finally dragged his mouth from hers, she instantly sagged to the floor.

Slade caught her before she actually hit the hard wood. "We're both gonna regret this," he said, panting and letting her down gently while straddling her. Regina's breath caught. His eyes were so bright she felt the heat as if they contained real flames. He caught her face again in his hands and his tone became reverent. "Never," he said harshly, "never have I seen someone so beautiful, someone so sexy. Not ever."

Regina moaned.

He claimed her mouth again. He claimed her with the same undaunting force he had used before, but Regina did not mind, for his passion, clearly overwhelming him, overwhelmed her. His kisses were all that she had dreamed, and so much more.

Her hands slipped and slid over his wet shoulders, clutching at them. She thrashed beneath him. She desperately wanted him to lay his big, hard body down on top of hers and complete the possession he had begun, but he did not. She desperately wanted to feel his maleness against her femininity, and she strained her hips toward his, but he refused to meet her.

He tore his mouth abruptly from hers. Close to weeping, Regina met his gaze, her nails digging into the skin of his arms. She felt swollen, close to bursting. She writhed helplessly. The sensation of the clinging wet silk, adhering to her every curve, added to her agony.

"Too fast," he panted. He moved his hands over her breasts, as if familiarizing himself with them. Regina bucked beneath his fingers. He thumbed her nipples, his panting harsher and louder now, and Regina whimpered uncontrollably. His hands slid down her belly, low and lower still. Regina tensed, surprised but filled with anticipation, with need.

Slade's glance met hers again. He was dripping sweat and out of breath, kneeling over her, and his gaze was so intense it almost frightened her. His hands had stopped their quest just inches from her. Regina realized, in shock, that she was undulating her pelvis beneath his palms. Yet even in realizing what she was doing she could not stop her body from its reflexive dance.

"Yeah," he said hoarsely, closing his eyes. A second later his hands were between her legs, molding her nightgown to the deep cleft he had discovered there. His thumbs opened and explored her as if the silk was just another layer of her skin. Regina was immediately wracked with waves of mind-shattering pleasure.

When the spasms died, she became aware of what he was doing. He had pulled her nightgown up to her waist. Now his bare palms and naked fingers slid over her. His breath touched her. New sensations flurried to life within her. His finger slid inside her, tentatively. His wild gaze jerked to hers as she clamped around him. Regina thought that she might die, very soon.

"So beautiful," Slade said hoarsely, lowering his head.

Regina cried out when his tongue swept over her. She tried to tell him to stop, then immediately forgot about her objections. If it was possible for a man to worship a woman, then that was what Slade was doing to her. She began to shake. His tongue circled her delicately, relentlessly. She sobbed and gave in to another round of endless, powerful pleasure.

Instantly he rose above her, pulling her into his arms. The sensations had not yet died when Regina felt his engorged phallus straining against her thigh. He had shed his drawers. He was raining desperate kisses all over her face and finally on her mouth.

"Oh, damn," he gasped, meeting her gaze. "I already lost it, but it's still gonna be short, but sweet."

Regina barely heard. She did not understand and did not care to. She knew only what she desperately wanted. She jerked her hips up to meet his palm, rubbing herself frantically against him.

"That's not what you want," he told her, and she felt him poised to enter her, hard and wet. Shudders swept through him as he kissed her again, hard and deep. Suddenly his hands were anchoring her hips to the floor. "I'm sorry."

A scant second later he was driving himself into her. He was large, impossibly large, but there was only a brief moment of pain and then she felt all of him, pulsing inside of her so tight and hot and deep. He froze, panting. He kissed her neck once. She could not stand it. She dug her nails into his shoulders, moving against him.

He laughed, exultant. He moved deeper. He withdrew. He slid into her the way a pistol slides into a well-oiled holster, smooth and quick. A blast of pleasure followed. While he pumped himself into her, deep, hard, and thick, she wept and cried out and contracted violently around him. This time the pleasure was so intense that she nearly blacked out. Then he shouted too, and moments later he lay heavily on top of her, clinging to her.

A minute might have ticked by, or an hour. He slid to the floor. "Damn," he said grimly, sitting up. "Did I hurt you?"

Regina had been in a mindless limbo created by the intense physical release she had experienced three times. Slowly she opened her eyes to see him staring intently at her. The feverish excitement was still there in his eyes. Yet his expression was dark and worried. She smiled. She wondered if the bursting love she felt in her heart was there in her gaze and there on her lips. "No," she whispered. She touched his mouth with her fingertip. "Oh, Slade," she whispered. "It was so wonderful, you are so wonderful."

He tensed.

"Slade," she said again, sitting up. His eyes were wide, watchful. Regina gripped his shoulders, staring at his handsome, dark face, at his beautiful mouth. She stroked her finger over it again. She murmured his name again. She no longer cared if he guessed how she felt.

He caught her hand. His eyes blazed. "This is gonna be a long night," he said.

Chapter 16

Slade paused at the door to look back at her. He knew that she slept like a rock under normal circumstances, so after last night he thought she wouldn't stir for many hours yet. He himself had not slept for a second. Despite the exhaustion.

Grimly he reached down for his duffel bag and slipped through the door. It hadn't taken him long to pack the few things he had brought home with him, and it had taken him even less time to make the decision now propelling him. He crossed the courtyard quickly. He wanted to leave without anyone seeing him. He preferred to leave like a coward.

And as he bypassed the house he tried not to think. It was exceedingly difficult. In the front courtyard he set the duffel bag down. There was one thing he had to do before he left.

With long strides, he began marching away from the house, not toward the stables, but north, toward the family cemetery.

As he walked, images from last night rushed through his mind. He and Regina, equally insatiable. He did not want to remember. Not now, not ever. He began to sweat.

The cemetery was just over the hill, ten minutes on

foot from the house. The family patriarch, Alejandro Delanza, was buried there—the man who had started it all when he had received the original land grant from the Mexican governor. Beside him was his first and only wife, Slade's grandmother, Delores. They had had a son before Rick who had died in infancy, and Jaime's grave was the oldest in the lot. Rick had one other brother buried there as well, the victim of a tragic stagecoach accident while in the prime of his life. Sebastian's wife had returned back east to her family and had subsequently remarried. Slade's grandparents had just the three boys, no girls, and Rick had kept up the family tradition. And as Alejandro's oldest son had preceded him into the grave, so too had James preceded Rick.

A whitewashed split-rail fence had been put up in recent years, cordoning off the area. As Slade approached, his eyes went instantly to his brother's grave. He entered through the gate, his steps slowing.

More images tumbled through his mind. Regina had been in every position he could think of, and there had been so many that the images were blurred and fragmented. He was thankful for that one small favor. His stomach roiled, not for the first time.

A marriage in name only. What a joke.

He stopped in front of his brother's grave. Someone had put fresh flowers there the day before, white and orange roses cut from the bushes growing in the courtyard. Josephine, he thought. It was becoming difficult to breathe.

The headstone was white marble, and it was obscenely clean and new in comparison to the rest of the timeworn, wind-eroded stones in the cemetery. He stared at the inscription. JAMES WARD DELANZA, A NOBLE, LOVING SON. 1873–1899.

The words were blurring—or was it his vision? God, the inscription said nothing, yet it said everything. James had died so unfairly in the prime of young manhood. James had been noble, so goddamned noble, and he had been loving, not just a loving son, but a loving brother, a loving man.

While he, Slade, was a bastard and a traitor.

"James," he suddenly cried aloud. "I never intended to consummate the marriage, I never did!"

But regret was useless. He had a secret. The secret was that he had spent the past ten years living the most honorable and noble life that he could—to prove to anyone who cared to see that his father's assessment of him was wrong. To prove to himself that Rick was wrong. Yet now his life up until this moment was irrelevant. Last night had exposed the real truth. Last night he had exposed himself. He was a fraud. He was not honorable, he had never been honorable, the past was a pretense. James was the one in the Delanza family with all the honor.

He, Slade, was a selfish bastard, as Rick had pointed out so often. *She* saw him as a noble hero. It was not even laughable. How naive she was.

God, how could he have made love to her like that? How could he have forgotten, even for a second, that this woman had been James's fiancée, that he had loved her?

"I'm sorry," he cried. "James, I'm so sorry!" But even as he called out to his brother he was a traitor. For his head filled with its own challenging refrain. *But I love her too.*

He was aghast. It was not true. If he loved James, it could not be true. Last night he had used the woman, nothing more.

But it had not felt cheap. He had not felt cheated. Only now did he feel cheated.

He gripped the headstone, forcing James to the forefront of his mind. He had come here to ask for forgiveness. He had come here to beg forgiveness. He had not come here to delve inside his heart, to betray James once again.

"James," he cried, his face upturned. "I'm sorry!" He closed his eyes, listening to the morning's first birdsong. There was no answer from the grave. But had he really expected one? And how could there be one?

For his apology was not one hundred percent sincere. The stubborn rebel in him kept thinking that he had a right, too. That she was now his wife, that James was dead—dead, dammit, and that he needed her just a little too.

But he was stronger than he had ever thought. He forced himself to stand tall. He would fight the part of him that continued to betray James, and he would win. He had to win. He could not live with himself if he didn't.

"I promise," he managed harshly, hoping James could hear, "I promise . . . never again. It was a mistake. It won't happen ever again. She doesn't mean anything to me. I swear it."

Slade waited. James did not materialize. There was no response, no answer, no forgiveness. There was not even a sign that James might be present, and that he might be forgiving. And it was stupid to be expecting him to appear, because James was dead. Stone-cold dead. Ghosts were for children, not men. Slade realized that there were tears on his cheeks.

He covered his face with his hands. Somehow he would get past this. James was dead, irrevocably dead, and there was not going to be any forgiveness from that quarter. Maybe, if he were lucky, one day he could forgive himself.

He quickly turned his back on the cold gleaming headstone. It was time to leave. Not just the graveyard, but Miramar, and her. He had proved how weak he was, there was no way in hell he could stay here with her now. If he had fallen once, he would do so again. There might even come a horrible time when he did not regret being with her. He didn't dare stay.

He walked more slowly back to the house and crested the hill. The sprawling adobe hacienda came into view. He faltered. Standing there by the gate and his duffel bag was his father.

Slade recovered. He assumed an inscrutable expression. He did not need this, not now. He hoped his eyes were not red. He continued on until he had reached the courtyard entrance.

"Where in hell are you going?" Rick demanded.

"What the hell is this?" He jabbed a finger at the bag.

"I'm leaving."

"Because of her?"

Slade was enraged—because it was the truth. "My reasons are none of your damn business."

"Why the hell not? I'm your father, aren't I?"

For a moment he did not speak. "You lost the right to call yourself my father a long time ago."

Rick gritted, "Maybe you lost the right to call yourself my son, runnin' out on me the way you did!"

Slade was reminded of the night he had run away a decade ago. For a brief instant he had an inkling that his father had felt betrayed by that night, but then he knew it was his imagination—or a reversion to a child's wishful thinking. "Blame me, go ahead. You never do any wrong, do you?"

"I didn't say that." Rick jabbed his finger at the bag again. "You runnin' out on me?"

"Yeah."

"You runnin' out on me again?"

That night, ten years ago, Rick had let him go without any protest. But he had not been the heir then, just the pain-in-the-ass second son. His stomach clenched up, aching. A kind of dread-filled anticipation crept over him, unwelcome. It almost seemed as if Rick was upset. "If you want to look at it that way."

"How the hell else am I supposed to look at it?"

Slade shrugged as if nonchalant.

"You're not taking her with you!"

Slade tried to laugh. "Believe me, old man, she's all yours." It shouldn't hurt—he knew Rick, knew his old man couldn't care less about him—but it did. It hurt more than it had ever hurt before, undoubtedly because he'd let too many feelings out already this morning and his heart was still bleeding. "You've got it all now," he said harshly. "That should make you happy. You've got Miramar and you've got your heiress. I'm through with her and I'm through with you."

"You're a son of a bitch, you know that?" Rick said.

"I think you've said that once or twice before. And I know enough to take you literally. You know what? Leave my mother out of it."

"Like hell I will," Rick shouted. "She left me without thinking twice. *You are just like her*."

Slade was equally furious. He wanted to explode, he wanted to inflict pain. Like a wounded animal, he lashed out. "We both had you in common, didn't we? You drove her away, didn't you? She didn't leave you, you drove her away!"

Rick went white.

Slade moved in for the kill. "But you don't have that power over me. Not anymore, not now. Once you drove me away. Now I'm leaving only because I want to."

Rick recovered. His dark-blue eyes, so like Slade's, held the same rage, and the same anguish. "Good! Leave! You think I'm gonna fuss over it? You think I want you to stay? You think I need you?" He laughed harshly. "Like hell!"

Slade picked up his bag.

"You would only bring this place down over our heads with your damn-fool ideas," Rick shouted as Slade walked away.

Slade didn't answer.

Rick screamed, "Besides, I got her now, damn you! I don't need you, boy, and I never will!"

Slade flinched, but kept walking. He couldn't remain impassive, not inside, where it counted. His heart was hurting as if someone was twisting a knife in there, hard. Yet his strides were steady.

When he was at the entrance, Rick said, his voice suddenly too high, "When are you comin' back?"

Slade didn't answer. The answer was that he was never coming back, another cruel twist of the blade. Leaving Miramar forever was just as hard as everything else.

"You always come back," Rick called out, as if he understood what Slade's silence meant.

Slade didn't respond. And because it was the last time, he wanted to look back. But he didn't. And even though his mind was made up, even though he was moving away from the house with lengthening strides, inside he was waiting, waiting for a protest, a last protest, any protest—only it didn't come.

He reached the barn. He tossed his duffel in a wagon. As he hitched a mare up in the traces, he wondered if the heavy pain in his chest was because of his father, his brother, Miramar, or the woman he had left sleeping in his room. The woman who was his wife, the woman he had dared to love, just for one night.

Regina had never been happier. She woke up smiling, bursting with pleasure, unable to think about anyone or anything other than Slade. Slade, her husband, Slade, her lover.

She should blush, but she was beyond blushing now; indeed, she thought, she would probably never blush again. She dressed quickly, wondering where he was, wondering what they would say to each other after having shared such a wild, reckless, decadent night. Her body felt a bit sore, but her heart was singing. This was love, and she had never experienced it before.

While she dressed she imagined the various scenes that might occur when they next met. He would smile at her from across the room as she approached, a real smile, a slow sexy smile, one that alluded to just how wicked the two of them could be.

Or he would cross the room with fast hard strides and pick her up and whirl her around, laughing. Then he would kiss her and tell her how much he loved her. He would tell her that he would love her forever, and that he was the happiest man on earth.

He hadn't said that last night. Last night he had not said much, except for how beautiful she was; he hadn't said that he loved her. Of course, Regina knew that he did love her, in the same way, and with the same fervor, that she loved him. He had proved it with his hands and mouth and body, and soon, very soon, he would prove it with words.

Today was the beginning of the rest of their lives.

Regina danced with excitement as she finished putting up her hair. They were husband and wife, and they were lovers, but they would become so much more. They would get to know one another. Become friends. Begin to trust each other. Soon there would be a child. And then another, and another. They would be a warm, loving family. Regina glowed. She imagined bringing Slade home to meet her family, and she trembled with anticipation. Her mother and her sister would be impressed with his power, his charisma, and his looks. And she knew that her brothers would respond to him instantly, too. Although they were from different worlds, they were of the same heroic mold that sets apart most men from an exceptional few. Her father would not be happy at first, because he had not had the chance to approve of Slade, but he would eventually see Slade for the man that he was, and when he gave his approval, they would become fast friends. Regina might have had doubts before, but not anymore.

She laughed, regarding her face in the mirror. Her eyes sparkled like yellow sapphires, her cheeks were rosy with joy. She looked like a woman in love, she realized; she looked like one of the happiest women in existence.

It was the middle of the day when Regina rushed from Slade's room. She headed directly for the den, hoping that he might be there, relaxing while he waited for her. But the den was empty. So too was the living room and the dining room. Disappointed, Regina paused, wondering where he might be. She heard Josephine using a cleaver in the kitchen. Quickly she crossed the threshold and poked her head in. Josephine turned, and when she saw Regina her expression sobered even more. Regina was startled by such a response. "Good afternoon. Have you seen Slade?"

Josephine hesitated. "Not since this mornin', chile."

"Oh."

"But Rick says he wants to talk to you. He's in his study."

Regina brightened. Rick would know where Slade

was. She hurried from the kitchen, by now knowing her way through the house as if she were its mistress. With a start of pleasure, she realized that, as Slade's wife, she *was* now its mistress, or at least one of them. Miramar was now her home, and who would not be thrilled with a home such as this? She nearly skipped through the halls.

Rick's door was ajar and he saw her before she could knock or announce herself. "Come on in."

Regina entered, smiling. "Good afternoon."

"Sit down, Elizabeth." His voice was very sober, very firm.

At his words, guilt pierced her, deflating her happiness. "Is something wrong?" She could not breathe normally. Had Victoria or Edward finally told him that she was not Elizabeth? Did he know? Her mind whirled with astonishing speed. If Rick knew, she was going to have to tell Slade. Slade was her husband—she had to tell him the truth, and soon. In fact, after last night, she felt confident that she could tell him immediately. Yet despite her confidence, the thought was not pleasant. How could it be? The subject was not pleasant.

"Something's wrong," Rick said slowly, "but not so wrong that you should look like I'm about to shoot you."

Regina relaxed slightly in response to his brief smile. Yet looking closely at him, she saw that his smile did not reach his eyes and she grew uneasy again. Did he know after all? "What has happened?"

"Look, honey, there's no easy or nice way to tell you this, but Slade has left."

He spoke in English, but he might have been speaking a foreign language for all the sense he made. "Left?"

"Left."

"I—I don't understand."

"Slade decided to go back to San Francisco, where he's been living these past few years."

"I beg your pardon?"

Rick repeated himself word for word.

She said, "Without me?"

He hesitated. "Without you. He knows you'll be taken care of here."

It took a very long moment for her to actually comprehend what had occurred. And then her world crashed around her with sickening force.

"Honey, you're not going to faint, are you?" Rick jumped to his feet and was at her side in an instant. "Here, let me get you a drink. I think you could use one."

Regina was stunned and disbelieving. She did indeed feel precipitously close to fainting. "Are you saying," she whispered, "that Slade has left me?"

"Well, he hasn't exactly left you," Rick hedged. "He's just returned to his life up north."

Regina stared. She was numb, in a state of shock. *Slade had left. Slade had returned to San Francisco, without her, where he had been living before their marriage. Slade had just married her, but he had left. He had left her. After last night, he had left her.*

Through the shock, anger hissed.

"You all right?" Rick tried to hand her a glass of liquor, but Regina did not take it, didn't answer. She barely heard her father-in-law. Her mind came to life again. Slade had stated from the first that he was marrying her for her money, nothing more. She had married him for love. Last night she had gone to him in love. And he had taken her not the way a man takes his wife, but the way a man would take a prostitute. And today, today he had left her.

"Elizabeth, this doesn't change a thing. He's still my heir, and you're still his wife." Rick put his hand on her shoulder. "You still belong here, don't worry about that."

Angrily, Regina shook his hand off. "That bloody bastard!"

"Well, he can be that, at times."

"He married me and left me! He had no intention—blast him—of staying with me as my husband!"

"Well, I guess not."

"Damn him!" Regina shouted. Tears blurred her

vision. Had she actually loved him? Was it possible? Now she could see that she had been the biggest fool to think that he had returned her feelings. Last night he had not been returning her feelings, he had been using her! He had been slaking his lust with her! How she regretted what she had done!

"Look, he'll be back, he always comes back," Rick said, without his customary vigor. "And when he does, the two of you can work things out."

"When! Next year?"

Rick was silent.

Regina got up and paced wildly. She was a woman spurned, and never had she felt such intense emotion as she felt now. It was a wild, reckless, burning hatred. God, how he had used her! And the fact that she had been a stupidly willing victim did not excuse his actions, not in the least! But there was a solution. And it was very obvious. She whirled. "Where is he?"

"Frisco."

"Do you know exactly where I can find him?"

Rick looked relieved. "Yeah."

"Good!"

"You going after him?" Rick asked.

"Oh, yes." Regina smiled, but not pleasantly. "I'm going after him—to get a divorce!"

"Now hold on!" Rick cried. Again Regina shook off his hand. "Don't you go acting like a fool! Think of Miramar! This is your home now, Elizabeth, and that's what's important. Slade will be back and—"

"I'm not Elizabeth."

Rick froze.

"I'm not Elizabeth," Regina said, feeling a savage kind of satisfaction. Rick was not to blame for Slade's actions, she knew that, but she could not help herself. "My name is Regina Shelton, Lady Regina Bragg Shelton, and yes, I'm related to the Texas Braggs and the New York Braggs. My father happens to be the Earl of Dragmore, and my mother is a countess. I am an heiress in my own right. And I do not need you or Miramar, thank you very much."

"I see," Rick said slowly.

"And I don't need Slade!"

"You got your memory back pretty suddenly, huh?"

Regina was too angry to care at being caught in an act of deceit. "I remembered two days before the wedding. But I stupidly wanted to marry your son and it had nothing to do with Miramar." She saw Rick's expression change, saw it brighten, but that didn't interest her either.

"Well, I've learned my lesson," she said hotly. "I'm divorcing Slade immediately and going home, where I belong. And he can just go find himself another heiress to save his precious Miramar!"

Part Two

Exposed

Chapter 17

*T*he day after learning of Slade's desertion, Regina arrived in San Francisco.

It was half past the hour of four. Regina sat rigidly, hands clasped in her lap, filled with tension. Adrenaline had been pulsing in her bloodstream since yesterday's betrayal. Since she had learned what a real bastard her husband was, she had not been able to do anything but think of him. There were rings of sleeplessness around her eyes, which were also puffy from crying. Because along with the anger, there was so much pain.

Edward leaned over and patted her unsteady hands. He had volunteered to bring her to his brother; in fact, he had insisted he accompany her. The situation was also horribly humiliating—what bride was deserted the day after her wedding by the groom? Regina would have preferred traveling alone, but, of course, ladies did not travel alone. She had accepted. Her acceptance had been frosty. She was not just furious with Slade, but with his entire family, even if it were unreasonable.

Nevertheless, Edward was nothing but caring and sympathetic. It was slightly longer than an eight-hour journey by rail from Templeton, where they had caught the day's train. He kept a minimal amount of conversation going, just enough to distract her, and all of it carefully innocuous. His wit had even brought forth the ghost of a smile twice. Regina was no longer cool to Slade's brother. How could she be? He might have guessed the truth about her before she had told Rick yesterday, and he might have even shared that truth with his mother, but it no longer mattered.

His kindness was all that mattered. She looked at him gratefully, any anger she had been taking out on him gone. Even now, despite the fact that she had been uncommunicative and just short of rude all day, he was attempting to comfort her. Lord, how she needed comfort.

That thought threatened to undo her control. She turned her head away so he would not see how close she was to fresh tears. Now she needed self-control more than ever. When she finally confronted Slade, she would not weep.

Nor would she rail. Yesterday she had acted like a common shrew. She had shrieked and shouted at Rick, who was certainly not responsible for what his son had done. Today she would be cool and calm. Just because Slade failed to have any morals whatsoever, she did not intend to sink to his level. She was a well-bred lady. She would cling to her manners and gentility no matter how hard it was. She must. She must never let him see what he had done to her.

Regina managed a small smile for Edward's benefit, a fragile kind of thank-you, and glanced away. She had not only lost all of her self-respect with Rick, she thought, deeply ashamed, every time she recalled her wedding night and her behavior—her abandoned, enthusiastic, scandalous behavior—she quaked. If she could have just one wish, it would be that the night had never happened. Slade had only been using her— but she had loved him. At the time her love had been an excuse to indulge in all the unspeakable acts he had guided her toward. Today, there were simply no possible excuses for the past. Now when she had to face him he would also remember her behavior. The mere thought was mortifying.

It was also incredible that she had thought, even for a moment, that he had loved her, too. Never would she be so naive again.

The train was slowing, already entering the large glass-and-iron station. Through the dusty windows, Regina saw a hive of activity. Commuters were everywhere. Men were rushing to and fro in their dark suits and jaunty hats, hurrying to catch the trains that would take them home, whether it was the elegant, super-fast Owl, a nonstop to Los Angeles that traveled through the San Joaquin Valley, or just a local spurr to San Jose or Oakland. Regina's heart was pounding heavily. Soon she would confront Slade and demand a divorce. Soon, but not soon enough.

She shifted on her seat, adrenaline thrumming through her body more strongly than before. She could barely wait, yet anxiety filled her too. Nothing was ever easy with Slade, but she would persuade him to divorce her. After all, once she made it clear that he would not get her money, he would no longer be interested in the liaison. And she would not reveal to him that she was Regina Bragg Shelton, not until after he had signed the papers, because she did not want him to realize the extent of her wealth and connections.

That meant that she had to move swiftly. She did not plan to see him tonight. She intended to go directly to her uncle, Brett D'Archand, so that he could drum up divorce papers tomorrow. Brett was a fabulously wealthy man, which meant he was a very powerful man. She would not confront Slade until she had divorce papers in her hand, hopefully by tomorrow evening. And she would get his signature. If he dared to refuse, he would have a fight on his hands the likes of which he could not win. She would bring all of her family into it, she would bring all of their power against him.

He did not deserve an ounce of consideration from her, yet she shifted uneasily. Thinking of how he could so easily be destroyed by her uncles, her father, and grandfather combined was more than unpleasant. She had to be honest with herself. She despised him—she did. But it was not like her to seek vengeance. She could not. She did not hate him enough for that. She would settle the divorce herself. Somehow the idea of Slade standing alone against her family distressed her.

Edward did not know of her plans. She was not even sure if he knew that she intended to divorce his brother, although she thought that Rick would have probably told him. She turned to Edward, wondering what his reaction to her question would be. "Would you like to spend the night at my uncle's? It will not be an inconvenience—in fact, it will be a pleasure."

Edward looked startled. "Your uncle's?"

"Yes." She smiled. "Didn't you know that I have family here? Brett D'Archand, the shipping magnate, is my uncle. I will be staying with him, of course."

"Don't you think you should go to your husband?"

Regina's eyes flashed. "No, I do not."

Edward was silent for a moment. "I see. And when are you planning on seeing Slade? I mean, I can only assume that that is the reason we have come to the city."

"Tomorrow, I think." She was reserved. She did not want to encourage Edward into venturing more deeply into this topic.

Edward could only be gallant. "Would you like me to stay at your uncle's so I can take you to my brother tomorrow?" His voice was soft, despite her tone.

Regina bit her lip. How could he guess that despite the anger, she was just a little bit frightened at the thought of confronting Slade? "You really don't have to do that."

Edward smiled; he was handsome enough to cause the three matronly ladies sitting on the other side of the aisle, who had been stealing peeks at him all afternoon, to turn and stare. Edward gave them all a dimpled grin before continuing. "It will be my pleasure."

Regina couldn't help thinking that if Slade had one ounce of his brother's compassion she would not be in this mess.

The train finally stopped and they disembarked. A

steward brought their bags and helped them to the depot's doors, where Regina saw Edward slip him a silver half-dollar. Tipping was expected, of course, but she was surprised that Edward would be so generous— too generous, in fact. A nickel would have sufficed. And Edward had no wealth that she knew of.

Passengers were crowding the street. A dozen hansoms were lined up, waiting to pick up fares, while a crush of cable cars and horse-drawn trolleys offered slower public transportation to those who preferred it. Moments later they were in a cab and Regina had given her uncle's address on California Street.

"Nob Hill?" Edward asked.

"Yes," Regina said, knowing what he was thinking. Nob Hill was lined with spectacular and ostentatious mansions. It hadn't always been that way. When Regina had first come to San Francisco as a little girl, her uncle had resided there, his forty-room home towering over most of the other residences on the street. Several years ago Regina had returned to the city and was shocked to find her uncle's home now greatly reduced in stature, for massive mansions lined California Street, each one bigger than its neighbor.

"Charles Mann lives on Nob Hill, too," Edward said quietly.

Regina tensed. Because she had not discussed Slade, she did not even know where he lived, or where he worked, or what he did precisely. She hesitated, then was careful to keep her tone impersonal. "And Slade?"

"He rents a modest home on Gough Street, although he is hardly ever there. He works late at the office more nights than not, and even goes there at ungodly hours. And he often dines with Mann. I think his house is used solely for sleeping."

Regina swallowed. It was now close to six o'clock. She imagined that soon they might be passing by Mann's residence and that Slade might even be within. She was agitated at the thought. She realized she was perspiring slightly, although it was quite cool out because of the summer fog. "Where is his office?"

"His office is with Mann's, in the Feldcrest Building—which Mann happens to own."

Regina stared out the hansom's window, barely seeing Market Street as they crossed it. The evening rush to get home was not yet over and passing through the intersection took ten minutes. She knew nothing about her husband's life in San Francisco. She did not want to know. But she said, "I don't understand his relationship with this Mr. Mann."

Edward regarded her thoughtfully. "Mann took him in when he was a hoodlum of fifteen."

Regina tried not to be interested, but she was. "What is a hoodlum?"

"There are gangs which rove the streets of the city after dark—and sometimes during the day. They prey on the Chinese mostly, but also on other foreigners. Since the depression, there's been a lot of anger. People feel that the Chinese are responsible for the depression, for the lack of jobs. I doubt it's true."

"That's sad."

"Yes, it is. I personally think they're good for the city, they're hard and efficient workers, but I wouldn't state such an unpopular opinion publicly. Anyway, the hoodlums are nothing for you to worry about, not unless you go alone to Chinatown at odd hours." He flashed her his winning smile. "Slade came here when he ran away from Miramar as a boy. He was penniless and on the streets and he took up with a gang. Fortunately the gang chose to rob Mann. Mann is an interesting fellow, as you shall see. He's about sixty now—back then he was just out of his prime, but he also grew up in the streets, though it was New York City's east side, not San Francisco's back alleys. He chased the gang off, apprehending Slade. That's how their relationship began."

Regina did not want to be interested. She was very, very angry with her unscrupulous, immoral husband. But she felt a pang of sympathy for a boy who had been rejected so often that he had run away from home and taken to the streets as a 'hoodlum.' Despite herself, she asked, "What happened?"

"I guess Mann saw the good in Slade, or maybe he saw some of his own misspent youth. Instead of turning him over to the police, he took him home. Gave him a bed, a meal, and a job. Slade started out as a messenger boy. Today he runs a good deal of Mann's empire."

Regina blinked. "Just what is it that Mr. Mann does?"

"He made his money in the Comstock during the silver rush in the late fifties and early sixties. And he was smart enough to sell out before it collapsed. He didn't sit on his money either. During the silver-boom years, he owned half of Virginia City. Today he owns the Mann Grande Hotel, which is second only to Ralston's Palace Hotel, as well as the Rancho Nicasio, which is the largest ranch in Marin, and probably a tenth of this city's property. I hear he's a very big investor in the Octopus."

"The Octopus?" Regina said weakly. Slade was this entrepreneur's right-hand man?

"The Southern Pacific is fondly—or not so fondly—called the Octopus," Edward said. "It owns most of the state's transportation, thousands of miles of track, millions of acres of land, and is rather influential in state politics." He smiled wryly. "And that is an understatement, Regina. Anyway, Charles Mann is quite a somebody. He's one of the richest men in San Francisco."

Regina said nothing. But she was even angrier. How dare Slade! He presented himself as if he were one of those hoodlums, but he was no hoodlum—oh, no! Why did he go to such trouble to present himself as a down-and-out rebel when he was actually a respectable businessman?

Edward apparently was reading her thoughts. "Slade sheds his real life like a snake sheds its winter skin whenever he comes home. You might have some trouble recognizing him, Regina."

"That's neither here nor there," she said briskly. "Frankly, I wouldn't care if he was Charles Mann himself."

Edward winced.

"We're here," she said, recognizing her uncle's home. While Edward paid the cabbie, Regina alighted, trembling with relief. Brett's home loomed as a sudden and very welcoming refuge, and she wanted to fly up the walk and up the steep front steps and into his arms or her aunt's embrace. But she waited for Edward and the cabbie, who brought their bags.

Her relatives were expecting her, for she had sent a wire just after the disastrous interview with Rick in which she had learned of Slade's desertion, explaining that she was fine and she would be arriving in the city as soon as possible. Still, Regina was surprised when the front door was opened by her aunt herself.

Her aunt Storm, a very tall, stately, handsome woman in her late fifties, shrieked like a young girl and hugged her with abandon, pulling her into the foyer and leaving Edward to amble in on his own. Storm rocked her. Regina clung, finding herself near tears. How she felt like spilling her heart out to her beloved aunt!

"Where have you been?" Storm cried. "We have been sick, sick with worry! Do you know your poor parents are in the middle of the Atlantic this very minute, with no hope of receiving word that you are all right until they arrive in New York?"

"I'm sorry." Regina meant it. She spotted her handsome uncle standing behind his wife, looking both grim and relieved. She recognized the expression well; it was one her own father had worn often enough, although never because of her, but always because of her hoydenish sister—who was now a duchess. Then she remembered Edward.

"Oh, dear," she cried, pulling him forward. Brett now looked acutely suspicious. "Uncle Brett," she said, smiling brilliantly, aware he must be thinking the worst, "you can see that I am fine!"

"Yes, I can see, and I hope you have a damn good explanation for disappearing without a single word."

"I have a very good explanation, but first let me introduce my friend, Edward Delanza."

"Your *friend?*" Brett asked. He eyed Edward, making no move to shake his hand.

Regina's heart tripped. "He's not exactly my friend," she said, flushing. "He is my brother-in-law."

Edward had conveniently asked to adjourn to his room, claiming that he was very tired from their journey. Regina knew he understood her dilemma. She now stood in the center of the large library, wringing her hands. Her aunt was beside her, too shocked to sit down. Brett was the only one functioning—and he was pouring himself a double Scotch whiskey.

"Let me get this straight," he said, turning to face her. "You are married to Slade Delanza?"

She nodded.

"Let's go back. You jumped from the train during the robbery and lost your memory in the fall. And you were mistaken for this other woman, Elizabeth Sinclair, by the Delanzas this entire time."

She nodded again.

"When did you regain your memory?" Brett asked tersely.

"Just a few days ago," she whispered.

"I want the best damn doctor in the state, and I will have him here tomorrow." His expression softened. "Are you all right?"

"Yes."

Suddenly he frowned. "Delanza?"

Regina tensed. "Do you know of him?"

"I know him. Not well. We run in the same circles, obviously, but he keeps his distance from everyone except for Charles Mann. I actually know little about him, except for the fact that he's a hard worker and dedicated to his employer." Brett frowned again. "What in hell possessed you to marry so precipitously? It's not like you. Did you know who you were when you married him?"

Regina could not lie—there had been too many lies already. "Yes."

"For the life of me, I can't see you and him together,"

Brett said grimly. "And I still don't understand."

Regina did not say a word, trying to decide if this was the moment to drop the cannonball right in their laps.

"I can," Storm put in smoothly. "I think you both complement each other nicely." She smiled at Regina, but, being more astute than her husband, her look was also inquiring. "The ladies in this town are going to be very disappointed."

Despite herself, Regina felt her heart drop. "They are?"

"I think it's the mystery surrounding him that has half the women in this city interested in him. Of course, he *is* a handsome gentleman, which has never hurt a bachelor's prospects." Seeing Regina's tightly pursed mouth, she hastened to assure her niece, "He has never paid court to any lady that I know of. Indeed, I don't think he even pays the ladies any attention. Whenever I see him, he is with Mann and other gentlemen, in serious discussion. He is not a ladies' man, my dear."

Regina murmured, "It really doesn't matter."

"Regina," her aunt said, coming forward, "what is wrong?"

Regina took a breath. "It doesn't matter," she repeated firmly. "You see, I—I am divorcing him."

There was silence in the library.

Regina added nervously, "And I do so need your help. I need you to obtain divorce papers for me, as soon as possible."

Storm squeezed her arm. Brett said ominously, "What?"

"I am divorcing him."

"Did I understand correctly that you were married just two days ago?"

"It was a mistake."

"Regina, what the hell is going on here?" Brett demanded.

"It's a long story." She swallowed. "I am going to do this, Brett. I thought I could count on you. I had hoped I could count on you. But if you will not help me, I shall obtain the papers on my own. I am sure, being who I am, I can obtain them almost as quickly as you could."

Brett looked thunderous. "I didn't say I wouldn't help you."

Quickly Storm took his arm and led him toward the door. "Let us talk, darling," she cajoled. "Woman to woman. Let me handle this."

"You know your brother Nick is going to be livid about this marriage, much less a divorce," he said tightly, referring to Regina's father. "Make sure you get to the bottom of this, Storm." With a last look at Regina, he left the room.

Regina had heard his every word. She had no intention of revealing everything, and she did not want to think about her father. He would be very angry that she had married without his approval. How he might react to a divorce was almost beyond contemplation. She loved her father, but right now he was the last person she looked forward to facing.

Briefly she closed her eyes as her aunt took her hand. It was unbelievable that her life had come to such a pass. After a divorce she would never be able to recoup her reputation. Most women would never be able to marry again, or at least not respectably, but of course the Earl of Dragmore would see to it that she was remarried, and well, immediately. Regina plunked herself down on a long red sofa, very close to crying. If she thought about that she would lose the last shred of her control. "You have to get him to help me. Either that or I shall run all over the city to find myself a lawyer who undoubtedly will take great advantage of my naiveté in matters like this but will gladly draw up papers despite the fact that I am momentarily penniless."

"You are not penniless, dear." Storm sat beside her. "You know you need only ask for funds. Is this a lovers' quarrel?"

"No."

"Did the two of you consummate the marriage?"

She hesitated. "Yes."

"Did he seduce you, Regina? Is that why you married him in such haste?"

"No."

Storm regarded her, perplexed. "I have known you all your life, dear. This is something I could see your sister, Nicole, doing, but not you. You knew who you were when you married him, Regina. I can only think that you must have fallen in love with him," Storm said gently.

"No!" Regina shook her head wildly, tears spilling. "He is very handsome, he did turn my head." She looked up from her hands, her eyes overly bright. Having decided not to tell any more lies made an explanation difficult, for she could not blame the amnesia for her marriage. Perhaps the truth, in halves, would save her after all. "I believed he cared for me. But he did not. He married me in order to save his precious home. He married me for my money, not out of love. And now he has deserted me, Aunt Storm!"

And Storm became as grim as her husband.

At two o'clock the following afternoon Regina had her papers.

Brett and Storm had decided to help her. That Slade had married her for her money in order to save Miramar angered them as much as it now angered Regina. She had carefully omitted the fact that she had, at the time, been fully cognizant of his intentions. She had carefully skipped over the extent of her infatuation for Slade, which was how she now chose to label what she had once felt for him. Still, there was some skepticism on the part of her relatives. They were as aware as she was that such a spontaneous marriage, without her father's approval, was entirely out of character for her.

Her relatives also did not want her soliciting lawyers on her own, knowing full well that she would be an easy prey for blackmail. If a divorce was on the agenda, Brett intended for it to be kept hushed up. There would be no scandal for his niece. He was not, however, thrilled with her divorcing Slade as precipitously as she had

married him. He had tried to persuade her to wait for
her father's arrival in the city before engaging in such a
monumental, life-altering action. But that would not be
for another ten days or two weeks. Regina would not
even hear of it.

Regina had also begged her uncle not to intervene.
She knew both men too well. Brett had a temper and
he was angry; she could imagine him getting heavy-
handed around Slade. In such an event, Slade would
not budge. He would become obstinate if pushed to
the wall. She was even afraid he and Brett might come
to blows, for Slade's temper was even hotter than her
uncle's.

Regina could not relax. As he had promised, Edward
was at her side in the carriage they had taken from her
uncle's stable. The Feldcrest Building was new, Edward
had said, ten stories of granite and limestone on the
corner of Van Ness Avenue and Eddy Street. They had
long since turned onto Van Ness, a major thoroughfare,
traveling south. A cable car was ahead of them, slowing
them down. A horse-drawn trolley passed them, then
a beer wagon and a milkman's wagon. They managed
to cut through the heavy traffic and pass the electric
car. Regina saw an automobile filled with a quartet of
grinning young gentlemen, but she did not smile. Auto-
mobiles were becoming increasingly popular, although
they were outrageously expensive. This one looked very
much like the one her cousin Lucy owned, the Duryea.

Most of the buildings on this street were commercial on the street level and residential above-stairs, and
did not top three floors. But up ahead on the left she
could see a tall office building. She was certain that
that was their destination, and was proved right when
the driver turned their carriage left at the next intersection.

Her pulse was pounding. Even though it was a pleasantly mild day, she was perspiring. She kept seeing
Slade's dark face in her mind, his expression characteristically inscrutable or characteristically angry. She
clutched her reticule and a large brown envelope very

tightly in her gloved hands. In the envelope were the divorce papers he must sign.

They alighted and quickly entered the building, crossing the spacious marble-floored lobby and pausing at the elevator. Regina realized that she was out of breath. And it had nothing to do with the short walk across the lobby.

"Half of the tenth floor is given over to Mann's staff," Edward said as they rode up in the elevator.

Regina could not respond. Her throat was too tight.

Edward took her arm when the elevator doors opened. He led her up the hall, perhaps sensing that she needed his support now more than ever, which she did. The prospect of seeing her errant husband again was making her nervous. Edward walked past several doors, all with opaque glass windows, and paused at the last one on the left side of the corridor. He knocked.

Slade's voice answered. "Enter."

Edward swung open the door and stepped aside to allow Regina to precede him. Trembling, Regina paused briefly to collect herself. It was too late to back out now. For Slade had already seen her.

Chapter 18

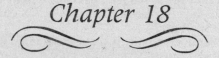

*H*e was sitting at a large desk with his back to a window overlooking the busy commercial traffic of Eddy Street. He was in his shirtsleeves, which were rolled up to his elbows, and buried in paperwork. Regina could see at a glance, however, that it was a fine white broadcloth shirt he wore, so different from those he chose at home, and that his dark tie was of equal quality, although it was carelessly loosened. Behind him a black wool suit jacket hung on a peg. He was staring at her.

She stared back, aware of the thundering of her heart.

In the next instant she saw that he wasn't alone. If she had been expecting him to be with anyone, she had been expecting to see him with Charles Mann. But he wasn't with another man. Standing behind him, her back to the window, was a tall, statuesque woman who would be considered beautiful by any standard in the world.

"*Hermano mio*," Edward said, grinning. "How convenient to find you here!" But his glance was sliding past Slade, and it settled abruptly on the brunette.

The woman regarded Edward, and then she turned to look at Regina.

Regina stood rigidly in the doorway, unmoving. The other woman was older than she, even older than Slade, but she was at that age when a woman is at her best—

in her early thirties. The very artfully applied rouge and powder enhanced her striking looks. Fresh hurt swept through Regina. Hard anger swept through her. Now she knew why he had been so eager to come to San Francisco.

Slade didn't get to his feet. Instead, a tight expression crossing his face, he leaned forward in his chair. "What are you doing here?"

Regina reminded herself that she was a lady. Ladies did not have tempers. The woman in the dark-red ensemble was definitely not a lady, otherwise she would not be carrying on with Slade outside of marriage, and that fact spurred Regina even more toward self-control. She would not stoop to either of their levels. Her voice was calm. She might have been addressing a stranger. "Forgive me if I'm disturbing you."

"Hello, Xandria," Edward said softly, as if he and Xandria were alone in the room.

Xandria was regarding Regina and Slade with wide, alert eyes. She met Edward's gaze only briefly before returning her interested attention to Regina. She had big blue eyes.

"What are you doing here?" Slade demanded again. He looked as if he might explode from his chair in an instant. He looked as if he wanted to throttle her.

"I have come on business," Regina said.

"What business?"

"Personal business. If you have the time."

He stared at her. Silence followed her words.

The woman, Xandria, broke it, moving briskly forward from behind his desk. "I see I had better leave."

Regina wanted nothing more than for her to leave. Her presence was threatening her control. She was trying very hard not to tremble, to hold onto her icy veneer. "Excuse me, but I do not believe we have met."

Xandria paused, then looked quickly at Slade as if for approval. Slade was standing. He said darkly, "Xandria, this is my wife. Elizabeth, this is Xandria Kingsly."

Xandria was obviously stunned.

Regina could almost feel sorry for her. Slade's mistress obviously had no idea that he had gotten himself married. What a bastard he was.

Xandria suddenly smiled. "How pleased I am to meet you."

Regina was taken aback. She did not move. Perhaps Xandria thought her naive enough to believe such theatrics, to think her relationship with Slade platonic. Regina extended her hand. "Likewise," she said stiffly. Inside she burned with the desire to scratch the other woman's eyes out. And to scratch her husband's eyes out.

Xandria looked from Regina to Slade. Her full mouth tightened. "I have an appointment," she murmured. Her voice was naturally low and husky. "Excuse me."

Regina barely nodded. Her face was as impassive as possible, but she could not stop herself from glaring at Slade. He matched her stare in intensity, in anger.

Edward jumped forward. "I'll see you out," he told Xandria. Regina stole a glimpse at him and saw the way he was looking at the Amazon. All men, she guessed, would buzz about this voluptuous woman like bees after honey.

Xandria gave him a long, assessing look. "Thank you."

She lifted a hand at Slade, then glided out. Edward, looking pleased, followed.

They were alone.

Suddenly all the sounds from the street outside drifted through the open windows. Bells and horns, the rumble of wheels on cobblestones, the clip-clopping of horses' hooves, a policeman's whistle, shouts. Pigeons cooed on the ledge through it all.

Abruptly Slade stood and came around his desk. "What are you doing here?"

"Maybe I should ask *you* that," Regina said very politely. At the moment she was referring to his tryst, not to his desertion.

"Obviously I am busy at work."

"Obviously."

His jaw clenched. "*What are you doing here?*"

"Perhaps you've forgotten," she said, the words com-

ing quite unbidden, "but a wife's place is by her husband's side."

"Not in this case."

The hurt crashed over her like a tidal wave. "No. Not
in this case. You have made yourself very clear."

"I never said I was planning on staying," he said,
but there was a catch in his voice and his eyes never
left hers.

She trembled. He had seen her anguish, but it was
too late. "You never said anything!"

"You never asked."

They stared at each other again. Regina was shaking,
feeling very near collapse. She wanted to vent her rage
and her hurt. She wanted to break things. She wanted
to have a tantrum. She wanted to hit her husband and
hurt him back. Most of all, she wanted to scream at him
wildly, scream the question she wanted answered the
most. How could he have left her after such a night?
How could he have abandoned her, deserted her?

But she did not give in to such self-indulgence. She
stood still, only the rise and fall of her bosom hinting
at the turmoil within.

Slade was somber. "I'm sorry."

She was going to cry. "I d-do not accept your apology."

He hesitated, then reached out to touch her. "That
night—it should have never happened."

She batted his hand away, fury apparent in her one
short movement. "Don't touch me."

He dropped his hands, clenching his fists at his sides.
"You have every right to be upset."

She did not bother to respond. "Upset" in no way
could even begin to describe her feelings. And she did
not want him to even guess at how distraught she
was.

"You shouldn't have come here, Elizabeth," Slade
said unevenly. "Why in hell did you come? I want you
at Miramar."

She gritted her teeth. "While you are here." With that
woman, in his other life. "You are a fraud."

Her accusation strained his expression. "I know. I know better than anyone."

She blinked. That was one response she had not expected. Yet she knew he had a deflated view of himself. Once, she had championed him; once, she had believed the best of him. Once upon a time she would have protested his statement. No more. Even if the insane urge to give in to old habits still dared steal into her heart.

Slade shoved his hands in his pockets, as if affected by her blurred stare. "I've hurt you. I didn't mean to."

She almost laughed. The sound came out choked, like a sob. "How thoughtful you are."

"All right!" he shouted. "But let me remind you that I did not come to your bed that night. You came to mine. I never had any intention of consummating our marriage. I wanted to be noble. But you threw yourself at me, dammit!"

She cried out. His brutally honest words were like a slap in the face. But so much worse was his statement that he had never intended to consummate the marriage. She reeled from his onslaught.

He paced away from her, to stare out of the window.

She was wide-eyed, still stunned. She fought to recover her wits. "You never intended a real marriage?"

He didn't turn to face her. "No."

She fought for breath.

He turned. "I guess I should have made myself clear. I assumed that you would be pleased about getting married, and that having a home and my name would be enough."

"Your assumption was wrong."

Slade grimaced. "Dammit, I'm sorry. More sorry than you'll ever know."

She didn't speak because she couldn't.

"I'll put you up in the hotel tonight. You can take the train back to Templeton tomorrow. Edward brought you here—he can take you home."

She had thought she understood this man a little. She did not understand him at all. "No."

He flinched. "You can't stay."

"That's right." Briskly she opened the envelope, hoping he would not see that she was batting back hot, stinging tears. She withdrew the papers. "I want a divorce, Slade, and I want it immediately."

"What?"

"I want a divorce."

He did not move, he did not respond.

"Why are you so surprised?"

Very slowly, lifting his gaze to her, he said, "Maybe I'm not surprised at all."

She did not like the dark, hurt look in his eyes. She was the one suffering. She did not care if he suffered too, he *should* suffer—she did not owe him one single drop of sympathy.

"I thought you wanted to be the mistress of Miramar."

"No." She felt like screaming at him that it had been a sham, that what she had wanted was to be his wife— to be not the mistress of Miramar, but the mistress of his heart. But that was an impossible dream. "I want nothing to do with you or Miramar."

He stared at his cluttered desk.

"I think you should know, I am not going to allow you to have a single penny of my inheritance."

"Is that vengeance?"

"Label it what you will." Her chin rose slightly. "Perhaps it is. Surely you can see that there's no point in continuing this marriage in name only."

"You no longer control your funds. A wife's possessions belong to her husband. Surely you can see that."

Perhaps in the case of Elizabeth Sinclair. In her case it was not so. Her father was giving her the inheritance upon her marriage. He had yet to do so. But she could not point that out to him. Not without revealing her true identity, which she preferred to avoid. Obviously he was intent on her money. If he knew she was a Bragg, he would never let her go.

Her hand trembled, holding the divorce papers. "Just

let me go, Slade. Perhaps we can arrive at a monetary settlement." Her lawyer had suggested that course as a last resort. Yet he had advised her not to even mention it. Sensing Slade's obstinance, she chose to ignore her lawyer's advice.

His expression hardened. "How much is a divorce worth to you?"

For some reason, she felt sicker inside than before. "I—I don't know."

His smile was unpleasant. "Why not?" He stepped toward her.

Regina took a step backward, not liking the look in his eyes or the expression on his face.

He crowded her, backing her up against the wall. "Why don't you know? I mean, if you're going to pay me off, you should have a price in mind."

Her heart was pounding. She did not want him this close to her. His proximity distressed her. So did his ill-concealed anger. "You make it sound so . . . sordid."

"Isn't it sordid?"

She closed her eyes. "Yes." Divorce was the most sordid event she could think of.

"How much?" he gritted. "How goddamn much?"

She was frightened. But her back was against the wall, so she could not move away from him. "Our lawyers—"

"No lawyers," he shouted, ripping the papers from her hand. "No lawyers, no payoff, no nothing!"

"What are you saying?" she cried.

He shoved his face close to hers. "I'm saying no. N-O. No."

She froze.

He bared his teeth. "This is what I think of your demand, Elizabeth." He held up the papers in both hands. Understanding his intentions, she cried out. Savagely, he tore them in two. And he smiled at her.

Hysteria won. "You are going to regret this! You are! When my father finds out, you are going to be dearly sorry! He shall see to it—"

"*Your father?*"

Too late, Regina realized her awful slip of the tongue. She blanched.

"George Sinclair is dead."

Regina pressed her spine into the wall. Her heart thudded. How could she have made such a mistake?

Slade gripped her shoulders, dragging her forward, up against him, thigh to thigh and chest to chest. "Who is your father? Who are you? Damn you!"

"Let me go! Let me go! I can explain!"

His hands found her face. For an instant she was afraid for her life. *"Who are you?"*

She wet her lips. She was impossibly dry, cotton-mouthed. If he wanted to, he could crush her skull. If he lost rationality, he would. "My name is Regina Bragg Shelton," she whispered. "I have remembered."

He stared, disbelieving.

"Oh, God," she whispered. "I . . . I was going to tell you."

He was clearly in shock. Then he tightened his grip on her face. "When? And how long—how long, goddamn you, have you known?"

She knew she was in jeopardy. A lie might save her, but only temporarily, for Edward knew the truth, meaning Slade would, too. She shook. "J-just be-before the wedding."

He stared into her eyes, furious but unmoving. *"God-damn you!"*

Regina shook visibly. "P-please release me." She would flee, come back another time. She was afraid of him.

He did not release her. Time stood still. Rage coursed through his body, lit his eyes. His gaze was murderous. He was unrecognizable.

"I'll come b-back a-another time."

His hands tightened on her face.

"P-please!" It was a cry of pain.

Abruptly he dropped his hands, spinning away from her. "Get out! Get out now! Get out now, damn you to hell!"

She was frozen.

"Get out!" he roared, whirling to face her. "Before I hurt you!"

Regina did not have to be told again. She fled. And from behind her, she heard a thunderous sound, the crashing of his desk as he overturned it.

Chapter 19

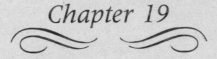

"This is a surprise," Xandria said.

Edward and Xandria had just stepped out onto Van Ness Avenue. He smiled at her. "A nice surprise, I hope."

She halted, regarding him with a look that was partly amused and partly seductive. "Are we talking about them—or you?"

Edward grinned. "We both know we're talking about me—and us."

"Is there an us?"

He had not taken his eyes from her for a minute. "What do you think?"

"I think you haven't changed one bit since you last tried—and failed—to seduce me."

Edward laughed. "Darling lady, I was not seducing you, I was consoling you, and gentleman that I am, I restrained myself from taking advantage of you in your grief."

Xandria was calm and still amused. "Edward, you were not a gentleman then, and I doubt you are now. And you did not restrain yourself—I restrained you."

"And of course, you have been regretting it ever since, lying awake at night, pining for me hopelessly."

She laughed. Then, suddenly serious and holding his gaze, she said, "Frankly, I have had a thought or two about you over the years."

Edward was also sober. "Hmm. That's a start. I hope they were indecent, improper, and scandalous."

"A lady never tells all, Edward."

They both smiled.

"It doesn't seem like four years, Xandria," Edward said. "I hope you have not gone and done something stupid—like remarry?"

"No, I have not. In fact, I have spent the past three years since coming out of mourning holding off any and all suitors."

Edward cast an admiring gaze over her lush, perfect figure. "And undoubtedly there were many."

She sighed. "Many, but none of them as honest as you. I fear my inheritance, both from Richard, my husband, and Father, was more of a lure than anything else."

"Don't sell yourself short," Edward told her. "Do you really have an appointment? And if so, may I escort you to it?"

"I have many appointments," she said with another wry smile. "I am the manager of the Mann Grande Hotel, you see."

"I'm impressed."

"And to think I thought you would only be impressed by a woman's figure and her face."

"Now you underestimate me. Is that your carriage?"

Xandria nodded, and they began walking across the street.

"You have changed," Edward remarked. "You are no longer the naive, grieving widow I met four years ago."

"So you have noticed?" She was pleased.

"I have most definitely noticed," he said, with obvious admiration.

"You have changed, too," Xandria said, unable to resist. "You are no longer a little boy."

"Darling, we both know I was not a boy, not even at eighteen, and I hope to reassure you soon that I am anything but little."

They paused beside her curricle. Xandria regarded him, no longer smiling. She had not one doubt he spoke the truth, and that she would soon be reassured. Very willingly, she was transported back in time, remembering being half-unclothed in his embrace and in the throes of hot, carnal desire. Heat unfurled in her loins.

Four years ago she had been a widow of several months. Edward had been a cocky, too-handsome youth. In retrospect she could understand how his kindness had turned into lovemaking. Fortunately for her, she had kept some of her wits, and had not let his hot kisses and hotter caresses go any further than that. Yes, she remembered very well. And he had gracefully accepted her refusal to culminate what they had started, and undoubtedly he had found satisfaction elsewhere.

The idea did not perturb Xandria in the least, although four years ago she had been shaken to the core of her being by their brief but passionate encounter. Then, there had been no small amount of guilt. How she had changed.

In the succeeding years, along with success had come confidence, and with confidence had come power. She was now a secure woman, one who had come to terms with who she was and her needs. She was a very content woman.

And she had not remarried out of choice. She was a wealthy woman and an heiress; she was also strikingly beautiful. Yet she discouraged every suitor, and as Edward had guessed, there had been scores of them over the past three years. It had nothing to do with pining for her dead husband, whom she had been fond of, but not in love with.

But it had everything to do with who she had since become. Xandria had worked very hard to achieve the success she had, despite her father's protests. She had started out at the bottom as a clerk, and it had taken two years to work her way to the top to become the general manager of the Mann Grande Hotel. She was a modern woman, a businesswoman, considered eccentric by many, and proud of it. Never would she marry again. That would mean giving up her life in order to manage her husband's household. It was unthinkable.

As it had turned out, she had discovered sometime after her husband's death that she possessed a strong libido. She was always discreet. Her father would never forgive her if he found out how she conducted herself. He was old-fashioned; he would not understand. She loved Charles dearly, and would never allow him to know the truth. So too, she cared for Slade, as much as she would if he were her real brother. But he was a prude. If he ever suspected that she had taken several lovers over the years, he would be shocked and disillusioned. Discretion was even more important to her than satisfying her appetite.

"Would you like to have supper with me tonight?" Xandria asked.

Briefly Edward was startled. Ladies, even eccentric ones, did not ask men out. Then his beautiful smile appeared. "I would love to have supper with you tonight, darling."

"Good. Is nine o'clock too late? We can dine in my office at the hotel. You can fill me in on what's going on with Slade and his wife."

Edward gave her a look. "I'm happy to fill you in any way you like, darling."

Despite herself, Xandria blushed.

Several hours later Slade threw down his pen with an oath. Ink splattered. He lunged to his feet and turned to the window. He stared down at Eddy Street but didn't see a thing. He could only see his wife's image there in his mind.

It was still unbelievable. That she wasn't Elizabeth Sinclair, that she wasn't James's fiancée—that she had never known his brother, his brother had never known her. Whenever he thought of all the sleepless hours of anguish, of the choking guilt he'd endured, he felt murderous.

She had put him through hell.

The lie had been monumental. There was no possible justification for it. And with the anger there was deep and bitter disappointment. She had the face of an angel, she spoke like an angel, she acted like an angel. But she was far from it. She was not a lady. Ladies did not lie. It was an act. She was an incredible actress, an incredible liar.

The betrayal was stabbing. He did not want to believe it.

He could not understand her motivation. He could not understand why she had married him once she regained her memory. After all, being both a Bragg and an aristocrat entitled her to a union far different, and far better, than the one she had made with him. Had she been infatuated with him? Perhaps, despite regaining her memory, she had still been filled with gratitude toward him. It did not really matter. She should have told him the truth. There was no excuse for such a deception.

She was also a far greater heiress than Elizabeth Sinclair had ever been. It was so ironic. It certainly made him pause. How could Rick, who had met Elizabeth, have made such a mistake? He did not think it possible. He was certain that Rick must have known her real identity and been gloating at the thought of a Bragg heiress marrying into the family. Not only had Regina deceived him, his father had, too.

He trembled with anger. Abruptly he wheeled and began pacing his office.

He was too angry now to care that he had hurt her by leaving her. Before her revelation, he had been unbearably moved by the anguish in her eyes; he had hated himself, even though he'd had no choice but to leave, thinking he'd made love to James's woman. Now it was almost funny. She didn't belong to James, so there had been nothing sinful in their liaison, in his love. Had he known who she was, he would have never left her. Had he known, there would be the bliss of paradise, not the pain of betrayal.

How far would she go to gain her divorce? For an instant he felt sick, realizing that even if she was not a lady, she must hate him very much to resort to an ugly, scandalous divorce.

His mouth tightened. He rebelled at the very idea. Which was ridiculous. There was nothing to be gained by staying married to her now. She despised him; he despised her. Such a marriage would be hell.

He tried to consider divorce. The sick feeling swamped him. It could not be possible, he told himself. After this betrayal, it could not be possible that he still harbored some affection for her. He refused to feel anything for her but anger and hate. Yet the truth was that hatred was an emotion that was out of the range of his grasp. No matter how hard he tried to summon it up, it eluded him.

He did not dwell on this failing, more disturbed than ever. He reminded himself that he had refused the divorce in a hot temper. That he didn't like being threatened, didn't like being bullied, and he didn't like being bribed, not by anyone, and especially not by her.

He also told himself that any feelings he still had for her were strictly carnal ones. And finally, here was the solid, undeniable truth.

He didn't have to think too hard or too long to remember every single detail of their wedding night. He instantly stiffened, aroused. The unbearable hunger he'd had for her had not dimmed. Indeed, guilt-free, it was stronger, more powerful, rawer than before. He sucked in his breath. It was the worst of reasons to remain married, but he would not be the first man who mindlessly obeyed the dictates of his cock.

He turned his thoughts away from sex with a great effort. She had hinted that she would fight him to obtain a divorce. He would be a fool to go into the ring with her father and the rest of her all-powerful family. Yet he had never turned away from a fight. If challenged, like all the Delanzas he fought, and he fought to win. But . . . the idea of battling her family distressed him, and not out of fear of the consequences.

Too upset and agitated to decide about a divorce now, he prowled his office, working off some of his anger and tension. He thought about his home. Miramar needed her. Or more precisely, her money. He would have no qualms now about using her after her deception. Undoubtedly, if he and she began a fight, it would not be easy to gain her inheritance. He had been in business long enough to know that her name alone would be enough to stall the bank until he could work out an arrangement with his wife. But the possibility existed that her family might choose to fight him indefinitely, and even her name could not buy Miramar that much time.

There was a brief, familiar knock on his door—a welcome distraction from his problems. Slade turned to greet his boss, mentor, and friend. Charles paused a beat before entering without permission. It was a long-established ritual. Charles knew there was really no reason to knock at all.

"It's getting late," he said in greeting. His iron-gray eyes were assessing.

Slade shrugged, knowing that this was not a social or a business call. "I'm buried."

"So I see." Charles smiled. "I never could understand how you can find anything on that desk."

After having overturned it, it was worse now than ever. "At least *I* keep records."

"Ah, but I keep everything up here." Charles tapped his dark bowler hat. "Besides, your kind of chaos is an indication of brilliance."

Slade flushed with pleasure. "Don't exaggerate."

"You know I don't exaggerate. Not unless I'm making a business deal. And you *are* brilliant. What would I do without you?"

"I'm not going anywhere, Charles."

"Good. I thought, perhaps, you might be returning to Miramar. Now that you're married."

Slade smiled in resignation and gestured to the seat in front of his desk. "So now we get to the point."

Charles didn't sit. He lightly clasped Slade's shoulder. "Let's go have a drink at the Palace Hotel."

"What? Not at the Mann Grande?" His tone was slightly teasing.

"I want to relax. More importantly, I want you to relax. And the Palace is closer."

Slade could easily refuse. He had not been productive since seeing Regina; he had intended to work very late in order to finish what he'd left undone. But he looked at Charles, needing very much to talk, and he agreed.

The Grand Court of the Palace Hotel was an atrium seven stories high and crowned with glass. Balconies looked down on the Court, often thronged with the hotel's guests, who were eager to catch a glimpse of what was going on below. The elite of San Francisco often chose to end their day there with a soft drink or something stiffer; then, too, the richest, most powerful men of the city might be caught there at any time of the day, engrossed in business and speculation. The wives of these men frequented the Court as well, especially in the afternoon. It was fashionable now to be charitable, and if these women were not immersed in gossip, they were plotting the latest gala in order to raise funds for any one of a dozen popular causes. The young publisher William Randolph Hearst often sent one of his newsmen there, or went himself, with the hope of sniffing out a story before it became a media jubilee.

Slade and Charles moved briskly through the Court. They were recognized instantly and both men nodded back at those they passed. Richly designed Oriental carpets were soft underfoot, while the many potted plants, all oversized palms, warmed up the very large, marble-floored atrium. Choosing a seating area in a corner well removed from the pianist, the two men made themselves comfortable, ordering bourbons on ice.

"Who is she?" Charles asked.

"Regina *Bragg* Shelton." Slade stressed her famous middle name. Had he said Rockefeller or Astor, he would not have surprised Charles more.

"Indeed! Slade, I am disappointed you were keeping your marriage a secret from me."

"Xandria tell you?"

"The instant she left your office."

He sighed. "Charles, it wasn't exactly a secret. And it wasn't a real marriage, not the way you're thinking. If it had been, I wouldn't have left her at Miramar."

"I was finding it hard to believe that you would leave your bride there."

Slade leaned forward as the white-jacketed Negro waiter brought their drinks. "I married her for her money, Charles, nothing more."

Charles was unperturbed. "Really? I find that somewhat out of character. You don't give a damn about money."

Slade explained Miramar's financial situation. He then proceeded to explain that Regina had had amnesia and everyone had assumed she was Elizabeth Sinclair, James's fiancée, himself included, and that he was to marry Elizabeth for her fortune. "It was to be a marriage of convenience only, because of James. I was giving her a home and, in her vulnerable condition, protection; she was giving Miramar the cash we so desperately need."

"That's quite a tale." Charles gracefully set his glass down. "Why didn't you come to me for help? I have many connections with many banks."

"Charles, if you could have helped, I would have. Don't forget, I have connections too, working for you the way I do. We can't handle another loan. I considered taking you on as a partner, but Rick would not hear of it. And even if we brought in a stranger, the kind of investment he'd have to make would give him a controlling interest in Miramar—and that's out of the question."

"What about a personal loan?" Charles asked. "Just between us. I would take your IOU. Slade, don't you know that?"

Slade was uncomfortable. "The thought had crossed my mind. But I don't think I could bring myself to ask."

"I know you can't," Charles said. "You've always given, but you never take. You've never asked me for anything, not in the ten years we've been friends. That's why I'm telling you that I would give you a loan, and you don't even have to ask."

Slade looked at him, trying not to reveal how moved he was. Deep inside himself, he knew he had been afraid to ask, afraid of being refused—afraid of not being important enough to Charles to be worthy of such aid. "Charles, we're talking about an incredible sum of money," he said unsteadily. "We need to make up two years of payments, and we need an influx of capital to turn the rancho into an agricultural operation, and we need enough capital to work for the next five years. At least."

"That *is* a large amount," Charles agreed. "I would lend it to you if you want me to."

Slade swallowed. "Thank you." He sighed. At least here was a way out of a crucial dilemma. Charles had come through for him. He should have had more confidence in their friendship, he should have known. "But it will be a last resort. Rick would object; in fact, he'd throw a fit. And it would be a long time before I could pay you back. Right now, I have some time. The bank will not move so soon after my marrying a Bragg. I'm going to use it for what it's worth."

"Bragg is a powerful name," Charles agreed. "I imagine she has the kind of inheritance you need."

Slade looked at his untouched glass of bourbon. Anger flooded him. "I might have had hesitations about taking her money once, but not anymore. She lied. I will never forgive her, never forget. Never will I trust her. She looks like an angel, but she is the farthest thing from it."

"What did she lie about?"

"She recovered her memory before the wedding." His voice was strangled. "I thought she was James's fiancée, but she knew she wasn't—and she didn't tell me."

Charles was still, then he leaned forward and gripped Slade's arm. "Let it out, son."

Slade shook his head wordlessly. Anger rendered him incapable of speech.

"Do you love her?"

He shook his head in denial. He did not, not anymore, and he would never admit to anyone that he had been foolish enough—and irreverent enough—to fall in love with her when he had thought her to be Elizabeth. He found his voice with an effort. "But I went through hell, Charles, thinking she was James's woman. Hell."

"So there *is* something there."

"Not love," Slade said harshly.

"I doubt you would be so upset if you didn't care for her."

"I have feelings for her, all right. The kind that belong in the bedroom."

Charles winced. "Are you trying to shock me? It won't work. I know you better than anyone."

"Sorry. I'm torn up. She wants a divorce. She *demanded* a divorce. We hate each other, but I don't particularly feel like giving her one." He didn't add that it didn't have very much to do with her money, either.

Charles patted his arm. "Why not let nature take its course? After all, she married you knowing who she was, and that certainly tells me something even if it doesn't speak to you. And you certainly could not have picked a better choice for a bride. Xandria told me she's not just lovely, but very genteel. Xandria has good instincts, as we both know, and she thinks Regina Bragg Shelton is perfect for you. I think a wife is something that has been long overdue, Slade. A wife and a family."

Slade was incredulous. "Dammit, Charles, she's not a gentlewoman. Xandria's wrong. Didn't you hear what I said? She's not a lady, she's a liar."

Charles smiled gently. "Son, if I were you, I would ask myself why she married you. Better yet, I'd ask *her.*"

Chapter 20

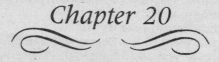

Charles was right. Slade *had* been asking himself why, his earlier attempts at explaining her behavior quickly becoming insufficient, and now he was going to ask her directly.

Determined, he rang the bell at the D'Archands' impressive home. It was late, past the supper hour, but this could not wait. He could not wait. The door was opened by a servant, one rightfully suspicious of him, for no one called at this hour uninvited. Slade announced himself. "And please inform Mrs. Delanza that her husband is here."

The butler's eyes flickered with surprise. "There is no one in residence by that name, sir."

Slade felt his temper ignite. She wasn't even using his name. He should have guessed. Obviously her intention was to gain this divorce secretly, so no one would even know she had ever been married to him. Not waiting for an invitation which would not be forthcoming, he strode past the butler and into the foyer. "Then tell Miss Shelton that her husband is here."

The butler was taken aback.

Before he could respond, however, Brett D'Archand strolled into the foyer. Slade knew the man. He was a smart businessman, yet an honest one. He was highly respected by everyone who knew him, Slade included. And generally, he was amiable enough. But not tonight. Slade braced himself for an unpleasant encounter.

"Looking for someone?" D'Archand asked wryly.

"I'm here to see my wife."

"Had you signed the papers today, you would not have to be here at all."

"But I didn't sign, now did I?"

D'Archand went to the point. "Why not?"

"I don't owe you an explanation. Where is she?"

"Let me confess something to you, Delanza. I am at a loss. It seems to me that you could be a very wealthy man if you were not working for Charles, if you were working for yourself. Yet that has apparently never interested you. But now you have married my niece for her inheritance. You never struck me as a fortune-hunter. Why?"

"As I said, I'm not going to explain myself to you. I have every right not just to speak with Regina, but to remove her from these premises. I suggest you get her down here immediately, before I decide to exercise all of my rights."

"You threaten me in my own home?" Brett was incredulous—and furious.

"Only because you give me no choice."

"Get out. Before I throw you out."

"I see I have no choice—unfortunately." Slade took a step forward. He would search the entire house if he had to, but he would speak with her this night.

Brett moved to intercept him.

"Stop it!" Regina cried, poised on the stairs.

Both men froze.

Regina swallowed, swiftly descending. "Brett, it's all right. If Slade wishes to speak with me, I will see him." Her gaze locked with Slade's. She was pale. "We never finished our conversation from earlier today."

Brett released Slade's arm. "You are not removing her from my home," he warned.

"That isn't—and wasn't—my intention," Slade retorted. But his regard was on Regina.

Brett relaxed slightly, looking from one to the other. "Fine," he said shortly. "Then I'll leave the two of you." But neither Regina nor Slade was listening to him. He suspected that they had not even heard him, and frowning, he turned and walked away.

Regina wet her lips.

Grimly, Slade stared at her.

"Why don't we sit in there?" She gestured at the open doors of a small, cozy salon just off the foyer.

Slade nodded, following her in. It was very hard to believe that this woman was not as she appeared. It was almost impossible to believe that she was not a proper lady—the very ideal of womanhood. It was not just her beauty, or her elegant and modest attire. It was everything. Her direct gaze, her demure airs, her gentle manners, her poise and grace, her femininity. Slade almost wondered if he had dreamed up her betrayal.

But of course, he had not.

And there was still the question he had come to ask. He turned and swiftly closed the salon doors.

"What are you doing?" Regina cried nervously.

He faced her, his expression intense. "I want to talk to you in private."

As pale as before, she nodded, trembling. She sat on the ice-blue sofa, clasping her hands in her lap, her knees pressed together. Slade realized she was more than nervous, she was wary, and perhaps afraid of him. She was so distraught that she had not even offered him a seat or refreshments. Not that the lapse mattered. He regretted throwing over his desk in his office as he had, knowing she had heard the noise and had undoubtedly guessed what he had done. He was angry—but he did not like her being afraid of him.

"Why did you lie to me?"

She gasped at the direct question.

"Regina—" He grimaced. "I still have trouble calling you by your name. Why?"

She shook her head.

Her knuckles, he saw, were white. He approached and sat beside her. She shrank away from him. Her eyes were wide, luminous. "Tell me," he demanded. "You must."

She lowered her gaze. "You rescued me, remember? I was g-grateful."

"So you lied to me in gratitude."

She pursed her mouth and shook her head again. "When I had amnesia, I grew fond of you. Or I th-thought so."

He was still. Except for his heart, which was pumping in mighty and painful bursts. "But it was an illusion."

She swallowed.

"Was it an illusion?"

"Y-yes. N-no. I mean, yes!"

"Make up your mind."

"All right, blast you!" she cried, greatly agitated. "It was a bit of everything! Does that s-satisfy you?"

"You were grateful. You were fond of me." There was no pain now. His words were a whisper.

Tears glistened. "I *was* grateful! I *was* fond of you!"

"And after you remembered that you were not Elizabeth Sinclair?"

"What does it matter?"

"You were still fond of me."

She stood and turned away, pacing. She had no intention of answering him.

"Admit it," Slade demanded. *She had been fond of him.* In full possession of her memory, she had still been fond of him—fond enough to marry him. Before, when overwhelmed with anger, he would have found any explanation irrelevant. No more. He was overwhelmed.

"No! It was a mistake," she cried, facing him.

He also stood, staring at her, in turmoil. "In other words," he said unsteadily, "you knew who you were, and still you wanted to be my wife."

Her shoulders shook. "It was only gratitude. And for a while, affection. Gratitude is not love. Affection is not love."

"No," he said, "gratitude is not love." He refrained from adding that affection was not far from the mark.

She turned away again, fighting tears. "What does it matter anyway? I do not wish to discuss my naiveté. I wish only to discuss our divorce."

The song in his heart was instantly silenced. She might have married him eagerly, but she did not want to be his wife now. She had come to her senses. "And I *don't* want to discuss divorce. Why didn't you just tell me the truth? We had already agreed to marry."

"I expected everyone to bring forth the real Elizabeth Sinclair once I made myself known. After all, Rick wanted the alliance with her, not with me."

Slade snorted. "Rick couldn't have been fooled, Regina. I'm certain he knew you were a Bragg heiress and has been counting your money for weeks."

She stiffened. "I have been wondering about that myself. It's horrible. But he must have known, Victoria undoubtedly told him."

"Victoria?"

"She knew. I'm not sure how. Someone went through my things and found my locket with my mother's— Jane Shelton's—picture in it, and my initials upon it. I am sure it was her. The locket was stolen the night you announced our engagement and she stormed away before supper. In any case, it could not have been too hard finding out the truth. Just the day after you brought me to Miramar, my uncle was in Templeton searching for me and posting a reward. Discovery was inevitable."

Slade was certain now that Rick had known, for if Victoria hadn't told him he could have gathered a few clues himself. "Damn him," he gritted. "Damn him." His father had also been responsible for the hell he had gone through in thinking he was marrying Elizabeth.

"I do not want to be another issue between you and your father," Regina said firmly, surprising him.

"You still care." The words were out before he could stop them.

"No. No, you are wrong, very wrong." Her furious gaze checked Slade's cascade of emotion, bringing doubt. "I only care about d-divorcing y-you."

"Then why are you crying?"

"I am—am n-not crying."

He could dispute her. Her eyes were tearing. He regretted leaving her now with every aching breath he drew. Hurting her had never been his intention. "Would it help if I repeated to you how sorry I am for hurting you?"

Vehemently she shook her head no. Tears streaked her radiant skin. She seemed even more furious at his words.

He hesitated. "If I'd known, I wouldn't have left you."

She laughed hysterically. "Words are free. Actions are costly. Your actions speak louder, and cost more, than any words could. *All* of your actions."

He did not comprehend her meaning entirely; indeed, he was afraid to. What was clear was that she now despised him enough to adamantly seek a divorce, and that she was judging him and finding him lacking on all counts. It hurt. It seemed he could not be immune to her condemnation, although he'd had so many years of practice at the hands of others he should be an expert at it.

It also seemed that her feelings for him had been tenuous to begin with. That would be perfectly logical. It would explain her about-face. But there was a possibility, a fragile one, one he should not broach, one he could not ignore. "Regina. You cared for me once. You could care for me again."

"No! I was sorely deluded!"

He stiffened. He slipped on an impenetrable mask. That she had once thought him to be some sort of hero had been a delusion and he was well aware of it. He was equally aware that there was a world of difference between them and that with her hating him now, he should do as she asked and give her a divorce and just walk away from her. Instead, he said, "We'll finish this another time."

"No!" she cried. "I want to finish this discussion now! Brett has a copy of those papers. Please sign them!"

He squared his shoulders. "No, Regina."

"No?"

He made his decision, an irrational and foolish one that was hopelessly against the odds. "I'm not going to divorce you."

"No? You have made up your mind?"

He walked to the door, where he paused. "I have made up my mind."

"Dear Lord, why? Why are you doing this?"

"Because James is no longer between us." With that, he let himself out.

Regina slowly descended the wide, graceful marble staircase, her hand on the wrought-iron banister. She gripped the smooth metal much too tightly. Why had Xandria Kingsly come calling on her? She anticipated what could only be a very ugly scene. She should have refused to see her, but for some reason, she could not.

She had not slept a wink the night before. Slade's visit had haunted her, appalling her, infuriating her. He had the utter gall to suggest she could come to care for him again—when he had deserted her, when he had this other woman in his life. It was a new day, but Regina could not stop dwelling on their confrontation of the night before. And now another confrontation loomed before her, one destined to be equally as distressing.

The majordomo, a short, impassive Japanese man, showed Regina to the morning salon, for it was just noon. The room was large and bright. Although the floor was the same tawny marble as the entire ground floor and the stairs, it was covered with a huge, custom-made Chinese rug that was vividly and predominantly gold. The entire room was done in many shades of yellow, so that despite the morning fog, the effect was inordinately cheerful.

Xandria was sitting on a floral-patterned chintz sofa. She wore a beautifully cut rose-red ensemble, the jacket fitted and designed to show off her small waist and full bosom, the skirts flaring just slightly after hinting at her full hips. Even her gloves, which she had removed, were a shade of rose. She smiled and stood up when she saw Regina.

Regina greeted her as politely as possible, given her stiff expression. Careless of whether they had refreshments, she sat on the other end of the sofa, facing her unwanted guest. She clasped her hands tightly in her lap. "This is a surprise, Mrs. Kingsly."

"I do not mean to intrude, Mrs. Delanza," Xandria said earnestly. "But I want so much to make your acquaintance."

Regina could not even begin to guess the other woman's motivation. And she'd had enough of this charade. "Let me be blunt, Mrs. Kingsly," Regina said coldly. "I have no idea why you would call on me. I can only guess you think me an utter fool. I assure you, I am not."

Xandria gaped at her.

Very angry and finally letting it show, Regina said, "I do not care one whit about your relationship with my husband. If Slade has not told you all, then I am happy to do so. I am divorcing him. As soon as that is accomplished, I shall be out of his life forever. And he shall be yours."

"Oh, dear," Xandria said.

Regina stood. It should not matter to her, but she hated the other woman. Jealousy taunted her. She should also be beyond crude speculation, but she wondered helplessly if Slade dared use his mistress as he had used her. The other woman had a certain look about her, a certain walk, a certain style, all timelessly seductive, and Regina did not doubt it.

"Mrs. Delanza, I fear you have jumped to a terribly wrong conclusion."

"Please." Regina gestured at the door.

Xandria rose gracefully to her feet. She was much taller than Regina. "I am not involved, in any way, with your husband! Except as a dear friend."

"Of course."

"Mrs. Delanza, Slade is like a brother to me! I have known him, and cared for him, for ten long years! Since he was a sulky little rebel! Do you really think we would carry on in such a manner beneath my father's nose?"

Regina was horrified as the woman's full identity began to dawn on her. "Who is your father?"

Again Xandria looked surprised. "Charles Mann."

The floor beneath Regina's feet felt as if it had tilted precariously. She sat down hard on the sofa. "Oh, Lord!"

Xandria sat beside her. "Are you all right?"

Regina could not believe the enormity of her mistake. She was red with mortification. She had been so quick to accuse and condemn. Uncontrollable jealousy had propelled her, not common sense. She was appalled with herself. "Oh! Please forgive me!"

Kindly, Xandria patted her hand. "There is nothing to forgive. Of course you could not know I was Charles's daughter. Stupid Slade! Why didn't he tell you?"

She bit her lip, not daring to look her guest in the eye yet. "He did not know what I was thinking." And she prayed he would never know she had made such a terrible mistake.

"Mrs. Delanza," Xandria said, suddenly smiling and amused, "do not fear. Your secret is safe with me."

Overwrought, close to tears, Regina finally met the other woman's gaze. Xandria winked. "Thank you!" Regina cried.

"I want nothing more than to be your friend," Xandria said simply.

Regina looked at her hands. "I see." She had to face the other woman, who had eased her heart immeasurably, and who was her co-conspirator now. "Mrs. Kingsly, I have erred greatly in my judgment of you. I am sorry," she began.

Xandria shrugged, smiling. "Do not dwell on it. I will let you in on my own secret. Other women do not like me. Especially because I am a widow who has chosen to remain unmarried. They see me as a threat. I can understand how you could make such a mistake." She laughed, the sound husky, genuine. "But it *is* funny. I can see that you do not know your husband very well."

"No, I do not."

Xandria gave her a pointed look. "Slade does not dabble in women."

A silence followed.

Regina could not restrain herself. Her aunt had said the exact same thing although in different words. "He does not?"

"No, he does not." Xandria stared at her. "Slade is not only highly moral, he is a prude."

Regina stared.

"You see, I have come here as Slade's champion."

Regina began to tremble. Slade's eyes, intensely passionate, and his haunting question—*Could you come to care for me again?*—seemed to threaten her resolve.

Abruptly Regina stiffened. She would not be seduced by his words. As she had pointed out to him, actions were significant, not mere words. She had mistaken his relationship with Xandria Kingsley, but he had deserted her. Had he cared one jot for her, even thinking her to be Elizabeth, he would have never been able to leave her after their wedding night.

Still, Regina raised her gaze to Xandria, when she should have sent the other woman away. But a part of her was thoroughly, breathlessly curious about what she might reveal about Slade. Cautiously, Regina said, "I do not think Slade is a prudish man."

Xandria laughed. "May I call you Regina? May we speak informally?"

Regina nodded, unable to stop herself from recalling their wedding night. There had been no prudery then.

"Slade is like a brother to me. If I were not so fond of him, and so concerned for him, I would not bother to impose upon you. I cannot tell you how delighted I was to find that he had finally taken a wife! And then I was shocked when I realized that he had not brought you back to the city with him, and worse, that you were living apart."

"He abandoned me, Mrs. Kingsly," Regina said simply, her color high. She regarded her hands, clasped in her lap.

"He hurt you."

Regina looked up. Her anguish, which just would not fade as easily as the anger had, showed. "Yes."

Xandria leaned forward. "Do you love him?"

Regina hesitated, afraid to inspect her own turbulent emotions. "I . . . I did. I . . . I d-don't know."

Xandria took her hands. "Slade is a dear, fine man! The two of you are made for each other! Trust me!"

"You are a stranger, even if a well-intentioned one. Please, do not ask me to trust you. Do not ask me to return to Slade. I cannot risk another broken heart, especially as this one is far from mended yet."

"Damn that Slade," Xandria said with a flash of anger. Then she sighed. "He is not an easy man. I know that as well as you. But could you not try a reconciliation? Slade is worth it, my dear. And if you do not go back to him, sooner or later you will lose him to someone else."

Regina was startled to find that the thought of losing him to another woman was very provocative. She did not like that idea in the least. "I don't know."

"Let me tell you about your husband, being as you do not know him that well. He is a dedicated, loyal man. Terribly dedicated and terribly loyal. He has been offered huge bribes to betray my father by Father's worst enemies, people who would love to see him fall, but he has refused. He has been offered great sums of money just to leave Charles, to work for the competition, but he has refused. Indeed, he works for Charles when he could be working for himself! Slade is selfless. He has no real interest in himself."

Regina could only stare.

Xandria saw her surprise, and her look became determined. "You did not know? He is loyal to me, too. If a man even looks at me the wrong way, well, Slade has dealt a blow or two, I am embarrassed to admit, on my behalf. You are his wife now. Even estranged, I can tell you that you have his complete loyalty." Xandria smiled slightly. "Which is why it's rather amusing that you thought me to be his lover. Slade would never break his marriage vows to you. Never."

Regina was helpless to stop the heady thrill that swept her at the thought of having Slade's fidelity—forever. "But he left me. That is not loyalty."

"I understand that he thought you were James's fiancée."

Ashamed, Regina nodded. How much had Slade told her?

"Slade is not a man who could marry the woman his brother once loved without being in turmoil over it. Assuming, of course, that he loved you himself."

"He does not love me."

Xandria raised an elegant brow. "That, of course, is something you would know, not I."

Regina met her stare. It was clear that Xandria thought Slade to be in love with her! "You are wrong," she said unsteadily. And there was no more fooling herself now. Her heart beat wildly with hope.

"Slade has been oblivious to all the fine ladies in this city for all the years that I have known him. There has never been a single romance, not one. And," Xandria went on candidly, "he does not keep a mistress. He does not even frequent saloons. He really is a most unusual—and much sought-after—man. But no lady has been able to win even his interest, much less his heart . . ."

Regina could supply the final missing words: *until you*. Xandria was determined to make a point. Regina was afraid to let her.

Xandria was barreling on enthusiastically. "And I cannot omit the fact that he is generous. So terribly generous! He is not a wealthy man, you must understand that, for he works for Charles on a salary. He is very frugal, he doesn't spend a penny on himself. He claims his needs are few. Yet what does he do with his savings? He gives most of it away!"

"He does what?"

"He is modest, so he will never tell you this, but the new orphanage in the Mission District was built solely by him. He alone contributed all of the funds necessary for the project. Over the years I have noticed that he seems to have a particular fondness for orphans."

"A fondness for orphans," Regina echoed. And she wanted to cry. Such an inclination was overpoweringly eloquent. Slade obviously identified with these poor homeless orphans.

Regina thought about the businessman she had confronted in his office, about the gentleman the fine ladies of San Francisco hoped to lure. She thought about the man who worked hard and loyally for another, not for himself, who lived frugally, who built orphanages. She did not know her husband. He was a stranger. It was as if Slade led a double life, and perhaps he did. Yet was it really such a surprise? Hadn't she seen his goodness from the start? Her very first impression of him had been that he was a hero and a gentleman, despite the facade he'd chosen to hide behind. Perhaps she knew all she needed to know about him after all.

"Do not give up on Slade," Xandria said softly.

Regina shook her head, until she was able to speak. "I knew, I knew all along, that he was a good man." She wiped her eyes. He was more than a good man, but damn him—he had left her, abandoned her, deserted her, making her life unbearable.

I would have never left you if I'd known.

Regina sucked in her breath. Could her masquerading as Elizabeth have really been so important to him? Did she dare take another chance on the complicated man who was her husband? There would be no in-betweens if she remained his wife. There would be only glorious happiness—or horrendous agony. Could she risk heartbreak again?

"If you sit here in your uncle's house you will never know him," Xandria said. "If Slade gives you your divorce and you return to England, you will never know him."

Regina looked at her, her resolve crumbling. Or had the disintegration already begun, yesterday in Slade's office, when she had first seen him again?

"Do not act in such haste." Xandria squeezed her hand. "And come to supper tonight. Come, please. Get to know your husband a little bit better before you decide what it is you will do."

That was only rational. It made perfect sense. But there was nothing rational about the incipient excitement flurrying to life within her breast. Mutely, Regina nodded, accepting Xandria's invitation.

Chapter 21

*I*t was five minutes past seven. Slade tried to look indifferent as he stole a glance at the Tiffany clock, set in heavy eighteen-carat gold, sitting on the white marble mantle. He poured himself a bourbon, his back to the center of the spacious salon where Xandria, Charles, and Edward sat, awaiting the last guest.

Edward and Charles were discussing one of Mayor Phelan's reform proposals, which was aimed at reducing some of the corruption in the city's government. Xandria was unusually quiet. Slade moved to one of the tall double windows, pulling aside the heavy emerald-green drape. He dimly heard the conversation. The afternoon fog had come in with the tide, but it was not thick, it never was, and he could clearly see the quiet street below. It was still light out, but by eight the sun would disappear and the city would be enfolded in twilight's mauve shadows.

She was late. He wondered if she were even coming.

Xandria had stopped by his office that afternoon to invite him for supper—and to inform him that his wife would also be a guest. Slade's reaction had been incredulity, excitement, and apprehension.

Yesterday he had made the decision not to divorce her. It had been spontaneous. Since then he had had plenty of time to dwell upon the myriad of possibilities a marriage might hold for them. He was torn. On the one hand there were dreams, unspeakable dreams, impossible dreams, and on the other cold, cruel reality.

Any feeling of betrayal for her deceit was long gone. She had not betrayed him. She had deceived him because she was afraid the real Elizabeth Sinclair would have married him in her stead had she told the truth. She had withheld her identity and married him because she had been fond of him. How easily he could forgive her!

But her feelings were in the past. Now she was furious and adamant about a divorce. Apparently she did not believe that had he known, he would have never abandoned her so cruelly. He thought that he could spend a dozen years convincing her—and it would not be too great a price to pay for their future. The thought would not leave him in peace: *if she had cared about him once, it could happen again.* He had always been a stubborn man, a determined man. It was a Delanza trait. Did he dare find out just how far his patience extended? For her, he thought it might span a lifetime.

But the circumstances had changed and he dared not delude himself for an instant. His wife was no longer an amnesiac named Elizabeth Sinclair. James no longer stood in their way, but now, it seemed as if the obstacles facing them might be even greater. She was a British aristocrat and a Bragg heiress. Under the best of circumstances, much less the worst, they did not suit each other. Even if he did succeed in bringing about a reconciliation, then what? She had already demanded a divorce just days after their wedding. Even if she did come to care for him again, how long would it last? A year? Two years, or even five? Could an upper-class noblewoman like her be happy with the kind of life he could offer her? Could she really be happy with him?

He was afraid. The possibilities, diametrically opposed, were both exhilarating and terrifying. What would the future hold? Happiness, or heartbreak?

It seemed as if he was determined to find out. Although it would have been safer, so much safer, to have signed those damn divorce papers, he was not going to do it. He could not bring himself to the point of irrevocably severing their relationship. He was unwilling to push her away, unwilling to walk away himself. Perhaps he was the one now being the fool. But it was too late, the die was cast.

Suddenly he spotted a luxurious carriage pulled by two fancy grays coming up California Street. His heart jumped. He was inexplicably nervous.

He turned as casually as possible from the window, straightening his necktie and cuffs. He had donned an elegantly cut tailcoat for supper, wanting to appear his best and hoping that his wife would be impressed. Meeting Xandria's eye, he managed a smile, hoping she couldn't see too much in his expression. The witch had dared to tell his wife that he was a prude. She had mercilessly teased him today with little bits and pieces of the conversation she'd had with Regina. She had even hinted that his wife would be amenable to his overtures. He could not believe it, but the mere thought generated no small amount of excitement. And bossy as Xandria was, she'd told him to be on his best, most charming behavior. Xandria was a busy woman, the least likely candidate to play matchmaker, but he was grateful for her interference today.

Regina was escorted into the salon by Mann's British butler. Slade tried not to stare as Xandria rose and swiftly went forward to greet her. As always, Regina was heart-stoppingly beautiful. And she had dressed, too. Her gold gown was worn off the shoulder, its fitted bodice crusted with topaz sequins, its draped skirts full and voluptuous. Her hair was upswept, revealing the long, elegant line of her neck, and her bare shoulders were smooth and round and an enticing shade of ivory. Her gown was low-cut but not enough to reveal any cleavage; still, it was enough to remind him of how she had felt in his hands on their wedding night. Regina looked exactly the way one would expect the daughter of an earl to look—elegant, sophisticated, genteel, and stunning. Not a hint of her passionate nature showed, and Slade could be sure that he was the only man to have ever glimpsed it, to have ever felt it, to have ever shared it. He gave up all his attempts not to stare. An unfamiliar and possessive emotion swelled his chest. Pride.

"Regina, I'm so happy you are here," Xandria said.

Regina nodded, her gaze slipping past her hostess to cling to Slade. "It was thoughtful of you to invite me."

"Please, come and meet my father. Charles, this is Slade's wife." Xandria was beaming.

Charles Mann took both of Regina's hands in his, holding them tightly. "May I kiss the bride?"

Regina returned his intent gaze. She had not been sure what to expect, but what she saw did not surprise her. Charles was an attractive man in his sixties with keen, intelligent eyes and a kind, warm expression. His grip was filled with both pleasure and acceptance. She sensed that he was everything she had imagined him to be, and more. She looked at Slade, standing rigidly by the windows, watching her. He had not moved since she had entered the room. Despite her doubts and despite the circumstances, she was glad he had found a man like this to be his friend.

Slade's eyes held hers. Her heart flipped in response. He said, "Go ahead, Charles."

Regina offered her cheek for the other man's kiss. Slade's look was intimate, matching his husky tone. She was trying to decipher his mood. She watched him as he crossed the room, his stride casual, yet heading purposefully to her. If her heart had somersaulted before, it was nothing like the acrobatics it now engaged in.

He was breathtakingly handsome, impossibly elegant, so urbane. He was, in short, devastating. She had never seen him in tails before. How could she have thought for a second that this man would not fit in with her friends and acquaintances back home? He would fit in anywhere; he would be at home if he had an audience with the queen.

He paused by her side, not making any attempt to touch her. "Hello, Regina."

For a moment they stared at each other.

Edward intervened. He strolled forward, standing beside Xandria. "I fear I shall interrupt this monumental reunion." He smiled at Regina, taking her hand and kissing it. "If my brother is at a loss for words, it is understandable. You are ravishing tonight, sister dear. When Slade shows you off to the city, there is going to be an uproar."

Regina blushed, but nevertheless found it impossible to keep her gaze from Slade. To her shock, he said softly, "He's right."

It was a compliment. Regina was so moved she almost burst into tears. Quickly she ducked her head, not wanting him to see how such simple praise could affect her so powerfully. She realized that she was putty in his hands. He had hurt her terribly; now he was pleasing her vastly. She was afraid, afraid he would hurt her again if she dared allow their marriage to continue. But how could she not give him another chance? And wasn't that what she was doing merely by being here now?

They sat in the salon with aperitifs. Although Charles took over the conversation, directing it at her, she was acutely aware of Slade, who had chosen to sit in a chair beside her. Despite the double life he led, she had expected to see some of the old Slade, but there was nothing volatile about him. The tension she felt emanating from him had nothing to do with anger. She was astute enough to know that it had everything to do with her.

"How do you like our beautiful city, my dear?"

"I love it. I always have. I have been here before, visiting my relatives, the D'Archands."

"Ah, yes. Fine people, Brett and his wife. Tell me, do you know the city well?"

"Not really."

Charles turned to Slade. "You are not thinking clearly, son. You are neglecting your beautiful bride to see to my affairs? That must be rectified immediately."

To Regina's surprise, Slade said, "I agree with you, Charles."

Charles smiled. "Why don't you show her the city? Take her to the Conservatory, wine and dine her on Kearny Street, tour our fabulous museums and art galleries. Take her to Chinatown." He smiled at Regina. "Have you ever been to Chinatown?"

"No."

"It's a worthwhile experience."

Regina glanced at Slade. She found the idea of his escorting her around the city exciting, even though she was supposed to be intent on obtaining a divorce. With every passing second, those intentions were fading.

She was staring at him. It was so hard not to. Slade was not the man she had married at Miramar, not completely, and seeing him like this was proof. She could barely tear her gaze from him. Every encounter they had had since her arrival in the city seemed to fill in the pieces of the puzzle he had kept hidden from her. She itched to know more, so much more, about him.

"What are you doing tomorrow?" Slade asked, his expression intense.

Regina was almost incapable of responding. "N-nothing," she quavered, his gaze making her shiver slightly. "I mean, I have no real plans."

"I'll pick you up at ten."

She should tell him no. She should, in fact, get up and leave the house at that very moment. Being with Slade was as dangerous as ever. The truth was, he mesmerized her, he fascinated her, and he had from the moment they had first met. He was making her forget everything, including how badly he had hurt her. Regina followed her heart, praying she would not regret it later. "I'll be ready."

Slade's eyes gleamed with emotion she was afraid to identify. She hoped it was more than triumph. And Charles clapped his hands in approval. "Very good! And you, Slade, I don't want to see you at the office for the rest of the week!"

Charles asked Regina to sit on his right at supper, as the guest of honor. He was smiling, clearly pleased to

be presiding over the small gathering of friends and
family. Slade casually took the other seat beside her.
She faced Xandria, who was stunning in a very daring
and very low-cut gown, one that was blood-red and
as straight as an arrow. Edward sat next to her, as
handsome as ever and impressively dashing in a white
dinner jacket and a black bow tie.

Supper was superb, an eight-course meal prepared by
Mann's French chef, who had previously been employed
in Paris. The service was flawless, as was the table.
It was set in Belgium linens with French crystal and
Waterford porcelain. The centerpiece was an exotic
tropical bloom that reminded Regina of orange-and-
purple birds. Xandria explained that the tropical motif
was the rage these days. Regina could have been dining
in any aristocrat's home in London.

Her husband was silent during dinner, but it was not
the kind of silence she had witnessed at Miramar. On
the one hand, he was relaxed in a way she had never
before seen him; on the other hand, she was certain
that he was as excruciatingly aware of her as she was
of him.

Conversation flowed freely along with the bordeaux
and sauvignon blanc, both from the Rothschild vine-
yards in France. Charles, Xandria, and Edward carried
on most of it. At the end of supper they lingered over
their dessert. Xandria said, "Father, why don't we all
enjoy an after-dinner drink together tonight?"

"I don't mind." Charles looked at Edward and Slade.
"Do you mind, gentlemen?"

"Not I," Edward said, turning his lazy glance on
Xandria. "I prefer the company."

She gave him a warm smile.

"You always prefer the company of females," Slade
said dryly. He was lounging in his seat. Regina's eyes
widened when she saw that he had placed his arm on
the back of her chair. His sleeve brushed the bare nape
of her neck.

"Unlike you," Edward retorted, "who is hard put to
notice even the loveliest of women entering the room."

Slade smiled. "I noticed tonight."

Regina's eyes flew to his. He had been drinking red wine quite liberally, but so had all the men. He did not appear in the least bit inebriated. And he *had* noticed her when she had arrived. He had been openly staring.

"Well, if you don't notice your wife, another man will," Edward said pointedly as they were served sherry and port.

Slade was unperturbed, shifting slightly, and Regina felt his knee against hers beneath the table. She could not even move. Her pulse had been waiting for just such a cue and seemed to riot. "If another man looks at my wife the wrong way, he will be more than sorry. And I am too polite to say in mixed company what his fate would be."

Regina turned and stared.

Slade smiled at her very slightly. She decided he was just a touch foxed. She was absolutely breathless. Whatever was going on? What kind of mood was this? What did his behavior signify?

Charles interrupted her thoughts. "May I have your attention," he said, tapping his spoon upon his empty wineglass. Everyone turned to look at him. In the dramatic pause that followed, Regina suddenly had an inkling of what was about to come.

Charles reached into his breast pocket and withdrew an envelope. "First I would like to toast the newlyweds."

Regina tensed. Her suspicions had been correct. She dared to look at Slade from the corner of her eye. His glance slid over her features one by one. She had actually expected some protest or anger, but his interest appeared to be focused solely on her, not on Charles. Then, startled, she felt his fingers glide over her bare shoulder, just once.

"Here, here," Edward said, standing. Xandria rose, too.

Charles said, "To peace and happiness, and, I hope, to love." He tipped his glass.

Edward and Xandria cheered and drank.

Regina blushed, not daring even to peek at her husband this time. He had not removed his hand from her shoulder.

Charles picked up the envelope. "This is one of the most pleasurable moments in my life," he said, suddenly gruff. "Slade, no real son could be dearer. Regina, you are a fitting bride for Slade, more fitting than you can know. This—" He waved the envelope. "—is a wedding present from both me and my daughter." He handed it to Slade.

Slade took the envelope, smiling slightly and apparently bemused. "Charles, you shouldn't have." He shook the envelope. "There's something heavy in here." He was wry. "A silver dollar?"

Charles laughed. "Go on, open it."

Slade turned to look at Regina, who was very still, her eyes fixed on his happy face. "There's something heavy in here," he told her. "Heavy and metallic."

She could not speak. But it was at that moment that she knew she wasn't going to divorce him. If he could be like this, then they had a chance. Then their marriage had a chance. And she was going to do her best to see that he stayed like this—a happy, contented man.

Slade opened the envelope and took out a key. His expression immediately sobered. He looked up. Very quietly, he said, "What is this?"

"Pack up your bags," Charles said, grinning. "Because that is the key to 1700 Franklin Street."

Slade looked stunned.

Regina gripped his hand. "What is it?"

But Slade did not look at her. He stared at the key. "That's the Henessy place," he said, so hoarsely his words were barely audible.

"You deserve it," Charles said softly. "A fitting home for such a groom and such a bride."

His hand, the key in it, trembled. "I can't possibly accept this." He still could not look up, not at Charles, not at anyone.

"The deed is already in your name. It is my pleasure, son."

Regina stared at Slade's profile. She thought that he was moved almost to tears. Gently, she touched his hand.

He blinked quickly and glanced at her, forcing a smile. His words were still low and rough; Regina had to strain to hear them. "It's a small mansion."

Regina nodded, hot tears spoiling her vision.

Slade finally raised his gaze to look directly at Charles. "I—I'm in shock. I didn't expect this. I don't know what to say."

"Slade, I am so very happy for you. Even though I suspect your destiny lies at Miramar, you will always have a home here, too. Close by, I might add." Charles smiled. His own eyes were moist. "But son, if you wish to sell it, I will understand. You know, too, that there is always a place for you here under my own roof."

Slade shook his head, at a loss for words. Regina dabbed unsuccessfully at her eyes. She didn't think she would ever be able to forget that moment. No wonder, she thought, Slade preferred San Francisco to Miramar. No bloody wonder.

Suddenly she realized that Slade had his arm around her shoulders and was pressing her to his side. "Thank you, Charles. I thank you, we thank you," he said hoarsely. And then he laughed, the sound rough but joyous music to her ears.

Chapter 22

~~~

*R*egina did not sleep. The evening spent at Charles Mann's played again and again in her mind. Slade had been relaxed as she had never before seen him. His easy smiles, his dry humor, his warm, intent regard were fast becoming cherished keepsakes. His slight, oh-so-possessive touch. And finally, the coup de grace, that unbearably heartwarming moment when he had realized the extent of Charles Mann's love.

Regina had been unable to restrain her own tears, tears she had shed for Slade, moved both for him and with him and relieved beyond belief that here, at least, was a father figure who loved him unconditionally.

Time after time, as sleep eluded her, she helplessly compared the evening to the several dinners they had had at Miramar. Time after time she compared Charles Mann, as unfair as it was, to Rick. The differences were heartrending. The warmth and caring that had flowed in abundance at the Mann household was the kind of ambience she expected among a family. She found herself regretful, she found herself angry. There was little warmth in Rick's home, at least as far as appearances went. Yet she knew Rick loved Slade as much as Charles Mann did—and more. She would gamble her entire inheritance upon it. Why in blazes couldn't Rick show it? Why did he have to taunt Slade, insult him?

Yet the Slade who prowled Miramar's confines was not abundantly likable. Why couldn't he relax and show Rick this side of himself? She was beginning to suspect that he deliberately pushed his father, that he sought to elicit Rick's insults. But why? And how had such a relationship come to pass in the first place? She was fiercely glad that Slade had a second family like the Manns.

Regina was determined to get to the bottom of the morass; she wanted answers. She wanted to see Slade and Rick in a relationship that, at the very least, did not resemble two fighting dogs being thrown into the ring eager to draw each other's blood. If there ever had been a reason for their animosity, there was no longer; it was time for both men to bury the hatchet.

Which Slade was the real Slade? She guessed that both sides were real, yet she did not think it was a matter of two different personalities. With a rush of heart-wrenching insight, Regina understood. She was reminded of a desert and a hothouse. In the desert only the hardiest, toughest species could survive; in the fertile garden of a conservatory the most fragile species could be coaxed into full bloom. Miramar was no desert, except emotionally. Slade had to be emotionally tough if he were to survive there. After all, he had been abandoned by his mother as an infant, left to a father who had favored his older brother and who seemed incapable of showing affection toward him. Yet with the Manns there was no need to be tough. His fragile feelings, his vulnerable side, carefully tended with love and compassion, could blossom, and they had.

Last night Regina had fallen in love with her husband again.

She heard the doorbell ring, echoing in the high-ceilinged foyer outside the salon. Breathless anticipation filled her. It seemed as if she had been waiting for Slade to come for her forever; actually, she had been waiting for this moment since the night before. How would they actually proceed from this new point in their relationship? For her it was a new beginning, and it seemed as if Slade felt the same way.

She was not sure what to expect. She was his wife, yet she was living apart from him, and she had asked for a divorce. He was calling upon her as if in courtship, yet only a few days ago he had abandoned her. So where did that leave them? If he brought up the subject of a divorce again, she would tell him that she had carefully thought it out and changed her mind. Yet she did not think she was ready to take on the full role of being his wife. She had been so badly hurt that she was still wary. He would have to earn back her complete trust.

Slade was shown into the salon. Regina ceased her anxious pacing before he came to the open doorway. Their glances locked instantly. Her eyes widened and her heart rate doubled.

She wasn't sure what she had expected, but it surely wasn't the highly fashionable statement he made. His white, double-breasted sack jacket was the latest trend, and coupled with pale off-white trousers, it was the epitome of classic, casual elegance. He even wore soft white sport shoes. His hair had been meticulously combed into place and was parted neatly on the side. He even carried a straw boater, although she could not picture him in it.

Regina realized that she was openly admiring him. Then she saw that he was too involved in gazing at her to have noticed, and she flushed with pleasure. For she had dressed with great care, too, hoping to please him. She knew the bronze-and-cream-striped suit she wore was flattering both to her figure and her complexion. And Slade was most definitely pleased; his gaze was bright and appreciative. Regina felt herself blushing, as if they had not shared every intimacy possible between a man and a woman. Yet when she smiled, she suddenly felt as shy as a debutante.

His smile was not the least bit shy. And his tone was equally suggestive. "Hello."

"Good morning . . . Slade."

He moved forward and took her arm. "It's cool outside. You need a wrap."

His concern, simple as it was, pleased her immensely, as did his possessive gesture. She was intensely aware of him as they left the house after retrieving a cape for her. He guided her down the wide, white stone staircase and past the carefully cropped green lawns that swept up to the city sidewalk. A small curricle awaited them with a dainty chestnut in its traces.

"I like to drive," he said, handing her up and then jumping in beside her. "Do you mind?"

She shook her head no. She was too aware of his body beside her, with only a few inches separating them. She gripped her hands in her lap. She had not forgotten their wedding night for one instant, although she had tried to ignore those particular memories whenever they intruded too far into her thoughts. Now she remembered just what it was like to be in his arms, naked, while he plundered her body. She shivered, trying to control her mind. He slapped the reins and the pretty chestnut mare trotted forward eagerly.

"I thought we'd drive through Golden Gate Park first, being as it's early." He glanced at her. His eyes moved over her face, lingering on her mouth.

"That's fine." She wanted to see the house on Franklin Street, their wedding present from Charles. She was afraid to ask, afraid it was too bold and sudden a declaration of her new intentions to remain his wife. She bit her lip. "What Charles did last night—it was simply stunning."

"Yes, it was."

Regina looked at Slade. "He loves you dearly."

"I'm very lucky," Slade said quietly. "He means a great deal to me, too."

She wondered if he were thinking of Rick, as she was. The two men were so different. She was saddened whenever she thought of the two lives Slade led. She shifted, unable to restrain herself. "Slade? Rick loves you too."

Slade tensed. His face darkened. When he looked at her his eyes were flashing with anger; the old Slade was back. "Don't ruin things."

Regina swallowed any further comments she might have made. She had not realized how easily she could chase away the happy man and bring forth the angry one. "I'm sorry," she whispered, meaning it.

"Don't be," he said roughly. "It's not your fault." Then he added casually, not looking at her, "I went there last night."

She did not understand. "Went where?"

He glanced at her, his gaze intense enough to rob her of her breath. "The Henessy place."

She was still. "I see."

He turned his head, staring out past the chestnut's ears.

"I would like to see it, too."

He jerked toward her. "You would?"

"Yes," she breathed, caught up in his gaze. "Very much."

Slade suddenly smiled, abruptly turning the mare in a tight about-face. There was something recklessly triumphant in his expression. "Good," he said. "Because I want to show it to you, Regina."

"That's it," Slade said quietly, making no move to leave the carriage.

Regina looked at the three-story house in front of them. The fog had evaporated and the day was brilliantly sunny. It was indeed a small mansion. The house was built of reddish stone and trimmed with white plaster. The front door was a temple front. The pediment above was detailed with a large round window and a curling leaf-like design, supported by two white columns. A tower stood behind it. The center of the house, which was asymmetric in layout, crescendoed to the roof which rose steeply above the front tower and above a second tower on the house's other side. Three stained-glass arched windows were set in pillars and plaster on the top floor. The roof was mansard.

Cornices, scrollwork, and rosettes divided each floor. The details would have been overdone except for the fact that the house was so grand. It was so very typical of the latest wave of architecture to hit the city, and Regina loved it instantly.

"Well?" Slade asked, tossing his jacket onto the seat between them.

"It's beautiful."

"I've always admired this place. It's grand but not ostentatious, detailed but not silly. You want to go in?"

Her gaze leaped to his. "Of course."

Slade helped her down. Regina thought his hands remained on her waist a touch longer than necessary, but said nothing, because his touch was no more unnerving than the complete set of circumstances they were in. He was her husband, but she felt inexplicably nervous around him; they were estranged, but she could only think of this house as their house. Still, he acted like a husband, taking her wrap from her shoulders while saying, "You don't need this." The sun had chased away the morning fog and he left his jacket behind as well.

They walked up the front steps. Regina was overwhelmingly aware of the man she was with. She fidgeted as Slade fitted the key into the lock. He glanced at her and threw open the door.

She wondered just what was on his mind.

"Oh," she said, glancing around the large foyer. The ceiling was three stories above them, making the entrance inside more impressive than it had seemed from the outside. The foyer was vast, appearing more so because it was unfurnished and the pink-and-white-checked marble floors carried one's eye relentlessly down the hall. The walls were painted salmon-pink.

There was a skylight above them, one that could not be seen from the street, and sunlight drenched them. Regina turned to Slade, realizing he was watching her very intently, his eyes gleaming. His look caused a prickle of foreboding. "This is beautiful."

He cocked his head and Regina stepped past him, accepting his silent invitation. She was growing more and more aware of the fact that they were alone in this huge empty house. Their footsteps echoed loudly on the stone floors, as had her voice when she spoke. She paused on the threshold of a ballroom with vaulted ceilings. A pair of heavy gilded chairs, terribly ugly, had been left behind, set against one wall. The other wall was mirrored; Regina thought that the effect was interesting. Tall French double doors faced them and looked out onto the house's gardens, which were terraced and abundantly in bloom.

Slade stood behind her, saying nothing.

Regina's nervousness increased. Swallowing, she walked across the room, leaving Slade standing in the doorway, and gazed out on the lawns. She could feel his eyes upon her back.

She turned slightly, and glimpsed him in the mirror. His expression was unguarded and fierce; hungry. The fine hairs raised on the nape of her neck. But she did not move.

In the mirror, she watched him slowly cross the room and walk up behind her. His footsteps resounded hollowly. Her skin felt tight. Her breasts seemed to tingle against the delicate lace of her underclothes. It was occurring to her that his intentions in showing her the house were not legitimate, or, if they had been legitimate, they were no longer. But she did not move. It had only been a few days since their wedding, but the interim felt more like long, agonizing years. She hugged herself, but did not face him. She didn't have to, for she had one eye on the mirror.

He stopped behind her. "Well?"

"I like it." Her words sounded choked. They echoed. Every nuance in her voice was magnified a hundredfold.

"So do I." His words echoed also. Then his hands touched her shoulders.

"Slade . . ." His touch was light, yet her body was quivering uncontrollably. His mouth touched the side of her neck. *Slade.* For an instant as she stood there while he nuzzled her, she thought she had spoken his name again. But she hadn't. It was the room, not only echoing her but mocking her, for her tone sounded like that of a seductress, husky and desperate.

"I like this," he whispered, his arms sliding around her. *I like this . . . I like this*, the room chanted back.

Regina stood stock-still, swept up by both the room's reverberations and the feel of his hard, aroused body pressing very firmly against hers. He continued to nuzzle her neck. Even had she the willpower to walk away, she would not have been able to, for he held her tightly, determinedly. She gulped air, gasping. The strangled sound chorused. His hands slid down her belly, splayed out. They paused above the juncture of her thighs.

"Slade," she protested very weakly. "Someone might walk in." *Slade . . . someone might walk in.*

His hand slid lower, cupping her intimately through the folds of her thin summer-weight skirt and petticoat. "I locked the door." The room chanted its refrain.

She shut her eyes, trembling. He had planned this, but the rocking motion of his large palm was making it hard to care. He extended his fingers and rubbed harder and lower. All of her clothing was silk, even her drawers, and the sensation was almost unbearable. Regina cried out. The room cried out.

Through the layers of fabric he delved between her legs, expert and relentless. She began to shake. And then she began to sob with pleasure.

Her cries echoed outrageously. Even when the peak had passed, Regina heard herself and was horrified. She tried to pull free of Slade but he had no intention of letting her go. Instead he was propelling her forward, but holding her so firmly that his body remained pressed against hers. "No, sweet, no," he panted in her ear, his phallus so distended that it stabbed her like a steel arrow. "Regina, don't say no, not now."

Regina, don't say no, not now . . .

His plea echoed not once but twice, the hoarse sexual need amplified in the waves of crushing, erotic sound.

Regina was pushed toward one of the gaudy gilded chairs. As he moved her forward he was also pulling up her skirts in the back, his hand sliding along the curve of her bare buttock and pushing down her filmy white drawers. Being in motion, she stepped right out of her knee-high pantalets.

He gave her no choice. His other hand guided her quickly, pushing her forward and down, and Regina found herself breathlessly bracing her palms on the hard wooden seat of the chair.

He kissed her neck wildly, also bracing himself on the chair, pressing his erection against her backside. Regina groaned, arching stiffly and allowing his hand to slip down her buttocks and beneath them. She cried out again when his palm slid between her legs. This time he pushed two fingers into her hard.

She whimpered uncontrollably. Her groans had yet to fade, and now her whimpers echoed dramatically, overlapping them. She was aghast, dismayed with the cacophany she was creating, yet her body was experiencing an urgency that was beyond any semblance of control. She pulsed heavily around his hand. She was only an instant away from begging him for even more; for the heavy, thick feel of his heat and hardness deep inside her. He thrust his fingers deep into her again and she could not stop herself. She wept amid another mind-shattering spasm.

Her sobs rang around them. "Yes!" Slade shouted frantically. "Yes!" His words resounded, blending with the fading strains of her echoing sobs. He slid the massive length of his phallus into her.

Regina cried out exultantly. The room reverberated as Slade held her hips and began a determined rampaging. Regina heard herself encouraging him, not once but three times, heard herself begging him, every plea she sobbed repeated in a near-endless chorus, as if the empty room had a mimicking voice of its own and was determined to outdo her.

Slade gripped her and surged into her. Regina convulsed again, sobbing his name, and Slade cried out.

The room was spinning around her. *Slade . . . Slade . . . Slade . . .* it chanted. She collapsed but Slade held her upright, his arms clamped around her to prevent her from crashing to the floor. She listened to the wild echoing of the room as her voice faded and finally died. She listened to herself, abandoned and in the throes of ecstasy.

She trembled. She remembered the mirror, one more unbelievable fact, and dared to peek to her side at it. She looked every bit as wild and wanton as she had sounded. Her hair had spilled free of its chignon. As he stood behind her, Slade had his arms wrapped around her rib cage, pressing upward against her breasts, making her appear dramatically voluptuous. Her skirts were up around her waist in the back, her buttocks starkly white and lush, pressed against Slade's naked groin. He wore only his shirt; he must have kicked off his pants at the crucial moment.

She closed her eyes. Heat flooded her. She should not have looked. And dear God, the noise. She would never forget those sounds. But just remembering, with the image of the two of them in the mirror, made her pulse heavily again.

"It was as good as the last time," Slade breathed against her neck. He kissed her there.

"Awful," Regina managed to whisper. "It was too awful." Then she winced, because the oversized ballroom was not through yet, and it eagerly repeated her words.

His arms tightened. "You were as excited as I was. Don't deny it."

You were as excited as I was . . . Don't deny it . . .

His tone stirred her senses. It was husky, low, and so obviously carnal when amplified by the empty room. She didn't speak. Denial would be ridiculous.

Slade shifted his face and she knew he was regarding them in the mirror. "Slade," she protested thickly.

He began lifting up the front of her skirt.

"No," she whispered, while the room whispered back, and despite herself, she turned her head and watched.

The luxurious fabric crept up her ankles and then her shins, revealing slim, curved legs clad only in pale hose. He bared her knees. She felt faint, yet was incapable of looking away. The garter she wore was frilly with lace and edged in purple ribbon. She opened her mouth to tell him he must stop, he must, but in the end she said nothing.

He lifted the skirt higher. Her naked thighs were ivory-white and lushly curved. Regina shook. Behind her, Slade's member rose hotly, pressing against her buttocks. He pulled the skirt up past her navel.

"No," Regina breathed, not meaning it.

No, the room breathed, desperation laced with desire. *No*.

Slade slid his free hand down the smooth white skin of her belly and into the brown hair at her groin. "You want me," he said thickly. He made no attempt to keep his voice down. As if he enjoyed the mocking walls.

She shook her head while his words were repeated in hoarse echoing tones.

He laughed slightly, roughly, sexually. His laughter echoed and swelled, reverberating around them, while his fingers spread her. Regina sagged against him. "Please," she cried wildly. *Please. Please.*

"Please this?" he asked roughly, delving deeper into her depths.

"Yes," she half-sobbed. She dared another glance at the mirror. She was no longer shocked and no longer appalled. Her body was too intent for her to be appalled.

He lifted her abruptly and sat her down in the chair. He did not pull her skirts down, but pushed them further up. Before Regina could protest he gripped her chin hard, kissing her mouth savagely. She gripped his face and kissed him back, their mouths fusing, their tongues sparring recklessly.

Slade suddenly slid to his knees on the floor. He pushed her thighs open wide. Regina cried out at the onslaught of his tongue. He held her open with his thumbs, his tongue a relentless, silent invader. Regina shook wildly, and accidentally glimpsed them in the mirror.

Too late. It was too late to protest and too late to stop. She gripped his head, flinging hers back, sobbing ecstatically, her wild cries filling up the room, amplified a hundred times over. When she slumped back in exhaustion, her cries continued to wash over them. He rose lithely to his feet, slid a hand under her to lift her, and thrust into her again. An instant later he yanked the chair from behind her so that her back found the wall. She rode up it, pushed there by his pounding. Seconds later that dissatisfied him, too. He sank to the floor, taking her with him. He plunged wildly into her again.

Regina was no longer tired. She gripped him savagely, crying out in encouragement, spurred on by the fever-pitch of his excitement and the mad echoing of the room. His heavy panting resounded. The slapping of their bodies reverberated. Her cries echoed. The room was filled with sound after sound crashing over them. His breathing reached a crescendo. Amplified as it was, it sent her over the brink. He followed, this time shouting his release.

Once again, Regina could not believe what they had done. She lay on the bare, cold floor, naked to the waist, Slade beside her. His arms were around her. One of his hands cupped her breast possessively.

She did not regret it. She was shocked at what they had done and at her own uninhibited participation, but she did not regret it. Not quite calm, not quite collected, she pulled her skirts down. She dared to look at Slade, and saw that he was amused. But it was not his amusement that startled her, it was the tenderness of his expression.

"You don't have to hide from me," he said softly. When his words echoed, he smiled.

"I don't want to," she confessed in a small voice. "But I think it's only proper."

He laughed then. She grew still. The lines around his eyes had deepened with his laughter. Then he grew serious, gazing back at her. "I'm glad you're proper, Regina. I want you to be proper. You are such a lady that I cannot really believe you would want me. But I never want to see propriety when we're making love."

Despite herself, she blushed. "I don't think you have to worry about that." She was thrilled. He could berate her for her passionate nature, he could find it defective, as many husbands would, but he did not. How lucky she was.

"No," he agreed, pleased, "I don't think so." He began plucking at her nipple.

Amazingly, her whole body began yearning for his touch and invasion again.

"I will never be able to get enough of you," he whispered. "You are so beautiful—and so perfect."

She was anything but perfect, as this moment showed, but she would not dispute him. Tears filled her eyes. "You are beautiful, too."

"But not perfect."

Her gaze, which had been on his lean hands as they stroked her, flew to his. She breathed in relief when she saw he was smiling. "No, not perfect. But it does not matter to me."

His eyes darkened. He gripped the lapels of her jacket and pulled her beneath him. Regina lay absolutely still. He leaned over her. "Am I forgiven?"

She did not have to ask to know he was referring to his desertion of her. "Yes."

He looked at her, his eyes blazing, then he began opening the buttons of her shirt, slowly and one by one. "I want you naked," he finally said, hoarsely. "I want to see you naked. This time, I want you naked in my arms when I take you—with nothing between us."

And his words rebounded, echoing loudly.

Chapter 23

*S*lade stepped through the door of his house on Gough Street. The hallway was shadowed even though the sun had yet to set outside. He flicked on a hall light but made no move to go up the stairs.

What in hell was he doing?

He had just left Regina at her uncle's after promising to call on her tomorrow morning. After they had left the Henessy place, the afternoon had been spent in smiles. He hadn't ever experienced such a glowing mood before; he had certainly never been so sated. The repletion was not just physical and he was astute enough to realize it.

But the glow had dissipated when he'd left her. In its place came doubt.

He had set them on a course today, one leading to a reconciliation. It would not take much to bring that about now. And he wanted a reconciliation. He wanted her. There wasn't anything he'd ever wanted as badly as he wanted his wife, and not just physically. But Jesus, she had already been prepared to leave him once. Now they were lovers again, with all the intimacy such a relationship entailed. He wanted to go farther, he wanted to get in deeper, but he was afraid.

For today had been capped with another monumental

decision. He could not take her inheritance. He could not use her. He would have to take the loan Charles had offered. And soon he would return to Miramar to begin the long, arduous task of transforming the rancho into a profit-making enterprise. If he reconciled with his wife, she would go back to Miramar with him.

A life of frugality awaited them there. It would be many years before he could begin to keep her in the manner she was accustomed to. Could she adapt to such a simple life-style? Could an elegant woman like her accept the duties of aranchero's wife? Could Regina be happy at Miramar? He hoped so. He wanted to believe so. But he could not be sure.

Frustration swept through him. Just when his life had never been brighter, it had never been darker. He was angry. It was like shooting in the dark at a ghost. He wasn't exactly sure what he was angry at, or who. It certainly wasn't Regina. He suspected it might be himself, for not being able to give her all that he wanted to give her, all that he should be able to give her.

He sighed and moved up the stairs, entering his bedroom. The small double bed was made up, but messily. He ignored a pile of clothing on the floor and began removing his tie. Stripping, he returned his jacket and trousers to the armoire, while his socks, underwear, and shirt fell by the wayside. He stepped into the small bathroom, running the tub.

Footsteps sounded in the bedroom. Slade shifted on the edge of the porcelain tub so he could see into his room. A small Chinese boy skidded to a stop. "Mista Slade! You home!"

Slade grinned. "What are you up to, brat?"

"Work-work in kitchen," Kim told him with a grin.

Slade doubted it. Kim couldn't cook, not that there was anything to cook with downstairs, although perhaps he was doing some cleaning. "There's a sack on the bureau with your dinner in it."

Kim's eyes widened with expectation. "Joe's Ribhouse ribs?"

"Isn't that what you asked for?" Slade stood and got into the tub.

"You want me washee back?"

"Get lost, kid," Slade growled. Kim was teasing him, though, because he knew Slade had never let him wash his back and never would. Kim ran out of the room, undoubtedly to feast on Joe's Ribhouse ribs.

Slade dressed to go to the office, even though it was late. He didn't really think he would be able to get any work done, not given the circles his brain was running in, but he felt compelled to try. He was silently moving down the stairs when his doorknocker sounded.

His heart immediately skipped. His first thought was that it was Regina. Yet he had just left her, not even a half hour ago. No, a lady like his wife would not come calling, especially at this hour.

He opened the door. His father stood there, a small bag in his hand. "Glad you're home, boy."

Slade was stunned. Rick had never visited him in the city, not once. Then he shrewdly realized that in the past he hadn't been married to a Bragg heiress whose funds Rick was undoubtedly itching to utilize. Slade stepped aside, somewhat reluctantly, to let his father in. "This is a hell of a surprise."

"I'll bet. Edward here?"

"Edward comes and goes. What do you want?"

"What do I want?" Rick set the bag down. "I spend all goddamn day on a hot train and that's the greeting I get?"

"That's the greeting you get. 'Cause I don't believe this is a fatherly social call."

"Well, it is," Rick said. "Do we have to stand in the hallway?"

Slade shrugged, following his father into the parlor which was just off the entryway. He never used this room. Which was why it was in perfect order.

Rick spotted the side table with its decanters and crossed to it, pouring them both drinks.

Slade hadn't felt like drinking all day, except for the single glass of wine he'd had with the late lunch he and

Regina had shared, but now he accepted the bourbon. "Let's not beat around the bush," he said softly.

"Okay," Rick agreed, settling down on the overstuffed sofa. He glanced around. "This place is shit."

Silently Slade agreed. Since he was only renting it, he had hired someone to furnish it for him. The decor was not to his taste. The sofa was too large, the fabric too bright; the wallpaper was too cute, the bric-a-brac unnecessary. The table on his left was cluttered with framed photographs, but he didn't know a single person in them. He sighed. He just didn't feel like a down-in-the-dirt battle today, if the truth be known. "Yeah, well, I'm rarely here."

"Where's the wife?"

Slade tensed. "So now we get to the point."

"She here? I want to say hello to the little lady."

"No."

"She's not here?" Rick stood, dismayed. "You didn't give her the divorce, did you?"

Slade clenched his teeth. "No, I didn't."

Rick was relieved. "Don't forget she holds the key to Miramar's future."

"I haven't forgotten. You knew all along, didn't you? That she was a Bragg heiress, not Elizabeth Sinclair?"

Rick's eyes widened. "I did not!"

Slade decided to debate the issue, which rankled. "I don't believe you, Rick."

Rick threw up his hands. "Dammit, all right! I guessed."

"You know what?" Slade was livid. "You are a son of a bitch."

"I did it for you!"

"You did it for yourself. You did it for Miramar!"

"I also did it for me and for Miramar," Rick told him firmly. "But if she wasn't such a perfect little lady, with you hot to trot on her heels, I wouldn't have done it."

Slade stared.

"You need that gal, boy, an' we both know it! You need a proper little lady for a wife, and a few cute little kids, too. You need the whole kit an' caboodle an' you have for years."

Slade's eyes narrowed. Rick was right, so goddamn right. He needed Regina Shelton. He needed her proper manners, her good breeding, her generosity, her compassion and her smiles. He needed her passion. He needed her, period. And if she would give him a family . . . his heart lurched. But it was all such a big *if.*

Slade crossed his arms. "I find it hard to believe that you would play matchmaker."

Rick grinned. "Well, I did. So believe what you want. But if you tell me you don't like her, I'll tell you you're a liar."

Uncomfortable with the idea of his father acting with anything other than selfish motivation, Slade changed the subject. "Charles offered us a loan."

"No."

Slade was well aware that Rick would hate the idea of being beholden to Charles. Borrowing from his friend still bothered him, but not as much as the idea of taking his wife's money. "I'm going to accept, unless you can think of another way to get enough cash to pay back the banks and operate for the next five years."

"No, goddammit!" Rick was furious. "I won't take a goddamn cent from Charlie Mann." He tossed down his drink, calming. "Your little wife is an heiress."

Slade said nothing. It wasn't Rick's business that he would not take Regina's funds. Rick had bamboozled him many times, so he felt little remorse in making this deal with Charles on the sly.

"Where is she?" Rick asked.

"She's staying with her relatives, the D'Archands."

"Well, that's great! A wife is supposed to live with her husband. You have to patch things up with her soon, boy." Rick left it unsaid that he was counting on her inheritance and counting down the days before foreclosure.

Slade coiled up tight. Deep inside he wanted nothing more than to have Regina living with him. He had almost asked her if she had changed her mind about a divorce, had almost asked her to move in with him. But he hadn't. That would be the final step, completing their reconciliation. It wasn't the doubt that had prevented him from asking her to return to him—it was the fear. "Listen, old man, don't get on my back. Your interest in my marriage may or may not be one hundred percent selfish, but it is *my* marriage and I'll handle it my way."

"*Are* you handling it?" Rick asked. "I don't see how you can be handling it with the two of you living apart!"

Slade took a sip of the bourbon. He remained calm with an effort. He really didn't want this additional headache right now. Saying nothing, he summoned up Regina's lovely image. It was infinitely soothing.

Rick seemed puzzled at his failure to respond. "So why isn't she here, where she belongs? Or rather, why aren't the two of you at Miramar, where you both belong?"

Slade set his glass down. "Can you really see her living at Miramar? For any length of time?"

Rick frowned at him. "What kind of question is that? Of course I can. What the hell is going on in that head of yours now?"

Slade had the urge to tell Rick everything, to spill his guts, but that was insane. "She's not exactly a country girl."

"So what? I haven't met a soul yet that didn't fall in love with Miramar, sooner or later."

Slade said nothing. Rick was prejudiced, but then, when it came to Miramar, so was he.

"Look," Rick said, jabbing his finger at him, "don't go tilting at windmills. Bring her home an' it will all work out. She's your wife now, or do I have to remind you of that, too? You both belong at Miramar, with me, not up here working for some goddamn stranger!"

"You don't have to remind me," Slade said grimly.

"Sure as hell doesn't seem that way. Have you even talked to her since she arrived in the city?"

"I've talked to her." Slade couldn't help it, he smiled, remembering. "I've seen her." He actually volunteered information, surprising himself. "We spent the day together. I took her to the Cliff House for lunch."

Rick beamed. "That's good to hear!" He came forward. "Speaking of food, I'm starved. Let's go get a bite to eat."

"I just ate," Slade said. "But I'm going back to the office. I'll drop you wherever you want to go." He turned and strode out of the room. His back was to his father so he did not see Rick's disappointment.

Regina looked at the small boy standing in front of her, holding out a note. "From Slade?"

"Yes, missee, from Mista Slade." He beamed.

Regina could not smile back. Dismay swept through her. Slade was already late. He was supposed to have picked her up at half past ten, but it was almost eleven. She didn't have to read the note to know that he was not coming after all.

Dear Regina, an emergency has arisen, requiring my immediate attention. If I can clear things up, I will call on you tonight. However, should you have other plans, do not cancel them on my account. Yours, Slade.

She balled up the note in her hand. Her disappointment was so vast it left her trembling. She couldn't help wondering if there had really been an emergency, or if he merely preferred work to her company. Since she had come to the city she had learned just how fond of working he was.

"Missee want to send note?" the boy asked.

Regina barely heard. Crushed, she shook her head. The boy bowed and backed out the door, then turned and ran down the front steps. She barely saw him as he veered abruptly and ran through the gardens, ducking beneath the hedge onto their neighbor's property.

Yesterday had been wonderful—too wonderful, in fact. After they had left the Henessy place, Slade had taken her to the Cliff House, where the views of the Pacific were stunning. They had both been unable to stop smiling and had gazed at each other until it was unseemly. Yet they had not really conversed. Regina had been waiting for him to discuss their relationship, hoping he would bring the subject up.

But he had not asked her if she still wanted a divorce.

He had not asked her to move in with him.

He had not asked about the future—their future.

She had been afraid to broach those topics herself. It was not appropriate; it would be terribly aggressive. As the man and husband, it was up to Slade to set the parameters and make up the rules, it was up to him to demand that their estrangement end. Yet he hadn't. After the wonderful meal he had simply taken her home. He had kissed her for a long time in the carriage before leaving her at the door, and at the time she had thought that he was sincerely fond of her. Now she wondered if it had only been evidence of his passion for her.

Regina turned and sank down on the settee in the foyer. She could not decide what to do. She wasn't sure he would even call on her that night. His words might have been a smoke screen. Perhaps he would be happier with separate living arrangements. It was done all the time in London.

Abruptly she stood. She wanted a real marriage. She had wanted a real marriage from the start, when she had thought herself to be Elizabeth Sinclair. She was almost prepared to throw convention to the winds and do what she really wanted to do—move into his house, even without his permission. She could not go that far. But she was his wife, and she had certain rights. Surely he could not be too upset if she went over there to take a peek at the situation.

And the situation was shocking.

The houseboy let her in. Regina blinked. The hallway was so dark in shadow that she could barely see.

"Mista Slade no heah," the boy said.

"I know," Regina said, moving forward and snapping on a wall-mounted lamp. "That's much better."

She looked around her carefully. The house was dark and drab; looking at the floor, she saw that it was also dirty. The hallway needed brightening, but that could be done with a framed painting or two and the addition of another mounted lamp. The floor was not just smudged but tired and worn. A good waxing would fix that. She began to smile.

She poked her head into the parlor. The furnishings were new but garish and the room itself was stuffy and dark. Regina swiftly moved to the lime-colored drapes and opened them. She was glad to see the street below and not the brick wall of a neighboring residence. She opened the window, letting in the fresh air.

"I can hep?" the small boy asked eagerly.

"You most certainly can. Does Slade use this room?"

He shook his head. "Nevah."

Regina was not surprised. The dust was an inch thick on all of the furniture, except for the small table in front of the sofa, where two unfinished glasses of whiskey sat. "Someone was here recently," she remarked.

"Mista Slade and fatha'."

"Mr. Mann?"

"No, Mista Rick."

Regina was surprised. Then she briskly moved forward. She pulled all the drapes and opened the other two windows. The room underwent a remarkable transformation, brightening considerably, but she was far from through. Eventually she would have to get rid of that horrid sofa, which she would not even contemplate moving to the Henessy place, but for now a few pleasing throw pillows would distract one's eye from the too brightly patterned green-and-gold fabric. The floor here also needed polishing, and the rug needed a good beating. She was cheerful. She could not, as Slade's lawful wedded wife, ignore this situation.

She strode down the hall and paused in the doorway of Slade's study. The desk was covered with papers and half a dozen glass paperweights. Books lined the shelves on one wall although several were on the floor, open, probably because there was no room for them on his desk. The houseboy hovered behind her. He said uneasily, "Mista Slade tell me nevah touch in heah. Nevah," he emphasized.

"Hmm, thank you for the warning. What is your name, child?"

"Kim."

"And you are Mr. Delanza's houseboy?"

Kim nodded as Regina shut the door of the study firmly behind them.

"I should like to meet the staff."

"Staff?"

"Yes, the staff. Especially the maids. If they wish to remain employed, they are going to start working immediately."

Kim looked uncomfortable. "No maids."

"There are no maids?"

"I clean."

"You clean?"

He nodded.

Regina was not pleased. Houseboys did not clean. Frugality had its limitations. Slade was taking advantage of the situation. She moved down the hall and glanced into the dining room. It was dark and stuffy, but Regina quickly drew the drapes and opened all of the windows. Obviously her husband never used his dining room, either. But where did he eat?

As they walked down the hall, Kim on her heels, it occurred to her that Kim might be expected to clean, but he apparently did not do his duty. And Slade apparently did not care.

"Is the cook in the kitchen?" she asked, already suspecting the answer.

Kim trotted after her. "No cook."

Regina paused. "Are you going to tell me that you do the cooking too?" She would be very angry with Slade if that was the case.

Kim shook his head. "No can cook."

"So how does Mr. Delanza dine?"

"Mista no eat heah."

"I see." She was beginning to get the picture. She

could just imagine what the kitchen must be like. She would not succumb to fear. She entered bravely.

And was relieved. There were only two dirty glasses in the sink. She soon saw why the kitchen was not a shambles. The icebox was empty. The pantry was empty. The cupboards were bare too, except for two plates, two bowls, two cups, and two saucers. She turned to Kim in amazement. "Don't you eat here?"

"Mista Slade bring me food from restaurants." He grinned. "No can cook," he reminded her.

"Might I presume that Mr. Delanza has only you in his employ?"

"What?"

"Are you the only one working for Mr. Delanza?"

He nodded eagerly.

She made a rapid mental calculation. She would hire one permanent maid and two temporaries, one butler, and, of course, a chef. But when she entered his bedroom and saw the pile of dirty clothes on the floor, she added a laundress to her list. "Who does the laundry, Kim?"

"Me," he squeaked. "But on Thu'sday. Today no Thu'sday."

Regina nodded. "I see." A smile wreathed her face. She must hire staff immediately. She had her work cut out for her!

"Missee mad?"

"No," she said, eyeing the bed now. It was much too small. She blushed slightly at her thoughts. She would definitely make improvements in this room as well. Slade would hardly be able to complain. "Tell me, Kim," she said as they returned downstairs, "how long have you worked for Mr. Delanza?"

"Four yeah," he said.

Regina froze. "How old are you?"

"Soon e'even."

She was indignant. "Why, that's sinful! Slade has robbed the cradle!" The boy was so clever she had thought him to be at least thirteen.

"No bad. Mista Slade ve'ey good."

"You like him?"

"Can do!" He nodded enthusiastically.

"But what about your family? Don't you miss your mother, your father, your brothers and sisters?"

Kim said, "Motha' die of clap. Fatha' chop-chop. Sista' no-good whore. No brotha'. Slade fami'ey."

She stared. "What is chop-chop?"

He made an imaginary gun with his hand and held it to his head. "Pow!"

She closed her eyes, moved. Kim was no ordinary houseboy; he was a homeless orphan Slade had taken in. She patted his head. "Are you happy, Kim?"

"Ve'ey!"

Slade stepped into his house and immediately wondered if he had somehow entered someone else's home.

The hall was brightly illuminated instead of lost in shadows. Two pretty floral paintings hung on the wall. The floors shone brightly, gleaming with wax. He sniffed suspiciously. There were strange odors emanating from the other end of the house. Someone was cooking beef, he thought, in his kitchen.

"What the hell?" he growled.

He prowled forward, past the parlor, then froze. He backed up a step, turning to face a vision in yellow.

Regina sat stiffly on the overstuffed sofa in a bright-yellow evening gown, her hands clasped in her lap, her eyes on him.

Slade stared. For a moment he felt as if he were in a dream, a very sweet dream. After all, in reality he did not have a beautiful wife to come home to, or a decent meal, or a clean, cozy home. But he wasn't dreaming. His mouth curved in a slight, disbelieving smile. "Are you real?"

At his husky teasing tone, Regina collapsed against the pillows. "Yes."

He set down his briefcase, shoving his hands in his trouser pockets. His heart was pounding. He looked around the room. The rug was brighter, the furniture free of dust; the drapes were pulled, revealing a foggy night, illuminated by the gaslights on the street below. He glanced at his wife. She was lovely, breathtakingly lovely. The sofa no longer seemed so ugly with her sitting there upon it. Then he realized she had adorned it with dozens of pillows, covering the ugly print upholstery.

A man entered the room, startling him. Tall, thin, and grim, he carried a silver tray, and on it was one glass, which looked as if it contained his favorite spirits, bourbon. "Who the hell are you?" Slade asked mildly.

"Brinks, sir." The man had a distinct British accent, a perfectly impassive expression, and an equally impassive intonation.

Regina was on her feet, wringing her hands. "Slade, this is Brinks." She hesitated. "Your butler."

"I see." He took the glass. "Thank you, Brinks."

Brinks said, "Will there be anything else, sir?"

Slade looked at Regina. "Ask my wife."

Brinks said, "Madam?"

"No, thank you. Oh—" She swallowed. "Slade, will you be ready to eat in forty-five minutes?"

He gazed at her. "I can be ready in forty-five minutes."

"Brinks, tell Monsieur Bertrand that Mr. Delanza is home and we shall dine at nine."

"Very good, madam." Brinks left.

Slade still gazed at his wife.

"I hope you are not too upset," she said breathlessly.

"I've been upset all day."

"You have been?"

He set his glass down. "I sent you a note but you didn't send a reply."

Her eyes widened. "I didn't realize you expected one."

"I did."

"I'm sorry."

"What's going on here, Regina?"

"I . . . I came over to see if you needed anything." She drew herself up defensively. "After all, I *am* your wife."

"You're making that clearer by the minute," he said.

She looked worried. "This place was such a . . . such a bachelor's suite."

He had to smile. "I imagine you're putting it mildly."

"Well, yes," she confessed. "I could not turn my back on your home! So I hired a maid, a butler, and the chef. I stole Monsieur Bertrand from the Crockers." She gave him a guilty but so-sweet smile. "But I believe he will be worth it."

"If the smells coming out of that kitchen are any indication, I would say so."

She looked at him hopefully. "Would you like to go upstairs and change into something more comfortable?"

He realized that she hadn't answered his question. What was going on? His gut was tight, even aching. Had she changed her mind about the divorce? It seemed so. It seemed as if she had come to his home and was there to stay. It appeared that she had taken the final step, made the final decision, absolving him of the responsibility to do so, ensuring their reconciliation. He was thrilled, he was dismayed. It was all happening so fast.

She was regarding him anxiously. The last thing he wanted to do was to disappoint her, or push her away. If she wanted him to go upstairs—and he imagined there were a few changes awaiting him there, too—he would. Impulsively he took her chin and kissed her softly on the lips. Then he wheeled abruptly and bounded up the stairs.

In his bedroom he paused on the threshold, wondering about her, about them. His utilitarian bed was gone. In its place was a king-sized brass bed, done up luxuriously in burgundy. How in hell could she have known that burgundy was one of his favorite colors?

He moved closer. As he tested it with his hand, imagining her there, in it, he saw the silk velvet-lapelled smoking jacket she had laid out for him. He never wore the garment, which had been a gift from Xandria a long time ago. He saw that she had put a similarly unused pair of slippers on the floor beside it. His heart, which had been beating unsteadily ever since he had spotted her there in the parlor, seemed to flip hard.

Slowly removing his tie, shirt, and jacket, he inspected the room. She had put a lace cloth on the dreary wood table by the window and a vase of fresh-cut lilies in its center. Their scent permeated the room. The decanter on the bureau, which had been almost empty, was refilled. The glasses on the tray were clean; taking a closer glance, he realized that they were also new. In fact, he didn't recognize the silver tray, either.

Soberly he walked into the bathroom. He found all of his toiletries neatly laid out on another large, unfamiliar silver tray. She had placed a potted fern in the far corner, and snowy-white towels hung from a brass rack which he had never seen before. She had also changed the single set of curtains, which had been somewhat mildewed. The new curtains were striped in burgundy and white.

She had made a lot of changes in his home, changes that were for the better. But he was frowning. How had she paid for all of these changes? He couldn't and he wouldn't undo them, not for a few dollars, but he had just made the decision not to take her inheritance and here she was spending it recklessly on him. Yes, he was pleased by her thoughtfulness, more than pleased, thrilled—but dammit, he could just see where this was going to lead them. Into a tunnel without light.

"Slade?"

Slipping on the smoking jacket, he jerked at the sound of her voice. Her hesitant tones brought him to the bedroom doorway. "Are you angry?" she asked.

"No."

She looked relieved.

He put his arms around her and held her hard. Already his body pulsed urgently. "This is like a dream, Regina," he said quietly.

She looked up at him, blinking back tears. "You like it?"

"I like it," he said hoarsely, wanting to say so much

more yet unable to. He took her mouth without warning, smothering her gasp of surprise.

Then she laughed happily, burrowing closer. "And . . . the bed?"

"Let's test it," he whispered, shaking. "Let's test it now."

"We can't!" She was aghast. "Monsieur Bertrand will quit before he has even started!"

"Regina, please," Slade said, lifting her in his arms. "Let me make love to you now."

She was silent, clinging to him.

"I need you," he whispered. Laying her down on the bed, he caught her face in his hands. "How I need you!"

"I need you too, Slade," she whispered, tears in her eyes. She started to speak and then bit her lip.

"No," he cried, sliding his hands over her shoulders. "Say it! Don't hold back. Tell me. Tell me you love me— even if it's only for now."

"Slade . . ."

He rained kisses on her throat, panting, his hands moving down her body. "Regina?"

"I do," she moaned. "God, I do. I love you, Slade."

Chapter 24

*T*he next few days passed quickly in a haze of happiness. Regina had not exactly intended to move in with Slade by organizing his home and staff, yet that was precisely what happened. After a fabulous supper, proving that Monsieur Bertrand was worth every penny, she again found herself in Slade's arms and in his bed. When she fell asleep after several impassioned hours, he did not awaken her to send her home. She was surprised to wake up that next morning with him—but more than a little pleased.

She expected Slade to remark upon their reconciliation. He did not. Perhaps, because they were married, there was no point in bringing up the unhappy past. He was the one who had refused her request for a divorce, after all. Perhaps he was afraid of where too blunt a discussion might lead. Regina was. She was on tenterhooks. But she did know one thing. She did not want to return to her uncle's—she belonged in Slade's home, she belonged at Slade's side. She did not even want to leave his home in order to retrieve her belongings. The situation was too delicate. Slade saved her from having to do so. Over breakfast—in bed—he casually suggested he send a servant to fetch her things. Enthusiastically Regina agreed. It seemed as if they had reached an

understanding to carry on with their marriage after all.
Yet somehow the unspoken pact seemed tentative and
tenuous.

During the next few days Slade did not treat her as
a wife, but as a bride. He gave himself a holiday from
his work in order to squire her about the city. It was a
honeymoon which Regina would never forget. He took
her to Little Italy and introduced her to pasta, which she
now craved. On the Embarcadero they dined at Maye's
Oyster House on fresh seafood and raw oysters, washed
down with iced beer. The Castle-Observatory on Tele-
graph Hill was not to be missed. They attended a show
at Lucky Baldwin's Academy of Music, which they so
enjoyed they returned for a second performance.

They took the Marin ferry to Sausalito and cycled
on Siamese-twin bicycles along the shore. They went
horseback riding in Golden Gate Park and boating on
Stow Lake. One afternoon they even went to the Sutro
baths. Regina had never seen anything like it. There
were six kinds of bathing—salt, fresh, warm, cold, deep,
and shallow—and the museum there was filled with
charming curios and contests for people of all ages.
Slade talked her into trying the slide, which was one
of the most thrilling experiences of her life.

And during it all was their passion. It had not faded
one whit. Slade was a merciless man. He did not like
being confined to their bedroom and he admitted it
candidly. Regina tried not to remember making love in
their carriage, not once but on two separate occasions,
and she tried not to remember his hot kisses behind
the slide at the Sutro baths. He had made love to her
on Ocean Beach, too, in a hurried but thoroughly sat-
isfactory manner, and they had just escaped discovery.
And he had taken her in the ruins of an old mission just
south of the city.

Thinking about him made her breathless. Thinking
about him made her wish that he was home today and
not at the office. She blushed scarlet with another vivid
recollection. Yesterday Slade had insisted that they stop
at his office to pick up a contract, one he wanted to

read that evening. Yet once in his office he had not even bothered to look for the papers. Instead, his smile promising, he had pushed her on top of his desk, sending files and folders flying to the floor. He had lifted her skirts, kissing away her protests, and made love to her on top of his paperwork. Regina fervently hoped that no one had any idea just what had been going on in his office that day. She suspected that Slade's assault had been well-planned; that he had never intended to retrieve a contract at all.

He was impossible. How she loved him. If only she could be sure that he loved her, too.

And she was not sure. His passion for her was boundless, so Regina could not help thinking that he must be fond of her as well. Yet men had mistresses all the time, mistresses they dismissed in the blink of an eye. Regina could not understand it, but it was evidence that a man did not need love to feel passion. She wished that Slade would tell her, just once, of the feelings he had for her. But he did not.

And to compound her worry was the fact that, despite the excessive physical intimacy they shared, there was little emotional intimacy outside of the bedroom. Slade was not giving all of himself to her. She was certain that he kept some sort of guard up around her, that he was careful to restrain his feelings, that he did not want to become too involved with her, his own wife. Slade had gotten a declaration of love from her, but Regina was beginning to fear that she would never get such a declaration from him.

She told herself that it was unimportant and that she could live without it, as long as she had him. But she could not stop herself from yearning for more.

When Slade returned that night after his first day at work since they had reconciled so subtly, Regina greeted him at the door herself. She was all smiles. Seeing her, he smiled just as widely.

She took his briefcase and his arm, pulling him into the foyer. "Hello! How was your day?" She leaned close, dropping the briefcase.

Slade took her shoulders in his hands. "Is this the greeting I'm going to get every day when I come home?"

"Yes," she whispered, her palms sliding along his strong neck.

"I guess there's something to be said for marriage," he joked, kissing her. Regina clung to him. It felt as if days had passed, not hours, since she had last seen him.

When the long, scandalous kiss had ended—after all, servants were about—Regina pulled Slade into the salon. "I have something to show you!"

"I'll bet," he said wickedly.

She gave him a look, then pointed at the couch.

He went still, his smile fading. He eyed the couch, which was covered with different swatches of fabric. "What's that?"

"Samples," she said happily. "I'll do your suite first. In our new home on Franklin Street. What do you think?" She rushed to the couch and held up a swatch of moss-green velvet. "For a soft, comfortable reading chair? And this—for your sofa? And of course, I know how you like burgundy, so I thought maybe you'd like this for the bed." She waved a paisley print and regarded him eagerly.

Slade said nothing.

Regina put down the fabrics, her own smile vanishing. "You hate it? All of it?"

"No, I don't hate it."

"I don't understand."

His jaw flexed. "We're not going to move into the Henessy place."

She was stunned. "But why not?"

He said tightly, "Because I can't afford it."

Regina stared. Finally she shook the cobwebs free from her brain. "Of course you can! We have my inheritance, remember? Father will be here any day now, and he'll transfer the funds to your bank and—"

"No."

She blinked. "Excuse me?"

"I said no."

"I don't understand, Slade." Not liking his hard, closed expression, she sat down on several of the samples. She began to tremble.

"I'm not going to take your inheritance."

"*What?*"

He paced across the room to pour himself a drink. "I don't want to take your money."

It sank in. A thrill swept through her. He did not want her money, not now, when he had married her for her money in the first place. "Why not?" she whispered.

He glanced at her. "I have pride. I don't want to use my wife or her money."

"Oh, Slade." She stood, wringing her hands. It couldn't be all pride. He cared for her.

Regarding her darkly over his glass, he sipped his bourbon.

In the next instant, the enormity of what he was doing—the ramifications—struck her hard. "But—Miramar? You need the money to save Miramar!"

"I've borrowed some funds from Charles."

Regina sat back down, trying to think. "So Miramar is safe?"

"It won't be easy." He stared at her. His tone seemed to hold a warning. "The next five years will be tight. We'll have to live simply, frugally. But by then I hope to start showing a decent profit."

"I see." Regina gazed at him. "Isn't it silly to live like that when we have all the money we could ever need—"

"No. I said I'm not taking your money and I mean it."

Her temper flared. "This is ridiculous! And what about the Henessy place?"

"We'll close it up. Maybe I'll sell it. I'm thinking about it. If I don't, in five or ten years we'll be able to open it and use it for vacations and weekends. Until then, if you want, I can keep this house for you to use when you come to the city."

"Slade." She stood. "This is ridiculous. We have a fabulous home and I'm not going to allow you to sell it!"

He faced her. "You're not going to *allow* me to sell it?"

She knew she should back down, but she would not. "No."

He stared, not responding, anger hardening his expression.

She was trembling, she did not feel brave, but she forged on. "And to close it up for ten years! Please reconsider. You knew I was an heiress when you married me—you married me because of it! Why should we struggle and live like paupers if we don't have to? It's ridiculous!"

"That's the third time you've said I'm ridiculous." His tone was dire.

"No! That's not what I—"

He cut her off. "We're not going to live like paupers, Regina. At least, not by my standards. But maybe by *your* standards we *will* be in poverty. Do you want to leave me?"

The last question was out of context. He said it so simply and swiftly he took her by surprise. "No! Of course not!"

"Then it's settled," he said, setting his glass down unnecessarily hard. He turned and strode from the room.

Regina sank onto the couch. For a moment she was still, her lips quivering. Then she picked up one of the samples, the moss-green velvet, and hugged it to her breast. A tear wet it.

Slade had said the issue was settled, but as far as she was concerned, nothing was settled. To the contrary, she had the terrible feeling that he had just opened Pandora's box.

Xandria was impressed.

A butler had shown her into the parlor and within moments, a maid had brought her a tray of tea and cakes. She looked around at the room, smiling. The monstrous couch had been replaced, the organized clutter, which was so unlike Slade, had vanished, and a new Oriental rug was underfoot. The few changes had brightened and cheered up the room considerably. She was so glad that Regina had returned to Slade last week, and her abilities as a decorator were not why.

They hadn't advertised their reconciliation, though. Xandria had not seen Slade since the dinner party she had given for the newlyweds. She would not have known their estrangement had ended had Edward not told her— at a rather startling time. She smiled in recollection of the moment he had chosen, when she was shuddering in his embrace, her shirtwaist undone, her corset pushed down, her skirts about her waist—in her office, for God's sake. With her clerk right outside the unlocked door, in the middle of the workday. Edward seemed to thrive on danger as well as love. Not that Xandria minded.

And then the devil himself walked into the room.

Xandria sloshed the tea she was pouring over the rim of her porcelain teacup. Her body also remembered him, too well, instantly. "What a surprise, Mr. Delanza."

He grinned. "Good morning, Mrs. Kingsly."

They shared a look. Xandria knew he was recalling the fact that the sun had awakened them both in one of the Mann Grande's hotel rooms, and that before she had slipped out, unseen, he had brought her to a wild, keening orgasm. For the sake of convenience, Edward had chosen to take up residence there, instead of with his brother. It made every rendezvous so much easier. Xandria would never bring a man home to her own apartments, even though her staff would undoubtedly be discreet.

"You are looking rather sleepy today, Mr. Delanza. Have you passed a difficult night?" she asked innocently.

"Very difficult, madam. You see, I was pressed hard to entertain a certain friend of mine, one who showed no respect for the time—indeed, one who seemed intent upon the particular entertainment I offered, too intent to care about my need for sleep."

"Perhaps you need a different friend, Mr. Delanza."

His mouth quirked. His eyes moved over her warmly, stripping her naked. "I do not think so, madam. This particular friend knows how to entertain as well as how to be entertained. In fact, even now I look forward to our next meeting."

By now, she knew exactly what that meeting would be like, but not when it would be. Fire licked her thighs. His words were enough to inflame her. She really was a shameless hussy, but Edward was a shameless rake. They were well-suited. Then she saw the gleam in his eye.

"Don't you dare!" She held up a hand as if to ward him off.

Ignoring her, he approached. "Why not?"

She tried to push him away. "Regina will be here in an instant."

Grinning like a very naughty boy, he continued to ignore her, pulling her into his arms and kissing her deeply. When he had finished with her, she was breathless and ready for him. "You are a bastard, Edward," she said without rancor.

"And you are my kind of woman," he returned warmly.

They both heard the approaching footsteps. Edward distanced himself from her, another grin lighting up his face. "You look very pleased with yourself," Xandria said, somewhat scoldingly. A glance in the mirror showed her that she was flushed; several wisps of her hair had escaped its coil and were curling around her face.

"I am," Edward said. "But I am also pleased with you."

It was impossible not to be thrilled. Fortunately she was an experienced woman, or this unrepentant charmer would have her falling head over heels in love with him. She felt sorry for any young woman foolish and naive enough to cross his path.

Regina appeared in the doorway. "Xandria, what a wonderful surprise. Edward and I have just finished a late breakfast. Would you care for anything?"

"No, no, I'm fine." Xandria regarded her hostess intently. She wasn't sure what she had expected—probably a glowing bride. But Regina was not glowing; she looked tired.

Edward kissed Regina's cheek casually. "I had better take myself off," he said, throwing one last look at Xandria. He strolled from the room.

"I'm so glad you have come," Regina said, the two women settling down for a chat. Xandria praised Regina for the improvements she had made upon the house. Regina seemed glad to detail all that she had so far done.

"How is Slade?" Xandria finally asked, trying not to watch Regina too closely.

Regina smiled, but it was not wide. "He's fine. He returned to work yesterday."

"And how are you?"

Regina smiled again. "I am fine, just fine."

"You seem tired."

"Well—" Regina hesitated. "I've been so busy, re-organizing Slade's home and—and shopping for the Henessy place."

"So the two of you are going to move in there?" Xandria was delighted.

Regina sighed, her pleasant facade falling away, her expression now openly troubled. "I do not know. I do not know."

"What's wrong?" Xandria touched the other woman's hand.

"Nothing, really. Slade is just being stubborn." She paused. "I think we are going to have to close up the Henessy place for a few years, until Miramar is on better footing."

"I see." Xandria was silent for a moment. Whatever was going on was not her concern, even if she would dearly love it to be. "Is there anything I can do to help? If Slade needs a good set-down, I will gladly deliver it."

Regina chuckled. "No, but thank you, Xandria." Impulsively, she reached out and squeezed the older

woman's hand. "I'm glad you care so much for Slade.
And I'm glad we are becoming friends."

"So am I." Xandria smiled and faced her hostess more
squarely. "Would you mind very much if Father and I
held a party in celebration of your marriage?"

Regina's eyes sparkled. "I do love a party."

Xandria laughed. "So do I! Then it's settled. We shall
plan it for the following Friday night. A gala. We shall
invite everybody who is anybody. You do know that
this marriage is the talk of the town? People are dying
to meet you, and I am dying to show you off! You are
about to become the reigning queen of the city, my
dear!"

Regina stood at the window and waved to Xandria
as she stepped into her carriage on the street below.
The light smiles she had worn during Xandria's visit
were gone. Her brow was furrowed, her mouth tight,
her heart troubled.

She told herself that everything would be fine in
time. It was normal for married couples to have dis-
agreements. But the distance she had sensed Slade was
keeping this past week had been more in evidence last
night during and after supper. It was only when they
had retired to their bed that he had turned to her,
making love to her in a manner that was almost fren-
zied. And after having just had their first real argument,
her responses had been equally as wild.

This morning while she had lingered in bed and he
had dressed to go to work, she had noticed him looking
at her intently. She had smiled at him but he had not
been able to smile back. Kissing her cheek before leaving, he had told her he would not be home for supper
that night. He had a business engagement.

Regina knew her husband well enough to know that
he was still troubled by the issues that had been raised
the night before, as she was. She was quite certain that
Slade was not coming home for supper because of the
issue of her inheritance that now lay between them. He
would put a physical distance between them now, she

thought in dismay, as well as an emotional one.

She still could not believe that he would refuse her inheritance when it could solve most of their problems. She hoped he would come to his senses. In a few days, when he had simmered down, she would have to delicately raise the topic again. But if he did not change his mind she would have to accept his decision. But she certainly would not leave him just because they would have to lower their standard of living. It was unbelievable that he might think so.

He had not said when he planned for them to return to Miramar. Obviously it would be soon. On the one hand, Regina looked forward to returning and was thrilled at the prospect; already she loved the rancho and, more importantly, it was where Slade belonged. On the other hand, she was filled with worry. Unless they solved the issue of her inheritance first, these first seeds of conflict would be nourished by the additional problems awaiting them there. Regina was thinking of Slade's relationship with his father. Her feelings had not changed. She had sensed from the start that it would be impossible for them to live at Miramar with any amount of happiness unless Slade and Rick came to some understanding with each other. Whatever was the real cause of the conflict between them, it had to be uprooted and laid to rest.

Regina sighed. Just yesterday afternoon she had been blissfully happy. Now she was worried and more than just apprehensive, she was afraid.

She was about to turn away from the window to prepare to go to her aunt and uncle's. She had not seen them since she had reconciled with Slade. She had sent them several notes explaining the situation and that divorce was no longer an issue, but she owed them a personal reassurance that she was fine. Before she could move she saw a carriage stopping in front of the house. She recognized it; it belonged to Brett. She smiled ruefully. Apparently they were coming to her, determined to find out for themselves if all was truly well. Brett stepped down from the carriage. Regina leaned forward to wave, about to call down to him in greeting. But the words died in her throat.

For the man was not Brett. It was her father, the Earl of Dragmore.

The Countess of Dragmore rushed into the house first. Regina cried out in delight, embracing her mother warmly. The countess was petite, even smaller than her daughter. When Jane pulled back from Regina, she was crying openly. "What happened to you? I have been so frightened!"

"I am so sorry, Mother!" Regina hugged her again.

Her father gripped her shoulders, meeting her gaze sternly. "This convoluted tale was just explained to me by your uncle. Thank God you are all right!"

"When did you arrive?" Regina asked.

"We arrived in New York last week. Brett wired us that you were fine, but refused to answer any of my numerous inquiries. We raced here, Regina, undoubtedly setting a world record for transcontinental travel. I have just left Brett and Storm. We have had a long discussion. I believe I am beginning to make sense out of this fairy tale. Are you truly all right?"

Regina nodded, her eyes wide and watchful.

Nicholas Shelton's expression darkened. "Good! Then I can blast you for putting us through hell! Is it true? That you had amnesia? That is why there was no word from you when you disappeared during the train robbery?"

"It's true, Father. You know I would never disappear like that on purpose."

"Not you, no. That is something your sister would do, but not you."

"Nicholas," Jane rebuked softly, "Nicole is a very proper lady now."

Nicholas eyed his wife. "Darling, believe me, despite her being a duchess, she is no more proper now than she was before she was wed. Hadrian is constantly sweeping up crumbs of scandal after her." He turned back to Regina. "Explain to me how you married this man. I was told by Brett that you regained your memory before the wedding. I can not understand this, Regina. You have never been one to be impulsive or irresponsible."

Regina swallowed. There was no mistaking her father's ominous tone. But she had known that it would eventually come to this. Nicholas was not happy with her marriage. "Father, he is a good man."

"Did he or did he not marry you for your inheritance?" Nicholas was brutally direct.

Regina froze.

"Well? Brett said that you told him that he married you for your inheritance."

Regina swallowed. "But that is in the past. He does not want my money now."

"Oh, really? Well, that's good, because if you remain married to him, I am cutting you off without a single shilling."

Regina gasped.

"Nicholas!" Jane cried. "Can't we at least sit down and discuss this civilly?"

"I find nothing civil about some fortune-hunting rake seducing my daughter and marrying her behind my back!"

"He did not seduce me," Regina whispered, horrified. This was worse, so much worse, than she had imagined it would be.

Her father was a very clever man. "He may not have seduced you before the wedding, Regina, not with love-making, but he must have done so with words. And can you tell me he has not seduced you now? I understand that you came to your senses and left him, intending to divorce him. Obviously he succeeded in luring you back to him. We shall wait while you pack your bags."

Regina had been about to protest her father's gravely erroneous assumptions. She stiffened. "Excuse me?"

"You have made a mistake but it can be corrected." His tone softened. "You do not have to fear for your reputation, darling. I will take care of everything. I can obtain a swift divorce, and when you return home, you shall be married immediately. Any scandal will be swept away quickly enough. The Marquis of Hunt is eager to marry you. He will be the next Duke of Cardham, Regina. With such a husband you have nothing to fear."

Regina was in shock. "I am not leaving Slade! Slade is my husband! Nothing will change that."

"A divorce will change that."

"No!"

Nicholas struggled for control. Jane touched his waist. "Nicholas, this is not the way, please! I know you are upset, but you must calm yourself so we can discuss this rationally!"

"I do not see what there is to discuss. That bastard has deceived and seduced my daughter, Jane. He is not going to get away with it."

"He did not deceive me! I knew he was marrying me for my money and I agreed anyway! Please, Father! I love him!"

"You loved Hortense, too."

"No," Regina cried, "I never loved Randolph! I just thought I did."

"Need I say more?"

His implication was clear—that she only thought herself to be in love with Slade now.

Regina knew she could not win a war of words with her father. But she would win this battle. She had to. Taking a deep, calming breath, she said, "Please, Father, come into the salon and sit down. We can talk about this. I can explain. Soon Slade will be home and you will meet him and see for yourself the kind of man that he is. Please."

"No, Regina. There is nothing to discuss except your divorce."

Regina took another breath, this time for courage. "Then there is nothing to discuss at all. Please leave, Father."

Nicholas was stunned. "You are defying me? You are defying me and ordering me to leave your home?"

Tears crept into her eyes. She could not recall a single instance in her life when she had ever disobeyed her father. "Yes, Father, I am afraid so."

Slade did not lift his head. "Enter." He flipped through the pages of the file he was reading. When he had finished, he handed them to his assistant. "Run these over to Rob Levine immediately, Harold."

"Yes, sir," the young man said. He hurried past the newcomer and out the door.

Slade looked up. The instant he saw the man he knew, without having to be told, that he was Regina's father. It had nothing to do with the slight resemblance he saw in his features, but it had everything to do with instinct. And the man had an unmistakable aura of power and authority, well-suited to an earl. Slade straightened and cautiously stood. "Mr. Shelton?"

Nicholas's expression was dark. "You are clever, Delanza," he said bluntly. "But then I expected you to be clever. Any man who could talk my proper, intelligent daughter into marriage in the space of a few short days would have to be very clever indeed."

Slade prepared to do battle.

"Or did you seduce her?" Nicholas demanded. "She says that you did not, but I have doubts."

"I did not touch her before the wedding," Slade said tightly.

"How noble of you."

"When is the hanging?" Slade asked.

"Now," Nicholas shot back. "Make no mistake about that. My sister and brother-in-law told me that you married her for her money. Regina admitted it. Thank God she is not capable of lying to me. I have an aversion to fortune-hunters, Delanza."

Slade gripped his desk until his knuckles were white. If attacked, he was used to fighting back. Yet he did not want to fight with his wife's father. "You're making this very difficult."

"Am I? I should hope so. I want to see you squirm."

"No," Slade gritted. "You do not understand. You're making it damn difficult to be polite, you're making it damn difficult not to get down in the mud with you, dammit."

"Feel free," Nicholas said coldly. "I would relish the opportunity of smashing in your nose."

"But I don't want to smash yours."

"Why not?"

"Because you're Regina's father."

Nicholas studied him. "Even if you do not fight with me, it won't change a thing. I intend to see my daughter divorced from you and married to a man who suits her. If she remains your wife—and you can be sure that I control her inheritance—you won't get a cent. So feel free to try and smash my nose." Nicholas tensed, eyes blazing.

Slade shook his head. "I need money to save my home and it's no secret. And in case she didn't tell you, I was honest with her from the start. Regina knew why I wanted to marry her and she accepted me anyway."

"I find that to be proof of your powers of seduction."

Slade gritted his teeth. "I'm tired of your slander. Chew on this, Shelton: I don't want her inheritance. I've made other arrangements. So feel free to cut her off."

"I don't believe you."

"Five minutes ago I would have cared what you believed, but not now."

"She is going to divorce you, Delanza. I intend to see to it."

Slade hesitated. "If Regina chooses to leave me, I would not stop her."

Nicholas stared. "Why?"

Again Slade paused.

Nicholas was ruthless. "Why? Because without her money she is worthless to you, right?"

"Wrong! I do not want her money! I've told her that! The truth is, Miramar is no fancy English castle. It's a working rancho. There will be no galas and balls, no need for fancy gowns and glittering jewels. It's a simple life."

"Jesus!" Nicholas exclaimed. "My daughter will be miserable if she stays with you!"

Although Slade had secretly worried that might be so, he found himself defending their marriage. "She knows what's ahead. I've been honest. She knows the next few years will be tight."

"This is all the more reason for you to allow her a divorce," Nicholas said, quietly now.

Slade just looked at him.

"I will not give you her money to help you out. She will be unhappy. I know my daughter, Delanza. Ever since she was a little girl she's disliked country living and cherished city life. As a woman she loves fine things—couture gowns, jewelry, works of art, French wines, I could go on and on. She is not a woman who would be happy or fulfilled living on an isolated rancho."

Slade found it hard to respond. "I make her happy." The words were almost a whisper.

"Perhaps you do." Nicholas regarded him seriously. "But for how long?"

Regina's father was verbalizing Slade's own darkest fears, fears that had been growing uncontrollably ever since his wife had returned to him. "Get out," Slade said.

"If you really care about my daughter, you will let her go. I have already arranged a marriage for her at home to a man who will one day be a duke. Regina might think she is happy now, but she deserves more than you can give her."

"Get out," Slade said again, furious. "Get out!"

Nicholas's eyes gleamed with triumph as he strode to the door, where he turned and paused. "I think you do care for her after all. Then you will have to do what is best for her, won't you?"

Chapter 25

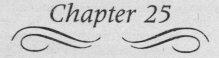

"Madam, Mr. Delanza is here."

Regina had been closeted in the parlor for the past hour, ever since the terrible confrontation with her father. She had not moved from the sofa where she had all but collapsed. She couldn't believe what she had done. She had not just defied her father, but ordered him to leave her home.

Upon hearing Brinks's words, Regina shot to her feet. It was mid-afternoon and she thought that Slade had decided to come home early to be with her. How she needed him now!

But it was Rick Delanza who walked past Brinks and into the salon, followed by Victoria.

Regina's face fell. Quickly she composed herself. "Rick, Victoria, how nice to see you."

Victoria gave her a skeptical look, then glanced disdainfully around the small salon. Rick enfolded her in a bear hug. "I'm sure glad to see you here, gal."

Regina recalled the last time she had seen Rick, when she had been furious and intent on divorcing his son. In the next breath it occurred to her that the last time she had seen Victoria she had been masquerading as Elizabeth Sinclair, and that the other woman had been well aware of it. Her eyes turned to Victoria.

Victoria's smile was cold. "Hello, Regina. What a pleasant little home."

Regina stiffened. Rick shot his wife a warning glance. "I came up here to visit you and Victoria insisted on coming. We both are happy to see that you and Slade have worked things out. Aren't we, honey?"

Victoria's eyes darkened but she nodded.

Regina almost laughed. They had barely begun to forge a solid relationship, much less work things out. The numerous pitfalls besetting them did not generate optimism. In fact, she felt perilously close to tears.

Rick studied her. "We're family now, remember?" He threw his arm around her. "You can tell me what's bothering you. Someone die?"

His kindness and loyalty were so unexpected that Regina was overwhelmed. And in her distress, his strength was so welcome. "No. No one died."

"Can't be that bad then." He gave her an encouraging smile.

Victoria said, "I think the honeymoon is over. If it ever began."

Regina was furious. But she remained calm, tamping down her temper with great will. "Victoria, do sit down. It is so nice of you to pay a pleasant social call. Would you like some tea?"

Victoria sat, shrugging.

"What time does Slade get home?" Rick asked.

"He'll be late tonight. But you can find him at the office."

"Actually, I didn't come here to see him. I saw him last week. I came to see you." Rick smiled. "We both did. We want to know when the two of you are coming home."

"I don't know. We haven't really discussed it."

"Perhaps they'll stay here in the city," Victoria interjected. "There's a rumor going around that Charles Mann gave the two of you an incredible mansion for a wedding present. Is it true?"

"It's true." Regina saw Rick flinch. "But we won't be staying there, we won't even be opening up the house.

Slade intends to return to Miramar, I just do not know when."

Victoria stood. "I cannot believe you—a Bragg princess—would be happy living as a ranchero's wife."

"Cut it out, Victoria," Rick warned.

Regina also stood. "I am happy with Slade, wherever he is, whatever he does."

"You do not seem happy to me."

Rick whirled. "I thought you said you wouldn't start."

Victoria ignored him. So did Regina. "Did you know who I was before the wedding, Victoria?"

She smiled. "You may have fooled everybody else, but you didn't fool me."

Regina glanced at Rick briefly before responding. "Was it you who went through my things?"

"Yes, it was. Your locket ultimately gave you away." There was no mistaking the cool triumph in her eyes.

"If you ever invade my privacy again, you will be sorry."

Victoria laughed. "*You* accuse *me* of wrongdoing? You were the one playing a charade, my dear. And it wasn't very noble of you, either."

"Why didn't you say something?" Regina asked.

"Because although I knew you weren't Elizabeth Sinclair, I did not know you were a Bragg heiress. I thought you to be nothing more than a fortune-hunting impostor! Unfortunately, I was wrong."

Regina seethed. But Victoria was Rick's wife, and the two of them were going to have to get along if they were to live together in the future. "Victoria, you cannot change who I am, no matter how you might wish you could. We are going to have to put our differences behind us. Can you not agree to that?"

"No, I can't," Victoria snapped. "And maybe I can't change you, but I probably don't have to. Once you get smart you'll realize that you belong here in the city, not on the rancho. Why don't you and Slade just move into your fancy mansion and live it up on your money?"

"That is not possible, Victoria," Regina said. "You see, I know that Miramar is Slade's passion. And I love Slade so much that I am determined that we live there for the rest of our lives. It cannot be any other way."

Openly angry, Victoria stormed from the room. Regina stared after her. She had forgotten Rick was present until he spoke up.

"She'll come around. You okay?"

"I'm fine."

Rick smiled. "You have more spunk than a body'd ever know. Don't you go worrying about her. She's mostly bark and little bite."

"I'm not," Regina said truthfully. She had too much on her mind to dwell on Victoria's animosity, however misguided it might be.

"Honey," Rick said, grimacing, "let's sit down."

Curious, Regina settled down on the sofa, wondering what Rick was about to reveal. He coughed. "I got a confession to make."

She did not move.

"You know, I like you, I like you a lot, and I have from the moment I laid eyes on you. I don't have to go an' tell you this." He shifted. "I sort of knew the truth too, right from the start."

"Sort of?"

"Okay, I knew who you were, your chaperone told me before she died."

"Oh, Rick."

"Honey, it's not as bad as it sounds!" He held up his hands. "I mean, I was motivated at first by the thought of how an heiress like you could save the rancho. But then I saw how you looked at Slade—and how he looked at you. I mean, if ever two people were meant for each other, it was the two of you."

Regina bowed her head, moved.

"What's wrong? Are you angry with me?"

She shook her head. "I cannot be angry with you, Rick. I like you, too, I always have." She managed a smile. "And I believe you, because I know how much you love Slade."

He reddened. "Yeah, well . . . now that Victoria's gone, why don't you tell me what's really going on?"

Regina was almost ready to confide everything in her father-in-law. He could be a difficult man, but she was seeing another side of him, one that was genuinely compassionate. However, Slade would not be pleased if she shared their problems with his father, and she owed him her loyalty, so she shook her head. "It's nothing, really."

Rick appeared disappointed, perhaps in her lack of trust.

Regina changed the subject. "Xandria Kingsly and Charles Mann are having a gala in honor of my and Slade's marriage this Friday. Will you be coming, Rick?"

Rick scowled. "Is that an invitation?"

"It most certainly is."

"Yeah, well, I'm not going to any gala."

Regina's smile died. "Why not? Can't you stay in town for a few more days?"

"I could but I won't. I didn't come here to argue about some damn gala."

"Why did you come, Rick?"

He took a breath. "Regina, I'll be blunt. I want you and Slade to come home. I'm asking you to come home."

Regina was motionless. Her heart sped. No matter how worried she might be about the unresolved issues between her and Slade and her and her father, she was thrilled with what Rick was saying. He wanted his son to come home. "You must ask him," she said firmly.

"Hell, you're his wife. Tell him it's time for him to return home, where he belongs."

Regina sat very still. Gently she said, "You must tell him that you want him to come home, Rick."

Rick looked uncomfortable. "I didn't ask him to leave in the first place. I sure as hell can't ask him to come home. But you can."

Regina shook her head. "I will not ask him for you."

Rick was on his feet. "Are you a stubborn little thing, too?"

"I can be. I sincerely hope that pride is not what is standing in the way of your having a decent relationship with your son."

Rick gasped. "Missy, you are out of bounds!"

"Perhaps I am."

Rick was incredulous. "I am not about to beg him to return! He left of his own free will. Not just once, mind you. Sometimes I think he hates my guts! Even if I did miss him—and I'm not sayin' that—I would never tell him!"

Regina stood, greatly perturbed. "I think you had better start being honest, Rick. First with yourself, then with your son."

"You're a meddler, you know that?" Rick's eyes flashed angrily.

"Someone obviously has to meddle here. Why won't you come to the party Friday? Your son is the guest of honor. I am sure he would be pleased that you came. He might pretend otherwise, but deep inside, I am sure he would be thrilled."

"I wouldn't set foot in Charlie Mann's place for a million dollars!"

Regina realized then how threatened Rick was by Slade's relationship with Charles Mann. He was hurt and he was angry. She wondered how long he had kept his feelings hidden. Slade had left home ten years ago. She hoped that Rick had not allowed his emotions to simmer for that length of time.

"Rick." She took his hand. "Charles Mann is not Slade's father. He is only a good friend. You are his father and that is not ever going to change. Slade cares about Charles, but that doesn't mean he doesn't need you and your love."

Rick was livid. "That boy doesn't know the meaning of family or love! Just like his damn mother never knew it either! You know his mother was a whore? She was so beautiful I thought if I married her and took her home I could turn her into some kind of lady. Hah! She didn't have one ladylike bone in her body. When she took off, I didn't beg her to come home, and I'm not begging him. He is just like his damned mother!"

Regina was pale with shock. Yet she knew that Rick's words were not true. Slade was a moral man, unlike his mother. She shook her head, unable to speak, thinking too vividly of how Slade seemed determined not to let her into his heart. Perhaps his determination had something to do with his being abandoned as a baby by such a woman. The realization overwhelmed her with purpose—purpose to stick by her husband no matter what.

"If he wants to pretend Charlie Mann is his father, why the hell would I care? It don't change the fact that he belongs at Miramar. But I'll be damned if I'll set foot in Mann's place!"

Regina watched him stomp to the door. She made one last effort for the sake of father and son. "Rick, you can try to pretend that you don't care, but we both know it's a lie. The only one who doesn't know is Slade. Don't you think it's time you let him in on the secret?"

The silence in his office was deadly. His business dinner had long since ended, and, unable to face going home, he had returned to the Feldcrest Building. Usually a cacophany of sound filled the floor, the hum of voices, the clacking of typewriters and teletype, the ringing of the telephones. Tonight there was nothing, just the heavy beating of his own heart.

He could not shake the encounter with Nicholas Shelton from his mind. He knew that Shelton was right. Every goddamn word he'd said was right. Regina had been born with blue blood, she had been raised to take her place among the British aristocracy, she deserved a duke, not an impoverished ranchero. She was happy now, but for how long?

For how goddamn long?

Slade paced his dimly lit office, finally pausing by the window, bracing his hands on the sill. The street below was gas-lit, but there was little traffic; two prostitutes loitered, a single pedestrian hurrying toward them, one lonesome hansom rolling by. He stared at

it all without seeing any of it. He told himself that
no matter how right Shelton was, he was not going
to do the noble thing. He was not going to end his
relationship with his wife.

He was not.

He had to face all of the brutal truth. He loved her.
He had for some time, perhaps since they had first met.
She was everything he'd ever dreamed a woman could
be, and so much more. He did not want to go home to a
dark and empty house, to a dark and meaningless life.
Having had all that she could offer, having had the very
ideal of a marriage, he could not face life without her.

He would not. No matter what, he would not sever
their union.

He straightened, sighing in relief. He resolved not to
think about the future, to live in the present and to do so
greedily. But as he left his office, he was not appeased.

He suspected that he was much more noble than he
had ever thought himself to be.

Regina paced their bedroom in her nightclothes and a
dressing gown. Another glance at the clock showed her
it was a minute past midnight. She sighed. She wrung
her hands. Where was Slade?

Lights from the street below caught her attention. She
ran to the window, but was disappointed when she
saw an automobile slowly driving past. Slade would
not be coming home in a motorcar. Then the door to
their bedroom opened behind her. She whirled. Slade
stood in the corridor, regarding her.

She bit off her cry and her question. Unable to smile,
she merely stared back at him.

He entered the room, shutting the door behind him.
He took off his jacket, saying quietly, "You didn't have
to wait up."

Truthfully she answered, "I couldn't sleep."

He stared at her, removing his tie. Watching him,
desire sprang forth so intensely that Regina felt weak-
kneed. When she was in his arms all of reality's harsh-
ness was stripped away. His embrace was a sanctuary,

the rest of the world vanishing into irrelevance. She felt
desperation wash over her, a desperate need to fuse
with him, to be reassured and healed. But she did not
move.

He slipped the tie from his neck and began unbuttoning his shirt, not taking his eyes from her. Regina
hugged herself. "How—how was your day?"

"Rotten."

She bit her lip. She knew her father very well. She
had worried all day that he had gone to confront Slade
with his demands for a divorce and with his heartfelt
threats. Such a scenario horrified her. She could so easily imagine the two men she loved most in the world
casting furious words at each other and then resorting
to physical blows. "Wh-what happened?"

"Do you know that your father's in town?"

"Slade," she cried. She rushed to him. When she put
her arms around him, holding him as tightly as she
could, he responded just as passionately, hugging her
hard in return. "Father went to see you?" She lifted her
face from his chest.

"I don't want to talk," he said. Abruptly he caught
her face in his hands and began kissing her. Her body,
already weak, shuddered under his onslaught. Slade's
tongue determinedly sought out hers. A second later he
had her in his arms and then they were on the bed.

"I missed you," Regina cried as he opened her dressing robe and, untying the ribbon straps, slid her nightgown down to her waist. Hot kisses fell across her bare
skin, her breasts and nipples.

"I missed you too," Slade returned, his hands intently
moving up her legs beneath her thin silk nightgown.

Their eyes caught and held. Regina was instantly
breathless. Slade desired her so greatly she did not
think it possible for him not to love her a little. And
maybe, just maybe, he loved her with some of the same
kind of passion he felt for her physically.

They kissed. Slade fumbled between them, unbuttoning his pants. Laughing, hysterically happy, Regina

helped him. She guided his shaft toward her. A moment later Slade was moving deep inside her while she gripped him blindly, oblivious now to everything except the moment and the man she loved.

Her release came so quickly, with such force, it took her by surprise. Slade made a sound both sexual and triumphant. An instant later he was crying out in abandon, in a way she had never heard him before.

They held each other. Regina lay blissfully in her husband's arms. Then reality began to intrude. Painfully. She did not want to be reminded of the day's events, or of anything else, but it was impossible not to be. She stared at the ceiling, no longer happy.

Slade stood and shed his shoes and clothes. He twisted to look at her, somber.

Regina swallowed, adjusting her nightgown. "Did Father call on you?"

Slade's jaw flexed. "I wouldn't exactly say it was a social call."

"What happened?"

"We had a chat."

She could read nothing in his inscrutable expression. "Father came here also. He isn't happy with our marriage, not right now, but he will come around eventually." She heard herself; she did not sound confident.

"Will he?"

"Yes, he will, I am sure of it!"

Slade sat down on the bed. "Why are you trembling? Why are you close to tears? What did he say to you?"

She did not want to tell him the truth, hoping that her father had not made the same demands on Slade as he had on her, even though it was doubtful. "I have never seen him so angry. I d-did not expect him to be so angry."

He stared at her.

She managed a smile. "It's natural for him to be angry, and it's natural for me to be upset. Please don't worry about Father, p-please."

"You are such a diplomat."

"No, I'm not."

"You are obviously worried about him, obviously very distressed."

"I'm not worried. Not really. It is stressful, but that's all."

"Is that all?"

"Yes!"

"Don't lie to me, Regina."

She winced.

"I don't like coming between you and your father, I don't like it one damn bit."

Her eyes widened. "Slade, Father and I have a good relationship. This will pass. Maybe not as quickly as I'd hoped, but it will pass."

"Somehow you don't seem confident."

She did not respond. He was right. She wasn't confident. She had never disobeyed her father before, had never seen him angry with her, and wasn't sure how it would all turn out. But she must never let Slade see her doubts. She changed the topic. "*Your* father was also here today."

Slade's eyes widened. "What the hell did he want?"

"Slade! He wants you to come home. He wants *us* to come home."

"He ask you to tell me that?"

"Actually, he did, but I told him he had better speak for himself. I thought you would want to know that he was here, and why."

"Don't get involved."

She stiffened. "Don't get involved? I'm your wife!"

He pulled the covers up over them both, his eyes dark. "Regina, you *are* my wife, but that doesn't give you the right to meddle."

"*Meddle?*"

"I don't even want to think about Rick right now," Slade snapped. "And if he has something to say to me he can damn well say it himself."

Regina was silent, hurt. But she was also angry. She sat up abruptly. "Your father loves you, Slade. The two of you must work things out, or living at Miramar will be a nightmare."

Slade was incredulous. "I just told you not to meddle!"

She hugged herself, teary-eyed. "What is it you expect of me, Slade? To warm your bed? Obviously. To run your home? Obviously. But not to become involved in your family—or with you?"

He threw off the covers and stood up. "What the hell does that mean?"

"It means exactly what I said." She was defiant. "You want me to be a housekeeper and a mistress, but nothing more."

He stared at her. It was a long moment before he could speak. "Just what is it you want to be to me, Regina?"

Now she cried. "If you don't know, then I am not going to tell you."

He watched her cover her face with her hands, then he said, very quietly, "Just what is it you want me to be?"

She was incapable of responding. Slade left the room. He did not return until after she had fallen asleep.

It was the day before the gala. Regina paced nervously in the salon. She hoped she was doing the right thing. She was afraid that the evening would turn out to be a disaster. For she had invited her parents for supper.

She had not seen her father since his arrival in town, which had been the very same day that he had confronted her and demanded that she leave Slade. But she had seen her mother every day since then. So Regina knew that Nicholas was still adamantly opposed to her marriage.

Jane had been the one to suggest a small, intimate gathering for the four of them. "You cannot let this impasse with your father continue, dear," she had said. Jane was always sensible. "Perhaps if Nicholas gets to know Slade he will change his opinion of him."

Her mother was privy to all of Regina's feelings. They had always been close, now more so than ever. Regina was thrilled when Jane had come to see her the next day and had confided in her instantly, not just about her love for Slade, but her doubts about him, too. Jane seemed certain that all would work out for the best. "If he does not want your money, darling, he must be seriously in love with you."

It did not seem possible that Jane was right. If so, then why was there this increasingly apparent gulf between them?

Slade and Regina had spent the past few days tiptoeing around each other and carefully avoiding the subjects threatening their marriage. Slade was spending more time at the office, leaving earlier and coming home later, which decreased the waking moments they spent together. Since they still made love each night, the time available for conversation had diminished considerably. There was less chance to venture into dangerous territory. Regina could not blame Slade. She also did not want to discuss anything right now which would upset their marriage any further.

Slade knew she had invited her parents for supper. She had found a moment to tell him last night. He had accepted it rather stoically. He had promised to be on his best behavior.

"That's not necessary, Slade," Regina had told him.

He lifted a brow. "You have my promise, Regina. Come what may."

His words left her with a bad feeling, one which haunted her all that next day.

Nicholas and Jane arrived promptly, as Regina had expected. She was very nervous. She hovered behind Brinks as he took her mother's coat, regarding her father anxiously. He was watching her just as intently.

"Thank you for coming, Father."

"Why would I refuse an invitation from my own daughter?"

"You're not still angry?"

"I *am* angry. But not as much as I am hurt." His eyes were dark. "I still cannot believe you ordered me from your home."

"I can barely believe it myself," she whispered. "Please, let's try to have a pleasant evening."

"I did not come here to wage war."

Regina sincerely hoped not. "Let's sit in the salon while we wait for Slade."

They followed her into the salon. "He's not here?" Jane asked.

"Earlier today he sent me a message that he might be detained a bit, but that he would try to be on time."

"Does he know that we are your guests?" Nicholas asked dryly.

"Yes, Father. I would not do something behind my husband's back that had the potential of upsetting him."

Nicholas sighed. "Regina, when will you come to your senses? Every day that you stay with him will only make it more difficult for you to finally leave."

Her spirits crashed. "Are we going to argue over this again? Tonight? You met Slade. Couldn't you see what a fine, responsible man he is?"

"He was not exactly what I expected," Nicholas admitted. "But he cannot give you the kind of life I know you need."

"How poorly you think of me!" Regina cried.

"I know my own daughter," Nicholas flared. "I know you will not be happy living at that Miramar! Were you or were you not unhappy, bored, and restless every time we resided in the country at Dragmore?"

Regina bit her lip. "But that was different! That was before I fell in love with a man whose entire life is wrapped up in his home!"

Jane intervened. "Nicholas, you do know your daughter, of course you do. But daughters grow up and become women. Regina has grown up. It's so very obvious. She has led a perfectly charmed existence because we were determined that she have everything she could possibly want. Now she has had to face adversity and make difficult choices. You should be proud of her, darling. Your daughter is selflessly in love with Slade Delanza, and willing to support him in whatever he has to do."

Nicholas grunted. "I am proud of you, Regina, you know that."

"No, Father, I don't know that. It seems to me that you are angry with me and grievously disappointed."

"I am angry that you have chosen a husband without my consent. I am disappointed that you would think so lightly of my opinion. I do not want you to make the biggest mistake of your life."

"I'm not. I assure you."

"I am not at all convinced, as your mother is, that you really love this man, having seen you infatuated a dozen times since you came out of short skirts. I am certainly not convinced that you love this man enough to give up all you are accustomed to."

Regina hesitated. This was her chance. She seized it. "Father, I don't have to give up all that I am accustomed to. Not if you would give me my inheritance."

Nicholas was silent.

"Father, we need that money, we truly do!"

"That is obvious."

"Do I have to beg?" Regina cried. "What do I have to do to convince you to give us my inheritance? Please, Father, please!"

Nicholas regarded her intently. A sound from the doorway made them all turn. Regina was surprised to see Slade standing there, not having heard him approach. She rushed to him. Seeing that he was rigid, she grew apprehensive. How much of her argument with her father had he overheard?

"Darling," she cried, taking his hand, "I'm so glad you could come home early after all!"

His glance flicked to hers. Regina stiffened. There was no warmth in his eyes; in fact, Slade seemed to be holding back his anger with a considerable effort. "Come," she said, faltering. At all cost, they must present a united front to her parents. "I know you and Father have met, but I think we should redo the introductions. And you have never met my mother."

Slade said nothing, allowing her to lead him forward. As Regina introduced Jane, she stole worried glances at him. Maybe she had imagined his anger. His face was expressionless, his thoughts unfathomable.

"Father," she said anxiously, "would you and Slade please at least exchange gentlemanly handshakes?"

Nicholas's jaw tensed, but he extended his hand. "Hello, Delanza."

Slade took it, equally wary. "Shelton. Welcome to our humble home."

"You're angry with me."

In his shirtsleeves now that her parents had left, Slade folded his arms, and leaned against the door to the salon. "Now what makes you think that?" he said coldly.

She tensed. She had known he was angry all night. But he was more than angry, for he had studied her as one would an odd, just-discovered specimen under a microscope. Indeed, he had studied them all. And he had not spoken except when spoken to. Regina had done her best to carry the conversation, helped by her mother. Nicholas had also said little, intent on assessing Slade. The evening had been an unmitigated disaster, with Slade truly seeming to be nothing short of a boor.

Although she had known he was angry, she had not known he was this angry. His words dripped icicles. If he were not her husband and they were not newlyweds, she would think him to be more than hostile, to be hate-filled.

Regina had taken off her shoes, which she carried in one hand. They had seen her parents out moments ago. Now she paused, almost afraid to approach her husband, which she must do in order to pass him and exit the door. "I'm sorry," she said softly, meaning it.

"Just what are you sorry for?"

She flinched beneath his hostile regard. "I'm sorry I invited my parents for supper. I had no idea it would be such a miserable evening."

"Of course you didn't. In the course of your *charmed* life, this is probably the first 'miserable' evening you have ever spent."

She dropped her shoes. "Were you eavesdropping?"

"A man can't eavesdrop in his own home," Slade said. He strode to the bar, where he poured himself an oversized bourbon. Regina had stopped counting the number of drinks he'd had hours ago. She had never seen him imbibe so much and with such determination. Yet he did not appear drunk.

"If you did not want me to hear something I shouldn't, then you should have thought about the consequences of speaking openly in *my* house," he added vehemently.

She flinched. She tried to decide if he was drunk. Some men became nasty when drinking. She had never been afraid of Slade before, but her instincts were surging forth now to warn her against him. For his anger was directly aimed at her. "Slade, I am sorry, for everything. Please." Making an instinctive decision, she approached him. "Let's go to bed." She touched his arm.

He batted her hand away. "Don't touch me."

She backed up. "I think you've had enough to drink."

He stared. "I'm not drunk, not by a long shot. Not yet. But believe me, I will be before this frigging night is through."

"What have I done?" she whispered.

"You've done it all." He tossed off the entire glass. "Get out of here. And don't bother waiting up. Sex is the last thing on my mind tonight."

Regina cried out. His crude words were a crushing blow, an intentionally cruel one. She could not believe he would say such a thing—and refer to all the glorious intimacy they had shared so disparagingly and so callously. "Why are you doing this? Why do you want to hurt me?"

He eyed her silently.

"If you're trying to make me hate you, it won't work." Her control was gone. She cried, but silently, tears streaking her cheeks. "You see, you can be a bastard but it won't change anything. I'm your wife, for better or for worse."

If he was aware of her shocking language, a first for her, he gave no sign. "I wonder," he said harshly. "Wife—or martyr?"

She shook her head in confusion and denial.

"*I don't want a martyr for a wife.*"

"I'm not! I'm not!"

He turned his back on her. "Get the hell out of here, Regina, before I say any more. Get out now."

But she didn't move. She was breathless, her heart fluttering in fear, but she was no longer afraid for herself. She was afraid for their marriage. They had reached a crisis point, and even if she did not understand how they had arrived here, or even why, she knew they had to talk about it immediately. She was not even aware that she was crying. "Please tell me what I have done," she implored. "Please, Slade."

He whirled. "Damn you! Dammit! If you won't leave, I will!"

She gasped as he rushed past her and into the corridor.

"No," she cried, racing after him. He flung open the front door. "Slade, wait! We must talk! We must!" She knew with certainty, with all of her heart, that she must not let him walk out that door—and out of her life.

But he ignored her. And the fog instantly swallowed him up.

Chapter 26

She dressed with the utmost care.

Lifting her bright-pink skirts, she slid the sheerest silk hose, translucent and white, slowly up her long legs. Garters trimmed in white lace and dark rosebuds followed. Finally allowing her palms to fall free of her thighs, she sighed, dropping her skirts. Her skin was deliciously alive.

Elizabeth Sinclair turned to face her reflection in the mirror.

She smiled. Seduction always stirred her blood. It was only a possibility today, but even the mere possibility stimulated her.

She was strikingly beautiful and she knew it. She smiled at herself, pleased. Slade Delanza could not be indifferent. No man was ever indifferent.

Adusting her rose-red felt hat and taking up her matching gloves, she left her hotel room. Downstairs the doorman hailed her a hansom. Elizabeth ordered the driver to the Feldcrest Building on the corner of Van Ness and Eddy.

Settling back against the worn leather seats, she let her hands slide over her belly. It was too bad it had come to this. If she weren't pregnant she would not have to marry. She sighed, unable to regret the past year—or the past years.

She had been sent away to school in London by her father when she had been thirteen. Remembering, Elizabeth smiled. She had been caught in the stable with the strapping young Irish groom—and they hadn't been doing anything that had to do with horses, but everything that had to do with riding.

Kevin hadn't been her first lover and he hadn't been her last. But he was one of her fondest memories because he had been directly responsible for her being sent away. She had hated the small-town life of San Luis Obispo for as long as she could remember. She was thrilled to be sent to London.

The elite private academy for young ladies was no match for Elizabeth. She quickly learned how to slip away at night. She had always looked—and acted— older than her years, and she quickly became a part of London's thriving nightlife.

She continued to present herself as a proper, devout young woman by day. When she came home she let no clue slip that she had not been reformed by the academy. She agreed to the betrothal, having little choice. When she met James Delanza she decided he was nice enough, if a bit boring. Still, he was very attractive, and she imagined the first few years of their marriage would be quite enjoyable.

Her father had died last summer. Elizabeth was sorry, she had loved George, but his timing could not have been better. For upon his death his entire fortune passed to her and she no longer had to wait until she was wed to receive her inheritance.

Never a fool, Elizabeth continued her charade. She spent that summer in San Luis Obispo mourning her father, while James came to see her every weekend, attempting to comfort her. Unfortunately his idea of consolation and hers were quite different. As soon as she was scheduled to return to London for her last year at the academy, she did. Eagerly. But she did not set foot back in the school. Instead she set herself up in a lavish town house, living a life that was an imitation of that of the British nobility she consorted with.

She would have stayed in London indefinitely, despite her looming marriage, when an affair ended abominably. This time, for the first time, Elizabeth was the one jilted, coldly and callously. Her lover had been an earl, both powerful and handsome, and Elizabeth was as in love with him as a woman like her could be. She was shocked and furious. She even tried to reason him out of it, to no avail. Not only was he through with her, he had the audacity to tell her that he was getting married—and that *he* was in love with his bride.

Elizabeth returned to America in a huff. She sent James a letter ending their engagement as soon as she arrived in San Luis Obispo near the end of May. Her stepmother had remarried, and Elizabeth, shedding all pretenses of amiability, rented a small mansion which would make Susan green with jealousy and hired a large staff, leaving abruptly and in open triumph. She soon took another lover, but found it hard to shake the earl's image from her mind.

Once she had realized that she was three months pregnant, she knew she could not continue as she was and that she must act swiftly. It was one thing to pretend to be a proper woman while doing as she pleased, it was quite another to be unwed and obviously pregnant. Her lover was married or she might have demanded that he wed her. Because time was of the utmost consideration, Elizabeth decided to go forward with a union with the Delanzas.

It was for the best that James Delanza was dead. He had not taken it well when she had broken their engagement. Being an expert when it came to men, she was well aware that he had been terribly in love with her, but she had crushed him as one would a fly, the way the earl had crushed her. In the process she had revealed too much. Had he survived the flood, it would have been impossible to reconcile with him.

Rick had two other sons. Elizabeth would not consider the younger one. Although she was an heiress, she was too vain to even consider marrying Edward, who had nothing, not even the hope of one day owning Miramar. She was certain Rick would still favor an alliance between his oldest son and her. She had always known that Miramar needed her inheritance. Little could have changed in the past two months. And by now everyone at Miramar was just over the shock of James's death. Indeed, her timing was probably perfect.

Elizabeth smiled. Her excuse for visiting Slade would be to pay her condolences—which were long overdue. He would be instantly attracted to her, of course, and she would use it for all that it was worth. If he were still distraught over his brother's death, she would comfort him the way that James had never comforted her. And she would work fast.

Regina's heart was in her throat. She was sick to her stomach. She made no effort to disembark from the hansom. The driver twisted to look at her. "Lady, this is it. The Feldcrest Building. You owe me twelve cents."

"Yes," Regina said hoarsely, fumbling for the change. She gave it to him and stumbled to the curb. She was loath to go into the building.

Slade had not come home last night. She had not slept a wink, crying until she'd had no tears left, afraid that their marriage was crumbling before her very eyes. In the past days as their relationship continued to deteriorate, it was only their lovemaking that offered hope, that still bound them together in intimacy. Last night was the first time since they had been living together as husband and wife that Slade had not slept with her. It seemed ominous. And she still could not understand how they had spiraled so viciously to this conclusion. Not so long ago they had been happy. Or had it only been the illusion of happiness?

Regina did not know, and she was afraid of the answer.

All night and all day, as she had alternately mourned

what was happening to them and contemplated how they might surmount such straits, images of Slade as he had been last night, utterly cold and totally distant, haunted her. If his goal had been to bar her from his heart, she knew that he had finally succeeded. But if his goal had been to make her hate him, then he had failed.

For she meant what she had said. She was his wife, for better or for worse, and she did not take such vows lightly. The promises she had made had come from her heart, as did the resolve which now filled her.

She swallowed, feeling sad and frightened. Slade had not come home last night; there was no excuse for such behavior, but she would not even mention it. She would not shriek or scold when she saw him. She would handle this crisis with all the dignity she could muster. She could not let him continue to slip away from her—she could not. She intended to fight for her marriage. She would begin by inviting him out to lunch.

Resolute, Regina entered the high-ceilinged lobby. She approached the elevator quickly, where another woman was waiting. After the elevator had arrived, Regina entered behind the stranger. Regina was immersed in her own thoughts, but she noticed that the woman pressed the button for the tenth floor. Only Charles Mann's offices were there, and she regarded the woman curiously.

The other woman stared back rather haughtily. Regina looked away. She had seen enough. The other woman was strikingly beautiful, about Regina's own age, a bit taller, more voluptuous, and very fair and blonde. There was an air about her that was very sophisticated—in that way she reminded Regina a little of Xandria.

Regina had barely slept the night before and she knew that she looked terrible. Her face was pale and her eyes were puffy. She had probably never looked worse. Normally Regina would not compare herself to another woman, but today she could not help feeling dowdy next to the stranger.

When the elevator stopped on the tenth floor, Regina

politely let her exit first. She could not imagine what such a woman would want with someone from Charles Mann's office. The other woman had removed her gloves and Regina had already noticed that she did not wear a wedding ring, so obviously she was not visiting her husband. Perhaps one of the clerks was a beau. Trailing behind her, Regina frowned when the woman appeared to be going all the way to the end of the corridor. There was only one office at the end of the hall and Regina froze in her tracks.

Why would this woman be visiting Slade? What business could she possibly have with him?

The woman paused in front of the desk where Slade's assistant, Harold, sat. He had not seen Regina yet, who lingered halfway down the corridor, and when he saw the young woman he immediately became flustered. Even from a distance, Regina saw Harold turn beet-red when confronted by her beauty.

They spoke. Harold got up and went into Slade's office. A moment later he returned and ushered the woman inside. He closed the door to Slade's office and took his seat.

Regina moved forward. "Good day, Harold."

He started. "Mrs. Delanza! I did not see you."

Regina did not waste words. "Harold, who is that woman who just entered my husband's office?"

"Her name is Elizabeth Sinclair, ma'am."

Regina sat as still as a mannequin at her dressing table. Her reflection was pale and ghostly white. She gripped a pearl-handled brush in her hand. She had been putting up her hair. On the bed lay the gown and underclothes which she would wear that evening to the gala at Charles Mann's.

She could not concentrate on the task at hand. Her mind was spinning crazily as it had been all afternoon. She had thought herself to be that woman, Elizabeth Sinclair. For a week or more she had lived as that woman, as Elizabeth Sinclair. And then, when the amnesia had disappeared, she had masqueraded as her as well.

She could not help being touched with guilt for purposefully assuming the other woman's identity.

They did not really look alike. There was no real resemblance between her and Elizabeth Sinclair. Yes, they were both blonde and pretty, both slender and petite. But there was no way that anyone who had ever met either one of them could mistake them for each other.

Of course, Rick had already confessed that he had realized the truth from the beginning, and Regina had long since forgiven him. No one else at Miramar had ever laid eyes on Elizabeth, except for James, who was dead.

What was she doing here?

The question had drummed in her brain all day until her head was aching from it. Regina could not help thinking that she was here to take what should have been hers from the very start—both Miramar and Slade.

She stared at herself. Her face was drawn, her expression tense. Her fear was ridiculous; she was Slade's wife, and that was irrevocable. But Elizabeth Sinclair's advent into their life could not have come at a worse time. It was one more blow for her to survive, and after the series of blows already dealt to their marriage, she felt almost incompetent to deal with it.

But she would.

Her thoughts were interrupted when Slade knocked briefly on the door, then pushed it open. Regina stared at him in the mirror. He paused in the doorway, staring back. Finally he said, "Isn't the gala tonight?"

"Yes, it is." Her voice was amazingly calm. Was he going to tell her about the visit from Elizabeth Sinclair?

He walked into the room, closing the door behind him. He went straight to the armoire, where his tuxedo, freshly pressed, was hanging on the door. He began to undress. Then, his shirt balled up and clenched in his hand, he faced her. "Aren't you going to say something?"

She looked at him. "About what?"

"About last night."

"What do you want me to say?"

"I don't know. Something. Anything. Most women would be having a fit, or be in tears, or be in bed with the covers pulled up over their heads, sulking."

"I'm not most women."

"Don't I know it."

She hesitated. "All right, I'm sorry you stayed out last night, sorry and disappointed."

He winced. "You *would* know how to make me feel even worse."

"You *should* feel guilty, Slade. If you want to apologize, I would accept."

"You know what?" he said roughly. "I *am* sorry. Damn, but I'm sorry for everything."

She was afraid he was not referring to last night, but to their marriage. She found she could not respond.

He turned his back on her to pull off his pants, his movements hard and abrupt.

Dismay crept over her. "Aren't you going to tell me?"

"Tell you what?" He pulled on a dressing gown.

"Aren't you going to tell me about the visitor you had today?"

He froze. "What?"

"Elizabeth Sinclair."

He moved toward her, meeting her eyes in the mirror. He paused behind her. "How do you know that she came to see me today?"

"I saw her. We met in the elevator, so to speak. I had hoped to have lunch with you, but when I realized who she was . . . well, I was upset."

"So you left."

"Yes."

Slade moved to her side so he could look at her directly. Apprehensive, Regina turned to face him. "What did she want?"

"I don't know."

"What did she say?" She was trembling.

"She gave me some stupid song and dance about how sorry she was about James. It was a big fat lie. That woman doesn't have a drop of sympathy in her blood for my brother," Slade said angrily.

"Are you sure?"

"I'm sure. She told me that before James died they had an argument and broke it off mutually. Which was why she didn't arrive in Templeton as scheduled."

"But no one knew," Regina said.

"That's right!" Slade cried. "She was lying through her teeth, Regina. James was head over heels in love with her, although after meeting her, I can't figure out why. James would have never broken up with her. She obviously broke up with him just before he died. But why, why didn't he say something?"

"Because he was hurt?"

Slade hit the wall with his hand. "Damn it! It kills me to think that James died with a broken heart. Damn her!"

Regina, having heard so much about James for so long now, felt as if she had known him, and she was also moved. "Maybe you're wrong, Slade."

"No, I'm not. She left lickety-split when she found out I was married. In fact, when she found out about you, she changed as fast as a chameleon. If you want to know what I really think, I think she was sniffing around me for one reason and it had nothing to do with James—it was for the purpose of marriage."

"I knew it," Regina said faintly.

He gave her a dark look and stalked away. Regina stared at the mirror, not seeing her own reflection or his. She had been right. Elizabeth had come here to claim Slade and her place at Miramar. It did not make sense, not after she had ended her engagement to James. But it was the only explanation for her sudden appearance in their lives. "Why would she break it off with James and then decide she wanted to marry you?"

"I don't know and I really don't care," Slade said shortly. "Forget her, Regina, she's the past."

He was right. Elizabeth was now the past. Regina had wondered about the other woman for some time, and slowly she began to relax. Some of the questions which had plagued her were answered, and she supposed the others would never be resolved. But it didn't really matter.

Elizabeth had come here, dramatically entering their lives, to claim Slade and her place at Miramar. But she had come too late. After the masquerade, after having assumed her identity, and even having believed herself to be her for a while, Regina was glad to have finally been confronted with the mysterious other woman. Her sudden reappearance in their lives could have been destructive, but as fate would have it, she could be easily dismissed instead. She had touched their lives more deeply than she would ever know, for if not for her, Regina would have never been taken in by the Delanzas, she would have never married Slade. Her role in this drama was over, once and for all. Perhaps in the back of her mind Regina had worried all along about the real Elizabeth Sinclair. She realized that she was relieved.

It was one of the most beautiful, and one of the most painful, sights he had ever seen in his life.

Slade stood on the edge of the dance floor, blending into the festive crowd but feeling apart from it. The huge ballroom of the Mann mansion was filled almost to capacity. The men were clad in tailcoats, the women in brilliantly hued ball gowns, feathered boas, and glittering jewels. The vaulted ballroom was alive with the buzz of conversation, laughter, and the rich, vibrant strains of a string quartet. White-jacketed waiters passed around exotic aperitifs, and banquet tables in the back of the room were laden with equally exotic food. Xandria had chosen a tropical motif for the ball. The floral arrangements were tall, exotic orange and purple blooms, and thirty-foot palms graced the four corners of the room. Slade was barely aware of these details as he stood watching the dancers whirling in clouds of billowing, jewel-like colors. For among them was his wife.

She was dancing with an acquaintance of his. She had been dancing for the past half hour. Slade was certain that his wife had taken to the dance floor to escape him.

They had ridden over to the Mann mansion in silence. He was well aware that his marriage had unraveled. Regina, once carefree and gay, was pale and withdrawn. Her attempts at light conversation were forced. Overwhelmed with what he had done earlier that day, Slade could not respond to her overtures. But as soon as they had arrived, Regina was transformed. He had watched her in amazement. She moved among the crowd with animation and enthusiasm, as if there was nothing at all wrong in her life. She had learned the art of social conversation well. She conversed with strangers as if they were old and dear friends. She had the knack of putting everyone immediately at ease. She was gay, beautiful, and bright. Everyone instantly adored her, falling hard for her charm.

He admired her. He had always admired her, from the very first, but now more than ever. This facade of hers could not be easy to maintain. He knew that she was strained from his rude behavior last night, behavior he still regretted, and from the brief advent of Elizabeth Sinclair into their lives. While the meeting with Elizabeth had left a bitter aftertaste in his mouth—he had taken an instant, overwhelming dislike to her—she could be easily dismissed from his thoughts. Last night could not be so easily forgotten.

He would never forget the sight of Regina begging her father for her inheritance, he would never forget the sound of her pleas. Despite the fact that he had told her he would not take her money, obviously she could not bear to be parted from it. He did not condemn her for her materialism. She deserved to live like a princess; no woman deserved it more.

Shelton's words haunted him, too. Apparently he, Slade, was not her first infatuation, and, like Shelton, he doubted he would be the last.

It would be easy to believe what he wanted to believe—that she loved him. It would also be very foolish.

They were so different. He had known it all along, but now the differences were glaring. Seeing her here at the gala, moving so easily among the elite of San Francisco society, was the final proof. She loved this kind of life and all that it involved; he hated it. He hated this nonsense, he always had. He was a simple man with simple needs. A life at Miramar was all he'd every really, secretly coveted, until Regina. But Regina thrived in this glossy, glittering setting. How could he have thought for a moment that she would be happy living with him at Miramar? Here, at last, was proof that he had done what was right.

Turning, Slade walked away, into the crowd.

Regina finally refused her fifth or sixth dance partner, not having to make up an excuse, for she was truly tired. The evening seemed endless. Once upon a time a night like this would have delighted her. Now it took all of her well-bred schooling and all of her determination to present an amiable facade to the guests who had come in her and Slade's honor.

She did not see Slade,. which was just as well. His increasingly withdrawn demeanor was frightening her. With every passing hour he grew more distant from her. Regina did not know what she was doing wrong. She was cheerful and bright, including him skillfully in every single conversation, even when it was all too clear that he did not want to be included. She was growing desperate. This evening should have been the perfect opportunity for the two of them to regain some normalcy in their marriage, as they had to present a united front to all those they met. Yet it was just the opposite case. Dread had long since beat its way into her breast.

Exhausted, Regina headed toward the powder room. She looked for Slade as she moved through the crowded ballroom but did not glimpse him. Her parents were in attendance, and they waved at her, trying to entice her to come over to them. Regina signaled them that she would return in a moment. But she did not want to speak with them tonight. They would take one look at her and demand to know why she was so unhappy.

She *was* unhappy. She was unhappy and frightened. How were she and Slade going to continue if their relationship kept on worsening? How could she stop this perilous downslide when she did not even understand it?

She was moving past the open doors of the terrace when a movement in the shadows outside caught her attention. The terrace was illuminated with dozens of paper lanterns, strung up and glowing like small incandescent moons. She paused, her gaze settling on a very familiar outline.

Rick had seen her too. Shrugging sheepishly, he came out of the shadows and met her inside.

"You came!"

"Yeah, well, hell." Rick looked uncomfortable. "You have a way about you."

Regina smiled. It was tremulous, but her first real smile of the night.

"You don't look good," Rick said bluntly. "You've had enough for tonight. Slade should take you home."

Tears were misting her vision, tears that had nothing to do with her own heavy heart. She pointed toward the dancers. "He's over there somewhere. Go to him, Rick."

Instead of moving, Rick said, "I shouldn't be here."

"No," Regina said, "you *should* be here." She took his arm. She had been going to the powder room for a brief respite, but this was more important. "Come with me."

Reluctantly, Rick allowed himself to be led across the room.

They finally found Slade standing alone beneath one of the potted palm trees. It struck her then that his lonely stance beneath the tree in the corner of the room was as purposeful as his self-inflicted exile in San Francisco, and as meaningful.

He saw them. His eyes widened.

Rick nodded at his son. "Fancy turnout."

"I don't believe this," Slade said. "I've been living in the city for ten years, yet until last week I never saw you here, not once. Now, in one week, I see you twice. I don't understand."

Rick shoved his hands in his pockets. "I came to the city to speak with your wife. But since she won't ask you to come home, I realized I'll have to do it myself."

"*What?*"

"You heard. You're gone and Edward's gone." He shifted. "I can't run the place alone."

"Sure you can, Rick. Even when James was alive, you were running it alone."

Regina came to life. "Slade, your father has just asked you to go home!"

"I heard him. I'll think about it," he said to Rick.

"What the hell is there to think about?" Rick asked angrily. "You prefer this crap to Miramar? That's real. This is a fairyland and nothing more!"

"Maybe I'll think about how long it took you to ask me to come home—and why you want me at Miramar now—when you never did before."

"Stop it!" Regina cried. "Why can't you both put your damnable pride aside and admit that you need each other? Why? Oh, to hell with you both!"

She turned and fled, finally pushed over the edge. She had had enough. She ran through the crowd and found herself alone on the terrace under the dozens of paper moons. She gripped the cold iron railing, refusing to cry. "Damn you," she whispered, cursing Slade. "Stubborn bloody fool." If he refused to make peace with his father, would he refuse to make peace with her, too? What would it take for Rick to get through to him? What would it take for her to get through to him?

"Regina?"

She tensed. Her father was the last person she wanted to see. "Please go away."

"I can't, not when you are so upset." He put his hand on her shoulder. "Why isn't your husband here comforting you?"

Regina turned to face him. "Because we're having problems. Isn't that what you want to hear?"

Nicholas sat beside her on the bench. "Do you want to tell me?"

"No, not really."

"I love you, Regina. Saying 'I told you so' is the last thing on my mind."

Regina covered her face with her hands. "I still love him, although things are so bad now and I don't know why. But I know that we can work through this. I know I can make him happy—that we can be happy." She raised her head to stare defiantly at her father. "If you've come out here to gloat, if you think that I'm going to run out on him just because everything isn't perfect, then you're wrong."

"I did not come out here to gloat," Nicholas said. "Your mother is right, Regina, you *have* grown up since we last saw you."

"That's right, Father. In England I was a naive, inexperienced girl, a nice enough girl, but a spoiled one. No more. I am going to stay and fight for what I want, and what I want is Slade."

"You know, I'm proud of you."

Regina gasped. "What did you say?"

"I'm proud of you. Perhaps you do sincerely love this man. The daughter I left behind in Texas would not have withstood the adversity you have, or the adversity now besetting you. I barely recognize you, Regina."

"I take that as a compliment."

"It *is* a compliment. You have changed, become strong. God, it's so hard to let go. Your mother has been harping on me that I have to let you live your own life, make your own decisions, whether good or bad. I'm used to being in control, but I'm going to let go."

"What are you saying?" she cried.

Nicholas sighed. "I am apologizing. I fear I overreacted to your marriage when I arrived in town and was confronted so abruptly with it. But at that time I was expecting to be greeted by my young daughter, not by a full-grown, mature woman. I will respect whatever decision you make regarding your marriage."

She was speechless.

Nicholas took her hands. "In other words, I will support your decision to remain with Slade Delanza."

"Father," she cried, hugging him. "Thank you so much for having faith in me."

"You deserve it. Of course, I'm not going to withhold your inheritance, either."

Regina hugged him again. "Of course! I knew you would come around. Thank you, Father. Not just for the money Slade needs, but for trusting me to do the right thing."

They arrived home at midnight, having left the gala in full swing. Regina's spirits had lifted. Her father had come around, so much sooner than she had thought he would. She was elated. Now she truly felt like celebrating. But when she tried to take Slade's hand, he would not let her.

When they were alone in their bedroom he withdrew, walking away from her to face the night-darkened window. Regina decided that now was not the time to discuss her father or her inheritance. But it was definitely the time to discuss their relationship. "Slade, can we talk?"

He turned slowly. His face was grim. "Yes, let's talk."

She went still. "Why do I have the feeling that you're going to say something I don't want to hear?"

"You know me well."

"Slade, I don't know you half as well as I long to."

He took a breath. "This isn't easy. I don't want to hurt you. You may not believe this, but I have thought this out at great length." He seemed incapable of continuing.

She was terrified. For she knew, instinctively, what was coming. "No."

"Regina, this was a mistake from the very beginning."

"No," she managed, "no, don't start, it was not a mistake—I love you!"

He flinched. "Regina, we cannot go on like this. I cannot go on like this."

She cried out.

"It would be best if you moved back to your uncle's tomorrow," he said firmly, striding to the door. "Tonight I'll sleep in the study." He paused. "I'm sorry."

"No." She finally found her voice, although it was high and desperate. "Don't be absurd. I love you. We have been having a few bad days, that's all, I—"

He gripped the doorknob, his knuckles white. "It's too late. I filed for a divorce today."

Part Three

Revelations

Chapter 27

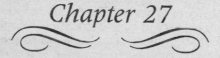

*O*ne month later, Slade locked up the house on Gough Street. He was finally returning to Miramar. It had taken him a month to dispose of his affairs for Charles and to find a replacement and acquaint that gentleman with his responsibilities. Not only had he locked up the house which he had rented for so many years, but he was handing the keys back over to the landlord. There were too many memories there now and he didn't plan on ever returning. But even so, he knew the memories would haunt him for a lifetime.

Regina had left him. She had left him the night of the gala, shortly after he had told her that he had filed for a divorce. That was a night he would never forget, one he wished he could forget. For when her shock had subsided, there was fury—so much fury.

"How dare you forsake our vows!" she screamed. A second later she had thrown a vase at him. Any temper she had ever had she had always controlled with ladylike rigor, but now she cast all such considerations aside.

He flinched, shocked at the display but saying nothing because there wasn't much more he could possibly say.

"You are nothing but a coward, Slade Delanza, turning tail at the slightest sign of trouble! And you are also a fool, because we could be happy, we could be so very happy, if you would only let us!" She was sobbing. "But I don't have enough strength for the two of us, not anymore. Goddamn you!"

She had rushed away, running down the stairs, stumbling on the skirts of her ball gown. Slade found himself racing after her, torn in two, desperately wanting to call her back. But she was already fleeing through the front door, without pausing even for a coat, and disappearing into the night.

Slade wanted to go after her. He'd wanted to shout the truth at her, that he loved her with all of his heart. He was ready, so ready, to forget his resolve. But images of that evening danced in his head, images of her in her couture gown with her fabulous pearls, waltzing in the arms of bankers and politicians, flitting through the crowd, a beautiful and perfect social butterfly. He did not call her back. He did not go after her. It was better this way for her, for she was returning to the life she had been born to; soon she would marry her duke. And it was better for him. It didn't feel better—his head ached and his heart hurt—but the pain would be so much worse years from now, when she walked out on him.

Pocketing the key, Slade stared up at the empty, shuttered house. God, a month had gone by but the pain was still so raw. He felt as if he were bleeding inside. Would he ever get over it? Would he ever get over her?

He walked down the front steps, his vision suspiciously blurry, to the hired carriage waiting on the street. Slade saw that Kim had already loaded their bags. Usually Kim was hopping with excitement when embarking on a trip with Slade, but not today. He had been uncharacteristically somber ever since Regina had left. Slade had not been able to hide his torment from the little boy, no matter how hard he had tried. And Kim was such a source of comfort, dogging his steps and rushing to do his bidding as if fetching the newspaper might end Slade's misery and bring light into the darkness of his life. Slade didn't know how he would have survived the past weeks without Kim underfoot and without his clever little ploys, all aimed at making Slade smile. And Kim had made him smile, more than once, despite it all.

But Kim was more upset than Slade had guessed, because one night Slade found him crying in his bed. Slade was stricken with guilt for distressing the child who was like a son to him. But Kim confessed that he missed "missee wife" also. Slade had cried then too, but secretly, so that Kim would not see.

Now he managed a mostly cheerful smile for Kim's benefit as he approached. "Okay, pal," he said. "We've got one stop to make, to say our good-byes to Charles and Xandria, and we're on our way."

Kim returned his smile hesitantly. "Tonight we be at Mi'a'ma'?"

Slade slid his hand into the boy's cap of silky black hair. "You bet." He lifted him into the carriage, jumping up himself. "Tonight we'll be at Miramar." He signaled the driver and they were off.

Slade tensed. They were going east on California Street, and coming into view was the D'Archands' home. There was no reason for him to tense up, because she was not there and he was well aware of it. Too late, he wished he had told the driver to take a different route.

His hand slid into the pocket of his suit jacket. His fingers slid over a letter so worn it was falling to pieces. He had read it a thousand times, he would read it a thousand more. It was, of course, from his wife.

Dear Slade, I am going home. Perhaps one day you will find the courage to come home, too. Your wife, Regina.

The note had arrived four days after he had told her he was divorcing her and she had left his house. Upon reading it, he had been stricken. He had almost given in to his impulses and run to her uncle's and asked her to come back. Of course, he was stronger than that. He was more like James than he had ever thought; he was selfless and noble after all.

He knew she had returned to England with her parents and that they were no longer in the city. She had gone home.

But even while he knew she had returned to England, he brooded about the fact that she had never gone forward with his motion for a divorce. Technically they were still married even if they were separated by a vast ocean. She had signed the note *your wife, Regina,* a blatant reminder of the fact. What did it mean? It bothered him. It bothered him because secretly he could not help clinging to that fact, as if it were some sort of lifeline.

He told himself to be logical. She had left the city furious with him, furious and hurt. There had not been time for her to solicit lawyers and legal advice and to deal with the paperwork and bureaucracy necessary to finalize a divorce. Every day he expected an inquiry from her lawyers in London. No inquiry came.

He brooded, too, upon the rest of her use of language in the brief letter. Why hadn't she said that he would one day *return* home? She had said he would one day *come* home, as if he would be coming to their home, or as if he would be coming home to her. She had also spoken of his needing courage to do so, when her last parting words had been to accuse him of being a coward. It did not make sense. It almost made him think the impossible. He refused to succumb to fantasies. She had gone home to England to marry her duke—she was not at Miramar, waiting for him with patience, devotion, and love. But if such a fantasy were true, he knew he would not be able to send her away a second time.

But it wasn't true; he was a lovesick fool, and the more he indulged in daydreams, the worse it got. He had to try and forget her, but that was like asking the sun and the moon and the stars to disappear.

God, how he missed her.

Charles and Xandria knew he was coming and they were waiting for him. Edward was with them. Slade was not surprised. Despite his own desolation, he was aware that his brother was keeping company with Xandria. There was at least a ten-year difference between them, and Slade could not fathom what was going on in Xandria's mind. But where once he might have judged her, he had no more judgments to make. He hoped that Edward's friendship might make Xandria realize that it was time for her to find a man to seriously love, and to marry.

Charles was somber; Xandria was teary-eyed and sniffled into a handkerchief. "I'm not crying because I'm selfish," Xandria said, hugging Slade. "But of course I will miss you. I'm crying because I am glad that you are finally going home where you belong."

"*Touché,*" Edward said emphatically.

Slade stepped back from Xandria. "I feel I owe it to Regina."

The others were startled into silence.

Slade reddened. "The one thing she couldn't stand was my fighting with Rick. Call it her legacy if you will. But I am going home, and Rick and I are going to settle things once and for all."

Charles stepped forward. "It's about time, Slade. Try not to judge your father too harshly. Remember, even fathers make mistakes."

Slade grimaced. "It won't be easy, but I am really going to try."

Charles embraced him. "There's nothing you can't do when you put your mind to it. You are as determined as you are smart. The next time I see you I fully expect your differences with Rick to be a thing of the past."

Slade wasn't quite as hopeful as Charles. "Well, we'll see. Charles, I want to thank you again for the loan. You can't have any idea how much it means to me." He meant it. He was no longer thinking of selling the Henessy place to generate more cash. Regina had loved it. He recalled all too well how adamant she had been against his selling it. That was her legacy to him, too.

Edward accompanied him to the railroad station. They left Xandria and Charles waving farewell on the street. Slade looked at his brother, seated beside him in the carriage. "Why do I get the feeling you have something on your mind?"

"Because I do. When are you going to get smart and go after her?"

Slade tensed.

"You love her. It's obvious. Don't be stupid and stubborn. I don't know what happened or why she left you, but go after her."

"Don't get involved in this," Slade warned.

"But I *am* involved, up to my eyeballs."

He looked at his brother very carefully. "What does that mean?"

"I knew all along who she really was."

Slade stared, shocked.

Edward touched his arm. "I didn't tell you because I knew that you needed her. You need her. Admit it. At least admit the truth."

"All right!" Slade was furious. "I do need her, but she doesn't need me. Does that satisfy you?"

"No! That woman is in love with you, you jackass, and she has been from the word go!"

"Leave it alone."

"No. I won't. I didn't tell you who she was because I wanted the two of you to marry and find each other and find happiness. But you had to push her away. Don't you understand?" Edward cried. "After ten years, I thought to atone for my sins, I thought I'd finally be free of the guilt!"

"Atone for your sins? Be free of the guilt? What guilt?"

"I've never forgiven myself for causing you to run away in the first place."

Slade was slack-jawed.

"I chased you away from Miramar. After that night, you never came back. When Regina appeared in our lives, with you now Rick's heir, it seemed that finally you were going to return to us. She seemed like a gift from fate. For me, holding my silence about her secret was a way of making up for all those years you were so unhappy."

"You goddammed fool," Slade cried. "My running away had nothing to do with you! I can't believe you've been blaming yourself all these years!" He was horrified.

Edward held up a hand. "Logic has nothing to do with the feelings a small boy has. Anyway, it doesn't matter. *You* matter. You deserve to be happy; you need her. Go after her, dammit. Find her and bring her back to Miramar so you can be happy and I can feel I've paid for my mistakes."

"You sonofabitch," Slade said, deeply distressed. "*It wasn't your fault.* Somehow you have to believe that. And—I am going home, and it's for good. But as far as Regina is concerned, know this. She's happy now, and that's more important to me than my own happiness. It would have never worked, Ed."

"God," Edward said, "you *are* a fool. Maybe I'll have to take matters into my own hands—again."

"Don't you dare," Slade said tersely.

Edward raised his hands in mock defeat. But there was no sign of submission in his eyes.

Slade had wired ahead to Templeton so that when he arrived at Miramar with Kim it would not be a surprise. But Slade had not expected his father to walk out of the house to greet him as he jumped down from the buckboard. Rick was smiling, albeit somewhat cautiously.

Once, and it seemed like so long ago, Slade had thought he would finally come home with Regina at his side as his wife. She wasn't at his side but he felt her presence as if she were close by. Heartache, never far from the surface, swept through him. He nodded at his father. "I didn't think I'd rate a personal greeting."

Rick hesitated. "You do."

Slade gaped. Then his eyes narrowed. "You get knocked on the head recently or something?"

"Not exactly," Rick said wryly. "Although a little birdie's been chirping in my ears for some time now. It's a miracle I haven't gone deaf."

Slade had no idea what his father was talking about.

They each grabbed a bag and walked into the courtyard, Kim running ahead to explore after receiving a nod from Slade. Despite the failure of his marriage, Slade couldn't help feeling a thrill to be back home. Miramar was in his blood, he could never be replete without it.

Just outside the doors to his room, Slade said, "Do you think we'll have early rains this year?"

"I don't know. The weather has been strange. The late-spring rain, the flood, that summer storm." Rick paused, and Slade knew his father, too, was thinking about James. "Don't think we can take a chance. We'll round up the herds and bring them down before the end of the month."

Slade agreed. Then he said, knowing that he was triggering the confrontation they must have, "But I won't be helping."

"Why the hell not?"

" 'Cause I'm going to be clearing land. In fact, tomorrow I'll be going back to town to put up help-wanted posters. I'm going to hire a dozen men. I figure I've got a month left as long as the bad weather doesn't set in early. I want to be ready to plant as much acreage as possible early in the spring."

Rick threw down Slade's bag. "You still have that crazy damn idea! Over my dead body!"

Slade said tightly, dropping his own valise, "We have no choice. What do I have to do to convince you of the facts?"

"We are not farmers, dammit! We can slaughter more beef. I've thought about it and I've been talking with packers in Chicago. They're eager to do more business."

"I'm happy to slaughter more beef, but that's not going to solve our problems."

"Maybe if you hadn't sent your wife away we could solve our problems, as we originally planned, without becoming farmers!"

"Leave Regina out of this!" Slade shot back. "And 'we' never originally planned anything. I always planned to take over this ranch and make it profitable!"

"How?" Rick challenged. "By borrowing more money from Charlie Mann? That's just what we need, more damn debt!"

"I did borrow thirty thousand dollars from Charles," Slade said coolly, "and we have enough capital to operate for a few years. Either we take Miramar into the future and make the rancho profitable, or we'll be facing bankruptcy again. If you object, then not only will I leave, I'll take the cash with me." It was a bluff, because Slade wasn't leaving, but he also knew Rick could not allow him to leave with the money. "I paid off our old debt, but I imagine the banks will lose patience with you again pretty quick once you fail to make more payments."

"You are a sonofabitch."

Slade looked at Rick. "I mean it. We're going to do things my way. I put the thirty thousand in my own account. You can't touch those funds. If I leave, the money leaves. You have no choice." He kept his voice calm, which was no easy feat. He knew Regina was right. Living at Miramar would be a nightmare if he and Rick did not reach some kind of understanding. At the very least he and his father must be able to work together. But with his mind—and his heart—he knew that was only a superficial solution that could not heal the wounds that were so very old and went so very deep.

Rick was furious. He paced around the courtyard. "You are a heartless bastard. Blackmailing your own father!"

"I'm sorry it has to be this way. You need time to think it through?"

"I guess I have no damn choice," Rick gritted. "Fine, turn us into farmers. My pappy's gonna turn right over in the grave. Why in hell did I ever ask you to come home?"

The words hurt. They shouldn't, but they did. But there would be no going back from this point, because Slade had come home to stay, and he was determined to get to the truth—no matter how painful it might be.

"You asked me to come home because you need me," Slade said bitterly. "Because you need the money I've acquired. Not because you have any feelings for your second son!"

Rick paled.

Slade was stricken with a sudden, wrenching insight. He wanted this man's affection more than he wanted almost anything, and it made the moment even more painful.

Rick recovered first, his face suffusing with color. "You're the one with no feelings for me!" he shot back. "You're the one who left me! I didn't leave you! Remember?"

Slade shook with long-repressed emotions: anger, pain, need, desperation. Regina chose that moment to come to him, so strongly it was as if she were present. She had wanted to reconcile father and son from the moment she had first set foot on Miramar soil. "You didn't try to stop me."

Rick was incredulous. "You were determined to go. Determined! When you decide to do something, boy, nobody can stop you and we both know it!"

Slade stared at his father. He was acutely aware that he had come home, finally and irrevocably. Miramar had always been his great love, now only second to his wife. He had given her up, but he was not going to give up Miramar, his last chance at happiness, even though it would be incomplete without Regina. Fleeing Miramar—fleeing Rick, his feelings—has no longer an alternative. He was afraid. The feelings had been buried so deeply for so long.

There was no turning back. "But you should have tried." Slade faced his father, feeling at once a tough man of twenty-five and a vulnerable boy of fifteen. "You didn't care enough to try."

Rick was ashen. "How in hell would you know what I feel?"

"You had James. Who was perfect. You didn't give a damn about me." Suddenly his control shattered. "I want you to admit it! I want you to be honest! Once you admit it we can go forward, as business partners and nothing else. We can forget we're father and son." Slade had never been more furious. "Admit it!" he shouted. "Admit it, damn it, admit it now!"

Rick was speechless.

Slade erupted. He reached his father in a stride and grabbed him by the fabric of his shirt. Rick was taller and bigger than he was, but he was so angry he lifted him several inches off the ground. "Coward!" He realized he was echoing Regina's words and that this situation was almost exactly the same as the one in which he and his wife had confronted each other. Only then it had been an ending, and now he prayed that this was a beginning.

Rick finally knocked his hands away. "*You* left *me!* You were the one with no feelings, no loyalty, no love! You left me, dammit, just like your damn mother left me!"

Slade was shaking. For one aching heartbeat he stared at his father, the man who hadn't cared enough to stop him from leaving when he had waited so desperately for some indication, any indication, of affection. But none had been given then, and he knew none would be forthcoming now. "*You* let me go!"

"Was I supposed to beg you to stay?" Rick cried.

"Yes! Yes!"

Slowly, painfully, Rick said, "You're your mother's son, and so much like her. I loved your mother. She broke my heart, Slade. Then you did the same damned thing."

Slade was speechless.

"I didn't beg her to stay when she left me, an' I didn't beg you. I don't regret not begging her, but I've been regretting not begging you for the past ten years."

"God," Slade whispered. "I thought you hated me."

"How can a man hate his own son?"

"But you were always pointing out how perfect James was, while I could never do anything right."

"I was on your back because you were too much like her and I was afraid you'd fail me the way she did. But it boomeranged. I wanted to beat that rebel streak out of you. Instead, stubborn as you are, it just grew and grew. I didn't have to worry about James or Edward—but I spent sleepless nights worrying about you."

"You worried about me?"

"I've been worrying about you since you were three months old."

"That's when she left."

"That's when she left," Rick said heavily.

Slade was shocked.

"The funniest part is that you look like her, but it's taken me a long time to figure out that you're not like her at all. You're a Delanza through and through."

Slade bowed his head. "No, I'm not like her at all." His voice wavered.

"What I'm trying to say is I'm sorry," Rick said. "I'm sorry. I've been sorry for ten years!"

Slade stared at his father. "Why in hell couldn't you say so sooner?"

"Maybe I just didn't know how," Rick whispered. "Maybe I needed that little bird chattering away in my ear to make me realize my priorities. Maybe I had to lose one son in order to realize I can't take a chance on losing another."

Slade had to wipe moisture away from his eyes and take a deep breath. Never in his wildest dreams could he have imagined Rick revealing so much love. He was overwhelmed. But so was Rick.

Rick coughed. "I'm gonna go get a drink. After all this jawin' I sure as hell need one. I'll see you at supper."

Slade nodded, still unable to speak, still reeling, aware that he needed a long private moment to recover his composure, too. He watched Rick walk across the courtyard and go inside the house. He took a shaky breath. But he wasn't about to recover his composure, not just yet. For he turned toward his room, picking up both bags, and looked up.

Regina stood there, tears streaking her cheeks, crying silently. And it wasn't a dream.

Chapter 28

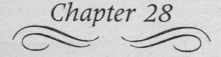

*R*egina could not stop crying, but her tears were those of happiness. Despite the anguish of the past month she was thrilled that Rick and Slade had finally found the courage to delve into the past and unearth the truth of their love for one another.

She wiped her eyes, watching Slade tremulously, waiting for him to recover from the shock of finding her here at Miramar. This was the moment she had been anxiously awaiting—Slade's homecoming—and she was afraid and apprehensive. How could she not be? She expected him to be very angry with her for her defiance of him and his wishes.

But she would face his anger. She hoped she would be able to diffuse it. The night of the gala she had said things she regretted, but she had also spoken the truth. Slade had chosen to end their marriage rather than fight for it—a cowardly way out. That night she had been pushed to what she had then felt to be her limit. The tension and stress of the days prior to the gala, coupled with Slade's astounding statement, had provoked her into her spontaneous eruption and flight. It hadn't taken her very long to recoup her strength. Not even an hour later, in her mother's arms, she had known she would not divorce Slade, that she would not and could not let him destroy their marriage or their future. She intended to fight for what she wanted, no matter how hard or how long that fight might last. And she wanted him. He was worth it.

Now Slade was stunned, as if confronted with a ghost. Only seconds ticked by before he moved. He gripped her arms, pulling her close, his eyes wide and incredulous. "What in hell are you doing here?"

"Waiting for you," she said simply.

He inhaled hard. She felt him shaking, but then, so was she. "I thought you went back to England!"

"I was afraid to make myself too clear in my letter," Regina told him softly. "But you cannot chase me out of your life, Slade. Maybe you had better state your intentions now." She lifted her chin, preparing for the worst—afraid of the worst.

Slade's grip tightened. "You've been here this entire time?" he asked in amazement.

"Yes."

"This is like a dream."

"I am no dream," she whispered. "Just an imperfect woman, one who has made mistakes, a flesh-and-blood woman, one who misses her man."

He groaned, pulling her into his arms.

Regina threw her arms around him. She was filled with many conflicting emotions, not the least of which was a good deal of anxiety over what his reaction to her would be. But there was also boundless joy in being with him again, and there was acute physical awareness. She fully intended to do whatever she had to do in order to remain with him at Miramar. He was not indifferent to her. Not emotionally and not physically. She pressed more fully against him. She turned her face so she could kiss his jaw. "I missed you, Slade," she said.

Immediately he lifted her into his arms, kicking open the door to his bedroom. "I missed you too. I've been miserable." He kicked the doors closed and slid onto the bed, Regina still in his arms. An instant later she lay beneath him, staring up into his beautiful midnight-blue eyes. They were dark with passion, but Regina also thought that they reflected a painful kind of joy and a desperate kind of relief.

"How in hell did I survive this past month without you?" Slade asked roughly, stroking his hands over her hair and then down her arms.

Regina gripped his shoulders. "Probably the same way that I did. Day by day."

Their glances locked. "Yeah," he said hoarsely. "Day by day."

It was then that she had an inkling of his real feelings for her. Briefly, she glimpsed his passion, his soul. "What are you waiting for?" she whispered.

"You," he said. "I think I've been waiting for this moment and for you."

A wave of desire crashed over her. "Kiss me. Make love to me, Slade, please."

He did not need any further encouragement. He took her face in his hands and kissed her. It was thorough and endless. Regina was instantly reminded of the first kiss he had given her on their wedding night. She had never thought she would be kissed like that again—as if she were dearly loved and had been dearly missed for a very long time. But she had been wrong. He was kissing her that way again.

His kiss spoke volumes. Slade had said he missed her; she could not doubt that it was true. But what she really wanted to know was if he loved her, and this kiss was making her think that maybe, after all, he did.

"Sweetheart," Slade murmured thickly a long time later, "I think I've been a fool."

Regina agreed but was not given the opportunity to speak. Slade was sliding his big body into hers. She wept. She wept because she loved him and in their physical union she could sense the kind of completion she would not ever feel unless she gained his love in its entirety.

Regina woke up with a start, confused. Long shadows had cast the bedroom in semidarkness. Recollection swept through her. She sat up. Slade was gone.

Fear gripped her.

She took a calming breath. They had both dozed off in each other's arms after he had made love to her twice. But making love was not enough; they needed to reach an understanding. Slade had admitted that he missed her, and he had made love to her as if he loved her, but he had had such passion for her before and that had not stopped him from trying to end their relationship. Regina was not leaving. And she wanted him to know it and accept it.

She got up, washed quickly, and straightened her clothing. She went in search of her husband. She imagined that he might be in the den enjoying a before-dinner drink, but only Rick was there. He winked at her, but Regina could not smile back at him.

Rick spoke up, saving her the effort of a search. "He went outside and headed up the path going north."

"Thank you!" Regina hurried away from the house. The path ran parallel to the ocean, which was just out of sight, hidden by the sharp spine of a hill. The track soon crested a small rise. Behind her, the house was no longer in sight. Regina froze when she saw the small cemetery below her. Slade was there, standing in front of one of the headstones.

She approached more slowly, fearful of intruding. It flitted through her mind that there was a irony in his choosing to find solitude in a cemetery and perhaps comfort from a dead man. Or was he here to bury his emotions? That thought angered her. Slade had been fighting his emotions since they had met. She refused to allow him to bury his head in the sand any longer—and his heart along with it. She would slowly and surely coax his feelings out of him, even if it took the length of their lifetime.

Slade's hands were in his pockets, his head was bowed. She wasn't sure if he was praying, grieving, or thinking. Her skirts rustled, announcing her approach. He didn't move. She came up behind him, hesitating only a heartbeat. Then she stepped forward, obeying her heart and her instincts, looping her arm in his and pressing against him.

He was tense. He didn't say anything and neither did she. He accepted her presence; for the moment that was enough. They stood in silence for a while, the sun setting now with finality. Gulls wheeled above them before fleeing through the incoming mist. Shadows slid out from the tombstones, long and eerie. A chill crept in with the dusk.

Finally he faced her, his eyes intent and probing.

Regina managed a brave smile. "Hello, Slade."

He reached out a hand. Gasping with delight, she gave him hers. He gripped it firmly. "Did Edward have something to do with you being here at Miramar?"

"Edward? No."

"I didn't think so." He stared at her. "If I sent you away, you wouldn't go, would you?"

"No, I would not go."

"I guess you're here to stay."

"I am."

His mouth slowly turned up. A single last ray of opalescent light slid over the ridge and Regina saw that his cheeks were wet and that he had been crying. "A man can only be a fool for so long. I know when to shout uncle."

"I beg your pardon?" she whispered.

"I haven't been happy. I want to be happy, Regina." His voice was unsteady.

"Let me make you happy! I can! I will!"

He almost laughed, the sound rough, then pulled her close and threw his arm around her. "I think you already have."

She sighed in relief and leaned against him. He would no longer fight their marriage, he would no longer fight her. She wanted more, she wanted him to openly love her, but she could wait for that. She was inspired with confidence. She smiled, gazing past her husband at the green ridges surrounding them, the jewel-like crown of Miramar. "Look," she whispered. "Miramar is smiling at us."

Indeed, it seemed that way. The inky night swirled over the hills and they seemed to come alive, pulsating with mystical, magical joy. But it was only the tendrils of fog, of course, along with her imagination.

Life soon slipped into its own unquenchable rhythm. There was a lot of work to be done, and both father and son relished the challenge. Slade had hired a dozen men within the first few days of his return. Every day he took the crew to the site where they were feverishly at work clearing the acreage he would put to the plow in the spring. Time was not on their side and everyone knew it. Bonuses would be given if half of the land was cleared in thirty days. And Slade did not stand idly by and watch. Regina soon learned that her husband enjoyed physical labor as much as he enjoyed mental challenges. Every night he came home exhausted but satisfied, and routinely he would discuss his day with her over the dinner table. Regina was an avid listener. She fervently hoped he would succeed in what seemed to her an impossible task.

Rick never said a word about the changes taking place on the rancho. Regina knew that Slade had resorted to underhanded tactics to win that battle, but she did not blame him. When push came to shove, she would unfailingly support her husband, and Rick would always have to be pushed hard when he was opposed to something. Yet he worked hard alongside his son, as caught up in the race against time as everyone else.

Edward returned home a few days later. Everyone was happy to see him, Regina included; he was a ray of bright sunshine and she imagined that he would always be welcome wherever he went. Victoria was ecstatic. And Edward was the perfect son, patiently enduring her pampering, all smiles and indulgence.

Victoria had tolerated Regina with cool disdain since Regina had come to Miramar at the end of the summer. Regina could only assume that Victoria had finally accepted the finality of her marriage to Slade.

As for Regina and Slade, they slid so easily and so nearly effortlessly into a domestic routine that it might have belonged to them in another lifetime. For a few days there was some awkwardness and tension between them. But Regina was eager to please her husband, to bring comfort into his life, and Slade seemed to want to get closer to her now. He left her with reluctance every morning and returned home to her eagerly every night. He shared all of the happenings of the day with her, his triumphs and his disasters, his hopes and his fears. Regina had always sought to be close to him, and now that he no longer held himself at a distance, their passion grew and the camaraderie they had shared just after their wedding during those first days in San Francisco blossomed anew.

It quickly became obvious to Regina what had happened to them in San Francisco. For whatever reason, Slade had been intent on wrecking their marriage by pushing her away from him. She could not understand why. He was a complicated man, so she might never know the whole of it unless he volunteered the information himself. But as the month passed she began to have suspicions. Several times he mentioned her lifestyle in England, watching her closely and awaiting her response intently. Regina finally called him on it. "Are you waiting for me to tell you that I miss my home? Or that I regret returning to you?"

Slade winced. "Do you?"

It was then that she understood him. He was afraid that she would become dissatisfied with her lot, cast in as it was with his. "No, Slade. I do not."

He studied her and slowly smiled. His next words were proof that she was right. "I think I misjudged you, Regina."

"I think that you have," she responded, moving into his arms.

By the first of October the roundup was completed and all the herds moved to more sheltered terrain to wait for the first onslaught of winter. Slade had finished clearing two hundred acres and it did not look as if he would meet his goal of three hundred, half of what he eventually hoped to put to the plow, before the rains. The days were growing shorter. All the men were working in a frenzy now, trying to finish the obviously impossible project. Time was running out if they hoped to clear all the land, for once winter set in the ground would become muddy and impassable.

Toward the end of October Regina stood by the window watching the first few drops of rain begin to fall. Tension filled her. The sky was dark and gray. It was almost dusk and she prayed these few sprinkled drops were not the beginning of the rainy season. Just last night Slade had said they needed another two weeks.

Victoria came to stand beside her. "They didn't make it," she said quietly. There was no animosity in her tone. If anyone coveted the richness that Miramar could one day bring the family, it was Victoria. "It's going to rain."

"Maybe not," Regina said hopefully.

Ten minutes later the drizzle became a downpour.

An hour later the men came in, exhausted, soaked to the bone, muddy and dismayed. Regina took one look at Slade's grim face and flew to his side. His eyes told her that the winter had indeed begun, before they had finished what had been impossible to begin with.

Everyone was somber at the supper table that night.

Regina spoke into the dismal silence. "Well, clearing two hundred acres is nothing short of a miracle. You will be able to plant those acres at the first sign of spring."

Slade said nothing.

Rick said, "Wasn't no miracle, honey. There's no such thing."

Slade looked up.

Edward said, sipping a glass of red wine, "Slade, I believe you have just been indirectly complimented for a job well done."

Slade was still, his fork poised over his plate.

Rick said, "Well, hell. It was an impossible job, an' it was mostly done."

Regina looked at Slade, smiling. Although Rick and Slade had apparently settled past misunderstandings, Rick's praise was rare and she knew her husband cherished it when it came. But she had no chance to judge his reaction. For suddenly Josephine screamed.

She screamed from the kitchen as if someone was committing bloody murder.

And she screamed again.

Chaos erupted. Everyone leaped to their feet and rushed toward the kitchen. Regina found herself behind the men while Slade led the charge. He burst through the kitchen door and abruptly froze. His brother and father collided against him.

Regina could not see past the taller men. Frightened, her heart thundering, she gripped Slade's arm, standing on tiptoe, peering past him.

Josephine was prostrate on the floor. A big man stood above her. Regina cried out, thinking Josephine injured or even dead. She tensed, waiting for Slade, Rick, and Edward to leap forward to attack the intruder.

"Jesus," the big man said, white-faced. "What the hell is wrong with Josephine? She fainted when I walked in the door! And what the hell is wrong with all of you? You act like you're seeing a ghost!"

Regina gasped, suddenly thinking the unthinkable and praying for the impossible. Then a miracle unfolded before her very eyes as Slade rushed forward with a cry, not to attack the man, but to embrace him. *"James!"*

James had come back from the dead.

Chapter 29

Pandemonium erupted in the kitchen. Slade wrapped James in a bear hug. Edward pounded his back. Rick grabbed James's face in his two hands, shouting at him. "Where the hell have you been? Jesus! Where the hell have you been? We thought you were dead!"

Everyone was tearful, except James, who was stunned and bewildered. Regina was crying, but laughing too. She whispered her own quick prayer of thanks to God for such a wonderful miracle. Then she realized that Josephine had been forgotten in the ensuing reunion. She rushed to the prone woman. Kneeling, she felt for her pulse. Josephine had only fainted; already she was stirring.

It was then that Regina felt a distinct warning tingle racing up her spine. The four men were shouting at each other incomprehensibly. James was saying something about a letter. Warily she looked up. One person was not participating in the spontaneous celebration.

Victoria stood in the doorway. Many different emotions played across her face, but not one of them was joy. Regina shuddered. Nor did Victoria appear the least bit surprised. A horrible thought dawned. Yet it was indecent. Regina told herself that Victoria could not have known that James was alive and kept such a secret to herself. Her imagination was running away with her.

Victoria realized that she was being watched, meeting Regina's penetrating stare. Her eyes were angry, yet an instant later a smile transformed her features.

Regina was frozen. Her heart pounded painfully. This woman was somehow involved in the mystery surrounding James.

Josephine moaned. "Lawdy, I'se seen a ghost!"

Regina stroked her brow. "No, dear, James has returned, but not as a ghost, as a mortal man."

Josephine cried out and Regina helped her to sit up. "James!" she shouted, furious. "I'm gonna whip you so bad you won't sit fer a week! Come heah, boy!" And she started to weep. Josephine had been the only mother James had ever known and she had loved him as she did any of her own children.

James was such a big man that he lifted the sobbing woman effortlessly to her feet. "God, I'm sorry. You all thought I was dead?" He looked horrified.

"Now I'm gonna kill you," Rick said, boxing his son's ears. But then a grin split his tearstained face. "What the hell happened? Where the hell have you been?"

James opened his mouth to respond and then he saw Regina. "Who's this?"

Instantly Slade pulled Regina forward, his arm around her. "This is my wife, Regina."

James was incredulous. "You're married?"

"I'm married," Slade said, with no small amount of pride and pleasure. *"What the hell happened to you?"*

"I wrote one letter and sent two telegrams," James protested. "I don't understand!"

There was a moment of sober silence. Regina could not help regarding Victoria, who was the only one to offer an explanation. Cheerfully, she said, "Mail gets lost all the time. And old Ben at the post office is drunk more often than not. Welcome home, James! How wonderful to have you back!"

James eyed her, obviously not buying his stepmother's

welcome for an instant. "Ben Carter quit drinking last year. Or did he start up again?"

"Not that I know," Slade said grimly.

"Let's go inside," Victoria said. "You're dripping all over the floor. Here, let me take your poncho. You must have quite a story to tell!"

Regina was sick. Something most definitely was wrong. She knew what was wrong. Somehow, for some reason, Victoria had intercepted the letter and the telegrams. But why?

She did not know, could not even guess. And she did not dare speak out. It was not her place to do so, and there was a chance she could be wrong. Later, privately, she would mention her suspicions to Slade. God, how hurt Rick would be if Victoria had known that James was really alive. Then she thought about Edward. He would be devastated to learn of such treachery.

They moved into the den. Supper was forgotten. Josephine and Lucinda brought in steaming-hot coffee for everyone and a plate of hot food for James. Neither woman returned to the kitchen; instead they hovered happily around James, just as everyone else did.

While he ate, before he launched into an explanation, Regina studied him. He was a very handsome man, a Delanza trait. He was bigger than Edward and Rick by several inches, and not just taller, but more heavily built. Yet there was no fat on his hard, powerful frame. His hair was the rich brown of mink, his eyes another shade of Delanza blue. He was certainly a man to set female hearts fluttering.

But the most obvious resemblance among all the men was their charisma. When James entered a room everyone would sit up and take notice. Regina had seen the same thing happen again and again with Rick, Edward, and her own husband Slade.

Rick was sitting on the sofa on one side of James, Slade on the other. Regina sat beside Slade, holding her husband's hand, ecstatically happy for him. Edward had pulled up an ottoman, so close that his knee almost brushed James's. Lucinda and Josephine had pulled up chairs and sat beside Rick, crowding him. They were even closer to James than Rick's wife. But Victoria sat in a chair on the other side of the seating area, distinctly removing herself from the family group, which Regina found disturbing and significant.

"Enough food," Rick growled. "I want to know where the hell you've been. We found your horse downriver after the floodwaters subsided, his leg broke, dead, caught in two uprooted trees. We already knew you'd disappeared. Jesus! We looked for you, not wanting to find you, afraid to find you dead!"

"Jesus," James said, pushing his plate away. He leaned back on the sofa, not looking very pleased. "But you didn't find me! If you had gotten my letter you would have known right away that I was fine."

"When we didn't find you and after a month went by, what could we think but that you were dead?" Rick said.

"Why did you take off without a word?" Slade asked.

"I got a letter from Elizabeth."

"What kind of letter?" Rick asked.

James's smile was bitter. "What kind do you think? It wasn't a love letter."

A silence fell after his words. Slade broke it. "Hell, James. I'm sorry."

"Yeah, well, don't be. Best thing that could've happened to me."

"So that's why you took off in the middle of the damned storm," Rick said grimly.

"I was mad. And disbelieving. And hurt. Stupid fool that I was, I figured I'd go to her personally and demand an explanation. I wanted to believe she was just having the usual last-minute jitters, and that once she saw me, she'd fall right into my arms and everything would be fine." He laughed harshly. "Boy, was I wrong!"

"You got her letter and took off in the storm and lost your horse in the flood," Slade said. "What happened afterwards?"

"I needed another horse so I stole another one out of old man Curtis's fields to make it to Templeton to catch the train to San Luis Obispo. When I realized the train wouldn't be coming until the next day, I just kept riding. Nothing was going to stop me—I was too damn mad. I rode until I could rendezvous with the Southern Pacific, which I picked up in Serrano."

"You rode almost the entire way?" Edward interjected.

"I wasn't just mad," James said ruefully, "I was crazy, too. I didn't send a telegram home until I got to San Luis Obispo, after I had seen her." His mouth twisted but the smile failed. "I can't remember what I said. She had changed so much—I was shocked, I guess."

Edward broke the ensuing silence. "I saw her, James. About a month ago I went down there to see her stepmother, and Susan sent me to Elizabeth." He hesitated. "You shouldn't be so upset. No woman could have been worse for you."

James was silent.

Slade said, "I saw her, too. Recently. Edward's right. She was bad news."

James looked at his brothers. Then his fist hit the table hard, sending his plate to the floor. "She had to tell me all of it. I think she enjoyed telling me all of it. She's a whore at heart and she always has been. Do you know why she was sent to London in the first place? Because she'd been caught in bed with some stable-boy! Somehow Sinclair hushed it up and sent her off to what he hoped would be a prison! She was thirteen! It wasn't even the first time! Boy, when George arranged the marriage was he laughing behind our backs!" James was shaking. He released a deep breath and stared up at the ceiling.

Rick was on his feet. "Goddamn George! If he wasn't dead I'd wring his neck right now! How in hell did he cover up such a scandal? George always was too damn smart!" Rick planted himself in front of his son. "Thank God, James, that she called it off. That tramp isn't fit to clean the horseshit off your boots."

"Amen," Edward said.

James didn't speak.

"You've been gone a long time," Slade said quietly. "Where have you been?"

"I drifted south. I didn't much care where I went. A few days after I'd seen her, when I was in Los Angeles, I sent another telegram so no one would expect me back anytime soon. Later I posted a letter from Tucson, explaining. When I wound up in Guadalajara two weeks ago, I decided it was time to come home and finish things."

Slade eyed him. Regina wondered what he meant.

James shook his head. "I don't understand what happened to the letter and the telegrams."

"Neither do I," Rick said furiously. "And it's one hell of a coincidence all three never made it here."

Slade spoke. "I'm going to get some answers. I'll go to town tomorrow to talk to Ben."

Regina tensed. She glanced at Victoria, who was nonchalant. But when the other woman saw Regina's expression, she shifted. Regina looked away, despairing. Dear God, she knew she was right.

"I know about the letter," Lucinda suddenly cried. "But not about the telegrams."

Everyone looked at her.

"What?" Rick shouted. "You kept that letter from me?"

Victoria was on her feet. "Lucinda, what kind of stupid ploy is this? And what are you doing here? Don't you have chores to do?"

Lucinda glared at her. "You're a mean woman and you deserve this. I have to tell the truth!"

Regina cringed. Rick grabbed the maid's arm. "What the hell are you implying?"

"Rick, I saw the letter in Victoria's bureau, hidden among her clothes."

A shocked silence filled the room.

"No!" Victoria shouted, livid. "She's lying because she hates me! She's always hated me. Haven't you, you lying bitch?"

Rick looked at his wife in bewilderment.

Edward stared at his mother in disbelief.

Slade took Lucinda's hand. "Tell us what happened."

Tears filled Lucinda's eyes. "I wanted to say something right away! When I found the letter by accident I recognized his handwriting, so I read it. But she came in and caught me!"

Victoria made a strangled sound.

"She threatened me, Slade! Then she paid me off." Lucinda almost broke into tears. "I was more afraid of her threats to see me thrown off the ranch than I was interested in the money. We fought about it. She hit me. I knew she'd do as she said, have me beaten up and taken away, if I spoke up."

"You should have come to me," Slade said.

"I was afraid! This has been my home since I was a child! Would you have believed me or her?" Lucinda cried wildly.

It really didn't matter. Slade turned to Victoria, his eyes filled with fury. Regina immediately moved to the stricken maid, putting her arm around her. Lucinda should have spoken up, but she could easily imagine her being thoroughly intimidated by Victoria. Regina had not a doubt that Victoria's threats to do her bodily harm had been real.

"You've gone too far, Victoria," Slade said. "I guess you intercepted the telegrams too."

Rick was staring at his wife, shocked. But it was Edward who was paralyzed. He hadn't moved, he hadn't even flinched, nor had he spoken. Now he said, his voice high and boyish, "Mother?"

Victoria rushed to him. "Oh, Edward!" she cried, clasping his hands. He stared at her as if she were a maddened stranger. "I did it for you! For you! And what was so bad? I didn't kill James! He went away, deserting us all! I didn't know Elizabeth was just a little whore. I thought she was coming here to marry James. Rick wanted her to marry Slade, but I realized that with James gone, she could marry you!"

Edward did not so much as blink.

"Don't you see? Slade would come for the funeral and leave. But you would be here and Rick would have asked you to marry her to save the rancho. Then this would all be yours! I did it for you! And was it such a terrible lie? Just what was so terrible?"

Edward suddenly lunged to his feet, throwing her off him so violently that she crashed into the chair behind her and almost fell to the flooor. "*Get away from me.*"

"Edward!" Victoria reached out to him, pleading.

"Get away from me!" Edward shouted. He whirled, knocking over the ottoman he had been sitting on. He moved so swiftly that no one had time to react. He was out the door, his strides so long and fast he was almost running.

Everyone was in shock. Slade was frozen. Rick sank down on the sofa, his face buried in his hands, looking old and defeated. Regina felt pity for them all, but especially Rick and Edward. Abruptly she gripped Slade's arm. "Call Edward back," she said urgently.

Slade looked at her. "No."

She started to protest.

"No, Regina, he has to deal with this himself."

And then, through the beating rain, they heard the sound of thundering hoofbeats. Regina ran to the other side of the room, which faced the grounds and the stables. Pushing aside the drapes, she saw Edward on his black stallion galloping down the drive, away from Miramar.

Victoria screamed when she realized what was happening. She rushed past Slade and into the downpour. Her sobs were heartbreaking. Regina ran after her. The woman stumbled into the outer courtyard and through the gate, calling after her son. Regina skidded to a halt, the rain pelting her fiercely. Her clothing quickly became soaked. Slade had followed her and he paused beside her. "Go inside before you get sick," he said quietly.

Regina looked at him questioningly. No matter what Victoria had done, she could not be immune to her grief.

And apparently neither could Slade. "I'll get her," he said softly.

Regina hurried to the sheltering overhang of the roof, watching as Slade walked slowly through the torrential rain to Victoria. She had fallen to her knees in the mud. Her anguished sobs did not abate. "Edward! Edward! Please come back, please! Edward!"

Edward was no longer even in sight.

Slade bent and lifted her to her feet. "He'll come back," he said quietly. "In his own good time, he'll come back." And he led her inside the house.

Hours later the rain had become a steady downpour, blanketing the night. Regina stood by the window in their bedroom, staring out at the drenched silvery darkness. Slade came up behind her, his warm, strong hands slipping over her shoulders.

She leaned back against him. "Edward didn't have a coat or a hat."

"He'll be okay."

"I can't help worrying. And hurting. He should be with us now, not out there alone in that cold godforsaken night."

He kissed her cheek. "You have a heart of gold, Regina. Edward is a strong man. He needs time to adjust."

Regina was silent a moment, letting a single tear drift down her cheek unchecked. Her heart cried for the entire family, but she could not help but be thrilled by Slade's praise. She turned to face him. "Poor James. What about him?"

"Poor James," Slade echoed grimly. "He's a very bitter, angry man. I barely recognize him. For five long years he loved a woman who did not exist. He was even faithful to her. He needs time, too."

Regina embraced her husband. "What about Rick?" She closed her eyes against the image of how he had appeared the last time she had seen him. After Slade had led Victoria back inside, he had gotten up and left the room, locking himself in his study. He had appeared dazed and very, very old.

"Rick's tough. He's a survivor. He's been through a hell of a lot in his life, he'll get through this. But he's gonna toss Victoria out, mark my words. He's forgiven her a lot over the years, but he won't forgive her this."

Regina leaned against Slade, hugging him. "God help me, I even feel sorry for her. She's lost her son, now she's going to lose her husband and her home."

"You are amazing, Regina. I think it's your generosity that I admire most." His hands slid around her. "I love you. I love you more than you'll ever know."

She froze, stunned. "I beg your pardon?"

He laughed roughly, caught up in the onslaught of his emotions. "If you think I can say those words again, you're wrong. This isn't easy for me, but I realize how much you want to know how I feel. I guess," he said softly, "I'm finding the courage to finally tell you."

She started to cry. She hugged him. "You have no idea how happy you're making me! I've dreamed of hearing you tell me that you love me, Slade!"

"Hasn't it been obvious?"

"Obvious?" She laughed, delirious with pleasure. "Only a month ago you wanted to divorce me!"

He sighed. Finally he cupped her face in his hands. "Can't you understand? I was trying to do what was right."

She blinked at that. "To this day, Slade, I have not been able to fully comprehend your motivations."

"I thought that your father was right, that you should return home, live in a castle and marry a duke."

"Oh, you foolish man!" Regina cried. "Father no longer feels that way, Slade. We settled our differences the night of the gala. He has given us his blessing."

Slade looked stunned. For a long moment he didn't speak. "God, I'm glad! I've agonized over my coming between you and your father!"

"You needn't agonize anymore." She hesitated. "He has even given me my inheritance, which is in a bank account in your name in San Francisco."

He stared. When he said nothing Regina was relieved, because he could have protested. "Oh, you foolish man," she said again, this time cupping his face. Tears filled her eyes. "You thought me so shallow that I needed to live in the lap of luxury? Have I proved myself to you yet? Do you realize how wrong you were?"

He swallowed. "Yeah, you've proved yourself, Regina, and I feel like a big fat fool."

"I think you do understand what love is all about," Regina said softly. "It is about compromise. When a woman really loves a man, she is willing to give up what she must for him and for their marriage—with no regrets."

He kissed her lingeringly. Then he rested his cheek against hers. "You're incredibly wise for one so young, Regina. Yes, I've come to realize, through you, what love is all about. Before, I was trying to be selfless in giving you up instead of selfish in keeping you."

"But love is both selfish and selfless, Slade," Regina murmured. "Are you saying that you loved me so much that you thought to make me happy by sending me away?"

He winced, regarding her seriously. "In retrospect, especially after the past month, it seems absurd."

"It was very absurd!"

"This month has made me realize how I misjudged you. I'm so sorry. You appear as soft and fragile as a hothouse rose, Regina, but it's an illusion. There's nothing that's not strong and determined about you. I've watched you thrive these last few weeks here at Miramar. You've bloomed. You've never been more beautiful and you've never seemed happier."

"I've never been happier," Regina said. She almost told him why she was thriving, then decided he should continue to think for a while that her glow was due only to him and her happiness and being at Miramar. She caressed his cheek. "I love you. I loved you from the moment we met, which is why I kept my identity secret and married you in the first place. And I never stopped loving you, not once, even when I was forced to leave you in San Francisco. There. I have confessed all." She regarded him through blurry eyes.

"You can confess to me at any time," he whispered,

taking her earlobe between his teeth and tugging it gently. "I will never grow tired of your confessions."

The next morning Regina overslept, exhausted both from the traumatic events of the preceding day and the emotional ecstasy Slade's declaration had generated. Of course, she was also well aware of the fact that most women were tired in the first few months of pregnancy.

It was still raining. There was no sign of it stopping. In the kitchen a solemn Josephine told her it might rain ceaselessly for weeks. "But then you'd be surprised," she added. "When it looks like it could nevah get bettah, suddenly the sun is shinin'."

Regina looked sharply at the Negress. She had not one doubt that Josephine intended her words to have a double meaning. "How is Rick this morning?"

"He's real upset and he's real mad. I only seen him like this once in his whole life an' I been heah since I was a chile."

Regina's heart twisted. "When Slade's mother left?"

Josephine nodded. "He nevah let on, but he loved Victoria despite her bad ways."

"He's a very strong man. He'll get through this."

"That he shore is an' he shore will. He'll be hisse'f, but it'll take some time."

"And Victoria? Is she all right?"

"Don't you go worryin' bout her, Miz Regina. Last night she done drank herse'f to sleep, she did. She's passed out cold. You let her be." Josephine was unforgiving. "She shoulda been tossed out of heah long ago."

Regina wasn't certain that she agreed, for Rick and Victoria had been through twenty-three years of marriage. She was glad that it was not up to her to forgive and forget Victoria's betrayal, and she worried about Rick and Edward. She was about to ask Josephine what she thought about Edward's flight when the sound of Rick shouting drew her attention. Exchanging a concerned look with the housekeeper, she ran into the dining room. Rick was in full temper, and his anger was directed at James. "What the hell has gotten into you now?"

"You heard me," James said calmly. But he was wearing a stubborn expression, one Regina recognized, having seen it on all of the Delanza men. "I only came home to get a few things. I'm not staying."

Regina moved close to Slade, taking his hand, noticing that he was pale. Rick pounded the table. "I won't have it!"

James remained calm. "I'm not staying. That's final. But I wish you would understand."

"I understand, all right! First Slade left me, now Edward, and now you!" Rick crumpled into a chair. "What have I done?"

Slade was on his feet and around the table, placing his hand on his father's shoulder. "Rick, Edward didn't leave you, he left because of his mother, and you know it. And I'm home now, to stay. James is hurting, Dad. Listen to what he has to say."

Rick looked up, his eyes wet. He blinked furiously. "Hell! Go on, you got something to say, say it!"

James took a breath. "Once Miramar meant something. Once there was a future. I worked hard for years for that future. No more. It's meaningless to me now." His tone became pleading. "Rick, can't you try to understand how I feel? For the past five years I've been building a home here, a home for me and Elizabeth and our children. My dreams weren't dreams, they were delusions. Well, never again. Those dreams are dead and buried. I can't stay. I don't know where I'm going and I don't give a damn, but I do know I can't stay here. Everywhere I look I'm reminded of what I once wanted—what I almost had." He laughed bitterly. "What I thought I almost had."

Rick bowed his head. "You think I'm so callous I don't understand? You want to know the truth? Last night I couldn't sleep, not just because of Victoria, but because I knew, I already knew, you weren't going to stay." He lifted his head. "Go. Go. Find what you need to find, do what you have to do."

James breathed in relief. "Thank you." Then he smiled at both Slade and Regina. "Besides, the future—Miramar—belongs to them. Isn't it obvious?"

* * *

Ten days later the rains stopped. The gray skies cleared. The sun appeared. The hills around them were no longer baked yellow from the sun, but lushly green. Yet no one was pleased. James had made it clear that he would leave on the first clear day they had.

Victoria was gone. She had disappeared without even a note, although she had taken several trunks. Rick seemed to be relieved. Regina thought that it was better this way; he was spared having to send her away. And there had been no word from Edward, although they had learned that he had taken a northbound train in Templeton. Slade told her that he thought Edward might have gone to San Francisco, finding temporary solace with Xandria. Regina fervently hoped so.

What was left of the household gathered to wish James well and see him off. He was in good spirits. Slade had said that James had to find his own destiny, and Regina agreed. Rick was resigned, but Regina knew he clung stubbornly to the belief that one day James would return to stay.

Josephine hugged him, weeping. Lucinda moved into his arms and kissed him demandingly on the lips, clinging. James returned both her openmouthed kiss and her warm embrace, causing Regina to look away, blushing. Apparently they had formed a *tendre* of some sort for one another.

It was Regina's turn. In less than two weeks she had grown very fond of James, and thought of him as a friend and brother. She gave him a hard hug. "I'm so glad we have met," she told him earnestly. "I wish you the best, James, only the best."

James winked at Slade. "It looks like my brother has made out like a bandit."

Regina lowered her voice. "You must promise me to come back in six months."

James's eyes widened.

"I haven't told Slade yet, but I am going to tell him tonight. You shall be an uncle."

James whooped and gave her an exuberant hug.

"What did she say?" Slade asked suspiciously.

"She'll tell you in her own good time," James returned, smiling.

The men said their good-byes. More unashamed hugs followed, with many more promises. James mounted up. Regina slipped under Slade's arm, Rick on her other side. James gave them a wave of farewell and spurred his bay forward. Waving back, they watched him trotting away. He turned and lifted his hand one last time and disappeared around the bend.

There was a moment of silence.

"I guess he's got some soul-searching to do," Rick said. He sighed. Then he slapped Slade's back. "Let's see if we can't get some work done today, son." He strode to the barn.

Regina regarded her husband. "Sad?"

"No." He smiled. "I'm not sad at all. I heard what you said."

"You did!"

He lifted her off of her feet and spun her around. "Another generation of Delanzas!" Setting her down, he took her hand and lifted his gaze to the green mountains which rose sharply against the horizon. "Now I'm more determined than ever to make Miramar a part of the future—a part of *their* future." He looked past the house, where the winter-gray ocean butted up against the hillside. "I almost envy them. The twentieth century is dawning, Regina—new, different, exciting, filled with challenge, and with promise."

"You are a poet," she whispered, leaning into him. "You are a visionary."

He laughed. "I am a realist, sweetheart. And I think this is the perfect time to tell Rick. Don't you?"

"I wanted you to have the honors," Regina said, and hand in hand, they followed in his father's footsteps.

EDINBURGH
NOVEMBER 16, 1093

There was no time to mourn.

Mary knelt at the bedside of the Queen, her mother, numb with shock. She did not know how long she had knelt there on the hard, cold stone floor, nor did she realize that she still held her mother's lifeless hand. She had been raised a devout Christian, but now, when she needed comfort from God, if there was any comfort to be found, she could not summon up a single prayer. Her mind was blank, frozen.

There were no tears. It was as if her body were frozen, or as if she too, were dead. News of her father's murder had come three days earlier. He had been ambushed near Alnwick by the Earl of Northumberland's forces, routed and killed. In the battle her eldest brother, Edward, had been mortally wounded, dying shortly after their father.

Mary had not cried, for one blow had come too quickly on the heels of another. And then Queen Margaret had fallen desperately ill upon news of Malcolm's death; she had needed Mary more than ever. She had not left her mother's side in days, helplessly watching as the Queen slipped closer and closer to death. There had been no time to mourn then, and there was no time now.

Because forces of hatred and ambition and greed were closing in on her.

She realized she was holding Queen Margaret's hand. Mary released it woodenly. The Queen seemed serene in death, and even in death she was beautiful—a beauty that was far deeper than her fair skin and noble features. The Queen's real beauty came from true goodliness and holiness, it came from a loving, selfless heart. No one deserved to die less; no one had welcomed death more.

Mary listened to the keening grief filling the manor, echoing within its thick stone walls and reverberating from the courtyard outside. T'was not just kin grieving for their Queen, all of Edinburgh wept as well—and all of Scotland.

There had been so much treachery, Mary thought, aware for the first time in hours that her knees ached. She did not dare think further. More thought might lead to even greater grief, and she knew she could not bear such a burden. Not now. Not today.

If only she could pray. If only she could find comfort, as her mother had, in God.

She crossed the Queen's hands, and, staring at her mother, she thought she felt a flicker of anguish deep within her soul. The eerie sobbing filling the castle seemed to grow and echo and close in on her. Suddenly Mary wanted to keen too, wanted to scream and wail, and a hot rush of tears filled her eyes. She choked, barely able to breathe, her mother's face swimming before her eyes. No! No, she could not, must not, under any circumstances, fall apart now!

Mary was suddenly on the verge of collapse, and she turned away from her mother, shaking, desperately fighting the rising grief. The keening and sobbing of the castle seemed louder now, more pervasive. "Mother, I'm sorry," she gasped suddenly. "I love you so much and I'm sorry I've failed you—so sorry!"

There was no response, of course, and no redemption. It was too late, it would always be too late. Through the rambling of her thoughts, Mary knew she must make some effort to function. She wiped her eyes with the sleeve of her torn tunic. There was no question that more disaster was about to follow—she could only hope that there would be a brief respite. Too much was at stake. Lives were at stake; a kingdom was at stake.

As that slim stab of reality intruded into Mary's emotions, she became aware for the first time of another discordant sound faintly underpining the loud cacophony of the wailing Scots. It was like the gentlest rumble of distant thunder, but the sky was a clear and cloudless blue. It could only mean one thing. Mary froze.

Dear God, not so soon!

There would be no respite!

The door to the Queen's room crashed open and Mary jumped in fright. "Edmund's gone!" The voice of her brother, Edgar, fairly echoed in the silent, stone room. His face was very white and pinched, his eyes red and swollen. He, at least, had wept until he could weep no more.

"What do you mean?" With Edward dead, Edmund was now their eldest brother.

"I mean the bastard's gone! Gone!" Edgar was usually calm, unnaturally so for a seventeen-year-old, but he was nigh hysterical now. "And Donald Bane's the Tanist! The word just came! His army landed at the Forth of Clyde yesterday—they must be at the Avon now!"

Mary grabbed Edgar's arm. Donald Bane had been proclaimed King, and he had come out of his long exile in the Hebrides, with an army, to claim the throne of Scotland. Every single one of her brothers stood in the way of the succession—they must flee. "Where is Edmund?" Damn her rascally brother for deserting them now!

"Gone, gone, oh, God, I pray t'is not true!"

"You pray *what* isn't true?"

"It's said he's joined Donald!"

Mary gasped. Her senses reeled. That their brother should betray them now was incomprehensible. And outside, the thunder became louder.

"I fear, Edgar, that Uncle Donald is closer than the Avon River." She glanced towards the shrouded window. "Round up the boys. We must run." There was no doubt about it—a huge mounted army was rapidly approaching.

"We can not leave her," Edgar said, faltering, barely glancing at their mother.

"Of course not. Send me Fergus, order horses and a cart. Quickly, run!" She shoved him from the room.

She hurried to the Queen, panting. Mary pulled the covers of the bed up to wrap her carefully from head to toe, all the while listening to the growing sound of the earth quaking beneath the oncoming riders.

Another bloody war was about to descend upon this land, and her beloved country was once again at stake. Donald Bane could not ignore the fact that Malcolm had left four living sons who might one day seek the throne he had coveted his entire life. Only with their deaths would his dreams be truly secured. Hurrying, Mary covered Queen Margaret's face with a sheet. They would bury her at the Abbey of Dunfermline, where they would also seek a temporary refuge—should they manage to escape.

Fergus burst through the door. He was a big, savage man who had been with her father from the beginning—and till the very end. Giving Mary one long look, Fergus gathered Queen Margaret in his arms as if she were a weightless doll. Mary ran beside him as they hurried down the corridor. "What of Edmund?"

"He's no a part a this family any more," Fergus said grimly as they stumbled down the dark corridor. They rushed outside into the courtyard, where the bright sunlight momentarily blinded Mary. Her brothers were already mounted, her youngest brother

David, only thirteen, trying manfully to hold back his tears. Fergus laid the shrouded Queen in the back of a horsedrawn cart.

Mary suddenly froze beside her mount, aware that an utter quiet reigned in the courtyard, replacing the disharmonious chaos that had existed just moments ago. All sounds of grief and wailing had ceased. All the normal sounds of life were also absent—there were no crowing roosters, no yapping dogs, no children's chatter, no smithie's blows. Not even the jangle of their men's mounts sounded. Only silence echoed within the dark, timbered walls of the bailey. A strange, frightening silence, unearthly and unnatural. Mary knew that she was listening for something, but she did not know what. And then it struck her—the ominous drumming beat of the invading army had ceased.

She was too experienced not to know what that meant. The army had halted . . . to position themselves for an attack.

Fergus wasted no time, he boosted Mary roughly onto her mare. Mary strained to hear even a hint of the danger that lay outside the walls of Edinburgh, but she could discern nothing. "T'is Donald Bane, is it not?" she asked, high-pitched, breaking the stillness.

Fergus leaped onto his own big stallion. "Nay."

Mary wheeled her mount next to his as the big heavy gates were thrown open. "Then, who?"

The glance he shot her was long and dark.

Mary felt it all, then: fear, fury, hatred, and most of all, dread. For she knew now who, and what, lay out there, awaiting them, stalking them. She uttered one word to the strong man beside her. "*No.*"

"Ay, lassie, I'm sorry, I am," Fergus said softly. "T'is the devil hisself, Northumberland's whelp."

Mary heard her own moan of fear. Her mare moved briskly forward amidst the others, beside Fergus. Mary realized she had stopped breathing, and with effort she expelled her breath.

Fergus hated him, with good reason, and had always called de Warenne the devil. Mary hated him too. God help her, she hated him, and feared him, more than she had ever hated or feared anyone. The Earl of Northumberland's heir, Lord Stephen de Warenne. Her father's murderer, her brother's killer, and ultimately the man responsible for her mother's death.

He was also the father of her unborn child—he was also her husband.

And if he caught her now he would kill her. She was running for her life.

The Incomparable

"Lowell is great!"
Johanna Lindsey

ONLY YOU
76340-0/$4.99 US/$5.99 Can
"For smoldering sensuality and exceptional storytelling,
Elizabeth Lowell is incomparable."
Kathe Robin, *Romantic Times*

ONLY MINE
76339-7/$4.99 US/$5.99 Can

ONLY HIS
76338-9/$4.95 US/$5.95 Can

And Coming Soon

UNTAMED
76953-0/$5.99 US/$6.99 Can